JAYSIN
THE LAST WIZARD SAGA
SONG 3

TONY SHILLITOE

Cover art by Kirsi Salonen
Cover design by TS

Millswood Books

ISBN: 978-1-7641848-1-6

For Henri

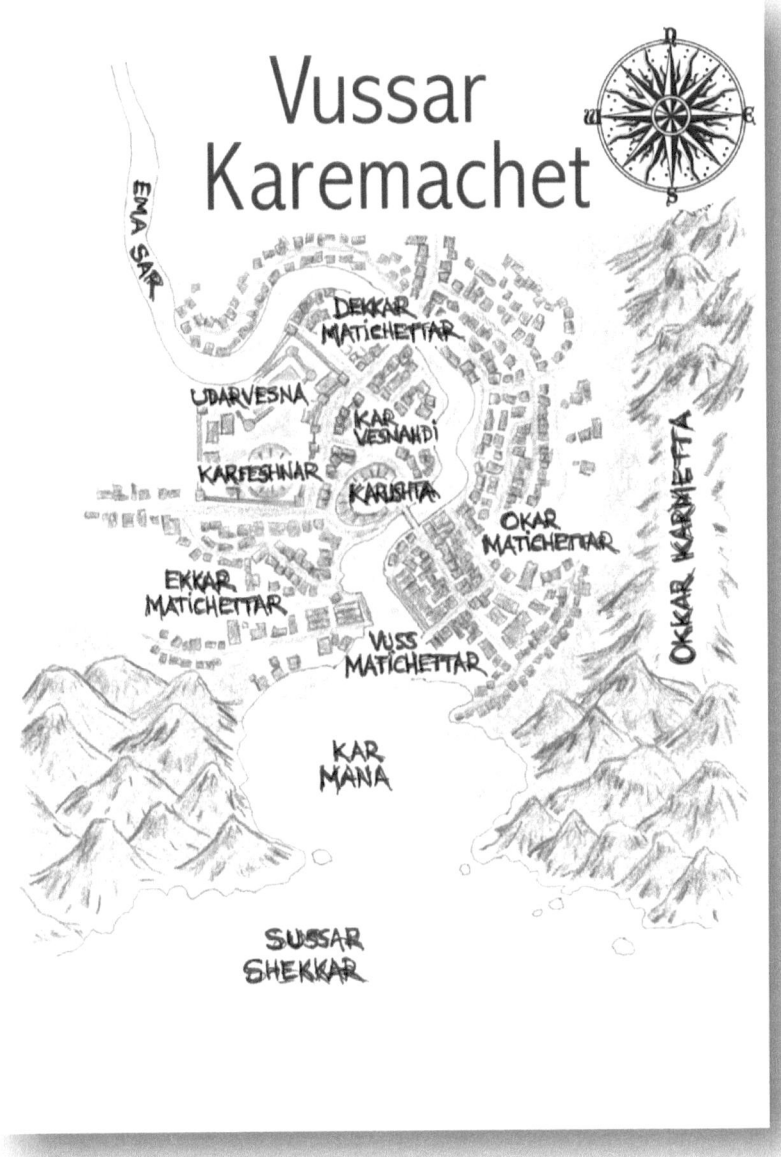

One

When he spotted the angular shape against the white peak of Jenjaka Mountain, Masha rose from his wooden chair and ignored his complaining knees. He hoisted the heavy wooden mallet with its fur wrapped head and estimated the dragon's bearing as he strode to the brass gong. The dragon was coming for Machutzka. He swung the mallet and struck the gong, its deep resonance resounding from his watchtower across the town and echoing against the perimeter stone wall – once, twice, thrice as was customary for warning the people when the dragon was on its way. After the third strike, Masha lowered the mallet and focussed on the dragon's flight. If it veered from the city, he would sound the gong five times to let everyone know they could go about their business again. If the dragon kept coming, his duty was to repeat the first alert to confirm the dragon's imminent arrival.

Of everyone in Machutzka, he was first to have the honour of seeing the dragon arrive and settle on the Dracovamin. He served Machutzka as Dracomeysa for twenty-two cycles, since ascending to the position at age thirteen, and he was one of five men who shared the role on a rotational schedule. His father and grandfather were Dracomeysii before him, although he only inherited the role when his two older brothers chose to train as Menuii warriors rather than step into the traditional family position. He considered himself blessed by the dragon to inherit the role, and doubly so since the dragon came to live near Machutzka after so many generations of waiting for the god to return. His father spent his entire life

1

waiting as a Dracomeysa and he never once saw a dragon.

The dragon was definitely heading for the city. Masha raised the mallet and struck the gong three more times before he leaned against the tower railing to watch the dragon glide to land at the city's central square.

Annoyed by the clanging gong, Jaysin lowered the vial of purple dust he was intending to blend into a mixture of Foxcross flower and Hasba herbal tea liquid. Three gongs. Harmi was coming. Machutzka was about to descend into pandemonium. People would stop working, close their shops and stalls, and usher their children and pets indoors before racing to the square to witness the arrival of their dragon god. The Mena would be hastily organising protocols for receiving the dragon and the Menuii warriors would be marching to the square to control the gathering crowd, his brother Chasse among them.

Jaysin looked at the colourfully illustrated Menin calendar on the wall behind his bench. It was the month of Bedan in the season of Goku – summer. If he was still in Harbin, this would be his fifteenth summer, but three years ago he arrived in Machutzka with his brother and sister and Harmi the dragon, and led by the Menuii warrior, Natias Hunda, and Machutzka was now his home.

He smiled at the memory of Natias' name. Unlike Harbin villagers, Machutzkan citizens had two names, one for themselves and one that belonged to their family. It was a strange culture. The people worshipped Harmi as a god, but no one in the city had heard of the Harbin gods – Varst, Procra, Ecg, Fler – or even the dragon gods, Arkamroth, Shaddho and Blitzart. *Actually*, he mused, *no one knew of Harbin*. His birthplace, from which he escaped, may as well have never existed.

The Machutzkans placed daily offerings at the Dracovamin, the dragon claw statue and seat in the city centre reserved for Harmi – food, gold, jewels, wine – and one of his daily tasks was to collect the offerings at sunset and transport them to the Dracoshaza jakusharm, the dragon wizard's home, where Tam and he lived. Tam redistributed the gifts among Machutzka's poor, and at first Jaysin thought Tam was being wasteful, but he realised how wise her action was because it enhanced her status among all Machutzkan citizens as generous and not greedy.

He didn't personally collect the offerings from the Dracovamin. Servants did it on his behalf. Collecting offerings was below his station – which was another aspect of Machutzkan culture he found interesting – social strata. People were defined by their wealth and their roles.

At the highest level were the Mena, the man and woman who were elected to their leadership roles for life by members of the fourth strata in Machutzka; the business and property owners or Menati. The second social strata belonged to the Menuii warriors. The third strata were the Machutzka Meysa, fifty administrators responsible for organising and overseeing all city matters, from tithes to sewage. A fifth level, the Bahsi, comprised everyone who worked for the business and property owners. People without Machutzkan citizenship, including the hawkers and poor living beyond the city walls, belonged to the sixth strata – the Pushka – and those who were homeless, unemployed or criminals filled the final strata, the Phah. He learned from his servants how those from the Bahsi level and up were treated with different levels of respect, but those in the Pushka and Phah were treated equally by everyone with disdain. Curiously, and a condition he relished, is that he sat outside the Machutzkan social strata, untouchable and important, because of his direct association with Harmi the dragon.

The second sounding of the gong interrupted his contemplation. Harmi was definitely on her way. Despite the freedom with his godlike status, he was expected to pay homage to the dragon like everyone else.

Jaysin crossed his workshop to the door and took his black cape from

3

a hook, sweeping it over his shoulders and lifting his braided hair from beneath the collar and hood. He perused his image in the full-length mirror. 'Gold chain,' he murmured and headed to the wooden dresser that was covered with an assortment of ornaments and jewellery. He selected a heavy, ornate gold chain with a dragon claw medallion, the one he always wore when Harmi made public visits because it emphasised his status as the Dracoshaza's brother, and he slid it over his head to drape ostentatiously across his chest. He collected a black staff that was leaning against the wall, assessed his appearance in the mirror again, and told his reflection, 'Ready.'

Jaysin opened the door and stepped into the corridor separating his workshop from his sister's chamber on the third floor of his home. Light spilled along the wooden floor from windows at either end of the corridor. A chamber was reserved downstairs for his brother, Chasse, but Chasse no longer used it, not since he moved into the Menuii barracks to demonstrate his commitment to his warrior friends. Jaysin still did not understand why Chasse would put aside comfortable luxury in the dragon wizard's house for rudimentary warrior-style quarters that were shared with others. He would never do that.

He stopped before a silver door that was etched with the gold image of a dragon and an emerald marking the dragon's eye. 'I'm coming,' his sister projected to his mind, and the door opened. Tam stood before Jaysin, her long white hair loose over her shoulders contrasting with her red robe. She held a black staff with gold ends.

'Can I open the portal?' Jaysin asked hopefully.

'Yes,' Tam affirmed.

Grinning, Jaysin held his staff with both hands and spoke the ancient words that Harmi and Tam taught him to generate energy for instant passage from the building to the dragon claw in the city square. 'Hrnetya zhemtaga otreva goust. Jakeyva enam wi. Ahtem!' The air crackled with static and a blue oval light shimmered into existence. Jaysin beamed with

4

delight and asked, 'What do you think?'

'You're learning a great deal,' Tam replied.

'I am,' Jaysin agreed, 'but is it good?'

Tam sighed, and replied, 'It's perfect, Jaysin. Why do you always ask?'

'I want to be the best,' he told her.

'Harmi is landing. We have to go,' Tam urged, and she stepped into the portal and vanished. Jaysin followed.

Bright daylight and crowd noise always irritated Jaysin. He blinked to allow his eyes to adjust as he appeared on the Dracovamin, a step below Tam, and patiently accepted the crowd's adulation at their appearance.

And then a hush fell over the crowd.

In the hiatus, Jaysin heard thumping wingbeats and looked up at the dragon descending to land on the claw statue behind him. Harmi was still a baby dragon in dragon years, but she was already the size of a large horse in her body and head, her wingspan twice that length and her tail almost twice her body length. Her grey belly scales and shiny red body scales gave her a regal appearance as she alighted on the dragon claw. She tucked her wings along her side, curled her tail around the black structure, and projected, 'Hello, Jaysin.'

'Hello, Harmi,' he replied telepathically. 'I take it there's news.'

'Not for here,' Harmi said. 'Later. I need to speak to the people.'

Jaysin shrugged at Harmi's dismissal and gave his attention to the crowd. Everyone in the central square was prostrated before the dragon and the city gong beat a slow and steady rhythm to solemnise the moment. 'Where are the Mena?' Jaysin asked. 'They're late.'

'They come in their own time,' Tam replied. 'In fact, here they are.'

Riders appeared on the boulevard to the left of the statue. At their head rode the Mena, the Man and Woman who oversaw the city, dressed in their traditional brown garments. Neither had a name. Their status by gender was an odd custom that amused Jaysin when he first learned that they did not use common names.

'It denotes them as representatives of the people,' Natias Hunda explained at the time. 'Who they are is unimportant. What they are is what matters.'

The explanation made little sense to Jaysin then, but, over time, he understood the intention behind the balance of gender and anonymity in leadership. 'Chasse is late,' he noted.

'He is here,' Tam corrected. 'Look to your right.'

Jaysin saw his brother marching toward the Dracovamin steps and nodded to him, quietly admiring, with a pang of jealousy, his brother's imposing muscular physique. Three years' of training with the Menuii moulded Chasse into a powerful warrior whose reputation was spoken of reverently whenever Machutzka citizens mentioned his name. 'You barely made it,' Jaysin chided as Chasse mounted the step beside him.

'Timing, little brother,' Chasse replied with a smile. 'All is in the timing.'

'A philosophical observation?' Jaysin retorted.

'A fact,' Chasse asserted.

As the Mena's entourage reined in, the crowd rose to their feet and a quiet susurration of voices rippled across the square. The Man, stocky in build, dark hair braided, dismounted, as did The Woman. She was taller, and lithe, her hair as intricately braided with coloured beads as The Man's, and both wore brown garments symbolising their bond with the common people. The Woman bowed her head before she asked Chasse, 'Do we have permission, Dracomenu, to speak with the Dracoshaza?'

Jaysin remembered the first time they encountered the Mena. Only Harmi understood the language when they arrived in Machutzka and she translated for Tam. Three years changed that dynamic. All three siblings could speak Machutzkan Menin fluently. In fact, Jaysin was learning four other languages through his studies and research, including Kermakk, the language of the Empire directly east of the mountains. And he was becoming proficient in dragon, thanks to Harmi.

'Amplify my voice,' Tam ordered, interrupting Jaysin's reflection.

6

He beamed, spoke an arcane phrase, coupled with a sweeping gesture of his hand, and the air around Tam shimmered. Knowing that his sister could easily cast the spell with Harmi's help, he was pleased that she asked him to do it.

'Harmi wishes to speak to the people,' Tam announced.

Jaysin watched the undisguised wonder in people's faces when Tam's voice reached them as if she was standing beside them. It was a good spell, a clever manipulation of energy vibrating the air. Harmi taught him the spell on her second visit to Machutzka.

'People of Machutzka,' Tam began, repeating Harmi's prompts. 'Listen carefully. I bring grave tidings and a warning. The Kermakk Empire is marshalling its armies. A great war is underway with their neighbours and Kermakk soldiers are scouring the land for recruits to serve in their Great Army. I tell you this news so that you can prepare for when the Kermakk soldiers come to Machutzka seeking your best warriors. You must choose your fates.'

Jaysin heard the crowd's shocked reaction that morphed into cries of anger and despair and disappointment. He turned to speak to Tam, but she was engaged with the Mena.

'What should we do?' The Man asked.

'Harmi says you must make your choices,' Tam replied.

'But what does the great dragon advise us to do?' The Woman asked.

Harmi tilted her head to look directly at the Mena, and The Man and The Woman lowered their gazes and their heads as Tam relayed Harmi's response. 'Harmi says that she has not come to advise you. The ways of humans are not her ways. She reiterates that you must make your choices. You must decide how you will respond to what is coming.'

'Yes, Great Harmi, Protector of the Menin,' The Man replied, without raising his eyes.

'Harmi has spoken,' Tam announced to the assembly. 'Go about your business.'

Harmi spread her wings and with a leap and down sweep of her wings she rose swiftly into the air, gaining altitude with each wingbeat. The collective gasps and awestruck cries of the Machutzkan populace echoed across the square.

Tam snapped her fingers to dispel Jaysin's amplification magic. To the Mena, she said, 'Gather the Meysa at the Great House after sunset, and we will join you to determine how we should prepare for this threat.'

'We will see this done,' The Woman replied.

'The Meysa will be waiting,' The Man confirmed.

The Mena mounted their horses and led their troop along the western avenue, their departure signalling to the crowd that everyone should disperse as the dragon ordered.

'Now what?' Jaysin asked, watching the people leave.

'We go home and wait for Harmi,' Tam answered.

'Is she coming back?'

Tam raised an eyebrow. 'I think that might be what I said.'

'No need to be sarcastic,' Jaysin retorted.

'I wasn't being sarcastic,' Tam replied. 'Harmi will join us after the city settles down. She has more news for us.'

'I'll send my warriors to their duties,' Chasse said. 'Then, I'll join you.' He descended to join the Menuii men and women who were diligently awaiting his command.

Tam uttered an arcane phrase and a portal crackled into being. 'I could have done that,' Jaysin said, unable to mask his disappointment.

'I know,' Tam agreed. 'It was my turn.' She stepped into the blue haze. Jaysin glanced at Chasse's back as his brother led the Menuii away, before he followed Tam through the portal.

8

Jaysin paced across the room and stood at the large window, gazing at the city rooftops. 'When exactly is she coming?' he asked impatiently, his back to the room. 'It's already mid-afternoon. I have things to do.'

'Like what?' Chasse asked.

Jaysin faced his brother. Chasse was tall for a warrior, but Jaysin was already taller by four fingers and he enjoyed the sense of superiority his extra height gave him. 'Experiments,' he said. 'Scribing. There is always more to learn.'

'Harmi is here,' Tam announced as she lowered a water jug.

Jaysin's skin prickled as it always did in the presence of powerful magic, and someone knocked on the door. Tam made a hand motion, the door handle turned, and the door eased open, revealing a woman wearing a green hooded cloak. The woman said, 'Hello.'

Chasse squinted and asked, 'Who are you?'

The woman entered and pulled back her hood revealing long red hair, saying, 'Surprised?'

Jaysin saw the smile on Tam's face as she approached the woman and he realised what was taking place, although that realisation added to his confusion, especially as the woman was the mirror image of his sister. 'Harmi?' he asked warily.

The woman accepted Tam's embrace, and when she disengaged she met Jaysin's inquiring gaze and replied, 'It is.'

'How?' he blurted.

Harmi laughed and moved to the table. 'It's an old spell of the Dragonkin, a spell buried deep in the memories of my forebears. I would never have recalled it if I wasn't already pondering the possibilities of taking human shape.' She bowed before Chasse and Jaysin. 'And here I am,' she added, as she straightened. 'What do you think?'

'Impressive!' Jaysin gasped. 'Amazing!'

'Why appear like my sister?' Chasse asked.

'The spell changes my shape and size to human form, but the only

9

human form that I can assume is Tamesan's because we are bonded,' Harmi explained.

'Except your hair is red,' Chasse noted.

'My scales determine my hair colour,' Harmi explained.

'But why do this?' Chasse persisted.

'To move through Machutzka,' Jaysin said, before Harmi could explain. 'It's obvious.' He beamed with excitement. 'Is it reversible? Can I learn to take dragon shape?' he asked.

Harmi shook her head. 'I don't think so. It's a dragon-specific spell.'

Jaysin frowned.

'I'm not sure you would like to be a dragon,' Tam suggested, touching Jaysin's arm.

'But I could fly, and breathe fire, and strike terror in the hearts of enemies,' Jaysin argued. 'It would be amazing.'

'And sleep in caves, and be hunted by humans, and be forced to live alone,' Tam countered.

'No one is hunting Harmi,' Jaysin retorted. 'The people worship her.'

'They worship me here, in Machutzka,' Harmi said. 'But only here. Everywhere else, my kind are hunted and reviled by humans, not revered.'

'What is going on in the Empire?' Chasse asked, unable to suppress his impatience with the chatter.

Harmi sat on a purple armchair and said, 'I can only relay what I saw from high overhead and heard from ordinary people in the marketplaces. I visited Ussaremmachet to the north. The townspeople are talking of a Great Army being gathered by the Karudar Marfek to be sent against the Five Kingdoms. In the Kermakk capital, the workshops are busy producing weapons and there is popular fervour favouring war. Artisans are building warships and the harbour is busy. Wherever I flew, east of here, villagers and townspeople and the city dwellers are mobilising, and young men are rushing to join the Great Army.'

'How does that affect us?' Chasse asked.

'In itself, that event is of little interest to us. The Kermakk political world is a passing phase in history,' Harmi replied. 'But I also heard and saw Kermakk soldiers swarming through the countryside, intent on press-ganging reluctant young men into the army. When I visited Sarchah, which is barely six days human travel from here, people in the marketplace told me the soldiers were determined to scour every part of the country to force young men to join the army against their will. I was informed that a local attempt to resist the conscription led to a massacre of thirty people.'

'I will organise observers and scouts to keep watch on our borders,' Chasse said. 'We may have to evacuate the city to protect our younger people.'

'That's drastic,' Jaysin observed.

'Hopefully it won't come to that,' said Tam. 'But I see what Harmi sees, and the Kermakk threat is real.'

'What can we do?' Jaysin asked. 'What if the Kermakk soldiers come here looking for – is it conscripts?'

'Conscripts,' Tam confirmed.

'We will drive them away!' Chasse asserted.

'You would lose,' Harmi warned. 'You have a thousand warriors. The Kermakk Great Army has a hundred thousand soldiers and warriors mobilised across the Empire.'

'We have to be smarter and evacuate Machutzka, like you first suggested, Chasse,' Tam said. 'If they find no one to conscript, they'll leave the city in peace.'

'Why is the Empire going to war with the Five Kingdoms?' Jaysin asked.

'Why do humans fight each other?' Harmi queried in response.

Jaysin shook his head.

'Greed and power,' Tam said. 'It's always about greed and power. Or pride. Or all three.'

'Is there anything else we need to know?' Chasse inquired.

'No,' Harmi replied.

'What are you going to do now?' Jaysin asked.

'Tamesan and I have research to undertake,' Harmi told him.

'Can I help?' Jaysin asked eagerly.

'Not this time,' Harmi told him, as she rose from the armchair. 'This is dragon business.'

'I'll take my leave then,' said Chasse. 'Jaysin?'

Jaysin looked at Tam and Harmi, adjusted his black cloak and deigned to follow his brother from the chamber, but in the corridor he asked, 'What do you want?'

Chasse smiled as he replied, 'Nothing, little brother. You weren't taking the hint.'

'What hint?'

'Tam and Harmi want to work without us in their way,' Chasse explained. 'You didn't hear that?'

Jaysin shrugged. 'I heard it. I was hoping they would acquiesce and let me stay.'

'I'm going to the barracks,' Chasse said. 'What are you going to do?'

'I'm working on an idea. I need time to develop it.'

'A new spell?'

'Yes,' Jaysin confirmed.

'Want to come riding with me this afternoon?' Chasse asked.

'Another time,' Jaysin replied.

'As you wish,' Chasse said, and he headed for the stairs.

Jaysin watched his brother descend before he went to his door. As much as the Machutzkan horses fascinated him, he wasn't interested in being lured into his brother's warrior exploits. He knew Chasse still believed that he would become a man in his sixteenth summer and follow the way of the warrior, but that was never going to happen. He had a very different future planned for himself. He turned the door handle, paused to stare at the wooden grip, and said quietly, 'Last time I do this.'

Two

'Why can't I be there?' Jaysin asked, frowning.

'Because you are not recognised as a leader in Machutzka,' Tam reminded him. 'The Mena honour you, but you are not invited to the Meysa meetings.' Seeing her younger brother's disappointment, she said, 'Besides, I always tell you what happens, and you don't have to suffer all the conversation and argument and diatribe.'

'Chasse will be there,' Jaysin murmured.

'Yes, he will,' Tam confirmed. 'You know his role. Without his consent, no one speaks to me, or Harmi.'

'But anyone can speak to me whenever they like,' Jaysin countered.

Tam raised an eyebrow. 'You are not exactly someone who seeks conversation, little brother.'

Jaysin winced at his sister's truthful jibe. She was right. Life was too short to suffer pointless discussions with unintelligent people. 'Be sure to tell me what is decided,' he said. 'I will keep myself busy reading and writing.'

Tam touched his shoulder affectionately, and said, 'You may be asleep before this meeting ends.'

'I'll be awake,' Jaysin replied.

Jaysin watched his sister leave. Harmi's news of the impending potential threat to Machutzka made him reconsider the focus for his learning, but he was determined to complete a small challenge first. He crossed to his table and studied the open pages. Although the language was unfamiliar, the illustrations confirmed the instructions explored the ability for a person to pass through a thin solid object. He spent several days unravelling as much of the language as he could, and that led him to search for a scroll in the Machutzkan library.

He straightened and smiled, remembering his joy when he learned there was a building in Machutzka devoted entirely to the collection and storage of texts. He happened upon the building while he was walking through the city streets four months after arriving in Machutzka. The frantic escape from Harbin, three years earlier, meant he was forced to abandon the precious book and scroll collection belonging to Eric, the Herbal Man. He did take five books in his backpack – the five he guessed would be of greatest value – but he had already mastered the spells and memorised the information within them. The Machutzkan library was a revelation.

'Our people donated all the texts and scrolls they found or inherited from their ancestors who lived in the times of The Great Dragon War and The Culling,' a heavy-set, greying woman with a snub nose told him.

'Why wouldn't they keep them?' Jaysin asked, peering past the woman's frame into the gloomy interior at shadowy stacked shelves and book piles on the floor.

'Most people don't read or write,' the woman answered. 'And even if they could, the texts are written in so many ancient languages that no one can read them.' She studied Jaysin and asked, 'Can you read?'

'Yes,' he said proudly.

She stepped aside and beckoned for him to enter and he was immediately enveloped in a musty atmosphere that reminded him of the Herbal Man's cave. 'My name is Shika Dimon,' the woman said. 'But everyone calls me The Librarian.'

'I am Jaysin,' Jaysin replied. 'My sister is –'

'I know who you are,' Shika interrupted, without pretence or acknowledgement of his rank. 'You are welcome to read anything in the library.' She moved to a small table and chair where the flickering flame of a metal oil lamp threw her plump, lined face into relief. 'If you want, you can borrow anything stored here, but you must promise to return it. This library represents the legacy of past centuries.'

'Can you read?' Jaysin asked as he lifted a book from the table.

'Of course!' Shika replied indignantly. 'My grandmother was a scribe in the old Kemze Court of King Fareem Katen Hadenya many years ago. She taught me to read when our family escaped from Kemze during The Purge.' She looked at the blue leather-bound book in Jaysin's hands. 'That is Gato's *The Eight Laws of Reasoning.*'

'You've read this?' Jaysin asked, opening the book.

'Yes,' Shika replied. 'It's in Menin, but a form much older than people use now. It's slow reading.' She grinned. 'It's actually very boring.'

Jaysin made a note to rapidly increase his understanding of the Menin language as he surveyed the collection. 'How many books have you read?'

'Quite a few,' she repeated. 'As I said, the languages are varied and ancient. I have read the easy ones written in Menin. And a small collection of Kemze and Kermakk texts that my grandmother brought with her.'

'Are there books about magic?'

Shika raised an eyebrow. 'I wouldn't know,' she said. 'Why?'

'I have a keen interest as the brother of the Dracoshaza,' said Jaysin.

Shika looked furtively at the door, her expression suggesting to Jaysin that she was deciding what she should say next, before she picked up the lamp and said, 'I will show you something.'

She led Jaysin between the tightly packed shelves and past the book piles to the rear of the room where a metal door dominated the wall. She halted before the door and said, 'Any book that might be concerned with magic is most likely stored behind this door.'

'Can I look?' Jaysin asked.

Shika's expression changed to disappointment. 'I swore an oath to keep this door locked.'

'To whom?' Jaysin asked.

'To the last dracoshaza who visited Machutzka.'

'When was that?'

'I was a young woman,' Shika replied. 'A long time ago.'

'But you have the key?'

Shika shook her head. 'The dracoshaza took it with him.'

'Was his name Eric?' Jaysin asked.

'He never gave his name,' Shika replied and added, 'and we do not ask impudent questions of a dracoshaza.' She gestured to the front of the room and she led Jaysin to the front door, where she politely said, 'You are always welcome. I am blessed that you came to me.'

Jaysin smiled at the memory of Shika ushering him out of the library that first time because her eagerness to make him leave only fed his hunger to return. And he did. He frequently visited the library in the intervening sun cycles, reading and borrowing books, while he painstakingly taught himself new languages in order to unlock the secrets within the texts.

He was impressed that Shika the Librarian did what she could to arrange the shelves and piles in her library in a semblance of order, but he quickly realised that the content and titles of many books and scrolls were beyond her linguistic talent. He hoped to find one that enabled him to penetrate the metal door at the rear of the library, and finally he found a key of sorts. Xanita's *Locks and Unlocking* contained the recipes of spells for manipulating locks. He learned and applied the spells, but to his immense frustration the door remained locked. Then he stumbled upon the scroll, which, in a very old language, detailed a spell for moving through solid objects. All he had to do was master it.

Jaysin glanced at the pages, and at a parchment beside the book, before he stood before his door, focused inward, imagined what he wanted to occur, put his hand on the door, stepped forward – and met impenetrable wood. He stepped back to study the door and stepped forward, placed his palm on the wood, breathed in, and bumped into the door. 'No!' he hissed as he stepped back again.

He strode to the table and unfurled the parchment and scanned the text again, searching for the flaw in his process. 'I have it right,' he decided. 'Again.'

He returned to the door and glared at it as if it was a recalcitrant opponent. *This spell*, he mused, *is taking longer to master than others and yet it is, in essence, simple to execute.* He placed his hand on the door, focused on the phrase from the parchment, gritted his teeth and stepped forward – and his forehead thudded on the wood. He cursed and sank to the floor. 'I am doing it right!' he yelled.

'But you are not relaxing,' Harmi observed as she appeared beside Jaysin's workshop table in Tam's physical form.

'Not funny,' Jaysin said grumpily.

Harmi sat cross-legged before him to explain. 'Passing through a solid object requires absolute stillness of the mind and the body. In order to move through the static particles, your physical form must be flexible, adaptable, calm. The door doesn't move or change. You do.'

Jaysin stared at Harmi. Given her comment, he wondered what it felt like for the dragon to be compressed into a human body. 'How long did it take you to learn how to do that?'

'Pass through a solid object?'

'No,' Jaysin replied. 'To take human form.'

Harmi blinked, and replied, 'Two, maybe three days.'

'And, what?' Jaysin asked. 'The spell simply popped into your mind?'

Harmi shook her head. 'No. Well, yes, but only because I was trying to resolve how I could easily navigate human settlements. It's one thing to observe the world from on high when the light is low and it is highly unlikely humans can see me, but getting among the people means I can glean greater information as to what is happening where and to whom and why. And that's when I recalled an ancient spell that my ancestors used in a place and time far from here to move among humans, so, I practised and refined it.'

'It's creepy that you look like Tam,' Jaysin complained.

'For now, it's all I can do,' Harmi said. 'I am studying ways to alter my human appearance, but it seems it has significant limitations.'

'Like what?'

'This, to begin with,' Harmi replied, indicating her appearance. 'And even if I can master how to look different to Tamesan, apparently I retain the appearance of the ancient ones who first created this spell. That form would make me appear very foreign to other humans.'

Jaysin looked at the door in frustration, and said, 'I've tried to relax. I still can't pass through.'

'Go deeper,' Harmi urged. 'Imagine that you no longer exist; that nothing can touch you, that you are free of your body. For a moment, let go of being you.'

Jaysin sucked in a deep breath as he approached the door and cleared his mind before he tentatively placed his hand on the wood.

'Stop.'

Jaysin turned to Harmi.

'Everything you did then was with an uncertain mind,' she observed. 'You are expecting to fail, so you will fail.'

'I should walk to the door expecting to go through?' Jaysin asked.

'In a manner of belief, yes,' Harmi replied. 'That requires discipline, preparation and practice.'

Jaysin rekindled the spell, walked purposely to the door and smacked his forehead on the wood. He slapped his hand against the door and swore.

'Practise,' Harmi reiterated. 'You will master it.'

'If I don't beat myself unconscious first,' Jaysin conceded, as he rubbed the red patch spreading on his forehead. 'Why are you here?'

'To listen in on tonight's meeting,' Harmi answered.

'You can do that without taking human form.'

'I can,' Harmi agreed. 'But it's easier like this. I don't have to land nearby, or hover overhead and risk drawing attention.'

'But you look exactly like my sister. You'll definitely be recognised,' Jaysin contended.

'I always wear a hood, and I'm careful,' Harmi replied. 'A woman walking around the building is less conspicuous than a dragon hovering above it.' She rose from her seated position and approached the table to scrutinize the book and scroll. 'Where did you find these?'

'In the library that I told you about,' Jaysin explained.

'And why this particular spell?' Harmi asked, lifting the scroll to read it.

Jaysin knew he had to be honest with the dragon because Harmi could read his mind if she chose. 'There's a metal door at the back of the library. Behind it are more books and scrolls –'

'Belonging to our ancestors,' Harmi finished. 'I remember. Eric locked it and took the key.'

'You remember?' Jaysin blurted and checked himself. 'Of course you remember. What happened to the key?'

Harmi chuckled and said, 'Claryssa swallowed it.' Jaysin's incredulous expression made her burst into giggles.

'That's seriously not funny!' Jaysin exclaimed. 'How is anyone ever going to access all that knowledge?'

Harmi stifled her mirth to reply, 'The knowledge in that chamber belongs only to a wizard and a dragon.' She cocked an eyebrow in the habitual manner Jaysin knew Tam used and it was unnerving. 'It is not wise for you to enter the chamber.'

'I could translocate into the chamber,' Jaysin suggested.

'But you don't know what's in the room,' Harmi warned. 'You know the translocation spell has limitations. Knowledge of the destination point. Distance. Height. If the door only opens into a cupboard, you will translocate into the wrong space beyond. If it opens to a stairwell, you will end up in the wrong place and fall or be embedded in a wall or ceiling. That could be fatal.'

Jaysin stared at the door. 'Guess I will practise this,' he said.

'Practise,' Harmi replied. 'But not on the chamber in the library. You are not ready.'

'I still have to pass through this door,' Jaysin grumbled, glaring at his workshop entrance.

'And I have to be excused,' Harmi informed him. 'The meeting with the Meysa is commencing, and I should help Tamesan negotiate a plan of action for the people.' She strolled past Jaysin and effortlessly passed through the wooden door.

'That is also not funny!' Jaysin yelled.

'Practise,' Harmi projected to his mind. 'For an instant, you do not exist in the physical realm as yourself. Let go of your ego.'

Jaysin walked to the table to re-read the scroll and ran his finger across the pages in the book before he moved to the window. The last vestige of sunset was a thin and fading pale-yellow line across the distant mountain peaks. Stars blinked in the cobalt firmament. He searched for the moon. Being the last week in the month of Bedan, he expected it to be waning, a sliver of itself, but it wasn't visible from his window. 'How do I stop being me?' he whispered.

He considered the scattered points of torchlight flickering in the city. At night, the Machutzkan markets operated like they did during the day, the vendors spruiking and selling wares, and people eating at stalls. He enjoyed shopping for trinkets and goods during the day, but he was warned very early to keep away from the night market. 'The Phah thrive in the shadows,' Natias Hunda warned him. 'They prey on the weak and defenceless.'

'I'm neither weak nor defenceless,' Jaysin retorted.

'They prey best upon the haughty and arrogant,' Natias said. 'Those who think they are above the Phah are the Phah's favourite victims.'

'But families eat there in the evening,' Jaysin argued.

'Local families. Known families. People who live and work in and near the market,' Natias explained. 'The Phah are thieves and robbers, but even they have a sense of what is fair and what is not. They do not harm the people they know.'

Jaysin obeyed Natias' advice and did not venture into the city after dark. He was confident, now, with so much magic at his disposal, that he would not be at risk if he did walk the streets at night, but he decided there was no need to do so.

He turned from the window to study the wooden door across the room. Harmi's warning to avoid the metal door in the library merely sparked his desire to learn what lay within the chamber beyond it. And he heeded her advice for making the passing spell work. *Let go*, he silently recited. *Let go*.

He walked across the room, relaxing his muscles, recalling the phrase recorded on the scroll before clearing his mind. *Ate ekam hooda shetra*, he silently recited. He kept his hands at his side, let go of his existence, emptied his mind of his desire – and passed through the door.

Three

Outside the Machutzkan library, Jaysin stopped to brush aside a fly that perched on his cheek before he looked up. The morning sun peered between scudding clouds against a light blue sky, but he knew the weather was changing. Later in the afternoon, rain would wash down from the northern mountains to turn the sky grey and muddy the city streets. Beyond the library entrance, with its wicker carving, Shika Dimon the Librarian would be shuffling or reading her books. *Will it matter if she sees me pass through the door*? he wondered.

A woman and two children approached with a beige dog trotting in their wake. The woman stared at Jaysin from beneath her orange cowl, her dark hair framing her face, and he thought he saw recognition sparkle in her eyes, but she herded her children past without acknowledging him. The dog, however, stopped to nuzzle the hem of his robe. He reached down to pat the dog's head. It sniffed his hand, licked him and padded after the woman and children. He liked that the Machutzkans kept animals as companions, a rare practice in his home village where animals were only kept or hunted as sources of food and materials.

Jaysin entered the library, anticipating Shika's greeting, but the interior was dark. 'Shika?' he called. When she didn't answer, he stepped further in, squeezing between the fusty book laden shelves and repeated, 'Shika?'

'Coming,' a voice answered from the rear of the room. Candlelight expanded on the ceiling and spilled along the narrow and cluttered aisle, and a familiar figure arrived. 'What are you looking for today?' Shika asked.

'I have a key to the door,' Jaysin announced, deciding that it didn't matter what the Librarian knew if he was the only one who could pass into the wizard's chamber.

Shika looked confused by his statement, and said, 'I don't understand.'

'Go to the metal door,' Jaysin instructed.

Shika retraced her steps along the aisle to the rear wall, turned left and walked to the metal door, holding her candle so that Jaysin could see as he followed. 'How did you get a key?' she asked.

'I am the brother of the Dracoshaza,' Jaysin replied. 'You said the last dracoshaza locked the door. I know how to enter the room.'

'Where is the key?'

'I am the key,' Jaysin replied.

Shika stared at him, expecting an explanation.

'I think I need you to leave me alone to open the door,' Jaysin said, reconsidering his plan.

'I promised to prevent anyone entering,' Shika reminded him.

'I am not anyone,' Jaysin retorted.

Shika hesitated, as if deciding how to respond to his assertion, before she asked, 'Should I leave the candle with you?'

'I won't need it,' Jaysin told her.

Shika shuffled away, glancing over her shoulder as she disappeared into the morass of shelves. The candlelight faded, and Jaysin was plunged into gloom.

I am not simply anyone, he mused. Recalling a spell that Tam taught him, Jaysin uttered 'Leoht' to conjure a light sphere and he set it to hover above the door. A magical light sphere, he decided, was a very practical spell and once he learned the spell he experimented with changing sphere size, the hue, its constancy. He examined how far from himself he could project a sphere, testing the spell's limits and variations. Tam entered his workshop unannounced, one evening, to discover ten spheres circling Jaysin's room, each a different shade and size, and she conceded he was improving the spell. He secretly wanted her to admit he was better at creating and manipulating the spell than either Harmi or herself, but Tam made no such concession. Her quiet confidence and sense of superiority annoyed him when he knew he was becoming more adept with magic than her.

He relaxed, recited the phrase for passing, let go of self – and smacked against the solid metal. His light sphere vanished.

Confused by failure, Jaysin checked his phrasing, whispered, 'Ate ekam hooda shetra,' relaxed his body and stepped forward. The metal door remained impassable. 'No!' he spat. 'I can do this!' He paced before the door, coaching himself. 'Calm yourself. You can't pass through if you are angry or self-conscious. Breathe. Relax.' He stood still and let his frustration dissipate. 'I am more than this,' he murmured. He formed the spell in his mind, imagined he was nothing, and pushed against the door. It remained impenetrable. He cursed, stamped his feet, and punched the embossed metal. Recoiling from the impact, he examined his scratched and stinging fist.

Candlelight crept across the floor. 'Are you all right?' Shika timorously asked as she emerged from between the bookshelves.

'Go away!' Jaysin snarled.

Shika retreated.

Jaysin slumped to sit before the door. His anger burned and he was embarrassed that the Librarian witnessed his failure. 'I know the spell. I've passed through doors. I've practised. I've tested. Why does it fail here?' he asked the darkness. 'Why?' He stared at the door, contemplating a renewed attempt, but he knew he would not pass through. *Is it because the door is metal?* he wondered. *Metal is denser than wood. Do I have to find a way to be even less in existence? Possibly,* he decided, but he suspected something else was at play.

Frustrated, Jaysin skulked between the bookshelves to the front of the library where Shika was seated on a stool, reading, with the entry door open to the street. 'What's the book?' he asked.

Feigning surprise at Jaysin's return, Shika replied, 'A Kermakk treatise on political will.'

Jaysin squinted. 'You find that interesting?'

Shika nodded. 'I developed a fascination for why cultural groups create norms around leadership based on ambition motivated by greed. There is an entire bookcase down the third aisle that I curated devoted to political philosophy, if you're interested.'

'No thank you,' Jaysin replied. He closed the entry door.

Shika peered curiously at him and asked, 'What are you doing?'

'Answering a nagging question,' he replied. He relaxed, formed the passing phrase in his mind, let go of his thoughts and self, and stepped through the door into the street. The sunlight was duller than when he arrived and dark clouds were piling over the distant mountains. He heard the library door open behind him.

'How did you do that?' Shika asked.

'I am the Dracoshaza's brother,' Jaysin replied haughtily, before he strode into the street and headed for his workshop.

'Where have you been?' Tam asked when Jaysin alighted at the head of the stairs.

Her expression warned him that something was awry. 'Finding my limitations,' he replied. 'Why?'

Tam glanced at Jaysin's wrist. 'Where is your bracelet?'

'I forgot to put it on,' Jaysin admitted.

'Always wear it,' Tam advised. 'I was trying to reach you.'

'Why?' Jaysin asked. 'What's happened?'

'Kermakk soldiers are marching into the Machutzkan hills. I tried to find you.'

'I was at the library,' he replied. 'Where is Chasse?'

'Shadowing the Kermakk soldiers with a party of Menuii warriors,' Tam explained. 'He's certain the Kermakk are heading here.'

'Do the Mena and Meysa know?'

'Not yet. Harmi only told me a little while ago. She's relaying messages from Chasse,' Tam told him. 'We are meant to meet with the Meysa and put the plans into operation.'

'No one's told me about plans,' Jaysin complained. 'I wasn't at the meeting, remember?'

'Come to my room,' Tam invited. She led Jaysin to her door, and opened it for him, and he grinned, knowing that, at least for himself, doors were no longer a barrier.

Tam's room was opulently furnished with green fabric and brown leather chairs and a long wooden table. The entry door wall was lined with shelves and books and a wide wooden door opened into Tam's bedchamber. The muntin-panelled window, framed with gold curtains and overlooking the city, let in dull light and raindrops spattered on the glass. Jaysin sat on a leather chair and waited for Tam to explain the plan.

'The plan,' Tam began, 'is to evacuate the city of men and women who might be considered recruits for the army.'

'Where will they go?' Jaysin asked. 'If the Kermakk soldiers are determined, they will track and find them.'

'You and I will weave a spell that hides their tracks,' Tam replied. 'The Menuii will hide the townspeople in the Machutzkan catacombs that are a short walk from the city.'

'It won't work,' Jaysin contended. 'The Kermakk will be like Mikane and his brothers and search everywhere if they are so intent on capturing recruits.' He glanced at the window as heavier raindrops began to fall. 'If I was the Kermakk,' he said slowly, turning to his sister, 'I would hold the rest of the city to ransom to make the others come back.'

'Yes. That's what Chasse and I argued,' Tam confirmed. 'The Meysa didn't agree. The Man told us that he knew the Kermakk ruler personally and he said that the Karudar Marfek would listen to reason if he spoke with her.'

'And say what?'

'He would ask that Machutzka not be involved in the war.'

'But The Man is here,' Jaysin said. 'The Kermakk ruler is in her palace, a long way away.'

'That's why The Man is journeying to Vussar Karemachet,' said Tam.

'How long will that take?' Jaysin asked.

'Chasse,' Tam uttered randomly, staring past Jaysin's shoulder into the middle distance. She looked directly at Jaysin. 'We have to hurry,' she urged, and she started for the door.

'What's wrong?' Jaysin asked, confused by his sister's diversion.

'They're fighting!' Tam yelled, and she bolted into the hallway.

Jaysin pursued Tam down the stairs and out into the rain and empty street, confused by her panic and asking, 'What's going on?'

'Chasse and the Menuii are fighting the Kermakk,' Tam hurriedly explained. 'We have to help them.'

'And how do we get to where they are?' Jaysin asked.

'We fly.' Tam summoned a portal. 'Come on,' she urged and stepped through.

Jaysin trailed in her wake and appeared at the Dracovamin. 'Why are we here?' he asked.

Heavy wingbeats pounded the air and Harmi materialised out of the falling rain, landing before them and lowering her belly to the ground. Tam clambered onto the dragon's back. 'Get on behind me!' she yelled, and she reached out as the town gong began ringing to announce the dragon's arrival.

Accepting his sister's hand, Jaysin climbed onto Harmi's back and quickly discovered that the dragon's scales were treacherously slippery and uncomfortably hard. As he settled behind Tam, he was conscious of water seeping into his crotch and legs.

'Hold on to me!' Tam instructed. 'Tight!'

As Jaysin slid his arms around Tam's waist, the world rippled with a burst of magic and he felt a powerful surge as Harmi's wings extended and beat the air. *Dragons use a combination of strength and magic to fly*, he reminded himself, and he was thrilled to be taking flight on Harmi's back. The city buildings sank beneath the rising dragon, but Jaysin's excitement was rapidly subsumed by a sickening rush of vertigo when Harmi ascended, and he was thankful that the stinging lash of cold rain on his cheeks at least stifled his nausea. He felt Harmi's heaving breath and muscles rippling, while the world became grey and miserable as they flew through a cloud and he pressed against Tam's back to combat a sharp chill that crept into his skin through his sodden clothes. He always hoped that he might ride Harmi one day, but he never imagined that he would be uncomfortably soaked to the skin and shivering like a wretch caught in a storm. And his intestines rose into his chest when Harmi banked and descended through the rain, and the grey, murky forest rose towards them.

The dragon tilted and shuddered when she touched down, and Jaysin slid from her scaly back to the muddy earth and onto his back. He rolled onto his knees, grateful to be on solid, if drenched, ground, but before he could appreciate the end to the ride an arm pulled him to his feet, and Tam urged him to move. He followed her up a steep rise into a stand of trees, glancing over his shoulder in time to see Harmi vanish into the rain.

At the crest, murky silhouettes huddled against trunks and behind bushes and Tam signalled for Jaysin to crouch beside one hooded figure wrapped in a green, wet coat.

Chasse's face peered from within the dripping cowl. 'They're not going anywhere in this downpour,' he announced, and he pointed down the slope into a wooded valley. A stream snaked through the trees, and a great number of soldiers, and horses and wagons were huddling beneath the boughs and foliage. 'The stream is rising,' Chasse continued. 'They have to climb further up the slopes to avoid being flooded, if the rain continues.'

'It's a big army,' Jaysin said.

'Our scouts estimate they have two thousand soldiers in the valley,' Chasse confirmed.

'Prisoners?' Tam asked.

'No,' Chasse replied. 'When they round up their volunteers, they load them in a cart and send them to Sarchah with an escort. From there, they take them downstream to Vussar Karemachet on barges to join the army.'

Jaysin looked around and said, 'We thought you were fighting with them. That's why we came.'

'We were,' Chasse said. 'At least, we fought with a scouting party.' As he pointed down the hill, Jaysin spotted dried blood on Chasse's extended hand. 'We were camped on the hillside, waiting for our scouts to come back. Instead, one of their scouting parties chanced upon us. We expected the main force to come up that valley from yesterday's reports, but they changed their approach late last night and came down this side of the hill. When their scouting party attacked us, we thought we had blundered into their army. Luckily, we hadn't.'

'So, we didn't need to come,' Jaysin said, shaking the rain from his hood, and looking regretfully at Tam.

'I'm glad we did,' Tam stated, frowning in return at Jaysin. 'Now we can see what we are facing.'

'They are well-equipped,' Chasse said. 'They have weapons that I've never seen before, large machines that hurl rocks and missiles, and they all wear metal armour.'

A tall and hefty figure approached and squatted beside Chasse, wiping his muddied hands, and Jaysin recognised Natias Hunda, the warrior who led them to Machutzka. 'War council?' Natias asked, appraising the siblings.

'Not yet,' Chasse replied.

'Because I was not here,' Natias said.

'I wouldn't hold a war council without your counsel,' Chasse responded, grinning.

'The young warrior is getting too clever with his new language,' Natias remarked. 'Warriors like straight speaking.' He patted his sword. 'And no speaking is even better.' He looked up at Tam. 'The Dracoshaza is here to help us send the whelps back to their leader. They will not stand in the path of the dragon.'

'There will be no dragon,' Tam said. 'We can't risk the Kermakk knowing Harmi exists. If they learn she is here, they will hunt her until they kill her. And all of us.'

Natias frowned and muttered, 'True. We will fight using the old ways. This I like.'

'If we can avoid fighting at all, we will,' Tam said.

Natias said to Chasse, 'They will not find the dead ones. They are buried and the mounds trampled to look like walked earth.'

'Thank you,' Chasse said.

'Now what?' Jaysin asked.

'We wait,' Chasse replied.

'Do we have to stay if all they're doing is waiting?' Jaysin asked, appealing to Tam.

Tam glanced at Chasse and Natias before replying, 'No. We can go back.' To Chasse, she said, 'We'll come back if it doesn't go well for you. Always wear your bracelet. I can hear you if you need help. Harmi has a plan in case the soldiers reach Machutzka. I'll explain it to you before Jaysin and I return.'

Chasse walked with Tam a few paces away from Natias and Jaysin, and Jaysin went to follow them, but Tam indicated that he should remain where he was. He shrugged and frowned to show his annoyance at being excluded.

Natias put a hand on Jaysin's shoulder and said, 'You are growing tall, young Jaysin.'

Although Jaysin was uncomfortable at the big man's friendly touch and considered shrugging Natias' hand off, he knew the gesture would insult the warrior. 'They don't think I'm old enough to be part of their planning,' he complained.

Natias laughed and removed his hand. 'Then what of a man like me?' he asked. 'Before I brought the Dracoshaza and Dracomenu to my city, I was an important man, respected for my wisdom and strength. Now, I am only another warrior led by the Dracomenu. I, too, should be annoyed that they do not include me in their discussions.' He waited for Jaysin to meet his gaze, rain dripping from his cowl, before he said, 'But I am not. We all have our roles. If we do what we are expected to do, those things we are good at doing, and that includes who does the planning and who does not, all will be as it should be. Am I not correct?'

Not really, Jaysin thought, but he pretended he was accepting the big warrior's sage advice. Tam and Chasse took all the glory in Machutzka. He was their little brother, treated by the people as an oddity, like he was in Harbin as a child. *I am more than people think I am*, he decided. *I will prove I am more*.

Four

Saturated clothes piled on the floor, pale skin shivering in the early evening light, Jaysin conjured warmth from the large granite stone in the fireplace and stood before it, rubbing his hands together and over his arms. The dragon ride was cold and dismal and cured him of heroic notions of flying majestically on the back of a great beast, and while he knew a better day might be more suitable his prime concern was getting warm. His next concern was getting through the metal door in the library.

Dry, dressed in red jerkin and brown trousers, Jaysin carefully braided his auburn hair in the Machutzkan fashion. When he was satisfied with his appearance, he draped his black cloak over his shoulder and recalled the interior of the library, especially the space between the shelves and the rear wall where the metal door stood. He murmured the arcane phrase for constructing a portal, watched the blue haze materialise, and stepped through.

He stood in the dark, listening. A board creaked overhead. Shika was awake. Jaysin remembered there was a rickety staircase in the rearmost corner of the building that he asked about on an early visit which obviously led to the Librarian's chambers. He waited until the room upstairs was silent before he conjured a light sphere to examine the door.

The metal had a faint patina of rust, giving the door an orange tinge in the artificial light. He searched for writing, embellishments, symbols, but apart from random manufacturing marks the door gave no clue as to how it could open. Except for the keyhole. *And the dragon ate the key*, he reminded himself. He knew the spell for passing through doors and walls. That wasn't the problem. Something embedded in the door was blocking him.

'The Dracoshaza cast a spell on the door.' Jaysin spun to discover Shika behind him. The Librarian held a candle holder in her left hand and her face was wrinkled into deep shadows. 'I knew you would be back.'

'Why didn't you tell me there was a spell on the door?' Jaysin asked.

'You didn't ask,' Shika replied.

'Then why tell me now?'

Shika smiled. 'I watched you try to go through the door using your magic,' she said. 'I guessed you didn't know what to do. But when I saw you go so easily through the front door, I knew you would come back until you worked out what was stopping you.'

'Do you know the spell?' Jaysin asked.

'What would I know about spells?' Shika asked in reply. 'There's no magic in these old bones.'

'Then how do you –,' Jaysin began, paused, and said, 'No need. The Herbal Man told you about it.'

'Who?' Shika asked.

'The dracoshaza you met,' Jaysin explained. 'Eric. He was a healer and herbalist. At least, he pretended he was.'

'He was a very kind person. I was no older than you when –'

'I know. You told me,' Jaysin said to curtail listening to another story, but a possibility suddenly sparked in his mind and he clenched his fist and yelled, 'Obvious!' He stepped to the side of the door and focussed on the wall. He whispered the spell phrase, relaxed, let his mind go blank and stepped forward – and hit the wall.

'Eric was a very wise man,' a familiar voice announced.

Rubbing his forehead as he turned, Jaysin saw that his sister, with her cowl up, stood beside an astonished Shika. 'Why are you here?' he asked.

'There were vibrations along the arcane web. They led here. And it's not Tamesan, it's me, Harmi.'

'What are you babbling about?' Jaysin asked, annoyed that the dragon was imitating his sister and was interfering again. 'What web?'

'There is so much that you don't yet know,' Harmi said. 'And that is why you are not ready to enter the chamber.'

'Eric put a spell lock on the walls?' Jaysin asked.

'A ward on the entire structure,' Harmi informed him. 'Mainly to stop ordinary thieves digging into the chamber. I don't think he anticipated someone like you trying to break in like you are, but what he did was effective.'

'You can go through, can't you?' Jaysin asked.

'If I ever really need to,' Harmi replied. 'But I don't need to.' She realised Shika was staring, open-mouthed. 'I remember you,' Harmi said. 'You have an honest heart. Thank you for protecting these treasures.'

'Do you know me?' Shika asked.

Harmi giggled. 'No, not me exactly. But I know of you.' She looked at the bookshelves, the closest flickering with candlelight, and said, 'You have a fine library. If I find more books, I will bring them to you,' before she returned her attention to Jaysin. 'I suggest you leave this obsession alone. Learn all the spells you can. When you have learned everything that you can, I will help you pass through the door. For now, Jaysin, go home. I need you to help Tamesan when the Kermakk army arrives. She will teach you what you have to do tomorrow and the day after that.'

'And you?' Jaysin asked. 'What are you going to do?'

'I will be ready to protect the people,' Harmi said. She said goodnight to Jaysin and Shika and walked into the darkness between the shelves.

Jaysin snapped his fingers to make his light sphere vanish and the dark closed in around Shika's candle. 'I'm sorry I disturbed you,' Jaysin said. 'It was rude of me.'

'I wasn't asleep,' Shika assured him. 'I thought it was a thief.'

'What would you do against a thief?' Jaysin asked.

Shika raised her right hand out of the shadows and she was holding a spiked club. 'Don't underestimate an old lady,' she advised.

'You know how to use that – thing?' Jaysin queried.

'I was married twice, both times to soldiers. They taught me a thing or two,' she told him.

'I thought you lived alone.'

'I do now,' Shika replied. 'But not always. A tale for another time. I will see you out.' She turned and led Jaysin from the library.

'The plan is simple,' Tam explained. 'When the army arrives, they will discover an abandoned, derelict site, the remains of a once great city, empty of people.'

Jaysin gazed out of the window at the morning light shining on the rooftops. 'And we will achieve this with a spell,' he said.

'It is a very powerful spell, an illusion that will extend over most of the city,' Tam confirmed.

'Which is where Harmi comes in,' Jaysin said. 'She hovers high overhead and acts as a conduit to spread the spell wide.' He turned from the window and approached his sister. 'Who thought of this?'

'Harmi, of course,' Tam explained, beaming. 'Apparently, wizards used it in the past to hide their towers and caves. Eric used it on Dragon Mountain to hide his chambers.'

'And you are sure it will work?'

'Have you a better plan?' Tam asked.

Jaysin shook his head. 'And if it fails?'

'We defend the city.'

'Let's hope we don't have to do that,' said Jaysin. He paused, before asking, 'Do you know how to break a lock spell?'

Tam's expression hardened, and she said firmly, 'Harmi warned you not to enter the chamber.'

Jaysin shrugged. Of course Tam would know. 'It was worth a try,' he muttered.

'Some things should be left in the dark places from where they came,' Tam said. 'Eric had good reason to lock away whatever magic is stored there. You should stay away from it.'

'Perhaps he should've destroyed it all,' Jaysin muttered.

'Perhaps,' she said. 'But knowledge is knowledge, even if it is knowing what should not be done. Knowledge should not be destroyed simply because it is dangerous.'

'Then why lock it away so that no one can read it? That's as good as destroying it,' Jaysin argued. 'How do we know what we shouldn't do, if we don't know what we shouldn't do?'

'I don't have an answer for you. Harmi knows what is locked behind the door. Perhaps even I do, if I choose to search our memories. Eric knew. I trust his judgement. You should, too,' said Tam.

'What if I don't?'

Tam ignored Jaysin's question. 'Time is short,' she said. 'We have a plan to organise. We need you to set up on the southern end of the city, in the Dracomeysa's bell tower. When I give the order, you weave the illusion exactly as I taught you. Keep absolute focus on the spell. If you break your concentration, the illusion will vanish, and the city will be in peril.'

'Wouldn't it be safer to evacuate and hide in the mountains, like the original plan?' Jaysin asked.

'You gave us the answer to that strategy,' Tam said. 'The Kermakk soldiers would ransack the city and still come hunting. This plan should send them back to their capital believing no one lives here. Go and practise the spell. We have two days before Chasse expects the army to arrive.'

'When will Chasse be here?'

'Chasse and several of his warriors are already back, preparing the people,' Tam revealed.

Jaysin crossed the room and stepped through the wall, into the hallway, and through the next wall into his workshop. He grinned with satisfaction, hoping his sister Tam saw how easily he passed through solid matter. The illusion spell she wanted him to practise was one he mastered a year or more ago. He remembered tricking Chasse with disappearing objects when they trekked through the mountains from Harbin. Since then, he embellished and tried alternative methods to create artful illusion.

His favourite illusion, one he did not share with Tam, was his ability to alter his appearance. He used the spell to walk through Machutzka on several occasions in the guise of an artisan, but the spell was fragile, easily disrupted by touch, and he was exposed twice through accidental contact with other people. And that was his concern with Tam and Harmi's plan for the city. Tam assured him that the spell variant Harmi knew was not affected by contact, meaning the soldiers could touch the walls and road and objects in Machutzka, and not dispel the illusion, because the spell's stability lay in the caster's concentration. He wasn't convinced, so he would experiment with what he knew to help enhance the spell's stability.

Jaysin translocated to a narrow alley near the library, startling a brindled cat that scampered over a rickety wooden fence as he appeared. He momentarily connected with the fleeing cat's mind and discovered a morass of scattered bewilderment. *Machutzkans keep pets*, he reminded himself. He liked the concept because he liked animals. However, tempted as he was to buy a puppy or a kitten at the market, he chose not to because he knew having a pet brought responsibilities he wasn't sure he wanted.

In the early months after arriving in Machutzka he practised mind-melding with animals in the streets – cats, dogs, horses – but all he managed to do each time was to startle the animals. Cats and dogs ran. Horses panicked and created chaos, so he quickly avoided communicating with them. The best creatures were young ones, unscarred by desperate living. He would spend his energy on a pet when the time was right.

Tam's and Harmi's phrases for conjuring illusion spells were different to those he learned from the Herbal Man's texts. He focused and repeated 'Darven kaa alemna chessar tupau,' while he recalled images of the market vendor whose guise he previously assumed when learning the spell. The air enveloping him altered texture and temperature, but in himself nothing changed, as he anticipated. The illusion wasn't what he could see, but what others were fooled into seeing when they stepped into the range of the spell. He could only judge the spell's effectiveness by people's reactions to him. He walked out of the alley.

People glanced at him, or ignored him, and that assured him the spell was working because when people normally recognised the Dracoshaza's little brother they stared or steered respectfully around him. Satisfied, he walked to the library and, finding the door open, he stepped in.

Shika stood at a shelf, rearranging books. Hearing a customer enter, she asked, 'Can I help you?'

'I want a book on potatoes,' Jaysin said, coughing and harrumphing to mask his voice, conscious that he sounded much younger than his illusory appearance should.

'Oh,' Shika said, approaching and appraising him. 'You can read?'

'Enough.'

'Do I know you?' she asked.

'I doubt it,' Jaysin replied.

'You do look familiar,' Shika said. She went to a pile and bent to sift through the books.

'Maybe in the market,' Jaysin said gruffly.

Shika straightened to face him and held out a dark bound text. 'This one's called *The Potato: God Food*,' she said. 'It might be useful. It's in Menin.' She squinted and added, 'Yes, the market. That's where I've seen you. Leather goods.'

'Thanks,' Jaysin said, as he turned to leave.

'Bring it back when you're done,' Shika urged. 'These books belong to everyone, but they need to be here for everyone to use them.'

'I will,' Jaysin promised and he walked into the street, grinning. *The illusion is working*, he concluded. 'Now to test its resilience.'

He waited until the street was almost empty. If the spell failed, he really didn't want to appear from nowhere in front of a crowd. The last time that happened, he received a scolding from his sister about how magic was not for making fools of anyone, including himself. He didn't need another reminder from her.

Seeing a young man in a beige smock and grey apron carrying a heavy sack of grain on his back approaching alone, the few people in sight far enough away for his experiment, Jaysin concentrated on his illusory self, stepped into the man's path and bumped into him. The young man stumbled, dropped his sack, regained his balance and abused Jaysin as he hefted his sack onto his shoulder. 'I didn't see you,' Jaysin grumbled apologetically. The young man shook his head and walked on with his burden, but his reaction confirmed for Jaysin that the illusion did not dissipate on contact so long as he held his focus. He was pleased, but he had to test it again.

Further along the street, he spied a couple embracing in a doorway. The man's broad arms were wrapped across the woman's back, and he was obscured in the shadows, but the woman was on the step in the daylight. Tall, muscular, her black hair was braided in the manner of the Menuii warriors. As Jaysin neared the doorway, he deliberately stumbled and dropped to his hands and knees, groaning.

'Are you all right?' the woman asked.

'Can you help me?' Jaysin pleaded, without looking up.

'Let me,' said the man, and Jaysin heard a voice he knew. Strong hands hoisted him to his feet, and he stared into his brother's face. 'Can you stand unaided?' Chasse asked.

Fearing his voice would give him away, Jaysin nodded. Two Menuii warriors emerged from a side lane.

'Are you unwell?' Chasse asked.

Jaysin shook his head again, forced a rasp into his voice, and replied, 'Thank you. I must go.' He walked away, remembering to adopt a faint limp for authenticity and turned into the next street. Spotting an inn, he veered into the entrance and searched for a vacant seat, choosing a wooden booth by a window that overlooked the street.

'A drink?'

Jaysin appraised the boy who spoke. Skinny, dark wavy hair, a lopsided grin, he guessed the boy was maybe ten years old. 'Chava juice,' Jaysin ordered.

The boy left to fetch Jaysin's drink while Jaysin returned to peering through the smeared glass. A ginger dog trotted by, ahead of a limber man wheeling a wooden barrow laden with vegetables, green leaves bouncing over the ruts and stones. Two women carried washing baskets, chatting as they traversed the scene. A youth was white-washing a shop wall, as much of the lime-based liquid on his clothes as on the target. In two days, the scene would have to appear deserted, decayed, if they were to prevent youths like the painter being carted off to a distant war.

At least he proved for himself that the spell worked. Even his brother couldn't see through it. He knew Chasse was in the city, but he didn't expect to find him in this street and especially not in the arms of a woman. *Who was with Chasse?* he pondered. *Why is Chasse here?*

'Chava juice,' the boy announced, startling Jaysin as he placed the mug on the table. 'Two bits.'

Money, Jaysin remembered. Because he was the brother of the Dracoshaza, he didn't need money. He had none with him. 'Oh,' he mumbled, fishing in the pockets of his garment. 'I dropped my coin bag.'

The boy picked up the mug and bluntly informed Jaysin, 'No coin, no drink.'

Jaysin rose and replied, 'No drink then.' He pushed past the boy and headed for the door.

Outside, he looked along the street to where he encountered Chasse, but there was no sign of his brother or the woman who was with him. He returned to the tiny alley where he first appeared, checked he was not being watched, generated a portal, and vanished.

Jaysin studied Chasse's broad shoulders when he entered Tam's chamber, seeing the brutal power in them, the result of Natias' persistent and rugged training during the years in Machutzka as he became a complete Menuii warrior. Chasse was examining a map on the table, but he turned, as if sensing Jaysin's presence, and asked, 'Are you ready for tomorrow?'

'I am,' Jaysin answered. 'Are you?'

Chasse rose from the chair, his red hair braided into a single chain down his back and his straggly beard also braided in the Menuii style, and he looked up at Jaysin, and said, 'You get taller by the day. Keep growing and you'll be taller than Natias.' He patted Jaysin's chest. 'Perhaps don't pick a fight with him,' he recommended with a grin.

'It would be unevenly matched,' Jaysin said, without attempting to mask his self-confidence. Chasse raised a questioning eyebrow. 'Muscle isn't all that wins a battle,' Jaysin posited. 'Are you ready for tomorrow?'

'The Menuii will be within the walls in case something goes wrong,' Chasse said. 'I trust Harmi's spell will make us redundant, and I don't mind that. The best battle is the one you don't have to fight.'

'Menuii philosophy?' Jaysin asked.

'Mine,' Chasse replied. 'I learned it on the dragonship.'

'And yet you still practise as though you would be willing to fight every day,' Jaysin noted. 'Ironic, isn't it?'

'Why do you learn magic?' Chasse asked.

'Because I'm good at it.'

'And I'm good at being a warrior,' Chasse replied. 'When you discover your gift and purpose, the world is different.' He tilted his head, as if studying Jaysin, before he added, 'You have a gift, little brother, but what is its purpose? Do you know?'

Jaysin shrugged and said, 'Tomorrow might be my answer to your question.' He looked around. 'Where is Tam?'

'With Harmi,' Chasse replied. 'Making sure their plan is ready. I thought you would be with them.'

'I know what I have to do,' Jaysin replied. He walked to the window and stared into the night.

The city was dark. The people were indoors, waiting, sleeping, lights and fires out in readiness for the arrival of the Kermakk army. No tell-tale trace of light or smoke could be risked. Jaysin knew Chasse's men methodically diverted or silenced the scouts sent ahead of the army and they planted false signs of tribal people attacking and disappearing with loot to give the impression the mountains were lawless and disorganised. The Kermakk knew Machutzka existed from trading goods that flowed into Sarchah, so he believed the planned ruse was a big gamble and he wasn't convinced it would work.

'What are you thinking?' Chasse asked.

Jaysin asked in return, 'Do you have a woman?'

Chasse blushed. 'Why do you ask?'

'There seems to be an endless stream of women wanting your attention when you are in the city,' Jaysin explained. 'Do you have one?' He grinned. 'Or many?'

'One,' Chasse replied. 'We will be bonded.'

'Married?' Jaysin asked. 'Menin don't marry. You know that. A person can be with whomever they choose.'

'Only everyone else. Not the Menuii,' Chasse replied. 'It's a Menuii

42

custom that Menuii bond with Menuii.'

'Why?'

'Warrior integrity,' said Chasse.

'And when will this bonding take place?' Jaysin asked.

'After this threat is over.'

'What's her name?'

'Kini,' Chasse told him.

'How long have you known her?'

'Since I chose to live in the Menuii barracks,' Chasse said.

'And you've kept it secret all that time?'

'It's not a big secret,' Chasse replied.

'I didn't know,' Jaysin said. 'Does Tam know?'

'Yes,' Chasse admitted.

'Then why haven't you told me?'

'It hasn't been necessary,' Chasse replied. 'You've been busy with your reading and magic.' He shifted on his seat and asked, 'What about you? Who is your favourite girl?'

'I don't have one,' Jaysin replied bluntly.

'There must be girls you like the look of,' Chasse said.

'Actually, there are none.'

'At all?'

'At all,' Jaysin confirmed. 'They don't interest me.'

Chasse held Jaysin's gaze as if expecting his brother to make an admission, before he acquiesced and said, 'We best get to sleep. My scouts say the army will be here by mid-morning and we need to be sharp and ready.'

'Where are you staying?' Jaysin asked.

'The barracks,' Chasse replied. 'We will be ready before dawn. You?'

'I'll be ready,' Jaysin said. 'I only hope this works.'

'You say that like you don't believe the illusion will work,' Chasse said.

'It's a big risk expecting the Kermakk to believe that a town as large as

Machutzka has been abandoned so recently,' said Jaysin. 'And an illusion spell needs everything to go right to avoid it being disrupted.'

'Harmi and Tam are never wrong,' Chasse asserted. He chuckled, and added, 'But we will be ready if something unpredictable happens.' He clapped Jaysin on the arm. 'Sleep well my not-so-little brother.'

Five

Jaysin chastised himself for not visiting the watchtower as part of his preparation because now he was walking through the town to the tower in the dawn instead of translocating. The streets were empty, save for occasional dogs who raised their muzzles inquisitively as he passed and cats who crouched warily or scurried out of sight. Heavy clouds hung over the western mountains and the air currents suggested the clouds would carry rain toward Machutzka later in the day. The sky looked as heavy as his legs.

Sleep did not come readily the previous night, broken by several pressing matters. First, he ruminated on his part in the massive illusion spell that Harmi and Tam planned to generate. He proved to himself that the illusion was immune to contact interruption, which lifted his confidence in the plan. Harmi would be soaring high overhead and able to sustain unbroken concentration. Tam, invisible to anyone who ventured into the illusion, stood in the palm of the Dracovamin sculpture to sustain the magic and he was aloft in a watchtower, both out of reach of the curious. Except for blind luck. The biggest threat was someone stumbling upon Tam or him while they were conjuring. That threat gnawed at his confidence.

Then, there was Chasse's confession concerning Kini and keeping Jaysin unaware of the relationship. What other secrets were kept from him by his brother or sister? Even as he grew older, they continued to treat him like a child. When would that end? Yes, he was younger – not his fault – but he had a right to know what was happening, especially if it affected him. If they were in Harbin, in one more summer he would be declared a man. Tam was already defying their parents at this age. Chasse was training to be a warrior. Why should they treat him as any different from them when they were fifteen summers? The differentiation goaded him.

And Chasse's imminent bonding and question about girls also sparked another turmoil within. He wasn't interested in girls. There were plenty to look at in Machutzka, if he chose to go searching, and he knew Machutzkan girls would happily accept his attention if he gave it, but he had no interest in them. Reading mattered more. Researching, experimenting and improving spells mattered more. Being alone and uninterrupted mattered more. Besides, Tam had no partner, and no desire for one, but no one questioned why her pairing with a dragon was enough for her. It was the same for him. He didn't want a partner. Girls were not even a distraction. *Why should they be?* he mused, as he approached the watchtower.

The watchtower door was unlocked, so he entered and climbed the stairs, weariness making each step feel like he was lifting grain bags for legs. To perform the spell, he needed to clear his mind of all interfering thoughts, especially of its exhaustion. His role in the city's defence was minor, compared to Harmi's and Chasse's and Tam's roles, because he was simply extending the spell across a portion of the city by connecting with Harmi and Tam on the arcane web and adding his power to theirs to complete the illusion. Harmi was the originator, the illusion creator.

'We won't see the effect, will we?' he remembered asking Tam when she taught him what he needed to know.

'No,' she confirmed. 'Only those affected will see it. Everything will look unchanged to us.'

He was mildly disappointed. He wanted to see what Harmi was imagining when she made the city appear derelict and empty.

At the tower summit, he watched the expanding sunlight spill across the western mountain faces. Snow gleamed on the higher slopes beneath the glowering rainclouds, and below the snowline the world was washed with gold. He faced the rising sun, shielding his eyes with his hand against the glare. Beyond the eastern hills lay the Kermakk Empire and cities much larger than Machutzka, cities filled with strange and new people and architecture and goods. One day he would journey there to learn and become part of a bigger world and a story greater than the mythology of Nakiades or the Machutzkan dragon fetish.

He lowered his gaze across the city rooftops. Tam would be on the Dracovamin. Harmi was already scouring the land from overhead, preparing for the Kermakk army to arrive and discover Machutzka desolate and abandoned. Chasse and his Menuii warriors were stationed near the open gateway in case the ruse failed.

Jaysin adjusted his bracelet for communication between the dragon, the wizard, the warrior and himself. His vantage point gave him partial view of the road leading to the main gate. He reached into his robe pocket and withdrew a handful of dried berries and nuts to chew. And waited.

'Time to create,' Harmi projected telepathically. Jaysin recited the dragon words and focused on searching for tension in the air that joined his conjuring with Tam and Harmi's illusion. The air thickened and Jaysin sensed a shimmer in the daylight.

'The illusion is in place,' Harmi confirmed. 'Keep your focus. No distractions. Stay firm. They are coming.'

Harmi's warning was followed by armour glinting in the morning sunlight as riders appeared on the inbound road. Behind the riders marched a thick line of soldiers, lances rocking to their marching cadence. The riders halted a short distance from the gate and the soldiers spread left and right across the field to face the wall. After a hiatus, five riders broke from the front rank and walked their horses to the gate, disappearing from Jaysin's view. 'Is it working?' he asked.

'Hold focus!' Harmi ordered.

Jaysin wanted to reply, *I can focus and talk*, but he stayed silent.

The riders reappeared, passing through the gate, and they reined in several paces within the walls. The lead rider rose in his stirrups, surveying what to him was a deserted and desolate city street. Jaysin expected the riders to venture deeper into the city, but they wheeled and cantered through the gate to re-join their company.

A conversation took place in the front rank of the Kermakk army. A solitary rider broke from the group and approached the gate, stopped, and called out, although his voice did not carry to Jaysin. He stood in his stirrups, called again, and waited. When he was met with silence, he wheeled his horse and returned to the army. Another period of time passed before the front soldier ranks parted to allow ten heavy machines to be wheeled forward.

'Focus!' Harmi ordered. 'They suspect a ruse. The Man is among them.'

'He has betrayed us!' Chasse projected. 'Why would he do that?'

'What are the machines doing?' Jaysin asked.

'The Kermakk intend to bombard the city,' Harmi announced. 'They're testing us. Stay focussed.'

'But the people?' Tam protested.

'Focus,' Harmi ordered.

Tiny figures clambered over the machines and wooden mechanical arms were winched back into position. The world seemed to hesitate. Then, in unison, the arms flicked forward, and ten boulders rose, tumbled through the air and crashed into the city, throwing up plumes of rock, wood and earth.

Jaysin's heart raced. He expected to hear cries from people caught in the deadly rain, but the city was silent. The spell held. *That should convince them to leave*, he decided. But, to his horror, the machines were moved by the soldiers, each one adjusting its angle slightly, the arms were winched back again, boulders loaded, and another deadly barrage released. As the second wave of boulders dropped on the town, the air crackled, and the spell broke. He concentrated, trying to reconnect with

Harmi and Tam.

'Sorry,' Tam projected, upset. 'I had to escape.'

Jaysin looked toward the centre square and the Dracovamin and saw an ominous dust cloud.

'What happened?' Chasse asked.

'The illusion is broken,' Harmi replied. 'The Kermakk know the truth.'

While Chasse and five companions hurriedly closed the main gate, the riders at the front of the army galloped back and forth, marshalling the troops, and a new war machine emerged from the ranks, pushed by a gaggle of soldiers, a large, wheeled contraption with a long shaft and an ornate metal animal head.

'Ring the gong,' Tam projected.

Remembering what was expected, Jaysin picked up the mallet leaning against the tower wall and swung it against the brass gong and the gong echoed its warning across the city. He took a final look at the Kermakk army. The war machine was almost at the gate and another avalanche of boulders rose into the air. Desperate cries echoed in the town. The battle was underway. He scurried down the stairs.

In the street, Jaysin stifled his panic, recollected his thoughts and created a portal to his workshop. As he appeared in his room and walked toward the window, the ceiling exploded, throwing him against the floor in a flurry of stone dust and wood chips. He lay motionless, letting his ears adjust, before he wiped dust from his face and sat up, pushing debris aside. The ceiling was ruptured with a massive hole, replicated in the floor where his worktable had stood. His heart raced.

'Are you all right?' Tam projected.

'Yes,' Jaysin replied. 'Where are you?'

'At the gate. It's nearly breached.'

'What do I do?' Jaysin asked, brushing dust from his black robe.

'Help us,' Tam replied.

'I can't fight,' Jaysin objected. When Tam didn't answer, he asked,

'Tam?' Her silence made him reach out to Harmi. 'Harmi? Where are you?'

'Helping,' the dragon replied. 'Hurry. People are dying.'

That's not my fault, Jaysin thought, but he generated a portal and appeared in the alley near the library. He expected a dramatic scene of smoke and flames, but the air was choked with dust that was enveloping the people who were fleeing for safety, some scrambling into buildings, others running for the southern gates. Two buildings along from the library, a tailor's shop façade was rubble and shattered wood and a massive boulder blocked part of the street. As he gaped at the size of the boulder, the air was filled with a low whistling, the earth shuddered, and he spun to see dust and debris rising at the far end of the street where another boulder struck. People ran past, faces stricken with terror, some streaked with blood. A tiny child wandered through the dust, disoriented and crying. Despite a momentary compulsion to rescue the child, he knew he had bigger things to do. Tam and Chasse were at the main gate and that's where he needed to be. He formed a new portal and translocated to the city entrance.

Jaysin appeared amid a brawling mass of Menuii warriors and Kermakk soldiers. A woman fell against him as he assessed the scene and a sharp weapon whisked past his shoulder. Kermakk soldiers had broken through the gates and the Menuii were fighting desperately to stop their advance. Terrified, Jaysin bolted for the nearest open space, dodging soldiers, warriors, swords, and axes, but, as he made it to a temporarily safe section of the street, the wall was breached further along and Kermakk soldiers poured through the gap. The town was falling.

He spotted Natias Hunda in the thick of the battle, beating down his enemies. An arrow jutted from the big man's shoulder, but Natias flailed his sword, driving back his opponents, unimpeded by the wound. Jaysin swallowed hard. This was no place for him.

He retreated into the doorway of a pottery shop, almost tripping over the body of a man sprawled inside. 'I don't know what to do,' he whispered, trembling. He ran through his repertoire of spells and remembered that Tam and Harmi taught him how to fashion an energy bolt. He recalled the phrase, stepped into the street, focused on a Kermakk soldier, pointed and shouted, 'Shasterna!' A bright bolt of energy whipped across the space, tore through the hapless soldier's back and continued on, wounding a Menuii warrior and passing through another Kermakk soldier's arm, before exploding against the wall. Startled by the effect, Jaysin slid back into the doorway.

The spell was too powerful and dangerous to use in chaotic hand-to-hand fighting. *What else do I have*? he pondered. As he considered his options, a Kermakk soldier burst into the shop, saw Jaysin and lifted his bloodied axe. Jaysin impulsively pointed and shouted, 'Shasterna!' and the shocked soldier jerked as a hole burned through his chest and he toppled backward into the street.

Heart pounding, Jaysin ran through the shop, into the back rooms, and out the rear door into a narrow alley that snaked between buildings. Part way along, rubble filled the way where a boulder crushed a house, but he clambered over the stone and followed the alley toward the next main street. As he reached the street, he saw a shape overhead and glanced up in time to see Harmi's tail sweep past and vanish in the direction of the main gate. He stepped out.

The street was empty. To his left, a half-buried boulder blocked the way and rubble littered the street. To his right, and to his dismay, lay several burning corpses. He squinted. Kermakk soldiers. Harmi was in the battle. There was hope. And if there wasn't, he needed to be safe. There was the library. He generated a portal and translocated.

Jaysin gazed out of Tam's shattered window at smoke drifting across

Machutzka's rooftops. In a street below, people were clearing rubble to make a pathway. A pair of men carried a corpse. A brown horse meandered aimlessly through the destruction.

'The Meysa want to meet before sunset,' Tam said. 'You should come with me.'

Jaysin turned to his sister and asked, 'Why?'

'It's time for you to take your place.'

'Why did the spell fail?' Jaysin asked.

'It was my fault,' Tam replied. 'I dropped concentration.'

'Why?'

'The Kermakk got lucky,' said Harmi.

Jaysin turned to the dragon who was seated in the purple armchair in the guise of his sister. 'How?'

'A boulder from the catapults landed precisely on the Dracovamin statue,' Harmi replied. 'If Tamesan hadn't leapt aside, she would not be telling us her tale. The statue was shattered.'

'I never meant to lose concentration,' Tam apologised.

'You are better alive than dead,' Harmi said, 'to both of us.'

Jaysin didn't miss the allusion to Tam's survival and Harmi's safety. 'Why didn't the Kermakk believe the illusion?' he asked.

'The Man betrayed us,' Tam replied. 'He told the Kermakk that Machutzka hadn't been abandoned.'

'You told me he was travelling to the capital to broker a peace deal with the Kermakk ruler.'

'It would seem he accepted a better offer,' Harmi said.

'And if I hadn't lost concentration, the Kermakk general might have dismissed The Man as crazy,' Tam added.

'You did what you could,' Harmi assured her.

'Where is Chasse?' Jaysin asked.

'The Menuii are pursuing the Kermakk,' Tam explained. 'They want to free the prisoners. Natias is among them.'

'I thought we won,' Jaysin said. 'We drove them away.'

Harmi rose from the chair, stood beside Tam, and said, 'They left because they got enough of what they were after. They took a hundred or more prisoners.'

'But I saw you fighting them,' Jaysin said. 'You could have killed them all.'

'Not without killing Machutzkans as well,' Harmi replied. 'They took prisoners and used them as shields against me. There was nothing I could do.'

'A spell?' Jaysin asked. 'You must have a spell that will incapacitate a large group. I'm certain those spells exist.'

'Those spells exist,' Tam confirmed. 'We haven't remembered them properly yet.'

'But we will,' Harmi asserted.

'You have no idea how weird it is having both of you talking to me like this,' Jaysin said. 'My sister, twice; one with white hair, and one with red hair. I thought one was enough.'

'I was about to leave,' said Harmi. 'I will shadow Chasse and the Menuii and help where I can.'

'You know this jeopardises everything,' Tam warned.

'How?' Jaysin asked.

'Word will get back to Vussar Karemachet that there is a dragon here.'

'Can we stop that news reaching the capital?'

'I doubt it,' said Harmi, and she shook her head. 'I've brought ruin upon these people, like my ancestors did.'

'We will speak to the Meysa to determine what we can do to compensate the people for today,' Tam said. 'Then we can decide where to go to from here.'

'Go?' Jaysin asked.

'We can't stay in Machutzka,' Tam told him. 'The Kermakk will come hunting for Harmi like they have always done. We can't stop an army.'

'But we just did,' Jaysin argued.

'Listen to what we said,' Tam advised. 'We didn't beat them. They left. They will come back.'

'Good luck with the Meysa,' Harmi said, and she vanished through the wall.

'Now what?' Jaysin asked.

'We help people clean up the mess as much as we can,' Tam suggested.

'What about my workshop? The Kermakk destroyed it.'

'Start there, then,' Tam replied. 'I'm going into the streets to help.' She motioned to form a portal and stepped through.

Jaysin stared at the fading blue haze. Machutzka was their haven. He was comfortable. He was learning to become what he believed he was destined to become. Now, with one lapse in concentration, the whole future was unravelling.

He walked to the wall, passed into the corridor and into his ruined workshop, and surveyed the mess. The hole in the floor dropped into Chasse's chamber, the one Chasse never used. Peering over, Jaysin saw the shattered remnants of his table jutting from the rubble and the catapult boulder.

He set to the task of collecting books and scrolls and brushing the stone dust from them before resetting them on the shelves. The battle reminded him that he needed to learn spells better suited to threatening situations. Shika uncovered one text he realised would suit his need, but he laid it aside at the time when he started learning passing spells.

Jaysin searched the bookshelves to find a thick leather volume with corroded copper inlay, lifted it out, dusted it, and read the embossed title: *Et Kar Ushta Ooshi*. The old Kermakk language translated to *The Great War Magic*. A compilation of arcane knowledge from multiple authors, the book was broken into eight sections.

He opened to the prologue, the yellowed fabric pages and spidery grey scrawl reminding him why he originally set aside the task of learning the spells within. Translating the archaic version of the Kermakk language would take time and persistence, and mistranslation was a certainty, meaning each spell would become a process of trial and error before it was correctly interpreted. He read the prologue opening line: "Power is not something you can take, but something you are given." The aphorism made no sense. The following exposition didn't add insight into the aphorism, and the final line of the prologue – "A life mistaken is less valuable than a life forgiven" – left him bemused by the clumsy philosophical meanderings of the writer, Adrit Mercanti Badilya.

His interest rekindled, however, when he opened the first section and translated the title: "Ways to Disable." He flicked through the pages to the second section and read its title, "Deadly Powers of Fire and Light." The third section translated to "Defending the Self." *How quickly can I learn these*? he questioned rhetorically.

Six

His heart sank. The dream plagued him for many nights after reaching Machutzka, but it eventually stopped. Now he was in it again, standing outside the ashen ruins of the Harbin Warriors Hall, his feet stuck in clay. His father lay on the ground in a pool of blood. A gaggle of men were driving people toward the water, and his mother's face appeared among them. She was pleading with him to go, to leave and never come back, but he wanted to run to her, only his feet were fixed in the earth. And instead of being driven aboard a ship, the men drove the people into the water, and they disappeared, one by one, Eesa being the last to sink beneath the surface. And he was engulfed in a wave of deep sorrow.

Jaysin woke to his bracelet tingling. He sat up on his bedding in the darkness and listened to the mindspeak. The meaning was garbled, but he recognised a distress call, and it came from Tam. 'Where are you?' he asked.

'Trapped,' Tam replied. Her mindspeak ended in a miasma of pain.

'Where?' Jaysin asked, but Tam was silent.

He climbed out of bed and passed through his bedroom wall into the shattered workshop. Rain tumbled through the hole in the roof. He conjured a light sphere. The floor on the lower level was flooding. He passed through the next wall into the hallway and darkness, and then through his sister's wall into her chambers where he conjured a new light sphere. Nothing was awry in the main chamber, but, as he opened the bedroom door, a ceiling beam swung down, narrowly missing him as it thudded against the floor. He retreated, afraid.

'Help,' Tam projected.

Tempering his emotion, Jaysin stepped over the collapsed beam and entered the bedroom and his trailing sphere revealed the collapsed ceiling across Tam's bed, with a massive boulder teetering on top. Rubble filled the floor and rain pelted in. 'Where are you?' he asked.

'Under,' Tam replied feebly. 'Help.'

Panic surging through his veins, Jaysin clawed at the wet stone and plaster, wrenching aside the smaller fragments, until Tam's foot appeared. He redoubled his effort, but the larger chunks were too heavy. He clambered onto the slippery pile and pressed against the boulder. Initially, he couldn't budge it, but he located where it was most precariously balanced and shoved hard. The boulder rolled and thumped against the wall. 'Tam?' he projected.

'Hurry,' she begged telepathically. 'Please. I can't breathe enough to speak.'

'I can't move the big pieces,' he admitted.

'Levitate,' she projected.

'How?'

'Makina hek agala pac.'

Jaysin focused on a large chunk of stone, placed his hand on it, and murmured, 'Makina hek agala'. Nothing changed. He realised his error. 'Makina hek agala pac,' he repeated. Nothing altered. 'It doesn't work,' he told her.

'Lift it,' she urged.

Jaysin took hold of the stone, lifted, and it rose like paper. He tossed it aside, chose another, repeated the phrase, and heaved the mass aside. Tam's bloodied leg appeared. His heart raced. 'It's working,' he projected. Tam was silent. 'Tam?' he asked. She did not reply. He sped up his process, shifting aside the rubble until he uncovered Tam's motionless body. 'Tam!' he cried. He reached in and touched her chest. A heartbeat. He focused on her, repeated, 'Makina hek agala pac,' and carried her from the room to lay her on the floor in the main chamber. 'Tam,' he pleaded, touching her face. 'Can you hear me?'

He ascertained she was breathing, but she was unconscious, so he nervously searched her body, finding cuts and blood across her torso and head. 'Healing spells,' he said, but none came to mind. Healing had not been a priority in his learning. He tore strips from Tam's nightgown to bandage the obvious wounds and he gently wiped blood from her face. 'I'll get help,' he said. 'I won't be long. I promise.'

Using his bracelet, he reached out psychically to Harmi and Chasse, but neither responded. Chasse was too far away in pursuit of the enemy. Harmi – he presumed she was shadowing Chasse's warriors as she planned and so she was too far away as well. Machutzka had healers, 'farnoo' in the Menin language. One lived near the library. He checked Tam's breathing and heartbeat, before forming a portal and translocating to the lane near the library.

Rain drenched him as he appeared. 'I should have worn a cloak,' he muttered. He strode out of the lane and headed for the intersection, trudging through mud and puddles and as he passed the library he made a mental note to return as soon as he acquired the healer's help. There would be books and scrolls devoted to healing. He would learn.

Jaysin turned the corner and tramped along the adjoining street, avoiding rubble from smashed buildings that reminded him the struggle with the Kermakk was only beginning. The darkness prevented him reading signs, but he conjured a light sphere when he guessed he was near the healer's house and searched until he found the healer's flowering bud symbol emblazoned on the wall by the door. He knocked. No one answered. He banged on the door. No one came. Frustrated, he recited the spell and passed through the door into the hall.

A startled man in a black nightrobe with a lantern, challenged him. 'Who are you?'

'Brother of the Dracoshaza,' Jaysin announced. 'I need your help.'

The healer lifted the lantern, recognised Jaysin's visage and bowed.

'Hurry,' Jaysin urged. 'Meet me at the jakusharm.' He didn't await a reply. He formed a portal and translocated to the entry of the library, passed through the door, created a new light sphere, and searched the shelves.

'What are you looking for?' the Librarian asked as she appeared at the foot of her stairs with her candle.

'Healing books,' Jaysin replied.

'Third aisle, five cases along, second shelf from the top,' Shika replied. 'What's happened?'

'My sister,' Jaysin said, heading for the books. He deciphered the titles in languages he understood. Several were illegible. 'Which books contain spells?' he asked.

'Third shelf, I think,' Shika replied. 'The strange languages I couldn't catalogue I put on the fourth shelf.'

Jaysin scooped an armful of texts from the third and fourth shelves. 'I'll bring them back when I'm done,' he promised. He pushed past Shika, put the books on the floor, conjured a portal, gathered the books and vanished.

Tam was still motionless when Jaysin appeared in her chamber. He put his books on the floor, generated a light sphere, and assessed his sister's breathing. Hearing knocking, he descended to the ground floor and opened the front door to find the healer shivering in the rain, his red healing bag clutched against his dark blue cloak. Wordless, Jaysin led the healer across the rubble, up the flights of stairs, along the corridor and into Tam's chamber. 'Do what you can,' he instructed. 'I will be reading.'

'Yes,' the healer said, his expression betraying his questioning of Jaysin's choice of action. He glanced warily at the light hovering above

Jaysin, before he knelt beside Tam, gently pulling aside her night clothes to examine her injuries.

Jaysin squatted on the floor and shuffled through the books, selecting one in the ancient Menin language titled *Treating Multifarious Vagaries and Injuries of the Wretched Flesh*. He flicked it open and poured over the pages. Dissatisfied with the content, he dropped it and selected another titled *Apothecarial Remedies*. Like the first, it was a ragtag collection of minor physical ailments. Jaysin looked up to see the healer was cleaning Tam's wounds and applying a dark green unction to each one. 'Is she better?' Jaysin asked.

The healer shook his head. 'I can treat the external injuries, but she is injured deep inside.'

'Do what you can,' Jaysin repeated, and he resumed searching the book pile, rolling over text after text, discarding those that were physiologically focussed, until he found a very old tome in an ancient language titled *Enchantments and Incantations for Bodily Reparation*. He thumbed through the pages, pausing to absorb information, discovered a spell scribed in the draconic script with illustrations suggesting the incantation allowed the user to work within the body of an injured being, and he memorised it. He looked at Tam and paused, thinking, *What if I get it wrong*? He re-read the pages devoted to the spell, tested his memorisation of the words against what he already knew of draconic language and expression, and shuffled to sit beside Tam and the healer. 'Where is her greatest hurt?' he asked the healer.

'Here,' the healer indicated, passing his hand above Tam's left hip. 'Here,' he continued, above her right ribs and chest. 'And here,' he added, holding his open hand over Tam's forehead.

'Which one should I fix first?' Jaysin asked.

The healer stared at Jaysin as if he didn't understand Jaysin's question, before he replied, 'The head is the cradle of the soul.'

Jaysin placed his open hands gently across Tam's cut and reddened forehead and left temple and the healer's unction, and whispered, 'Tefere e ne sefarin. Husta e ne def. Sefarin. Sefarin tefere ne def. Emestra hah shest.' Warm energy swept from his stomach and chest through his arms and into his hands, and they glowed with a green hue, startling him. He repeated the incantation and a second surge of energy moved through his body to his palms and into Tam. He rested his palms on Tam's head until the energy dissipated and when he lifted his hands away Tam's skin glowed with green light in the shape of his hands and fingers.

'I have never seen such – such healing,' the healer said quietly, eyes wide with fascination.

Jaysin placed his hands on Tam's chest and spread his fingers wide to embrace her ribs, preparing to repeat his enchantment, but what he felt within himself was intense exhaustion. The spell was draining his energy into his sister. He breathed in, focussed, and whispered the arcane sentences. As his energy rose and flowed into Tam, he was drawn into a vortex, his mind clouding. He was losing consciousness. He tried to fight the enveloping weakness and darkness. He tried.

'I'm sorry,' the healer was saying. 'I didn't know what else to do.'

Jaysin saw the man's grey bearded lips moving in the flickering lantern light, heard the apology, and asked, 'My sister?'

'The Dracoshaza is sleeping,' the healer replied.

Realising that he was on his back, Jaysin sat up, but the effort to sit was taxing and he shook his head to clear the fogginess. The healer knelt before him, holding a lantern. Jaysin studied the man's craggy features, salt and pepper straggly hair, and sparkling dark eyes. 'What is your name?' he asked.

'Deekum. Deekum Mak.'

'Help me up,' Jaysin instructed. Deekum took hold of Jaysin's left arm and helped him to stand. 'Thank you,' Jaysin said, and he removed his arm from the healer's grip. The healer had moved him away from his sister, so Jaysin returned to Tam's side. Her head was cushioned on a rolled robe, her white hair matted with blood and dust, her body covered by a grey cloak. He squatted beside her.

'Whatever you did,' Deekum said from behind, 'she is breathing easier.' He squatted beside Jaysin. 'She needs a lot of sleep and rest. Her body will take many weeks to heal.'

'We should put her somewhere comfortable,' Jaysin suggested, looking at the sofa.

'I would not move her,' Deekum recommended. 'The injuries within are unknown. Perhaps tomorrow, with others to help.'

'I have a way,' Jaysin said. 'Make the sofa ready.'

Deekum hesitated, as if he was deciding whether to trust Jaysin's intention, before he rose and moved to the sofa. Jaysin recited the levitation words, placed his hands gently beneath Tam, lifted her and carried her to the sofa. 'You are incredibly strong,' Deekum observed, as Jaysin lowered Tam onto the sofa.

'Thank you for coming,' Jaysin said, as he straightened to address the healer.

'Can you teach me what you did?' Deekum asked.

'It is only for the dragon family to know,' Jaysin bluntly replied.

Disappointment flooded Deekum's face, but he bowed respectfully and apologised, saying, 'It was not right for me to ask.'

'Again, thank you,' Jaysin said. 'I will take care of her. You can return home.'

Jaysin led the healer downstairs and into the rain. It was difficult to ascertain the time, but he guessed it was early morning, pre-dawn. He closed the door, and as he ascended the stairs he tried, again, to contact Harmi through the bracelet, but the dragon was unresponsive. And then chilly realisation swathed him. Tam and Harmi were bonded. Tam was injured and unconscious. Did her condition affect Harmi? What if the dragon was lying unconscious and unprotected in the wild? What if Kermakk soldiers found her like that?

He hurried upstairs and squatted beside the sofa in the lamp light, and whispered, 'Tam?' He touched her forehead and her chest. She was breathing restfully. 'Tam?' he projected. She did not respond. He tucked the cloak around her, before he straightened and considered his options. He needed someone to care for Tam because he had to check in with or find Harmi.

The conversations with Shika and Fern replayed in his mind as Jaysin rode in the soft rain through the battered city gates.

'The healer will come if you need,' Jaysin explained to Shika.

'Deekum Mak,' she said. 'I know him. He regularly borrows books.'

'I don't know how long it will take to do what I need to do. I'll come back as soon as I can,' Jaysin promised.

'The Dracoshaza will be safe,' Shika assured him.

'Who could take me to Sarchah quickly?' Jaysin asked.

'Can you ride?' Shika asked.

'I learned how to control a horse,' Jaysin replied. His mind flashed back to the first time that he saw horses when he arrived in Machutzka. Then, they were mysteries, but he recognised majesty in their bearing and elongated heads and he asked Natias if he could teach him to ride.

'I cannot,' Natias told him, 'but I will organise someone to teach you.'

And Natias was good to his word because he arranged for a Menuii warrior named Valin Corsin to tutor Jaysin throughout the first six months after arriving, and Jaysin learned to ride.

'Fern Chadra in the Dracovamin side market has good horses,' said Shika. 'See her. Tell her I recommended her. She's an old friend.'

Jaysin rode out of Machutzka in the wake of Fern's sons, Garva and Akanda, young men of a similar age to his brother. Labourers were repairing the town's stone walls and beyond the gates Pushka were reconstructing their hawker stalls and huts. The stench of death soured the morning air. Kermakk corpses rotted in piles, the Machutzkan people heaping the dead enemy outside the city as a sign of their contempt for the Empire.

Fern insisted that Jaysin be accompanied when he asked for a horse. 'The road is obvious to follow,' she said, 'but you will need to move quickly and my sons know how to make the horses work best in the harder sections. And, if you meet trouble, they are handy fighters.' He wanted to ask why Fern's sons were not Menuii if they were such good fighters, but he let the question slide and accepted their company.

The road into the hills climbed steadily. The rain was constant, but the horses were surefooted in the mud and the progress was easy. Jaysin pulled his hood lower to keep the rain from his eyes, and flirted with exploring the horse's consciousness, but he knew it would only confuse and alarm the creature, so he reluctantly abstained. As with the bond he built in Harbin with wolves and bears when he wandered the slopes of Dragon Mountain, he needed time and patience to establish the same trust with the Machutzkan animals. *Thoughts go in circles*, he pondered, remembering a text from the Herbal Man's library. *Everything is one day. One day should be now.*

The undulating and winding ride through the rain was broken at midday as the rain cleared when Garva held up a hand and gestured to indicate that they should dismount and move into the trees. Moments later, a wagon rattled along on the road, drawn by two horses. When Garva recognised that sitting beside the waggoneer was a Menuii warrior, he stepped onto the road. The wagon halted and the Menuii warrior drew his sword but he lowered it when Jaysin and Akanda joined Garva. 'Where are you going?' Garva asked.

'We have wounded to take home,' the Menuii warrior replied.

'How far away are the others?' Jaysin asked. He peered into the back of the wagon where a healer was tending to six sorely wounded warriors.

'We left this morning,' the waggoneer told him. 'The Dracomenu and the others were still chasing the Kermakk.'

'They're within two days of Sarchah,' added the Menuii warrior.

'Have they rescued any prisoners?' Garva asked.

'Those the Kermakk aren't killing,' said the waggoneer.

'I thought they needed conscripts,' Jaysin contended.

'They do,' the Menuii warrior agreed, 'but they sacrificed some of our people to warn the Dracomenu not to pursue them. You'll see the poor sods hanging by the road further on.'

'And the dragon?' Jaysin asked. 'Is she with them?'

'The dragon disappeared overnight,' the warrior replied.

'We have to keep moving!' the healer on the wagon shouted. 'These people need to get to Machutzka!'

The warrior resumed his seat, and said, 'You'll have to hurry to catch them before the Kermakk make Sarchah.' The waggoneer shook the reins, and the horses wrenched the wagon into motion. 'May you fight under the flames of the dragon!' the warrior called, reciting the Menuii blessing as he waved.

When Jaysin, Garva and Akanda remounted, they urged their horses into a steady canter.

Mid-afternoon, five more wagons appeared and rolled by, yelling greetings and good fortune as they bore their wounded cargo home. Jaysin hailed the trailing waggoneer, wheeled his horse and reined in beside him, to ask, 'Where did you camp last night?'

'There's a bend and a hummock before the stone bridge over the river,' the waggoneer replied. 'You'll know it when you see it. We were there last night.'

Jaysin wheeled again, urged his horse into a gallop and took the lead, drawing Garva and Akanda in his wake, but a short distance later his horse broke pace and limped into a walk.

Garva pulled alongside and advised, 'You can't push a horse so hard for so long. She's already developing a limp.'

Garva's caution aggravated Jaysin because he was determined to find Harmi, but he accepted the wise guidance and let his horse recuperate at her own pace, as frustrating as it was for him.

The sun cast long and deep shadows across the road and the trees as it settled over the western mountains, and the afternoon's vague warmth evaporated, and when the sky turned deep blue, and stars sparkled, the moon yet to ascend, Garva veered from the road into a clearing and announced, 'We rest here.'

'We should ride for as long as we can to catch up,' Jaysin reasoned.

'Our horses are tired. I am tired. My brother is tired,' Garva replied as he dismounted. 'We will rest here. We can start before sunrise to make up time.' Akanda slid from his saddle and bent to hobble his horse. Garva called to Jaysin, 'Do you know how to hobble your horse?'

Jaysin shrugged. 'I learned to ride. I never learned how to look after horses.'

'Here,' Garva said, handing Jaysin a short rope with hobbling loops. 'I'll show you.' He indicated that Jaysin should watch as he hobbled his horse above the fetlocks. When he was finished, he said, 'Now you can do it.' Jaysin used the rope to encircle his horse's legs and when Garva inspected his effort he clapped Jaysin on the shoulder, saying, 'One day, you will be a horseman.' He pointed to the middle of the clearing. 'I will make a fire and we can eat. Akanda is fetching wood.'

'I will go for a walk,' Jaysin said.

'Where will you walk?' Garva asked. 'It is dark.'

'I need time to think through matters,' Jaysin replied. Garva shook his head in disapproval, but Jaysin left the clearing and ventured onto the road, heading for the bend, guessing that they were close by where the waggoneer told Jaysin they had camped the previous evening. He needed time away from the horsemen. Garva annoyed him because he was treating him like his father used to treat him – as an incompetent boy who didn't measure up to his expectations.

A small creature startled Jaysin as it scurried into the undergrowth at the edge of the light, and he stopped to listen to the animal's progress through the bushes, wondering what business the little animal was undertaking. The starlight was not enough illumination, so he conjured a small sphere and made it float at knee height to reveal the road's undulations and potholes, before he continued. A few paces on, the sound of rushing water drew him forward.

As the waggoneer described, the bend led to a decline onto a stone bridge. To his left was a bare hillock. He climbed, and at the peak the moon's pale visage peeped over the horizon. He listened. Hand on his bracelet, he projected telepathically, 'Harmi?' and waited. He projected, 'Harmi – it's Jaysin. Where are you?' An owl hooted, a wolf howled nearby, but Harmi did not respond.

The wolf howl lent familiarity to the night for Jaysin, so he waited for the howl to be repeated and, when it came, he headed down the slope into the trees. Another howl broke the silence as he approached the riverbank, and another. He recognised the calls. Wolves on Dragon Mountain used the same language. The wolves were either hunting, or they had made a kill and were calling others to join the feast. Curious as to what excited the wolves, he pressed on, shadowing the river, aware of the brightening moonlight glittering on the water.

And then he heard the deep growl, the warning, and he froze. A shape materialised between the trees, shaggy, large, an alpha wolf. The animal shifted from shadow into the light, its eyes gleaming, but Jaysin stayed still and searched the animal's consciousness. Kill shapes. Anger shapes.

Blood. Fear. This wolf knew humans. And loathed them. The wolf was deciding what to do.

Jaysin generated calm shapes, submissive thoughts, pack shapes, the wolf language he learned above Harbin, but the wolf snarled, its teeth sparkling in the moonlight. Another shape emerged from the undergrowth beside it. And a third. Three adult wolves. Jaysin searched the second and third minds. They, too, were angry, but greater uncertainty ran in streams through their thoughts, making them subservient to whatever choice of action the lead wolf made. Jaysin focussed his thought on the first wolf again, generating soft images – a warm sun, a gentle breeze, butterflies, cubs. He remembered the Shadow Hunter pups. Pack images.

The lead wolf stopped snarling. He sniffed the air, before turning dismissively and fading into the trees. His companions followed.

Jaysin searched for wolf minds but the only ones were at a distance where the three wolves were headed. He sensed hunger, frustration, curiosity in their thoughts, especially frustration. Dousing his light sphere and relying on the moon and starlight, he crept through the trees by the river towards the wolf pack, preparing to respond if they decided to turn on him. He had one spell he would use if he needed safety that wouldn't hurt the animals. He admired wolves. They were clever, tenacious and they loved their own. He would not hurt them.

He reached a thick clump of bushes beyond which the wolves were gathered. On his knees, he peered through the leaves and witnessed the wolves circling and tugging in turns at a large creature lying on the riverbank, part of it in the water. A wolf pulled on a wing, growling and tugging with its teeth. Another grappled a limb. A third gnawed on a long tail. Horrified, Jaysin stood, shouted 'Hashar!' and the darkness exploded in a bright ball of light, sending the wolves yelping and rushing into the night.

Seven

The dragon was breathing feebly, in the same way that Tam was breathing when he pulled her from the rubble of the collapsed roof. Jaysin was grateful for the levitation spell that Tam taught him in her fading state because he used it to move Harmi out of the water and away from the riverbank. The spell worked, but he sensed Harmi was close to the spell's limit of size and weight.

He generated a light sphere and expanded it to illuminate the riverbank and surrounding space to keep the wolves at bay, while he methodically examined the dragon's body, wings, limbs and head for damage, thankfully finding none. Even where the wolves latched onto Harmi's wings and limbs, there was no evidence of trauma. He knew dragon scale was impervious and the frustrated wolf attack proved it, but he also knew what made dragons vulnerable – their wizards. And that meant Harmi's injuries, if she had injuries like Tam, were internal and invisible to him. The healing spells he learned required close physical contact with the point of suffering, but he could not identify those places on a scaled creature that showed no cuts, abrasions or bruises. *What happens when a dragon dies?* he wondered. *Do they decay or do they stay whole because their scaled exterior protects them from rotting?* Tam slept when Harmi slept during her crucial growth period. He figured Harmi was going to be unconscious for as long as Tam was unconscious.

The wolves howled their lament outside the circle of Jaysin's light. He knew they must have been excited to have so large a potential meal crash fortuitously into their territory and then furiously exasperated to discover it wasn't edible. His arrival aggravated their discontent, but if time and chance allowed he would make peace with them. Wolves were noble creatures.

He sensed impending rain because of the humidity and shadowy clouds blotting out the stars and moon, so he searched the riverbank for two large stones and placed them near Harmi's head and her body before activating warmth from them. He estimated he wasn't far from where Garva and Akanda were camped, but he was unwilling to leave Harmi unprotected with the wolves so close. He focussed on Chasse and projected to him, but his brother did not reply, probably because he was still too distant.

Jaysin settled against Harmi's side and felt the dragon breathing, her scales sliding softly back and forth, her big heart pumping steadily. The warming stones would be fine without him, but if he fell asleep the light sphere would vanish. He vowed to keep watch until dawn.

Jaysin woke. The world was dark and wet, except for the warming stone's soft amber energy glow. He conjured a sphere. Raindrops flashed through the circle of light. Jaysin pulled up his hood and searched for shelter, settling under a tree twenty paces from Harmi. He would not be dry, but he would not be saturated. Rain sluiced down Harmi's scales and pooled around her and the river whispered above the rattling rain. *There have to be spells for controlling the elements*, he mused. *I will find them. Harmi probably already knows them.*

He leaned against the trunk and recited the spells he knew, and his thoughts turned to the metal door in the Machutzkan library. *What is stored there that the Herbal Man wanted to keep hidden?* he wondered. *Why is Harmi determined I should not go in?* He wished he could keep the rain off the dragon, but he reasoned that her scaly hide was protection enough. *The wolves will be warm and dry in their dens*, he decided. *The dragon is safe, if damp.*

Soft golden morning light filtered through the canopy. The river babbled and an avian chorus echoed through the forest, chirps and cackles and squawks bouncing back and forth. Jaysin pushed to his feet, stretching out his muscle tightness and aches as he sucked in the crisp air, and surveyed the riverbank and tiny glade. Harmi's dew-kissed red scales sparkled. He approached and listened to the sleeping dragon's breathing, satisfied to hear its regularity.

Whether Harmi was internally injured like Tam, he still could not ascertain, but he remembered that Tam did not suffer when Harmi fell while she was learning to fly. The two were inextricably linked psychically, but seemingly not physically. Perhaps Harmi had no physical injuries after all – unless she fell from height when she lost consciousness. He reasoned that Harmi's recovery was dependent on Tam regaining consciousness. As he patted the dragon's nose, he recalled an image of Harmi masquerading as his sister and the memory made him smile. 'One sister is enough,' he murmured.

He pondered whether to leave Harmi sleeping to find Garva and Akanda, but the possibility that Harmi might wake while he was absent held him fast. Harmi awake meant Tam was awake. Perhaps the horsemen were searching for him. They wouldn't be far away.

Cupping his hands to his lips, Jaysin shouted, 'Hello!' and listened to his voice echo across the hills. 'Hello!' he shouted again. 'I'm here!' He waited. The birdsong was broken briefly by his interruption, but it resumed with gusto. Perhaps Garva and Akanda rode ahead, searching for him. 'Looks like you and I are waiting,' he said to the sleeping dragon. He dispelled the warming stones and gazed up at the blue sky streaked with clouds and was grateful the rain was gone, but he was hungry. 'I'll find something to eat,' he said.

He checked Harmi before he headed into the trees, but he stopped abruptly when a voice called, 'Hello!'

'Here!' Jaysin replied eagerly. His spirits rose and he listened to judge direction as the caller replied.

'Where?'

The voice came from the direction of the bridge. 'Follow the river!' Jaysin shouted.

The voice called three more times before Garva and Akanda appeared through the trees with the horses in tow. At the sight of Harmi, both horsemen dropped to their knees and bowed before the supine dragon.

Jaysin waited a moment before he asked the men to rise. 'The dragon is –' he hesitated, before saying, 'resting, and we must watch over her.'

'With great respect,' Garva began, 'but we must keep moving quickly if we are to catch the Menuii. They may already be near Sarchah.' He eyed the dragon as he spoke.

'You are right,' Jaysin agreed. 'Can one of you ride ahead and meet the Menuii and tell the Dracomenu what has happened?'

'I will ride ahead,' Akanda volunteered, looking to his brother for approval.

'Ride carefully,' Garva advised. 'Watch for Kermakk.'

Akanda bowed his head to the dragon, before he mounted his horse. 'I will return after I have spoken with the Dracomenu!' he called. He wheeled and rode toward the bridge.

'I was going to forage,' Jaysin said.

'I'll fetch food,' Garva offered. He bowed to the dragon before he headed into the undergrowth.

Alone, Jaysin checked Harmi again. She was sleeping soundly, so he sat on the riverbank, watching the water rippling over rocks as he recalled text from the healing books. In his haste to help Tam, he didn't pay attention to details like whether there was a time period for the healing to take full effect. He didn't read whether it involved extended periods of unconsciousness or sleeping. He was so lost in thought that he didn't see Garva return, until the man called, 'I will make a fire!' and Garva dropped kindling from his left hand.

Jaysin rose and offered, 'I can create a fire. What did you find?'

'These,' Garva replied, holding up two long-eared animals by the rear legs in his right hand. 'Rabbits.'

'Anything else?' Jaysin asked.

Garva shook his head. 'Why? You don't like rabbit?'

'I don't eat meat,' Jaysin explained.

Garva shook his head and dropped the rabbits on the earth. 'I will find plants for you,' he said.

'No,' Jaysin intervened. 'I'll make the fire and then I will go find the plants I like. You watch Harmi.' He held his hands above the kindling and uttered, 'Shaka hah!' and the kindling burst into blue flame before settling quickly into normal yellow flames. Jaysin enjoyed the shock on Garva's face at the display of magic. 'Tend it as you would any fire,' he said. 'I will be back soon.'

Jaysin appreciated walking through the forest beyond the makeshift camp because the familiar birds flitting through the trees, small animals and reptiles scurrying beneath the bushes and the flora reminded him of Dragon Mountain. He searched for and found a variety of herbs and Wereberries, and he stooped to dig mountain yams from between the roots of a giant Junya tree. He followed a runnel down a short slope where it trickled into a glittering stream that he guessed flowed to join the river, and he collected fungi gathered in the moss and on exposed tree roots. The forest was bountiful with the foods that Tam taught him to enjoy.

Pleased with his armful of fare, Jaysin turned to head back to the camp, but as he went to ascend the slope he spotted a tuft of grey fur and a tattered ear. The air stank of death. He twisted and rubbed his nose as the stench assaulted him and he listened for movement, before he crept forward to discover a wolf corpse between the broken limbs of a crude trap. A second corpse lay beyond the first with two arrows protruding from its sunken hollow side, and another dead wolf lay across the opening to a den. The scene angered him. He understood why the pack he encountered the previous night were antagonised by his presence. They were acquainted with the predatory nature of humans.

Jaysin started to skirt the den, driven back by the odour, until he heard a tiny whimper. He placed his foraged food on a log and, taking a deep breath and holding it, he lowered onto his chest to peer into the den. A fuzzy face peered back at him and growled. Jaysin grinned. He focussed on the pup's consciousness and discovered confusion and fear, so he formed wolf shapes and symbols of safety and friendliness, and cooed, 'Hello.' The pup's thoughts morphed into uncertainty and hunger. Jaysin widened his reach, searching for more wolf pup minds, but there was only the one. 'Stay there,' Jaysin said softly. He scrambled up the slope and jogged through the trees to Garva and Harmi.

At the camp, struggling to breathe from his exertion, he found Garva seated at the fire, chewing cooked rabbit. 'I need a piece of that,' Jaysin announced.

'I knew you couldn't resist,' Garva said, and he passed the rabbit to Jaysin.

Jaysin tore the hind legs from the offering, handed the remainder to Garva, and said, 'I'll be back,' before he trotted into the forest, leaving Garva staring at his back, bemused.

The pup is out of season, Jaysin reasoned, as he headed for the den. The three dead wolves revealed that a pack was involved, but normally the surviving wolves would take the pup and care for it. 'Unless the hunters drove them away,' he muttered, as he started the descent. But the pup was oddly out of season. Wolves whelped in the Machutzkan season of Ama, the Harbin time of Fler, but this pup was only a few weeks old, at least at first glance.

Jaysin held his breath from the decay of death again as he crouched to peer into the den. He held out a tantalising piece of rabbit and he projected what he remembered of wolf eating images. A tiny black nose appeared at the edge of the shadow and a snout and head followed as the pup was drawn to the food. A moment's hesitation ended with the pup snatching the morsel and chewing frantically while Jaysin prepared a second offering. The pup snatched the second piece and chewed gratefully. 'I can't leave you here,' Jaysin said, as he assessed the den and the dead adults. 'I'm surprised there's only you. What happened to your brothers and sisters?' He coaxed the pup further out with another portion of rabbit, and as the pup took the meat Jaysin picked it up it by the scruff and stood, inspecting it. The pup snarled, making Jaysin laugh. 'You are a fighter,' he said, holding the pup to look it in the face. 'Come on.' He tucked the pup under one arm, scooped up as much as he could of the plants, herbs and fungi he placed on the log, and headed for the camp.

Garva, crouching at the river to wash his hands and face, stared as Jaysin sat by the fire with the pup, and asked, 'Where did you find that?'

'Her family were killed,' Jaysin replied.

'It should have been killed too,' Garva stated.

Jaysin glared. 'It is wrong to kill wolves.'

Garva cocked an eyebrow, and replied, 'Wolves kill livestock. They carry away babies. Dead wolves are the only good wolves.' When Jaysin did not reply, he asked, 'What are you going to do with it?'

'Raise her.'

Garva laughed. 'It's not a dog. You can't master a wolf.'

'I don't intend to master her,' Jaysin retorted.

'You won't befriend it either,' Garva continued. 'Once a wolf, always a wolf.'

'I'll let her decide,' Jaysin said. He lifted the pup to stare into her dark eyes, smiled and carried her to his horse. He put the pup on the ground, saying, 'No wandering off,' and he projected another image of safety and closeness to the pup. She looked up. 'Stay close,' he said. He rummaged in the pack strapped to the horse and retrieved a bowl and his waterbag. 'Come on,' he said, and projected an image of following, as he walked to the fire. The pup trotted behind him, stumbling over a twig.

Garva watched with intrigue. 'How old is it?' he asked.

'Weaned,' Jaysin replied. 'Maybe a couple of months.' He squatted and put a handful of herbs and plants and fungi in the bowl and poured in water.

'Pups are born in Ama and No,' Garva said. 'This one is late.'

'It is strange,' Jaysin agreed. He placed the bowl over the fire to boil the water.

'You eat that?' Garva asked. 'No meat?'

'Yes,' Jaysin replied. 'You should try it.'

'I'll stick to rabbit,' Garva said. 'On that matter, your wolf and I agree.' He fished in his pocket, retrieved a chunk of rabbit meat and tossed it to the pup. She flinched and eyed the gift warily, but when she caught the scent she licked the meat and snatched it. 'You will need to be a hunter if you want this one to survive,' Garva said to Jaysin. 'You will need to be a wolf mother.'

The light faded quickly and heavy rain set in by mid-afternoon while they waited for the dragon to stir. Garva tethered the horses beneath the thickest branches, but the downpour drenched the animals and transformed the earth to mud. When the water streaming over Harmi's scales pooled around her, Garva dug a channel to drain the water into the river.

Jaysin squatted beneath a large tree, partly protected from the rain, watching Garva work until the rider retreated to a nearby tree to hunker down. Nursing the sleeping wolf pup in his arms, his hood pulled low, Jaysin vacillated between searching for Harmi's consciousness, forming safe and sleep images for the pup, and pondering what was unfolding in Machutzka and outside Sarchah for his sister and brother. Harmi's state suggested to him that Tam remained unconscious in Machutzka and he had no way of determining how long she would stay like that. Chasse and the Menuii must be on the outskirts of the river city. He hoped that Akanda reached and relayed the situation to Chasse, although he knew Akanda would be delayed by the weather. Everything was uncertain.

Jaysin stroked the pup, soothing it as it slept, acquainting it with his psychic presence, voice, touch and smell. The little animal's dreams were confused, brief images flickering between darkness and the scent of the den, his mother, other pups, fur and milk and regurgitated food, images broken with fear and loathing and loss. Jaysin observed the images and gently interspersed them with new images of comfort and his presence to calm the pup. He looked across to Garva, but the Machutzkan was huddled within his leather cloak and locked in his own thoughts while he sheltered from the rain.

As rapidly as the rain arrived, it stopped. Jaysin rose and the pup stirred, so he put the animal on the damp ground and laughed when the pup lifted its paws as if it didn't appreciate getting them wet. Jaysin projected the wolf image for 'Stay,' to the pup before he headed to speak with Garva who was standing and stretching. 'I don't know how long we will have to remain here,' Jaysin offered apologetically.

'Serving the dragon is our first order,' Garva replied. He gestured at the pup. 'I see your friend doesn't appreciate water.'

Jaysin looked down to find the wolf pup beside him, shaking its legs to remove moisture. 'She was meant to stay over there,' he confided.

Garva chuckled, shaking his head, and replied, 'And you are surprised a wolf doesn't do as you ask?'

Jaysin stooped to lift the pup, but as he straightened, a voice whispered in his mind, 'I am awake.' Seeing Garva's astonishment, he turned to find Harmi staring at him and Garva shuffling to kneel and bow his head to the wet earth.

Eight

The dragon adjusted her wings across her scaled back and drank from the river before she turned to the humans. She lifted her head and projected to Jaysin, 'I will go to Tamesan.'

'What about Chasse and the Menuii?' Jaysin asked.

'If Tamesan is healed, I will return,' Harmi said. 'But you should find your brother. He will need your skills.' She cocked her head and studied the wolf pup chewing Jaysin's foot. 'You have a new companion?'

Jaysin glanced down, as he replied, 'Her family were killed.'

'Then you are her new family,' Harmi said, shaking out her wings. 'What is her name?'

'I don't know,' Jaysin replied. 'She doesn't know either.'

'Give her a name that belongs to her,' Harmi said. As she spread her wings, the pup crawled behind Jaysin and he bent to lift her, sharing comforting images. 'When I can return, I will,' Harmi promised. She coiled her legs and launched, her wings and flight spell powering her upward, and her red scales sparkled in the late afternoon sun as she banked and raced towards Machutzka.

After Garva rose from prostrate reverence, Jaysin said, 'We have to find my brother.'

'I will prepare the horses,' Garva offered. 'What will you do with the wolf?'

'She comes with me,' Jaysin said, as the pup gnawed his left hand. 'I'll empty my bag and she can ride in that.'

'You need provisions,' Garva argued.

'I have enough,' Jaysin replied. 'Besides, we will reach my brother within a day, won't we?'

'Perhaps two, if all goes well.' Garva replied. He walked to the horses to remove their hobbles.

Jaysin emptied his bag and organised the pup, using safe and sleep images to make the pup amenable to nestling inside the bag. 'What is your name?' he said to the pup.

'You could call her Kante,' Garva suggested. 'It's likely she was born in that season.'

Jaysin held up the pup and stared into her eyes. 'Shar,' he said. 'Her name is Shar.'

'An auspicious name,' Garva said approvingly. 'A gift from the dragon.'

'She is indeed,' Jaysin agreed. 'I would not have found her if I hadn't come searching for Harmi.' To the pup, he said, 'Your name is Shar.' He tried to recall a wolf image to represent her name but, realising there was no image for a dragon gift, he chose the image of a wolf presenting another wolf with food. Shar wriggled in his grip.

'The horses are ready,' Garva announced. He held out an object wrapped in cloth. 'This is for your wolf.'

Jaysin accepted the wrapped rabbit corpse, saying, 'Thank you.'

Garva nodded, and said, 'We only have a short time to travel before it is dark.'

'We will travel in the dark,' Jaysin decided. 'I can light the way.' He mounted his horse and sat the bag with Shar in front of him. 'We're ready.'

Garva mounted and shook his head at the sight of the gangly red-haired youth in the dark cloak, clutching a rein in one hand and a bag with a wolf pup in the other, before he urged his horse to follow the riverbank to the bridge and the road.

As the evening faded, Garva held up his hand to halt and listen. Hoofbeats resounded through the landscape. He gestured for Jaysin to follow him into the trees and, moments later, a company of riders cantered by, Kermakk armour visible beneath their riding cloaks. Jaysin and Garva waited until the hoofbeats faded.

'Where are they headed?' Jaysin asked.

'How they have eluded the Menuii is more important,' Garva replied. 'Something is wrong.' He indicated his intention to move back onto the road, but he jerked his horse around and ushered Jaysin deeper into the trees.

'What?' Jaysin demanded.

Garva put his fingers to his lips and pointed to the road. Jaysin saw a Kermakk rider come into view, and another, walking their horses. They were followed by three more and then came a team of horses hauling a creaking wagon packed with wood and metal framework. More riders and four more wagons rolled past. Behind the wagons marched two long lines of soldiers.

When silence descended, Garva led Jaysin onto the road, saying, 'We must ride warily if Kermakk are in the area.'

'What was in the wagons?'

'War machines,' Garva replied. 'I fear for our people.'

'Harmi is with them,' Jaysin said. 'The Kermakk are no match for the dragon.'

'The Kermakk killed dragons in the past,' Garva replied. 'Let us hope the dragon is smarter than its ancestors.'

The night settled in as they rode on, clouds hiding the stars and moon and the road, but when Jaysin conjured a light sphere at shoulder height Garva reined in and warned, 'That is not wise.'

'Without it we can't see,' Jaysin argued.

'Then we will camp and wait for morning.'

'No,' Jaysin replied. 'We're wasting time.' He made the light sphere descend and hover a few paces ahead of his horse to reveal the road and prompted his horse to walk on.

'What if there are more Kermakk?' Garva asked.

'We'll vanish,' Jaysin said. He made the light disappear and the night closed around them. Example made, he reconjured the sphere, set it ahead, and said, 'You can follow.'

The pair rode deeper into the night along the winding road, enclosed by the forest shadows, following a small circle of light floating above the ruts and mud. Jaysin checked on the restless Shar and twice stopped to let the pup stretch her legs and urinate. The road crossed three wooden bridges, and for a time ran parallel to the river, the watery chorus filling the night, gleaming in the overflow of light from Jaysin's magical sphere. Cliffs and steep slopes lurked in the shadows. Exhaustion steadily seeped through Jaysin's body, until he was unable to continue. He slowed his horse and agreed with Garva that they should rest.

'Sarchah is close,' Garva assured him. 'If we rest the horses, we can reach the city before midday. Keep watch for a village beyond these cliffs.'

They crossed a stone bridge over the river where the cliffs fell away to become forest and a small wooden building appeared. Beyond it were half a dozen more buildings. 'What is this place?' Jaysin asked as he stopped.

'A logging and hunting village,' Garva replied. 'It's called Nekdonchet. I've never come this far.'

'Perhaps there's an inn.'

'They would all be asleep,' Garva noted.

As they rode into the village, Jaysin became aware of the odour of burnt wood and then he spotted embers glowing in the centre of a building. He widened the spread of his magical light and elevated it to reveal the road and building facades on either side – and a grim vision.

Before the ruined and glowing remains of what would have been the village inn, six bloodied and naked corpses hung by their arms on stakes, riddled with metal shafts. To Jaysin's eyes, two women and three men had muscular definition he associated with Menuii warriors. The sixth corpse was lithe, with long dark hair. A chill rippled through his being.

Garva dismounted and strode to the sixth corpse, touched it reverently and fell to his knees, howling with despair. Jaysin remained on his horse, taking hold of Shar who sat up in the bag, head cocked, staring at the source of the howl. Jaysin guessed the slaughter and destruction was the work of the troop they encountered in the afternoon, and it worried him that a Kermakk force was freely travelling the road when the Machutzkan Menuii were meant to have caught them. What was Chasse's fate if the Kermakk were still ransacking the countryside?

Garva rose, took out his hunting knife and cut the rope binding his brother to the pole. Although he felt compelled to help, the idea of handling a mutilated corpse repulsed Jaysin. Instead, he watched the Machutzkan rider lower the body and hideously extract each metal arrow, crooning to the spirit of his dead brother as he worked.

Shar whined, forcing Jaysin to dismount and release the pup. He projected wolf images for *Stay close* and *Safe* as he watched the little animal sniff and search and squat to urinate, glad for the distraction from Garva's task.

'I need your help.'

Garva's request interrupted Jaysin's respite. 'What do you want me to do?' he asked.

'Bring Akanda back to life.'

The unexpected request perplexed Jaysin. 'That's not possible,' he said. 'The dead are dead.'

Garva ceased his task and approached, bloody knife in his hand, stopped a few paces short of Jaysin, and said, 'You know dragon magic. Bring my brother back from the dragon's cave.'

'There's no magic to do that,' said Jaysin.

Garva took a step closer, lifting the knife menacingly, and he said in a voice charged with sorrow, 'I know the legends. I know the great god can resurrect the lost. Call the dragon. Save my brother.'

Seeing Garva's desperation, fear trembling in his own voice and flowing through his veins, Jaysin stammered, 'I can't.'

He held Garva's wide-eyed stare, fearing the rider might attack, until Garva dropped to his knees, his chest heaving as he sobbed. Shar trotted toward Garva, but Jaysin scooped her up, afraid the man would react irrationally if the pup touched him, and he stood back and let the rider cry his grief into the earth.

There were no survivors. The buildings were empty, and a closer survey of the charred inn revealed where and how the villagers perished. Reluctant as he was, Jaysin helped Garva pile the corpses and gather combustible fuel and he ignited the funeral pyre with a spell. Garva watched the flames consume their grisly fuel.

'We shouldn't stay,' Jaysin suggested.

'I will give my brother due respect,' Garva stated quietly.

Uncomfortable to be in the circle of light, uncertain as to the safety of the situation, Jaysin withdrew to the shadows and waited, nursing Shar, while Garva knelt before the fire. The pup fidgeted and wriggled until Jaysin let her down to sniff the earth, and when her sniffing was done she curled against his boot.

By the time the flames died, and Garva rose, Jaysin's legs ached from standing. Shar stirred at the sound of footsteps, so Jaysin lifted her and waited for the rider. 'I am going back to Machutzka,' Garva announced.

'But we have to find my brother,' Jaysin asserted.

'You do as your heart commands, and I will do as mine commands,' Garva stated bluntly. 'I am riding home.' He headed for his horse.

Jaysin wanted to argue, wanted to warn Garva that he was abandoning the Dracomenu, but he held his tongue while the rider mounted, wheeled his horse, and galloped out of the village ruins. The hoofbeats faded into the night.

Jaysin considered his options. Staying in the village was not one. He could follow Garva back to Machutzka, but to what end? Harmi was with Tam and their presence drew him toward the city, but he came in pursuit of Chasse, and he was compelled to find his brother, more so having seen the Kermakk threat everywhere. He failed to save his father and mother in Harbin, and the guilt of those failures hung heavily on him, even though he rationalised that he was too young at the time to do anything. He would not fail to rescue Chasse. Chasse had to be nearby if Sarchah was close.

He mounted his horse, dispelled his light sphere, and rode out of Nekdonchet into the night. Clutching Shar, sharing calming images to soothe her, he rode warily and wearily a short distance before veering into the trees and halting in a tiny glade. He was beat. *Even a short sleep will help*, he reasoned. He dismounted, put Shar on the ground while he tethered the horse, chose a patch beneath a tree, coaxed Shar to snuggle beside him, and fell asleep.

His muscles tightened as he sat up, and pain gripped his neck, back and arms. Bitter cold filled his limbs and fingertips. Grey light filtered through the leaves. He looked for the wolf pup, but she was not with him. He pushed to his feet, afraid Shar had wandered away, and concentrated, searching for a canine consciousness – and startled Shar, who came gambolling out of the bushes and stopped at his feet to sink her tiny teeth into his trouser leg and shake it.

Jaysin hoisted the pup to stare into her eyes. 'What were you doing?' he asked. 'Hunting insects?' She stared at him expectantly. 'Food,' he said, nodding. 'You're meant to be the hunter, not me.' He put Shar down and walked to his horse, rummaged in the pack for Garva's gift, unwrapped the rabbit and used his knife to cut small strips of meat. The pup gobbled the offerings greedily. 'Not too fast,' Jaysin advised. When the meat supply ceased, Shar licked her chops, shook, and trotted into the bushes to squat. Jaysin returned to the horse to stow the rabbit – and froze when a tall, armoured figure appeared between the trees.

'What have we here?' a voice uttered to his left, and three more Kermakk soldiers emerged from the undergrowth.

A bearded individual demanded, 'Who are you?'

'A traveller,' Jaysin replied hastily.

Another two soldiers appeared between the trees, holding weapons the Machutzkans called crossbows, the kind used to execute the captives in Nekdonchet. 'Travelling from where to where?' the lead soldier asked.

Jaysin struggled with a quick answer, but as he went to speak a crossbowman shouted, 'Look at that!' and turned his weapon. Shar was slinking toward him from the bushes.

As the crossbowman aimed and pulled the trigger, Jaysin screamed, 'No!', raised his hand and shouted, 'Shasterna!' An energy bolt pulsed from his palm and punched through the soldier, exploding in flames against the tree behind him.

The lead soldier drew his sword and, as the second crossbowman took aim, Jaysin conjured another energy pulse and loosed it. A crossbow bolt whistled past his left arm, shearing through his cloak sleeve, piercing his skin. Anger and fear seething through his shaking right arm, he generated a third pulse, tearing a hole through the lead soldier's armour and chest as the man charged. Jaysin wheeled on the fourth soldier who was frozen by the carnage, and repeated 'Shasterna!', the force throwing the hapless soldier against a tree. The last two terrified men bolted for the road.

Head spinning, life energy sapped, Jaysin heard horses galloping away as he sagged to his hands and knees: gasping for breath, fighting for consciousness.

Jaysin woke, staggered groggily to his feet, and he searched the glade for threat. Four soldiers lay where they fell. His horse grazed nonchalantly beneath a tree. Shar was gone, a crossbow bolt buried in the earth where he last saw her. He listened. Birds twittered and chirped, and a bright blue-winged rand flitted across his vision, the tiny bird chasing a yellow whirring insect. Wind rustled the canopy. His left arm throbbed. Dried blood streaks stained his arm and hand. He shed his cloak and gingerly examined his upper arm. The cut from the bolt wound was shallow and it had stopped bleeding. He pulled on his cloak and sighed. Tiredness saturated his core. The encounter taught him that there was a limit to his use of the magical bolts, each drawn from a combination of inert air energy and his internal source. 'Magic is harnessing energy,' he murmured, paraphrasing advice from a book he studied. 'Energy without and energy within. Energy is finite. Energy must be managed, conserved, and used wisely.'

He focused and searched for Shar, but the pup's mind was either out of range, or worse. Afraid she was fatally injured, he examined where the crossbow bolt was embedded in the ground, but there was no blood on the ground or on the bolt, so he deduced she wasn't injured. He looked for paw prints, but he had limited tracking skill, so he resorted to entering the forest in the most logical direction that Shar may have run, and he searched for her consciousness again. There was no trace. The loss bit deeply. He was ready to be the pup's mentor, her protector, and the bond was deepening – he knew it – but he failed her because he could not protect her from the violence of humans.

Dejected, angry, Jaysin returned to the glade and his horse and glared at the dead soldiers. The two who fled would tell others and they would be waiting for him, if he could not reach Chasse first. He bent over the lead soldier's corpse and studied the man, his clothing, his armour. If he continued on, he would use the illusion spell to disguise himself. He whispered, 'Darven kaa alemna chessar tupau.' As before, he felt the subtle adjustment in the air around him. 'I will be you,' he said to the dead soldier.

Satisfied the spell would work when he chose to cast it again, he dissolved the illusion and rummaged through the dead soldiers' pockets and possessions, collecting coin pouches, and taking rings and chains to use for bartering or payment. He retrieved a crossbow and studied how the mechanism operated. His brother trained with a bow for years after being gifted one by Keshaan, but this mechanical contraption seemed easier to master. He found a quiver of bolts and carried the weapon and ammunition to his horse. Booty secured, he removed the hobble, mounted, pulled up his hood, and rode for Sarchah.

Nine

Jaysin reined in before the junction to take in the vista. Four forested hills, almost small mountains, framed Sarchah to the south and east. Wooden houses and businesses sprawled along the roadside, and the southern buildings formed a narrow island between the road and the river that snaked in from the mountains. Taller stone structures and towers broke the roofline deeper in the city's heart and further along the river, but most buildings were one or two storeys and constructed from wood, thatch and tiles. The city was bustling at midday under a grey sky and thick smoke columns rose from workshops and foundries. Horses, wagons and people streamed along the main road from the junction uniting the west, the north and the central roads, carting and carrying goods in and out of the city.

His logic urged him to camp on the outer limits while he searched for his brother and the warriors, because the presence of Kermakk soldiers on the road, the dead Menuii in Nekdonchet, his narrow escape from the soldiers and Chasse's silence convinced him something terrible had happened to the Menuii, and he needed answers. He believed the answers would be found in Sarchah.

He anticipated casting his disguise to pass soldiers guarding the city entry, but, unlike Machutzka, no wall or great gate separated or protected Sarchah from the surrounding country. He searched the stream of people, but the only soldiers were in a group, standing and sitting, at the side of the north road and quite a distance from him on the west road. Jaysin pulled up his hood to hide his conspicuous red hair and prodded his horse forward to follow a laden hay cart into the city.

People he passed occasionally looked up, but most were too engrossed within their business to be bothered with him. He warily rode past four groups of Kermakk soldiers, his hood tightly pulled to cover his hair, ready to escape, but the soldiers paid him scant attention. Even if the surviving soldiers returned to the city and reported the deaths of their companions, he reasoned in a city so large it was possible no one had yet heard of the incident in the foothills. He was curious, however, as to why there were only men on the road and outside the buildings, and no women or children.

He reined in to study and memorise the features and bearing and clothes of a stall owner selling cooked meat. While he had memorised the dead soldier's appearance, he realised there was far less chance anyone would question a common citizen than if he adopted the appearance of a soldier. The ruse worked in Machutzka, so he was confident he could adopt the vendor's appearance as his illusion. Memorisation completed, he moved on, following the general flow of the travellers and merchants.

The road opened into a broad market square filled with colourful marquees and tents and temporary wood and canvas booths, and people jostled between the structures to the sound of hawkers' shouting and singing the scope of their wares and prices. He expected to see women in the market, but still there were no women or children and their absence bothered him as unnatural. He dismounted and led his horse into the throng.

'You!' a voice challenged.

Jaysin turned to see who was yelling and met an angry bearded face framed by a shaved head. The man wore a distinctive light blue shirt, under a dark blue jacket, and the man's trousers matched his jacket's hue.

'No horses!' the man yelled.

A glance confirmed for Jaysin that his horse was an anomaly in the lively market. 'Where can I leave my horse?' he asked, hoping that his Kermakk pronunciation and accent wasn't questionable.

The man squinted, scrutinising Jaysin, before replying, 'Take it to the hitching wall,' and he pointed diagonally across the heads of people to a street.

Jaysin obediently led his horse around the market perimeter to the street where he discovered a long and high stone wall with a variety of horses hobbled and hitched to wooden rails. The smell of horse dung and urine permeated the space, and the ground was moist underfoot. As he searched for a place to tie his horse, men pushed past him on their way to the market or to retrieve their horses. He selected a rail between a bay and a brown horse, but a heavy-set man in a loose fawn smock with his dark, grey streaked hair stowed tightly in a bun, approached, holding out a grubby hand, and informed him, 'One bit for the remaining daylight, two bits until midnight, three for the night.' He flexed his fingers.

Jaysin hesitated. Dealing in money was an unfamiliar practice. He knew a Kermakk bit was a coin, but as brother to the Dracoshaza in Machutzka he didn't need money because the people freely gave him what he wanted whenever he asked.

'Are you deaf, or do I need to call the Hakamati?' the man threatened.

Jaysin opened his saddlebag, retrieved a purse and fished out a gold coin. 'Will this suffice?'

The man's eyes widened, as if the coin surprised him, but he took it, saying, 'I'll make sure your horse is in excellent order when you return.'

The man's manner warned Jaysin that he did something wrong in the transaction, but he did not know what. Perhaps his Machutzkan or Harbin accent was evident. Perhaps the man recognised his foreign appearance. He wondered what a Hakamati was. He spotted an alley entrance along the street beside a high wall and headed for it.

At the juncture, Jaysin peered into the alley and was pleased to see it was empty of people, although full of discarded crates and baskets. Two white cats eyed him disdainfully before they scampered out of sight. He stepped in, recalled the image of the food stall owner, repeated the arcane phrase 'Darven kaa alemna chessar tupau' and felt the air texture thicken. He returned to the street, lowered his cowl as he walked slowly towards the man who was minding the horses, and stopped, testing if he showed recognition.

The man met his gaze and asked, 'Something I can do for you?'

Jaysin rasped, 'You look after the horses?'

The man repeated the prices he gave Jaysin earlier, and added, 'Do you have a horse?'

'Being curious,' Jaysin replied. Pleased that the man did not recognise him, he entered the market.

He weaved between the stalls that were selling a vast variety of goods – pots, tools, jewellery, food – and still he did not see women or children. Inquisitiveness piqued by the crowd of men heading towards the river, Jaysin joined in the flow and discovered that they were gathering around a stage on which stood armed guards and a tall, weathered and muscular individual in a red robe with a neatly trimmed, full grey beard, his hair tied in a ponytail. The man's gravelly, forceful voice carried to him.

'No fake bidders today! No hopefuls! You are either here to genuinely buy my goods or you're here to watch!' the man called across the crowd. 'Are we ready to begin?'

A ragged shout of 'Yes!' rose from the crowd.

The auctioneer spoke to his guards, and two descended behind the stage and out of Jaysin's view. Seeking a better vantage point, Jaysin shuffled to the left in time to see the men pushing a young woman in chains onto the stage.

'Let's start with a fresh piece of Okkari flesh!' the auctioneer announced. 'Healthy, strong, this one will suit a discerning owner looking for a servant who is pleasant on the eye and can be trained to do as the owner desires!' The terrified woman cowered beside the auctioneer, her dark hair loose and unkempt.

'Twenty bits!' a man shouted from the crowd.

'Are you mocking me?' the auctioneer challenged. 'Twenty bits?'

'Thirty!' another man yelled.

'For thirty bits I get my horse secured for ten nights!' the auctioneer replied. 'This young woman is worth more than ten nights with a horse!'

Laughter rose from the crowd.

'Fifty bits!' someone yelled.

'Eighty bits!' cried a new voice.

'At last someone recognises value when they see it!' the auctioneer declared. 'Do I get better than eighty?' He waited, but no one made a bid. 'Anyone willing to offer more than eighty?' he asked. 'Last chance!' he announced when no further offer came. He groaned, making it clear he was unhappy with the standing bid, smacked his left fist into his right hand, and yelled, pointing at someone in the crowed hidden from Jaysin, 'You, my friend, are a very lucky man! Sold to Kalan Vessenya for the paltry price of eighty bits!' He gestured to his companions who hauled the woman off the stage while he continued his spiel. 'The next offering is a young buck straight from the southern Yargu wildlands. Wiry, easy on the eye and guaranteed a good investment for a worker. Let's say we start the bidding at fifty bits!'

The auctioneer's companions pulled a youth onto the stage, his white skin glowing in contrast to his long jet hair. Jaysin heard murmurs ripple through the crowd.

Three separate voices shouted, 'Fifty bits!' and one spoke again, offering, 'One hundred bits!'

'One hundred and twenty!' yelled a second.

'One fifty!' the first replied.

'Impressive,' observed a man to Jaysin's left.

'Two hundred bits!' a new voice hollered. Loud gasps and appreciative murmurs greeted the bid, and heads turned toward the bidder.

'Someone understands the value of this very rare individual!' the auctioneer cried. 'Does anyone else?' He waited for a counter bid. 'No one willing to own this incredible opportunity?' the auctioneer teased. 'He can speak four languages!'

'Three hundred bits!' yelled a man, and applause rose as people peered in the bidder's direction.

'Three hundred bits!' the auctioneer repeated. 'Now we have a true indication of the value for this beautiful specimen of Yargu youth! Three hundred bits! Do I hear better?'

The bid stood. The auctioneer confirmed the sale, congratulated the buyer on his discerning judgement, and moved onto his next auction. A pair of girls, Jaysin guessed could be ten or eleven summers in age, were ushered onto the stage and the bidding hustle began again.

Fixated by the event, Jaysin watched five more auctions before he eased away from the crowd and headed for a wooden building at the edge of the market square with a sign above the door that proclaimed it in Kermakk as 'The Market Pot.' He only entered two inns in Machutzka in the past three years, one recently, and he didn't spend long in them because the atmosphere and people held no interest. He learned from Tam and Chasse that people went to the inns to drink and eat and gossip, and travellers passing through Machutzka could buy a bed for the night. He would see if the denizens of this place knew or heard of his brother and the Menuii warriors.

Thick swirling smoke in the drinking room stung his eyes when he entered and he coughed. As he refocused in the dim light, he saw several men standing and sitting in the room holding long stemmed smoking objects, which they lifted periodically to their mouths to suck in and exhale smoke. The activity puzzled him as to why anyone would do that or find it pleasurable.

A youth with lank brown hair cut short around his ears and wearing a dark blue smock approached and asked, 'What can I get you?'

As to what the youth could get him, he wasn't sure. 'I'm hungry,' Jaysin said, the aroma of cooked food teasing his nostrils.

'Stew or broth?' the youth asked. 'Stew is two bits, broth is one.'

'What's in a stew?' Jaysin asked.

'Vegetables and lamb.'

'Can I have it without the meat?' Jaysin asked.

'Why would you not have the meat?' the youth challenged.

'I don't eat meat,' Jaysin replied. 'Got any vegetables or fruits or nuts?'

The youth squinted at Jaysin and said, 'Everything has meat in it.'

Realising he wasn't being offered a choice, Jaysin said, 'I'll have a serve of the stew.'

'And a drink?'

'Water.'

'No water,' the youth said. 'Ale, mead or zikka?'

'I don't know those drinks,' Jaysin admitted. 'What do they have in them?'

The youth shook his head. 'Ale is grain, mead is honey, zikka is vegetable.'

'I'll have zikka,' Jaysin decided, pleased it was made from vegetables, although the others sounded good.

'Where you sitting?' the youth asked.

Jaysin surveyed the room. Only two spaces were empty: a small circular table with two stools in one corner and a ragged chair near the hearth. 'There,' he said, pointing at the table.

'Three bits,' the youth announced, holding out his palm.

Remembering the expression on the horse vendor's face, Jaysin fished in his purse and retrieved a gold coin, expecting the youth to either look askance or ask for two more when Jaysin handed him the payment, but the youth accepted the coin, and weaved between the men and tables to a long bench at the rear of the room, where a balding, thin individual with a long grey beard and coloured tattoos along his skinny arms was stirring a black pot.

Jaysin eased past several men and tables to a stool in the corner, from where he watched conversations and action unfolding, but as he studied the customers he became aware that the man behind the bench was analysing him.

The serving youth came back carrying a blue ceramic mug and, when he reached the table, he put down the mug and spread a pile of silver rectangular coins beside it. 'Your change,' he said perfunctorily, 'Seventeen bits,' and he walked away.

Jaysin looked at the pile and understood. Gold coins were worth twenty silver ones. He understood why the horse vendor was interested. He checked if anyone was watching, including the man at the bar, before he opened his purse and emptied the contents. Seven gold coins remained – one hundred and forty bits and the seventeen in change on the table. He had more coins in the soldiers' purses inside the bag on the horse, but he didn't know how much was in them.

'Stew,' the youth announced, placing a crude brown earthenware bowl and wooden spoon before Jaysin. The youth glanced at the coins and retreated. Jaysin scooped the coins into his purse and checked again that he wasn't being watched. He pocketed his purse, picked up the spoon and scooped the stew into his mouth. He was famished and the warm, gluggy mass tasted sensational, and although he was acutely aware of the meat flavour and aroma permeating the stew, because his hunger was greater he wolfed down the serving.

As he wiped his mouth, he observed what was happening around him. Men came and went through the front door. Two groups were playing games at their tables, one with a set of cards, the other group rolling small blocks with symbols on each of six faces. Both groups were animated and noisy, and coins changed hands. Three men in dirty grey smocks, smoking elongated objects and talking quietly, were perched on tall stools and leaned against the far wall under a framed picture of a strange two masted ship navigating a wild sea. Other men drank and talked at the tables. White smoke drifted through the noisy room and the youth moved between the customers and the bench, carrying meals and drinks, and taking money.

Jaysin lifted the chipped mug and sipped the odourless liquid, and coughed as it smarted his lips, tongue and throat. There was no recognisable vegetable taste. Aware that the man at the bench was staring again, he took another sip. The liquid stung his throat and his eyes watered, but he tried to suppress his distaste to avoid drawing attention, deciding that if he ever bought another drink he would choose the one made from honey. He wiped his finger around the bowl to extract the remnant stew liquid and sucked his finger in an effort to alleviate the bitter zikka taste lingering in his mouth. The mug was still three-quarters full, but he wasn't willing to drink it. He also ascertained he was unlikely to get information about his brother easily from the patrons, so he stood and approached the bench.

'Something you need?' the balding man asked. He put down the jug he was drying with a grey towel.

'Heard a curious story about Machutzkans,' Jaysin said, slurring to mask his accent and tone.

'What did you hear?' the man asked. He resumed cleaning the jug.

'There were warriors outside the city,' Jaysin said, gauging the man's reaction to his news.

The man cocked an eyebrow and said dismissively, 'You're a bit late with that news.'

'Are they still out there?' Jaysin asked.

The man put down the jug again, straightened to face Jaysin and replied, 'Beaten, caught, sold and shipped out.' He stared hard at Jaysin and asked, 'You from out of town?'

'I am,' Jaysin replied, hoping the man didn't ask from where because he knew nothing of places beyond Machutzka and the village where Garva and he discovered the executions.

'Thought as much,' the man said. 'Your accent is odd.' He paused to fill two jugs with a golden, frothy liquid for the youth, who carried them to the table where men were playing with the odd objects. Pouring finished, he asked Jaysin, 'Are you here to buy slaves?'

Jaysin wanted to ask what the man meant by slaves, but he replied, 'No. First visit to Sarchah.'

The man squinted and grinned. 'Word of advice, then,' he said. 'Don't go flashing gold around.'

Jaysin surveyed the room, before he asked, 'When you said the Machutzkans were sold and shipped out, what do you mean?'

'You are definitely new to these parts,' the man said. 'Where are you from?'

'North,' Jaysin replied.

'Not really a northern accent,' the man said. 'You're hiding something.'

Before Jaysin could deny the accusation, from behind he heard a voice shout, 'Hakamati!' and the tables where the men were playing games became a flurry of activity as the cards, cubes and coins were hastily cleared, while the young man who called the warning sauntered toward the bench and leaned against it beside Jaysin.

The entry door opened and four men wearing dark blue jackets and trousers like the man who yelled at Jaysin in the market entered and they surveyed the room. Two remained by the door, while two approached the bench, appraising the men at the tables.

'Nothing untoward going on here, Alban?' the shorter man asked.

'Same as every day, Raspa,' the man behind the bench answered. 'Nothing for the Hakamati to concern yourselves with.'

'We're looking for a traveller,' Raspa said.

Alban glanced at Jaysin. 'What's the traveller done?'

'Army wants him,' Raspa replied. 'You seen anyone today who might not be a local?'

'What's it worth?' Alban asked.

Raspa smirked and approached the table where the men were playing cards. He bent, lifted the boot of a patron to reveal a hidden card, and let the embarrassed man put his foot down as he said to Alban, 'Might save you being closed down again.'

Alban met the Hakamata's stare and asked, 'Any description?'

'Young. Red hair. Has too much money for someone of his station.'

Alban chuckled. 'Better send him my way, then, before you arrest him. I could do with a customer with too much money.'

Raspa laughed, turned to the room, and asked, 'Anyone seen a young stranger with red hair?'

The men shook their heads, some muttering, 'No.'

'If you do,' Raspa continued, 'the army wants him.'

'The army wants everyone!' a man shouted from the corner, and murmured agreement met the comment.

'They didn't want you!' another man responded, and laughter erupted.

Raspa shook his head, nodded to Alban, and led his companions from the inn. When the door closed, and the young man returned to keep watch at the entrance, Alban said to Jaysin, 'You'd be needing a place to sleep?'

'I don't know,' Jaysin replied.

'Your Machutzkan friends, those that were still alive, were shipped down river this morning,' Alban said. 'The next barge you can buy a ride on doesn't leave until dawn tomorrow.'

'I don't know what you mean,' Jaysin said quickly.

Alban shook his head. 'Your accent,' he explained. 'I recognise it now. Machutzkan traders come here regularly. I heard about the army attacking your city. Sorry to hear that. The Karudar Marfek might be He-Who-Cannot-Be-Named's mistress, but she's not popular around here. Some of these men lost sons and brothers and fathers to the Great Army. They have no love for the Empire or its wars.'

'I'm searching for friends,' said Jaysin.

'No need to explain,' Alban replied. 'You better go find your young friend with the red hair before the soldiers or the Hakamati do. And if you need a place to stay overnight, you're welcome to come back.'

Jaysin thanked Alban before he exited the inn and walked into the town.

Ten

Leaving The Market Pot knowing he was being hunted, Jaysin returned to where he quartered his horse to discover the horse being led across the square by a soldier and more soldiers talking with the horse vendor. A small crowd was watching the event unfold. He joined the crowd and he overheard a conversation that drove him deeper into the city for safety.

'Why are they taking the horse?' a stocky stallholder asked.

'Belongs to a murderer,' a thin man replied.

'How do they know that?' asked a third individual.

'Had an army crossbow strapped to it and army possessions in a bag,' the thin man explained.

'They think the rider is one of them Machutzkan rebels,' a broad-shouldered man with a long ponytail chimed in.

'How do you know that?' asked the thin man.

'Was speaking to the soldiers,' the broad-shouldered man told the listeners. 'Someone ambushed a team of them on the western road. This gear came from there.'

'Must have been with that Machutzkan lot the army routed,' said the thin man.

'Nah,' said the broad-shouldered man. 'He's from somewhere else. Has red hair and fair skin. Not a Machutzkan.'

'Have they caught him?' the stallholder asked.

'Haven't heard,' said the thin man. 'He's a dead man if they do. Soldiers are brutal with anyone who kills their lot.'

'Stupid to be carrying army gear in plain sight,' said the third man. 'Not a smart customer.'

'Machutzkans are generally dumb,' said the stallholder. 'Easy money when they come to the market.'

Jaysin eased from the gathering and headed into a street, walking as calmly as he could muster while his heart raced, fighting his instinct to run. The horse and his extra money were confiscated. As he learned at the inn, the army and Hakamati were searching for someone who looked like him in his undisguised state, so as long as he maintained the vendor's appearance he would remain hidden. *For how long*? he pondered. He never tested the longevity of the illusion spell, only its robustness. He was feeling energy seeping from him, but he couldn't decide if it was a consequence of sustaining the spell or the result of natural tiredness. He couldn't risk passing out like he did in the forest after fighting with the soldiers.

He walked a long time through the streets as the afternoon dissolved into evening and the grey clouds dropped their torrent on the city, turning the streets to mush. Gongs rang across the city as the sun sank, and men disappeared into buildings and dwellings, emptying the streets, and for a short while Jaysin was oddly alone in the street until the men began re-emerging in the evening light. The event fascinated him because he did not understand its purpose. Women remained absent from the streets. He tried to contact Harmi and Chasse, but both were too far away. He figured Harmi must still be in Machutzka with Tam, and, if Chasse was alive, as Jaysin believed he was, he was almost certainly shipped down river to the Kermakk capital.

Tiredness gradually overwhelmed him, so he sheltered under a narrow porch where he dispelled his disguise to conserve energy and pulled up his cowl to hide his red hair and foreign features. He remembered Alban's offer of a bed and knew it was as good an offer as he was likely to receive in the town, so he retraced his steps through the streets to the market square and the docks and waited patiently in the dark and rain for the markets to close and the inn activity to settle.

Lamplight flickered through the inn's window and spilled into the night. The front door swung open, and three men burst out, arms linked, singing a loud and crude ditty as they staggered across the dark square through the soft rain.

Sheltering under the eaves of a closed market stall, Jaysin watched two lantern-bearing Hakamati emerge from a side street and stop the revellers and a short exchange ensued before the revellers resumed their singing and disappeared along the street. The Hakamati crossed the square, stopping at stalls and holding up their lanterns to investigate. Two figures slipped out of the shadow of a stall and sprinted into a side alley before the Hakamati reached where they had been hiding. Jaysin was concerned the Hakamati would venture in his direction, but they veered away and continued onto a road out of the square. He headed for the inn.

Jaysin entered the smoky common room. Two lamps burned, one on the bench and one hanging from the centre of the ceiling. A solitary flame flickered among the glowing hearth embers. Two patrons at a table close to the hearth looked up as Jaysin entered before returning to their conversation and drinks. Alban sat behind his bench, smoking, but when he saw Jaysin he announced, 'Closing up!'

The men by the hearth rose from their chairs, one pausing to down the contents of a mug. 'See you tomorrow night,' his companion said, and he waved to Alban as the pair walked by Jaysin and exited.

'You've come for a room,' Alban said.

Jaysin lowered his cowl, revealing his face and red hair, and Alban nodded knowingly. 'Your friend told you to come here.'

'He said you would let me stay,' Jaysin replied, maintaining the charade.

'Where is your friend?' Alban asked, rising from his stool. He gestured for Jaysin to follow him through a narrow door behind the bench.

'He's busy,' Jaysin replied. He trailed Alban through the door into a small kitchen where an older woman with white hair and a younger one with long dark hair were busy.

'Seria, my wife,' Alban said, indicating the dark-haired woman. The woman lowered the pot she was drying to pull a shawl over her head, and bowed, and Jaysin noticed a flicker of surprise on her face. 'And my mother,' Alban added. The older woman continued stirring a mixture in a large bowl, ignoring the introduction. 'She has no hearing,' Alban explained. He selected a lamp from three on a small table in the kitchen, lit it, and said, 'Come,' as he opened another door into a corridor. 'This is where we have rooms for those who need accommodation. Overnight is five bits.' He stopped at the second door, pulled a key ring from his belt, unlocked the door and swung it open. 'You can have this room. A bed, bedclothes, a bucket for your needs.'

'What time does the barge leave?' Jaysin asked.

'Sunrise,' Alban answered. 'I will wake you early enough. Passage on the barge will cost you a gold coin.' He grinned amiably. 'Night cap?'

'What?' Jaysin asked.

'A drink to help you sleep.'

'Water,' Jaysin said.

Alban cocked an eyebrow, and said, 'I'll bring you a drink better than water.' He indicated Jaysin should enter before he withdrew.

The room was small, basic, cold. A single wooden bed rested against the wall, with green blankets and a grey pillow on top, and a small three-legged stool stood beside it, doubling as a bedside table. A wooden bucket was placed conspicuously beside the door. There was no window. A carved picture of an unusual white bird with a large orange beak hung crookedly on the wall opposite the bed. Jaysin unfolded the blankets. He was adjusting the picture when Alban returned with two mugs.

'Warm mead,' Alban said, handing Jaysin a mug. 'Nothing better for a goodnight drop.'

Jaysin held the mug near his mouth and inhaled the honey and herb aroma. 'Smells good,' he said. When he sipped, the mead eased down his throat in a warm stream, and he understood why Alban wanted him to try it.

'Good, eh?' Alban asked.

'Yes,' Jaysin replied. 'What is mead?'

'Honey wine,' Alban explained and asked, 'You never had it?'

'No,' Jaysin admitted.

Alban sat on the stool. 'You are from Machutzka, yes?' Jaysin nodded.

'They have fine drinks,' Alban continued. 'Customers brought some when they stayed. You have a drink called cheddah?'

'I don't know,' Jaysin replied.

'What exactly do you do in Machutzka?'

'I – I work in the library.'

'Library?' Alban queried.

'It's a place where books and scrolls are stored,' Jaysin explained.

'Oh,' Alban muttered.

Seeing Alban's confusion, Jaysin asked, 'You can read?'

'I do numbers,' Alban replied. 'Ledgers. Don't need to read. Nothing to read.' He snorted and gestured, 'Drink up.'

Jaysin took another sip, aware that weariness was spreading through his core. 'I was curious why I saw no women or children today,' he said.

'Where?' Alban asked.

'In the market,' Jaysin replied. 'Everywhere.'

'We keep our women and children safe from strangers,' Alban said. 'It's He-Who-Cannot-Be-Named's decree. Women go to market on Shebaal, but they remain at home the other days.'

'What's Shebaal?' Jaysin asked, exhaustion slurring his words. He took another sip of the mead.

'God's Day,' Alban explained. 'You don't believe?'

Jaysin wanted to ask, 'Believe in what?' but he struggled to assemble his thoughts, and he stared at Alban, mouth open, feeling the world fading, thinking, *I am an idiot.*

A vibrating puddle. Boards. He wondered when and why he fell on the floor. The puddle stank of urine. Repulsed, he lifted his head and tried to sit up, but his hands were stuck behind his back. He was naked. He wasn't in the room.

'This one's awake,' said a man over him.

Jaysin looked up at the silhouette against the deep blue sky. Hands grabbed his shoulders, hauled him into a sitting position, and pushed him against a hard surface.

'Welcome aboard, fekeer,' the man sneered, his cropped black beard framing thin lips. 'Enjoy the journey.'

As the man moved away, Jaysin realised he was hobbled like a horse and the hobble rope ran through an iron ring attached to the boards. He was sluggish, as if a heavy hand pressed on his body and his mind. His head ached. The air was chilly. 'Where are my clothes?' he asked. He was making sense of where he was. Boxes and bales were piled by his right side, and baskets and barrels filled the view to his left. 'Where are my clothes?' he repeated.

Another man appeared around the corner of the bales, his brawny arms covered with tattoos, his beard thick and full. 'Stop squeaking like a baby,' the man snarled, as he squatted before Jaysin. 'You've been sold. You're a slave, my friend. You don't own anything.'

'I'm cold,' Jaysin complained.

'Not surprised. There's frost on the grass and fog on the river.'

'Where are my clothes?' Jaysin repeated.

The man squinted, and said slowly, 'Did you not listen?'

'I heard you,' Jaysin replied.

'Good.' The man rose and put his boot on Jaysin's bare left foot and pressed down. Jaysin tried in vain to pull his foot from beneath the boot and squirmed and screamed in pain. The man lifted his boot. 'That's a little taste of what you will feel if I hear you whinge one more time about what you don't have. You don't have anything. Understand me?' He raised his boot.

'Yes!' Jaysin yelled.

'I won't hear your voice again, will I?'

Jaysin recognised the trap and shook his head.

'Good,' said the man. He turned his head, and said to whoever else was on the barge, 'This one's smart. Learns quickly. Should fetch a good price.' He grinned at Jaysin before he disappeared around the bales.

The pain in his foot subsided, but Jaysin couldn't stop shivering. He pulled his knees to his chest and leaned against a bale, hoping he could gain warmth from the scratchy material. The deep blue sky lightened and sunlight spilled across the cargo surrounding him, but he was trapped in the shadow and cold. He wished he had a warming stone. The spell only worked on dense material. He looked at the metal ring. He could conjure the warming spell on it, but it was too small to generate sufficient heat to be of use. The bails, bags, and baskets wouldn't sustain the spell.

He focussed and tried to reach out to Harmi and Chasse and Tam, until he realised he no longer wore his bracelet. Like everything, it was gone. He studied the red welt where someone wrested it from his wrist and over his hand, scraping his skin raw. *Why would Alban do that?* he pondered. *For money? Why? What did I do to him?* His fate, it appeared, was to be sold into slavery in the capital city. He needed a good spell to escape. Translocate was impossible. He didn't know where he was, and he was sure he was already too far along the river to focus on somewhere in Sarchah. The shackles stopped him from moving. He wished he chose to learn the simpler spells around unlocking instead of creating portals and illusions and passing through walls and doors.

The sun rose toward its zenith, but grey rain clouds loomed at the edge of his view and he wondered what would happen to him if the barge was caught in a downpour. He listened to the men discuss their women, their small adventures, what they intended to do in their stay over in the capital as they worked. Two men discussed the war raging in the east and rumours of a brutal battle costing thousands of lives.

Jaysin wished he was in the library, or in his chamber, reading and learning. He wished he was more alert, more wary in the inn. He was thirsty and hungry. 'Can I have water?' he asked, catching sight of a man's head over the barrels. The head disappeared. Perhaps they weren't going to feed him. He didn't know how long the river journey would take.

'Here,' a gruff voice said to his left. A broad-shouldered individual stepped around a stack of bales and squatted before Jaysin, holding a pitcher. 'Open up and I'll pour,' the man said.

Jaysin tilted his head, opened his mouth and the man trickled in water. Jaysin savoured the moisture.

'More?' the man asked.

Jaysin nodded, and the man repeated the routine. He went to leave, but Jaysin stopped him by asking, 'How long is the journey?'

The man looked up as a spot of rain dropped on his face. 'Not quite three days.'

'Do we stop anywhere?' Jaysin asked.

The man grinned through his greying beard. 'No point thinking of escaping. You won't be getting out of the ropes.'

'What if I need to piss?' Jaysin asked.

'Go ahead and piss,' the man said. 'Your mess. Your problem.' He put the pitcher on a barrel near Jaysin. 'I'll leave this here. Someone will give you another drink later this afternoon.'

'What about food?' Jaysin asked.

'Not even three days,' the man said, walking away. 'You won't need food.'

A raindrop splashed on Jaysin's face. And another. Thunder rumbled.

He huddled against the bales to escape the drops, but the rain intensified, drenching him, turning the world watery and cold. Shivering involuntarily, teeth chattering as he fought to stave off the chill seeping into his limbs, knees pulled against his chest, eyes scrunched tight, he wondered, *Are they going to let me die like this? What's the point?* He wrestled in vain with the rope binding his wrists behind his back.

And then an unexpected weight fell across his shoulders and legs, and he understood someone threw a canvas shroud over him because of the texture against his skin and the enshrouding darkness. Despite the shelter, he was already soaked by the rain, and puddles seeped under the edge of the canvas, and it took a long time for his inner heat to fill the air spaces. He closed his eyes and listened to the rain thrumming against his rough shelter. He wondered what would happen next, whether Chasse had suffered the same fate, and whether Harmi or Tam would ever find him.

His sleep was broken and sodden. He woke to stuffy air under the canvas, tried to stretch his legs and slid back into a wallowing stupor. Needing to piss, he had no choice but to let go and then he closed his eyes again and tried to sleep again.

He dreamed he was running from kids throwing stones at him in Harbin, but the background changed, and he was running from people throwing stones in a town. It could be Machutzka. Maybe. A dragon's shadow flitted across the earth at his feet, but when he looked up the sky was dark and

empty. *Someone reminded him of Chasse further along the street, but he wasn't certain, and the person who was Chasse, and yet wasn't, ignored him, and stepped into a thick mist.*

The canvas slid away. He opened his eyes to a lantern and a sense of a man holding it. 'Throw a dry bag over him,' a voice ordered. 'Don't want Alban to lose an investment.' Boots shuffled on wood, the lantern rose higher, and a heavy cloth landed on him. Silhouettes pulled at the thick cloth and tucked it around his shoulders.

'That should keep you warm,' a different voice said. 'Water?'

Jaysin nodded, shifting his legs to ease the cramping tightness. He rolled onto his left buttock to release pressure on his right and let the numbness dissipate.

'Here,' said the man backlit by the lantern, and a pitcher pressed against Jaysin's lips. He tilted his head and drank, grateful to soothe his parched mouth and throat. 'That should do,' the man said, withdrawing the pitcher. 'Another lot in the morning.'

'Where are we?' Jaysin asked.

No one answered. The silhouettes carried away the lantern and left him in the dark under his makeshift blanket. Boots clomped on the boards, receding, and voices faded. A dog barked twice in the distance. Water lapped against wood. As his eyes adjusted to the gloom, he was aware of very faint light glowing on the tops of the surrounding bales and barrels, its yellow hue and inconstant flicker suggested torches or lanterns.

A man yelled, 'Nambor!' and another answered, 'Here!'

Metal clunked to his right. The rain stopped, but he couldn't see stars or moonlight, meaning the sky was guarded by clouds. He heard a brief burst of distant laughter, and a different dog set to barking until it tired of its racket. The cloth was dry and warmer than the canvas. As uncomfortable as he was, he couldn't resist encroaching sleep. *Not that it matters*, he told himself. *I'm not going anywhere*. He was hungry. He closed his eyes.

A patchwork of grey and white clouds prevented the sun from warming the world. Jaysin swallowed, savouring the moisture in his mouth and throat. His captor took the pitcher to refill it, returned, and placed it beside Jaysin without speaking. Occasional conversations between the bargemen reached him; talk of weather, plans for the city, more talk about the war, but the men stayed away. He saw four different individuals, so he guessed that four men worked on the barge. He was hungrier than ever. They were giving him enough water to keep him alive, but no food. He wanted clothes. He wanted the shackles removed.

A man appeared, the kind one with the broad shoulders. He kneeled before Jaysin, and asked, 'Hungry?' He lifted a sliver of flat bread to Jaysin's mouth which Jaysin accepted, chewed and swallowed. 'More?' the man asked.

'Yes,' Jaysin answered.

The man tore a second sliver from the bread and fed it to Jaysin, and waited for him to eat, before he asked, 'Is it true your people worship dragons?'

Jaysin hesitated at hearing the seemingly random question, before he replied, 'No.'

The man lowered his head, as if thinking, before he lifted it and said, 'I was told all Machutzkans were dragon worshippers. That's why they live in the mountains.'

Realising his error, Jaysin said, 'Sorry. You're right. Machutzkans do worship dragons.'

The man squinted, baffled, and asked, 'Why did you say no to my question?'

'I was confused,' Jaysin apologised.

'Why don't your people worship He-Who-Cannot-Be-Named?'

'I don't understand,' Jaysin replied.

The man looked as if he was trying to peer into Jaysin's mind. 'He-Who-Cannot-Be-Named. You have heard of Him?' he asked.

Jaysin shook his head, wondering, *Is this man speaking of Varst*?

'Then your sale into slavery is a blessing,' said the man. 'He is rescuing you from the Dark One and giving you a chance at Redemption. You have been mightily blessed.' The man lifted his arm, opened his palm toward Jaysin, and said, 'Praise to You, He-Who-Cannot-Be-Named, for saving this lost soul and letting us bring him to Your understanding. Praise to You for Your bountiful gift of forgiveness. All praise to You, almighty, all-seeing, all-knowing.'

The man's ritual fascinated and unsettled Jaysin and he wondered why the man could not use his god's name? He watched the man touch his chest and his forehead with the heel of his hand, after speaking, and lower his head for a moment of silence.

When the man raised his head, he asked, 'What is your name?'

'Jaysin.'

'I am Norlin Drasmor,' the man replied. 'I pray you remember my kindness when you stand before He-Who-Cannot-Be-Named.' He smiled as he stood. 'I will bring bread and water again after sunset,' he promised, and he withdrew beyond the circle of bales and barrels, leaving Jaysin perplexed by the man's unexpected and odd visitation.

As the day wore on, Jaysin's discomfort and embarrassment amplified until he could no longer suppress his need to defecate. Wallowing in stench and waste, he was glad when a short afternoon shower washed across the barge, if only because it flushed away a little of his urine and excrement.

Norlin reappeared at sunset with bread and shook his head at Jaysin's situation. He left, returned with a bucket, and washed away the shit and piss. 'Don't be ashamed,' Norlin said, as he kneeled before Jaysin. 'Redemption always begins with a trial. This is His way of renewing your spirit. Be courageous, Jaysin. Build your faith in He-Who-Cannot-Be-Named.'

Jaysin accepted Norlin's mercies and was both interested in and annoyed by the man's proselytizing. Norlin repeated his blessing ritual before he laid the thick cloth across Jaysin for warmth.

'Tomorrow, you wake to a new life,' Norlin said, as he made to leave. 'Be grateful that He chose a new beginning for you, a fresh path to embrace His faith.'

Jaysin heard the other men laugh and taunt Norlin as he joined them.

'Saving another soul?' one asked.

'You know religion is only to keep idiots like you in line,' said another.

'Poor Norlin. Has to save souls to cleanse his own,' the third mocked.

Hunched beneath the blanket, Jaysin promised himself, *I will find a way out of this. I will not be a slave.*

Eleven

The bargemen forced Jaysin to his feet and marched him onto the wharf. He winced and struggled as his leg and back muscles adapted to movement after so long hobbled and cramped on the barge and the flurry of activity around him flustered his capacity to think. The rope hobbles stifled his stride and he stumbled, only to be straightened and pushed forward by his captors. He looked for Norlin, but the men escorting him were the other three bargemen. Dockworkers stopped to stare, briefly, and he was conscious of his lack of clothing as he was coerced toward a crowd. The men pushed him to the rear of a wooden dais where eight prisoners were lined up and under guard. All but one prisoner was trussed and naked. A woman with cropped dark hair, in a green smock, was unshackled. As he was added to the line, the woman ascended the steps onto the dais.

'This, my fine friends, is Lilla, a fully trained and experienced maid, a treasure, a maid worthy of a place in a fine household or business,' announced the auctioneer. 'Unfortunately, her current master has gone to the war and has no further need of her services. He puts her up for auction so that her talents can be enjoyed by someone else. Bidding starts at three hundred bits.'

'One-fifty!' a man yelled.

'Let's not be insulting,' the auctioneer replied. 'We're not offering inexperience here. Lilla can do what few maids, especially fresh ones, can offer.'

'One-fifty!' the bidder repeated. The crowd laughed and jeered.

'Two hundred!' a second bidder offered.

Jaysin listened to the auction banter, reflecting on the irony that when he witnessed the slave auction in Sarchah he was captivated that people could buy and sell other people so easily, and now he was about to be sold in the same way.

The woman finally sold for five hundred bits, the auctioneer decrying her worth was much higher. She walked off the dais and disappeared into the crowd with her new owner, an elderly man by his stooped stature and greying hair.

Each slave led onto the dais before Jaysin, two girls and four boys, sold for between a hundred and two hundred and fifty bits. And then he was shuffled roughly up the steps and placed on display. The crowd stared and commented, appraising him as the auctioneer introduced him.

'Last stock of the morning, and fresh off a barge from Sarchah, I give you a most unusual individual. Machutzkan, according to information we've been given, but we know by his height and hair colour and fine features that his origins lie deeper in the mountains, perhaps even from the west coast regions. Possibly intelligent, given his skin and muscle show no signs of heavy physical use, this one could be a valuable asset to a home as a manservant or eunuch for watching over your women and children.' The auctioneer finished appraising Jaysin by advising the crowd, 'I wouldn't be taking this one for hard work.' The men laughed. 'Let's start the bids, then, at one hundred bits.'

'Fifty bits!' a man shouted.

'Dagmar Elinas!' the auctioneer scolded. 'Go buy the pigs you're looking for and stop wasting my time.'

'Don't waste ours with weak offerings!' Dagmar shouted. 'I came here looking for more of those Machutzkan brutes. You give us the runt of the litter!'

'One hundred bits!' the auctioneer yelled. 'Do I hear a bid?'

'One hundred!' a man shouted.

'One ten!' shouted another bidder.

'One twenty!' yelled another.

Jaysin studied the crowd of bearded men. They wore robes of different hues, a handful were in coats and trousers, and many wore round woven red caps. A few were leaving, peeling off the back or weaving between those remaining to watch the final auction.

A man raised his arm and called, 'I offer two hundred for the lad!'

The auctioneer pointed at him, declaring, 'We have two hundred from Feshnar Mezzin! Do I hear higher?'

Jaysin gazed at the last bidder, the only man wearing a purple robe. His white hair was shaved short beneath his red cap and his white beard was trimmed close.

'A mere two hundred for this unspoiled treasure,' the auctioneer lamented. 'Is anyone going to bid?'

'No one bids against a Feshnar!' a voice called from the midst of the crowd.

The auctioneer shook his head, and announced, 'Two hundred bits and the slave goes to Feshnar Mezzin!' He exhaled dramatically, held one hand high, and said, 'Go, my friends, with the blessing of He-Who-Cannot-Be-Named to protect you. Today's selling and buying is done.' As the crowd dispersed, the auctioneer gestured to his associates who hauled Jaysin from the dais and held him until the bidder appeared with two bald men in grey robes.

Feshnar Mezzin appraised Jaysin closely, and said to a bald companion, 'Fetch something appropriate to cover his frame.' The man bowed deeply before he retreated.

'Do you speak Kermakk?' Mezzin asked.

'Yes,' Jaysin replied warily.

'Good,' said Mezzin. 'That will make it easier for both of us. What else can you speak?'

'Machutzkan. And my home tongue,' Jaysin replied.

'What is your home tongue?'

'I came from Harbin, on the coast,' Jaysin said. 'Ah nee shedder yo. That means "I was born there."'

'But you are not a seagoing warrior,' Mezzin noted. 'So, what did you do?'

Jaysin considered possible answers, but settled on, 'I tended goats.'

'Can you read?'

'Yes.'

'Good,' Mezzin repeated. 'Then I bought myself a bargain.' He paused when his bald companion returned with a grey robe similar to his own. 'Let him dress,' Mezzin instructed. 'Gabnar will untie you.'

The second companion walked behind Jaysin and loosened his wrist bonds and stooped to remove the hobbles. The first companion handed Jaysin the grey robe.

'What is your name?' Mezzin asked.

'Jaysin.'

'Put on the robe, Jaysin,' Mezzin requested. As Jaysin slid into the robe, Mezzin told him, 'Your first compulsion will be to run away. Please don't. Apart from the inconvenience that will cause me, and a minor investment loss, it will not go well for you.' He waited for Jaysin to adjust his robe, before saying, 'Let's walk.'

Jaysin was glad to be clothed and ending his humiliation on the barge and auction dais. He was glad to be free of the ropes. His wrists and ankles were chafed red and stung, and he was still adjusting to walking after being shackled for almost three days. The entire experience was dehumanising and the idea of one human owning another made no sense.

The docks were busy with workers lugging bales and baskets and rolling barrels and carrying crates to and from barges and warehouses. Amid the miasma of sound and odour, Jaysin could smell the ocean, reminding him of Harbin. He looked over his shoulder at the river and saw that it opened into a bay, where ships, some like the dual masted vessel that brought Mikane and his people to Harbin, sat at anchor with gulls circling their masts.

Gabnar led the party from the docks up a paved road, and the second companion followed, while Mezzin walked beside Jaysin. 'I take it you have never been to Vussar Karemachet?' Mezzin asked.

'No,' Jaysin replied.

'And you are not a Believer?'

The question perplexed Jaysin, so he asked, 'What is a Believer?'

'Every person who worships He-Who-Cannot-Be-Named,' Mezzin explained. 'To live in Vussar Karemachet you must be a Believer. Gabnar will teach you, and you will attend the weekly Gathering on Shebaal.'

'Where are you taking me?' Jaysin asked.

'To my home,' Mezzin replied. 'There, you will learn your new duties.'

'Did you buy any other Machutzkans?' Jaysin asked hopefully.

Mezzin shook his head. 'I missed an opportunity. I assume you know the others who were brought here?'

'One is my brother,' Jaysin revealed. 'His hair colour is like mine.'

'I did not see him. He also tended goats?'

'He is a great warrior,' Jaysin said proudly.

Mezzin shook his head. 'Then it's likely he was either sold to the army or bought by a Lekna.'

'What's a Lekna?' Jaysin asked.

'Lekna train fighters to compete in the Karushta. It's for popular and somewhat crude public entertainment,' Mezzin explained. He cleared his throat before adding, 'I never go.'

Gabnar veered left onto a wider street lined with merchant stores, some buildings three storeys tall, where men walked, rode horses and sat on carts, navigating the street as they went about their business. Jaysin studied the places they passed, memorising the road down to the docks. If he had a chance to translocate, he would remember potential destinations. Above the distant roofline, he glimpsed gold-capped towers and cupolas and wondered what lay in that area of the city. The absence of women and children still did not feel right. He also was aware that most men on the street were much older than himself.

Gabnar led the quartet into a street that angled and curved up another slope, again with a cobbled surface, and, apart from a lone white dog, it was empty. The dog jogged Jaysin's memory of Shar and his nagging guilt for abandoning the wolf pup. *But what else could I do*? he considered. *Nothing*, he decided, but he felt deeply sad for failing to protect the little waif.

Gabnar halted outside an iron grill gate set in a high stone wall. He produced a metal key, unlocked the gate and swung it open, and Mezzin ushered Jaysin through.

Beyond the gate, a small garden of fruit trees and green shrubs and coloured flowers was neatly arrayed in rows and a white pebble path led to the front door of a two-storey building with a white stone façade, multiple glass windows and stone steps leading up to a portico and double door. Gabnar locked the gate as Mezzin escorted Jaysin to the house, but Mezzin stopped at the base of the steps to address Jaysin. 'This is where you now live. There are important rules. You never enter the house by this front door. Only my family and my associates do that. Slaves go through the side door, which Gabnar will show you. You will only address me from this point on if I address you first. If I do not speak to you, you must not speak to me. Understood?'

Jaysin nodded.

'If you are asked to answer me, you will address me only as Zekk. In your Machutzkan language it means 'Master.' And only if I address you first. I will not call you by your name. You will be addressed by your role only by everyone in the house. Gabnar will show you where you sleep and eat and he will teach you your role. You cannot leave these grounds without my permission. You will wear the seal of my house on both arms. Gabnar will see to that this morning.' Mezzin coughed before he continued. 'This is the last time I will speak to you informally. You are my possession to do with as I wish. I would like that to be pleasant for both of us. How quickly you learn your place will determine how well you will be treated.' Mezzin gestured to Gabnar, who indicated that Jaysin should follow him.

Gabnar led Jaysin along the side of the house to a wooden door that angled into the earth beneath the house. He pulled on the metal handle to reveal a stone stairway and gestured for Jaysin to descend. The stairway opened into a large cellar lined with shelves stacked with foods and casks and jars and bags. A fireplace was alight in the wall immediately to the left of the stairs and a long table filled the centre. There were doors in the left and right walls and another staircase led up and into the house.

'This way,' Gabnar directed, and he steered Jaysin through the left door into a dormitory, while the second slave proceeded upstairs.

The austere dormitory with its eight wooden beds, four against each side wall, and stark but dirty white walls and ceiling, was uninviting. He looked for a hearth like the one in the main room, but there was none, which meant the room would be bitterly cold in Thahu. He spotted a wooden trough and a cloth hanging beside it.

'This is where you sleep,' Gabnar said. 'The third bed on that wall is yours.' He opened a large wardrobe by the door. 'In here, we keep our robes. You rise before dawn, bathe in the trough, give the morning offering, and dress in your robes. At the end of your day, you undress here, wash your hands and face, leave your dirty robe on the floor outside this door for the cleaners, give the evening offering, and go to bed.'

Jaysin was about to head for the assigned bed when he heard footsteps and, before he could turn, strong hands grabbed his arms and his captors dragged him through the door and laid him on his stomach on the long table and held him down. He struggled, until Gabnar said sharply, 'Stop being foolish! You are wasting your energy and ours!'

'What are you going to do?' Jaysin asked, fighting his fear.

'There will be a little pain,' Gabnar said. 'You will bear our Zekk's seal on your arms.'

'I don't understand. Let me up,' Jaysin pleaded.

He heard the fire being stoked, more footsteps and then searing heat bit into his right forearm. He screamed and tried to wrench his arm free, but whoever was holding it was stronger. And agonising heat lit up his left forearm, and he screamed again, the stench of burning flesh stinging his nostrils. Panic-stricken, he conjuring an energy burst from his right hand that exploded through the wooden floor. Cries of alarm rang out as his right arm was released. He tried to roll, but someone sat on his back and the agony in his arms was brutal. As he released another random energy burst from his hand, a heavy weight cracked against his skull and a voice screamed, 'Again!'

Jaysin was spreadeagled on his back on a hard stone floor. When he opened his eyes, he saw the wooden ceiling with cobwebs spread between the boards and beams. A black spider huddled in a corner. He tried to move his arms and legs, but chains clinked against stone and held him rigid. As he angled his head to the left, a heavy throbbing surged through his skull, making him groan and stop moving. He closed his eyes, trying to make the pain subside, and cautiously straightened his neck. He felt ill.

Time lagged. Footsteps came and went in a room beyond where he lay. He waited for someone to stand over him, but no one came for a long time. He needed to piss and knew he was in the same predicament as on the barge. There was no fighting the situation. He exhaled and let go and closed his eyes. Tam and Harmi would not know where he was, even if they were searching for him, and without the bracelet he could not communicate. As for Chasse, he could only guess at his brother's fate. The

Menuii were obviously routed by the Kermakk soldiers and some taken prisoner. Perhaps Chasse was among them. Perhaps he escaped the fighting and found his way back to Machutzka. Perhaps he was sold into slavery. Maybe he was forced to fight for the Kermakk Great Army in the east. He might be dead. Jaysin's mind raced through all the possibilities, all the outcomes, but slowly he brought his emotion under control and ran spells through his memory, exploring potential for change. *I have so much to learn*, he pondered. *What have Harmi and Tam withheld from me? What is behind the metal door in the Machutzkan library? I need to know.*

A door opened and footsteps approached. Mezzin's face stared down. He wrinkled his nose and said, 'Wash this filth away.'

A man – a servant because of the grey robes – appeared with a bucket and poured water over Jaysin's stomach, groin and legs.

Mezzin stepped back into Jaysin's field of vision. 'I imagine you are not very comfortable,' he said. 'This is the discipline room. I keep it for slaves who struggle to accept their places. I don't like using it, but sometimes slaves give me no choice. Understand this is not how you should be learning your trade.' He paused, as if awaiting a response, but Jaysin chose silence. 'So. You showed my servants you have a hidden talent. What else are you hiding?'

Jaysin stared mutely.

'As you choose,' Mezzin said tartly. 'I will ask the questions. Your answers will determine your fate. Understand?'

Jaysin stayed silent, uncomfortable, his robe saturated from the cursory wash, the watery chill prickling his skin.

'Where did you learn arcane skills?'

Jaysin did not reply.

Mezzin asked, 'If you were given a second chance to act appropriately, can I trust you?'

Jaysin considered the question's opportunities and risks, but he held his silence.

Mezzin shook his head. 'I didn't take you for stupid, but I was clearly wrong in my assessment. Nevertheless, it seems that you are worth a great deal more than a few bits in the slave market. That I do know.' He stepped out of Jaysin's vision and said, 'Make sure he is fed. Bind his hands behind his back and let him sit and stand. Keep a close eye on him.' Footsteps faded and the door opened and closed again.

Jaysin waited for the men to release the chains on his hands. He hoped they would release his legs so he could make an escape, but they tied his hands behind his back before they untethered his ankles and dragged him upright. A man placed a chair behind him and Gabnar appeared and pushed him onto it. A servant tied Jaysin's ankles to the chair legs.

'If Zekk Mezzin did not prize you as highly as he does, I would have smashed in your skull,' Gabnar snarled. 'Whatever oddity enabled you to shoot fire from your hands, it saved your life.' Gabnar leaned in close to Jaysin's face and said quietly, 'For now.' He straightened and said to a bald slave, 'Fetch water and bread to feed this one.' He looked down at Jaysin. 'I have work to do. Remember, fekeer, you belong to Mezzin. He holds your life in his hands. Pray to He-Who-Cannot-Be-Named that he has a purpose for you.'

The pain on his arms and his thumping headache steadily receded through the day like the afternoon light, and the room gradually melted into shadows and darkness. A gong sounded multiple times overhead in the house. The servant who brought bread and water came once. After that, Jaysin was left bound to the chair and alone. He called out, asking to relieve himself, but no one answered and again he was left to piss himself. *Is this what all slaves endure?* he wondered. *Why would anyone want to*

do this to other people?

Light spilled under the doorsill before the door opened. Mezzin entered, followed by two servants bearing lanterns, Gabnar, two soldiers and a portly man with a lengthy brown beard and a shaved head. Mezzin stood before Jaysin, noticed the puddle, and said brusquely, 'I asked that he be kept clean.' Gabnar barked an order at a servant who handed Gabnar his lantern and scurried out of the room. 'My apologies, Sheykermett Bahti,' Mezzin said with a faint deferential tilt of his head. 'I did not expect my servants to be so lax.'

'He's barely a man,' Bahti grumbled, squinting at Jaysin. 'You offer me a boy.'

'But he conjured energy that would kill a man,' Mezzin replied.

Jaysin watched Bahti walk around him, inspecting him. 'You say he came from Machutzka?' Bahti asked, returning to stand before Jaysin.

'Further west, originally,' Mezzin replied. 'He has the colour and features of the dragonship raiders.'

'Didn't our coastal friends put the raiders out of business?' Bahti asked.

'I wouldn't know,' Mezzin replied. 'That sounds like a political matter beyond my level.'

Bahti faced Jaysin. 'You understand our language, boy?'

Jaysin stared silently.

'He has taken to passive resistance,' Mezzin explained. 'Shall I have Gabnar persuade him to be more communicative?'

Gabnar produced a sharp instrument from his cloak and grinned menacingly at Jaysin.

'I speak your language,' Jaysin said.

Bahti's face remained impassive, but he asked, 'How long were you in Machutzka, boy?'

'Three years.' Jaysin replied.

Bahti nodded. 'Were you there when the soldiers came?'

Jaysin glanced at the two soldiers behind Mezzin and said, 'Yes.'

Bahti nodded again. 'I heard there is a dragon guarding Machutzka. Is that true, boy?'

Jaysin did not answer. Whatever game Bahti was playing, he refused to participate. He looked away.

'Can you do magic, boy?' Bahti asked.

Jaysin met Bahti's gaze.

'Are you a mas? A dracoshaza?' Bahti persisted. 'Where is your oozim? Where is your dragon?'

Think what you choose, Jaysin decided, and he maintained his silence.

Twelve

Jaysin did not know how much Bahti paid Mezzin, but he was taken from the city before sunrise and ferried aboard a dual masted ship in the harbour. This time he was locked in a metal cage, his wrists tied behind his back and ankles bound with iron manacles, and he was guarded by two Kermakk soldiers.

When Bahti inspected Jaysin's containment, he informed him, 'You will be a fine gift for the Karudar Marfek,' but Bahti disappeared below deck when a gong sounded and was echoed by deeper bass gongs across the city. The sailors and his guards also disappeared for a short time before they re-emerged to recommence their duties.

The ship's rocking made Jaysin queasy, and he wished the world would be still so he could adjust to the motion. Sailors untied ropes and hauled on hawsers to raise the spars and unfurl sails, and the early morning sky turned as the sails cracked in the breeze and the ship heeled to starboard and headed out of the river mouth into the wider bay. White gulls circled the mastheads and swept low across the waves toward the shore as the wind caught the sails and drove the ship from the land, and one man's gravelly voice bellowed orders that sent sailors scurrying to new tasks.

As much as the heave and sway affected his senses, Jaysin became absorbed in the ship. He never wanted to go on the dragonship journeys, even less so when he learned from Chasse how the southern summer journeys were not heroic dragon hunts but raids on villages and killing people, but the desire to sail over the ocean lay deep in his fibre, and now, for the first time, he was heading out to sea, and he was rapt as he savoured the salty ocean and seaweed tang.

By late morning, the overcast sky threatened rain and the wind shifted to the north-east, pushing the ship swiftly over the waves. A squall raced across the ocean and Jaysin hunkered in his cage as rain enveloped the vessel, but the squall quickly moved on, a receding grey wall heading south-west. Soaked, Jaysin shivered until the sun broke through the clouds and bathed the deck in warmth, and all the while the sailors went about their duties.

A short man, his head wrapped in a green bandana, a goatee adorning his ruddy chin, arrived with a bowl and fed Jaysin gruel with a ladle through the bars. The sailor didn't speak, and Jaysin wasn't interested in speaking, so the feeding proceeded in silence. The man tilted a mug so that Jaysin could sip water, though most of the liquid spilled before Jaysin could enjoy it. Task complete, the sailor disappeared down a hatch. Jaysin expected Bahti to emerge, but his captor remained below decks as the day wore on.

Mid-afternoon, a sailor perched in the crow's nest on the main mast cried, 'Cheznah!' and shipboard activity increased. Ropes were hauled and tied off and sails adjusted, and Jaysin felt the ship slowing as it tacked into the wind. Everything fell into a lull.

The sun was on the horizon by the time Jaysin sighted clifftops and distant forested hills over the ship's railing. The gravelly voice barked orders, the sailors lowered the sails and spars, and a heavy chain rattle was followed by the splash of the ship's anchor. Bahti appeared on deck, but he ignored Jaysin while he conversed with a small group of men before he went to the side of the ship and climbed over.

When the sun set, the gong sounded on the ship and the same ringing rose from the shore. The sailors retreated below deck for a short while and returned, but it was dark before Jaysin was taken from his cage and lowered over the railing into a longboat. As his escort heaved on the oars, Jaysin studied the lights sprinkled along the shoreline and up a low slope. Wherever he was, the town was smaller than Sarchah or Machutzka. His wrists and ankles were chafed and sore from his bonds again, and he was hungry and thirsty. The awe of being aboard a ship in the morning soon gave way to boredom by midday and he was glad to be heading for solid ground.

The longboat scraped alongside a pier and Jaysin was hauled up a short ladder onto the wharf. In the lamplight, he was bundled onto a dray and his leg chains pegged against the vehicle's side planks. The driver urged the four horses into action.

The dray rattled across the wooden planks onto a rough road that climbed the hill through a maze of silhouetted structures, some with windows framed by lantern light, and Jaysin glimpsed shadows of men moving through the night. The horses turned onto an avenue of manicured thin tall trees, covered from base to tip with leaves, the trees forming a tightly spaced guard of honour. Light cascaded onto the last section of the avenue and the dray halted outside a stone mansion lit with lanterns and torches.

Men in grey robes appeared, bald heads shining in the lights, and they unshackled Jaysin and marched him away from the large house to a smaller stone building. The slaves ushered him inside and half-carried him down stone steps into a chamber lit by a solitary lantern sitting on a wooden table at the centre. His leg chains were attached to rings on the floor and then the slaves removed the lantern and left. The light faded up the steps, a door clunked, and he was alone in darkness.

All day, he pondered what Bahti was planning for him and how he might escape. He hoped that Tam or Harmi would find him and castigated himself for thinking he could find or even rescue Chasse on his own. His bracelet was gone. None of his magic enabled him to break his chains. If his hands were free, he could use the energy bolt to break the chains. But they weren't. He was hungry. He needed to relieve himself and again he was subject to humiliation.

As a child, he was sometimes afraid of the night and the enveloping darkness reminded him of those childhood fears. The silence was absolute. When he stopped, he could only hear his breath and heartbeat. The air was cold and pungent with odours, a mixture of mould and something odiferous. He rattled his chains. They allowed him to stand and sit, awkwardly without hands for stability. He relieved himself at one extreme of his confined space and sat at the opposite length, pulling his knees to his chest for warmth. And he cried. He wished he was home, or in Shika's library where he was safe and happy. He wished he had never been so foolish to believe that he could find or rescue Chasse. He couldn't even save himself.

Jaysin woke. As his eyes adjusted, he recognised Bahti standing over him, flanked by bald men with lanterns. Stiffness tortured his body.

'It's time to talk,' Bahti said. He gestured to a slave who retrieved two wooden chairs from near the table and placed one before Bahti and one beside Jaysin. To another slave, Bahti ordered, 'Clean that mess and fetch a waste bucket for our guest.' He indicated for Jaysin to sit, and as one minion helped Jaysin onto the chair Bahti also sat. 'I understand you might not consider this comfortable accommodation, but I need to know quite a few things about you before I can determine if you are a burden or a risk,' Bahti explained.

'Where am I?' Jaysin asked.

Bahti stroked his brown beard, and replied, 'In good time. I will ask the questions first, and then, perhaps, there will be questions I may answer.'

Jaysin assessed the man sitting opposite, noticing a scar extending across Bahti's bald pate. The man's glittering bright brown eyes warned Jaysin that behind them sat a sharp intelligence and, although nothing about the overweight man suggested physical strength, the compliant presence of his grey-robed servants demonstrated Bahti had significant power.

'You came from a coastal village?' Bahti asked.

Jaysin was tempted to refuse answering the questions. What could Bahti do that he hadn't already done? *But I might learn about Bahti by answering*, he reasoned. 'Yes,' he replied. 'Harbin.'

'The infamous Dragon Fang.'

'You know my home?'

'By reputation,' Bahti said. 'Raiders. Minor nuisances. But you are no dragonwarrior.' He stared at Jaysin. 'We believed the dragons were long dead. But that's not true, is it?'

'I don't understand –' Jaysin started, but Bahti cut across his response.

'Do not lie to me,' he warned coldly. 'Our soldiers saw your dragon in Machutzka. We know a dragon is there. Your dragon.'

'I don't have a dragon,' Jaysin replied.

Bahti stood and kicked Jaysin's left leg sharply, spinning his chair. A grey-robed assistant twirled Jaysin's chair back to face Bahti. 'You burned holes into Mezzin's wall and floor,' Bahti said calmly. 'That makes you a wizard. And a wizard cannot exist without a dragon. Correct?'

'I'm not a wizard,' Jaysin said, fighting his fear, and he realised a possibility. 'If I was a wizard, would I still be sitting here, letting you do this?'

'A ruse,' Bahti said flatly. 'You're protecting your dragon.' He gestured to a slave, who produced a small black vial and a piece of cloth. Bahti leaned forward to keep Jaysin's attention, and said, 'We do know that, so long as you are conscious, your dragon can go about its business freely. Even when you sleep, it is free of you. But knock you unconscious and your dragon is also unconscious. And if your dragon is somewhere unsafe it can't defend itself.' He smiled cruelly. 'Of course, kill you, and your dragon dies. Very convenient – for your enemies. Most inconvenient for you and your dragon.'

Jaysin shook his head. 'I am not a wizard. I have no dragon.'

Bahti gestured to his slaves. One grabbed Jaysin's head and tilted it back while the other pushed the cloth over Jaysin's mouth and nose and tipped drops from the vial onto the cloth.

'In a few moments, you'll lose consciousness,' Bahti said, 'and whatever your precious dragon is doing it will also instantly stop. Let's hope it's not bad timing for the dragon.'

Jaysin fought through the grogginess clasping his mind as he struggled to focus his eyes on his antagonist. Bahti's pudgy face swam in flickering torchlight. 'Saving your dragon is easy,' Bahti said. 'The Karudar Marfek will make you a hero.'

'I don't have a dragon,' Jaysin mumbled.

'If you keep this stupidity up, you won't have a dragon,' Bahti said. 'Another round.'

The cloth. The pungent smell. Emptiness.

Cooked food. Vegetables. He could smell them. Fresh. Close. Darkness cloaked the chamber. He was hungry, brutally hungry. To eat. Drink. His lips were cracked. *How long have I been unconscious? How many times?* Fog shrouded his mind, but the sweet scent of food made his parched mouth water. Even the meat. He would eat it. But where was it in the pitch dark? He whispered, 'Leoht' and a light sphere appeared an arm span above the central table, bathing the chamber in its radiance. Steaming bowls sat on the table, but the table lay outside of his reach when he was standing in the chains.

'Hunger is a great motivator,' said a familiar voice.

Jaysin spotted figures in the shadows. Bahti stepped into the light.

'Do you want to eat?' Bahti asked. He sat at the table, picked a hunk of meat from a bowl, and lifted it to his lips. 'It smells good.' He looked at Jaysin. 'Want some?'

'Why are you doing this?' Jaysin asked.

'You know why,' Bahti replied.

'I have no dragon,' Jaysin stated. He wanted the food.

Bahti bit into the meat, chewed, and paused to say, 'You must be very hungry.'

'If I had a dragon, you would already be dead,' Jaysin said.

'So you said before,' Bahti replied, and he took another bite. 'I'm surprised to be still very much alive.'

Have I said that before? Jaysin wondered. *What have I said*? The fog closed in, confusing his thoughts, and peeled away. 'Please?' he begged.

'Swear allegiance to the Karudar Marfek and you can eat,' Bahti said. 'Help the Empire against its enemies and you can eat anything you want, as much as you want, whenever you want.' He licked the meat in his hand, savouring the flavour.

'I swear allegiance,' Jaysin said, unable to fight his desperate need to eat.

Bahti stared at him. 'And your dragon?' he asked.

'And my dragon,' Jaysin said. 'Please.'

Bahti nodded to a slave who approached, carrying a bowl. The slave kneeled before Jaysin, scooped a chunk of meat with his fingers and fed it to Jaysin who wolfed down the offering, almost choking as he swallowed. He waited in anticipation while the slave scooped a second serve.

'That is enough,' Bahti said. The slave returned the bowl to the table. 'I would hate for you to make yourself sick by scoffing food after such a strict diet,' Bahti said. 'So,' he continued, clearing his throat. 'We have an agreement. You and your dragon will aid the Kermakk Empire in its war against the eastern kingdoms. I will send a message to the Karfeshnar with this good news.' He turned to leave.

'What about my chains?' Jaysin asked hopefully.

Bahti smiled benignly. 'I trust you will keep your agreement. I don't trust that you won't try to escape. And I have to be sure your dragon will also be agreeable. Until I'm assured on all three counts, the chains remain.' He left the chamber with his entourage of slaves.

'What about more food?' Jaysin yelled. 'And I'm thirsty!' The chamber echoed with his voice, but no one answered.

Angry, dejected, his arms locked behind his back, his ankles bound to the chains and rings on the floor, Jaysin stared at the table beneath his hovering light sphere. *How long am I staying here*? he pondered. *What else does he expect*? The food aroma lingered. There were spells he could have learned that would have levitated the food to him. There were spells to break chains. He sighed and his head drooped. *They expect a dragon, and I don't have one*, he rued. He extinguished his light sphere and closed his eyes.

Bahti issued orders while his minions hauled Jaysin out of the chamber and up the stone steps, with his ankles hobbled and his arms braced behind his back. His eyes smarted when they dragged him into the mid-morning light and he squinted, the commanding stone mansion coming into view against a background of tall leafy green trees and blue sky pocked with puffs of white cloud. He became aware of a circle of men – soldiers – at least thirty, who held crossbows like the one he took from the soldier outside Sarchah, and he was ushered to the circle's centre.

Bahti stood before him and ordered, 'Call your dragon.'

Jaysin assessed the situation, wondering if Bahti was calling his bluff, or really was expecting him to call a dragon? *I have to get out of this*, he decided. There were horses at the mansion. He could visualise the place where they were tied almost a hundred paces away. *Further would be better, but I have no clear memory of anywhere else. I need my hands free.*

'We're waiting,' Bahti said.

'I'm trying to clear my head to make contact,' Jaysin replied. *I have to take a chance that these people have never seen magic*, he decided. 'I need my hands to make a calling circle.'

Bahti stared impassively. 'There are thirty crossbows aimed at you. One stupid act and you'll be a pincushion.'

Jaysin did not know what a pincushion was, but he understood the threat. 'Let me explain,' he said, fighting his fear. 'To summon my dragon, I need to create a contact point. She is far from here. I have to summon her across the – across the arcane web.' He was grateful that he remembered the term. 'To do that, I have to conjure a blue disc.' He glanced across the space to the horses. Two soldiers were leaning against the tie-rail, presumably tending them. 'I can't do it without free hands.' *I'll still be hobbled,* he thought. *This won't be easy*. He looked at the ring of soldiers. *And I'll have to be quick.*

Bahti gestured to a slave who stepped behind Jaysin and jiggled roughly with his bonds. Blood rushed painfully into Jaysin's hands as the wrist bonds were loosened and he shook his arms to restore circulation and relax tormented ligaments and muscles.

'Do what is necessary,' Bahti said, as he backed toward the edge of the circle. 'And don't be stupid.'

I could kill you with one energy burst, Jaysin thought angrily as Bahti moved away. *I might yet*. He sucked in a deep breath and mentally pictured the space beside the horses. 'Hrnetya zhemtaga otreva goust. Jakeyva enam wi. Ahtem,' he whispered. A sparkling blue oval portal appeared. He lunged.

Jaysin leapt to his feet beside the startled horses and glanced back at Bahti and his men who were milling where the portal appeared and vanished. Two soldiers lay writhing at the circle's edge, victims of colleague's crossbow bolts. Jaysin focused on the chain binding his ankle manacles and loosed an energy bolt that ripped the links apart and tore into the ground, shocking him with its intensity. The terrified horses whinnied and wrenched at their tresses and the soldiers minding the animals stared in open-mouthed disbelief. Jaysin raised his hand and the soldiers panicked and bolted. Aware that Bahti and his men were running towards him, Jaysin unknotted the closest reins, and when the reins came free he pulled himself onto the roan horse and grabbed its mane and neck as he urged it to gallop, smashing his face against its pitching neck as it bolted for the avenue.

Jaysin clung to the horse as the horse galloped into the town, but he lost his grip and pitched to the ground when it veered sharply left. Winded, arms and legs grazed and bruised by the fall, nose bleeding and mouth and lips numb, he struggled to his feet and looked up the incline to see who was pursuing, before he realised that nearby men on the street were staring at him.

He stumbled for the shelter of a narrow alley, hampered by his injuries and broken chains, and several paces in he burst through a part-open door, surprising men seated at a small wooden table.

'Who in the Unnamed are you?' a man demanded, rising.

Jaysin retreated into the alley and ran deeper, scattering three cats and causing a dog to bark ferociously from behind a green door. He looked over his shoulder to find the man who challenged him had stopped pursuing and was standing, arms akimbo, watching his escape, so Jaysin kept running, fighting his pain and breath as he headed for the end of the alley.

Emerging on a street, its length in both directions covered with clothes lines strung from building to building, he turned left and jogged until he spotted an alcove between two buildings crammed with bags and crates. A sign proclaimed the left building as a tanner's shop. The right building looked like a dwelling. He limped into the alcove and sank among the detritus, heaving to catch his breath as he shifted a crate to hide his presence. An irritated rat scuttled deeper into the pile.

Jaysin had no concept of where he was. His memory of the journey from the dock to the mansion and his prison was vague, tainted by travelling at night, blindfolds and the rounds of induced unconsciousness coupled with starvation. He was thirsty and hungry. He needed to eat and drink and rest. His nose and mouth ached from colliding with the horse's neck and the cuts on his body and limbs stung. Blood smeared the front of his garment.

Jaysin listened as he rested, anticipating pursuit. He decided he would fight if he had to, but the best option was to translocate, even if it was back into the alley he just traversed. He couldn't remain where he was. Bahti would be searching and he would disperse his men to find Jaysin because he was determined to enslave Jaysin and his alleged dragon to serve the Empire. 'Except I have no dragon,' Jaysin whispered.

He needed an illusory disguise. He saw more than enough of Bahti to assume his guise, but Bahti was an important figure, so adopting his appearance wouldn't work, at least not for long. He had to take the semblance of someone who would not attract attention. He recalled Gabnar easily enough. His guise might work. And there was always the meat vendor whose appearance he assumed in Sarchah. The vendor's appearance would be the best choice: neither a slave, nor a servant, nor someone important. *I need to hide in plain sight*. He would steal from the washing garments hanging in the street to clothe himself, using long sleeves to hide his slave branding.

When he was certain the street was quiet and he was safe, he recalled the vendor's appearance and whispered, 'Darven kaa alemna chessar tupau.'

Thirteen

'You want to eat, you need bits,' the innkeeper said gruffly. 'We don't feed vagrants.'

'I can work,' Jaysin pleaded. 'I can muck out your horse troughs or the stables.'

'Already got lads who do that,' the innkeeper told him.

'I'll do anything,' Jaysin said. 'I haven't eaten for days.'

'You a professional beggar?' the innkeeper asked warily, fingering the handle of a large baton shoved through his belt.

'No,' Jaysin said. 'Just unlucky.'

'Improve your luck by moving on before I beat you to a bloody pulp and feed you to my dogs.'

Jaysin retreated onto the street and glanced up at the sun. It was already late afternoon, and this was the third inn that he tried for food for the day. Water was not a problem. He slaked his thirst from a horse trough outside the first inn, but the owner chased him away when he asked for food. The second innkeeper laughed and said, 'If I see you again, I will call the Hakamati.' He passed a small market, but there were too few stalls to hazard stealing food and he was not an adept thief.

He stepped aside two times for soldiers and three times for Hakamati, careful not to act suspiciously or to give them cause to stop and question him. His illusion spell was holding, his guise seemingly effective, but his energy levels were dropping rapidly without sustenance or rest and he was afraid he would either lose his illusion or collapse if he did not eat soon. He could afford neither to happen. Even with the illusion spell, he had to move cautiously because the chain fragments attached to his anklets, invisible to observers, clanked on stone and dragged along the ground. He needed a blacksmith or someone who could remove them, but that would mean dropping his disguise.

Jaysin turned another corner to follow a descending street toward the docks when the aroma of cooking stopped him outside a dwelling. His mouth watered. Even though he knew it was foolish, he checked no one in the street was nearby before he peered through the open window. A black steaming pot was suspended by a tripod over a low hearth and a fresh bread loaf sat on a small wooden table near the hearth.

'Smells good,' a woman said. Startled, Jaysin stepped back, but the woman's blue shawled head and shoulders filled the window frame, and she said, 'I'm guessing you're hungry.'

'Sorry,' Jaysin apologised. 'I don't have any coins.'

'I'm not asking for any,' the woman replied. 'Do you want a serve?'

Licking his lips, Jaysin answered, 'If it's no trouble.' He glanced guiltily left and right, looking for soldiers and Hakamati. A man toting a sack walked by, but he showed no interest in Jaysin and two men on stools outside a doorway, two buildings along, were talking and smoking.

'Take off your boots and come in,' the woman invited.

Jaysin scanned the street again for anyone watching before he entered the blue daubed door. Removing his boots was problematic, he realised, because they were an illusion. His feet were bare. *How do I dispel part of an illusion?* he puzzled. 'My – my feet are – are dirtier than my boots,' he explained.

'Take off your boots and I will wash your feet,' the woman offered. She scooped a ladle of stew from the pot into a dark blue earthenware bowl and placed it on a small wooden table near Jaysin. The aroma made Jaysin salivate.

'I can't let you do that,' he replied. 'I'll take the bowl and sit outside.'

The woman's dark eyes gleamed, as she said, 'Sit and eat.'

'Thank you,' said Jaysin, glad the issue of the boots was resolved. He sat on a three-legged wooden stool and eagerly set to eating.

'How long since you last had a meal?' the woman asked, as she poured a golden, frothy liquid into a mug.

'A while,' Jaysin mumbled with his mouthful.

'Slow down, then,' the woman recommended, as she put the mug by the bowl. 'Or else you'll throw it all up and that would be a waste.'

As much as he wanted to gulp down the warm stew, Jaysin took a deep breath to control his impulse. Warm food was so good after being imprisoned. He scooped the next spoonful, savouring the vegetable and herb flavours, even the salty meat taste, and then he drank from the mug, noting the drink's bitterness. 'What is this?' he asked.

The woman cocked an inquisitive eyebrow. 'Beer,' she replied. 'You've never drunk beer?'

Fearing he blundered, Jaysin said, 'No, I mean yes, but I've not had any for a while.'

'Where are you from?' the woman asked, as she cut a thick slice from the bread and put it beside Jaysin's bowl.

'Sarchah,' Jaysin replied, remembering the vendor whose disguise he was adopting.

The woman chuckled as she took Jaysin's bowl and headed for the pot to refill it, and she said, 'You're starving, your accent is bad, and you're terrified of the Hakamati. So, you're not from Sarchah.' She ladled more stew into the bowl and returned it to the table. 'I don't care where you're from, and you don't have to tell me.'

'I'll go,' Jaysin offered, starting to rise.

The woman put a gentle hand on his shoulder to stop him rising. 'Stay and eat. I won't let anyone starve.'

'Why are you doing this?' Jaysin asked, as he settled on the stool.

'It's what I do. My name's Iris. I feed sailors who come into port and want a good wholesome cooked meal.' She winked and added, 'And if they have coin to spare, sometimes I give them something more.' She sat on a stool opposite Jaysin and lowered her shawl to reveal her long, dark hair. 'What's your name?' she asked and added, 'Your real name?'

Jaysin paused from eating and studied Iris. Older than him, older than his sister, her face was strong and attractive, although lines creasing her forehead and the corners of her eyes betrayed her age. Her dark hair complemented her dark eyes. Her face and her kindness suggested she was trustworthy, but he could not tell if he could risk his true identity with her. 'Markoo,' he improvised.

Iris looked as if she was assessing the validity of his reply, before she said, 'Why are you hiding?'

'I'm not exactly hiding,' Jaysin told her. 'I – I lost my work and I've been trying to find a place to start again.' He continued eating.

'What do you do?' Iris asked.

'I'm a vendor. I had a shop stall in Sarchah, on the road. I sold things, like shawls and bracelets and boots.'

'But why are you in Cheznah?'

'I thought it might be a good place to start a business.' He paused from eating to empty the mug.

Iris shook her head. 'You made a bad choice. Cheznah is a closed community. Sheykermett Bahti rules the island with an iron fist. Outsiders are welcome to trade and spend their coin, but they are not invited to stay.' She stared keenly at Jaysin. 'Except slaves. They are brought here and made to stay.'

Iris' gaze unsettled Jaysin because he felt that she guessed he was not what he was pretending to be. 'I'm no slave,' he said.

'Do you need a place to sleep?' Iris asked, rising.

'I have no money,' Jaysin said.

'It's free,' Iris replied, fetching the jug to refresh the beer mug.

'Why are you doing this for me?'

Iris sat again and waited until he met her gaze. 'He-Who-Cannot-Be-Named put kindness towards others deep in my heart,' she explained, 'especially those who need help. I have devoted my life to sharing this gift. As I said, mainly sailors visit, but now and then someone less fortunate, like you, also happens by.'

The offer of a place to sleep to recover his strength appealed to Jaysin, but he was suspicious and hesitated to accept Iris' offer because the last time that he accepted help he ended up in chains.

As if sensing his wariness, Iris said, 'I've never handed anyone over to the Hakamati or to Bahti's soldiers. That's not my responsibility. In my house, you are safe.'

'What about your man?' Jaysin asked.

Iris laughed. 'He won't be bothering you. He died five years ago on a battlefield fighting for another woman.'

The reference to another woman puzzled Jaysin, but he asked, 'You live alone?'

'I have two children; a boy and a girl,' Iris told him. 'Stay, and you'll meet them.'

'Where are they now?'

'Tasshja is washing clothes. Amin works on the docks.'

'I have to find a way back to the capital,' Jaysin said.

'Then you need to get aboard a ship again,' Iris replied. 'Without money, that won't be very easy.' She smiled. 'But you obviously got here, so perhaps you know a way to get back.' She gestured for Jaysin to follow as she opened a door into a small bedroom with an open window. 'You can rest in here until you're ready to leave,' Iris offered. 'If you want more to eat, come out and help yourself. I always have a stew on the fire.'

Jaysin closed the door and went to the window. It opened onto a small grassy yard adjoining the rear of other buildings and the late afternoon shadows made the space appear cold. A scruffy tan dog stared up at him. 'Hello,' he said to the dog, but the dog remained fixed and staring. He examined the room. The warm stew and beer placated his hunger, but exhaustion loomed, and the bed beckoned, so he lay on the bed, let his disguise evaporate and slid into a deep slumber.

Jaysin felt the presence before he opened his eyes. Peeking, he discovered a girl in a dark blue smock with long brown hair studying him. He opened his eyes properly. His face ached, especially his nose.

'I don't know how you got in here,' a familiar voice said, 'but don't be afraid.'

Panicking, Jaysin sat up, remembering that he was no longer cloaked in his illusion. Iris stood by the door. Warm sunlight angled across the wall from the window.

'What's your name?' Iris asked.

There was no escaping the question. 'Jaysin,' he replied. He could translocate to the street and run. *How long did I sleep?* he wondered.

'Hungry?' Iris asked.

He was hungry. He remembered eating in disguise, but he was still hungry. 'A little,' he said.

'Tasshja, fetch a bowl of stew,' Iris said.

The brown-haired girl moved away from Jaysin's bed and eased past her mother, but she kept watching Jaysin until she left the room.

'That's my daughter,' Iris said. 'She wants to know who painted your hair.'

'My hair?' Jaysin asked, his hand automatically rising to touch it.

'Red hair is rare in these parts,' Iris explained. 'You're from the western shores. Red hair is more common there.'

'How do you know that?' Jaysin asked.

'Anyone who lives near the sea knows about the western raiders,' Iris replied. She looked at Jaysin's ankle shackles and loose chain remnants. 'I know someone who can remove those,' she said. 'When did you climb through the window?'

Jaysin glanced at the open window. 'Last night,' he replied, recognising that Iris wasn't associating him with his former appearance as the vendor.

'There was another man in here,' Iris said.

'It was empty when I climbed in,' Jaysin told her.

'And someone made you a slave,' Iris said, looking at Jaysin's arms.

Jaysin looked down at the symbols burned into his skin and felt the residual memory pain. He pulled down the sleeves of his stolen shirt.

'You're not the first slave I've helped. I doubt you will be the last,' Iris told him. Tasshja returned, holding a steaming bowl. 'Take it to the young man,' Iris told her daughter. Tasshja handed Jaysin the bowl and a spoon, and stepped back beside her mother, burying her face into Iris' side. 'I think my daughter is taken with you,' Iris teased, and Tasshja pushed her mother in reply. 'Fetch Jandis Neyma,' Iris told Tasshja. 'Tell him bonds need breaking.' Tasshja glanced at Jaysin before she retreated into the main room.

'Who is Jandis?' Jaysin asked.

'A man who knows how to fix things,' Iris replied. 'Relax and eat.'

Jaysin scooped a spoonful of stew, but before he put it in his mouth he asked, 'Do you know which ships sail to the capital?'

Iris sat on the bed beside Jaysin and said, 'A ship goes every day. *The Divine Wind*. Sheykermett Bahti travels on it to Vussar Karemachet to conduct business.' She waited for Jaysin to finish a mouthful before she asked, 'Why would an escaped slave want to go to the capital?'

'I'm searching for my brother,' Jaysin replied.

'It's a big city,' Iris said. 'If he's been sold like you, he could be in any one of a hundred households or businesses.'

'He's a warrior,' Jaysin said. 'I heard he might have been bought by a Lekna.'

'That would make your task easier, if your brother has survived the Karushta.'

'Chasse would not die easily,' Jaysin asserted. 'My brother is not an ordinary man.'

'*The Divine Wind* sails for Vussar Karemachet at sunset,' Iris said. 'Getting aboard will be impossible for an escaped slave.'

'I have a plan,' Jaysin said. 'I need clothes like a sailor would wear. Where could I find some?'

Iris laughed. 'I have clothes you could use,' she said. 'Some of my visitors are careless.' She assessed Jaysin. 'You might even get away with the bruises on your face. Did your owner hit your nose?'

Jaysin touched his nose gingerly, as he said, 'I hurt it escaping.'

'Let me look at it,' Iris said, and she leaned in to examine Jaysin's nose, gently pressing around its perimeter and across the bridge. He winced when she pressed one point. She sat back. 'It's not too bad,' she said. 'You might be lucky. The swelling should subside after a few days. The bruising will take longer. I don't think it's broken.'

'You are a healer?' Jaysin asked.

'No,' Iris replied, grinning. 'But I've seen quite a few broken and bruised noses, and cheeks and ribs over time. My clients and visitors often arrive with an injury. I've learned how to treat them, that's all.' She rose. 'Would you like a beer?'

Remembering the drink and its bitter but soothing taste, Jaysin answered, 'Yes.'

'I'll fetch a mug. Jandis should be here shortly. Finish your bowl.' Iris withdrew.

Jaysin spooned another mouthful of stew and ate as he considered his situation. The light outside revealed it was early morning, so if the ship sailed in the evening he had to stay safe for the full day. If Iris could find him clothing appropriate for a sailor, all he had to do was use an illusion to look like someone else. The real challenge, once aboard the ship, would be avoiding being revealed as a fake. He knew nothing about sailing, or the work of sailors, other than what he observed from his cage, and that taught him very little. The risk was immense.

He heard a male voice in the adjoining room and put down the bowl, readying to cast a translocate spell, but Iris led a non-descript thin man into the room, announcing, 'This is Jandis. He has no love for the ruling classes.'

Jandis stepped forward, hand out in a gesture of friendship. He had a thin face with a black goatee and bushy eyebrows. 'Happy to help, lad,' Jandis said. 'The Empire has taken all three of my sons. I owe the Karudar Marfek and her cronies nothing.' Jandis dropped onto one knee to inspect Jaysin's anklets. 'Standard issue,' he said, and Jaysin saw the tool bag Jandis carried. 'You've got some serious chafing there, lad, so it will sting when I cut these off. I'll have them off quick. You need to put your foot down there and hold still.'

Jaysin gritted his teeth as the man set to breaking and cutting the anklets with a hammer, chisel and saw, and he stifled a yelp when the saw's heated blade burned his skin and flinched when the metal gave way and scraped his raw abrasion. Tasshja watched the process from the doorway.

'Now for the other one,' Jandis said.

Jaysin swapped his feet and Jandis carefully cut the second anklet and chain away. 'Terrible things,' Jandis said, studying Jaysin's raw skin. 'I've seen so many of these turn septic before I've been able to free the slave.' He stood and said to Jaysin, 'You certainly upset the Sheykermett, lad. He has soldiers and Hakamati searching everywhere for you. You stirred up a hornets' nest.' He turned to Iris. 'I'll have Amin keep an eye out for the Hakamati. I'm surprised they haven't been here, yet.'

'I'll hide him in the den,' Iris replied.

'Good,' said Jandis. 'I'll alert the rest. We'll keep the soldiers and Hakamati running in circles.' He patted Jaysin on the shoulder. 'You've brightened my day, lad. We like giving Bahti grief.'

Jaysin watched Jandis leave, memorising his features and figure, wondering why the man was so keen to help him, especially with it being risky.

'Come on,' Iris urged, taking Jaysin's right arm. 'I'll get you into the den and then we can clean those wounds.' To Tasshja, she said, 'Fetch a candle.'

Iris led Jaysin into the main room and through another door into a large bedroom dominated by a bulky bed covered with a patchwork blanket and festooned with multiple colours and shapes of pillows and cushions. Iris pushed the bed aside and pulled back a strip of purple carpet to uncover a metal ring and trapdoor. She opened the trapdoor, revealing wooden steps dropping into the dark. Tasshja appeared with a lit candle. 'Take the candle,' Iris said to Jaysin. 'I will come down in a few moments to dress your injuries and bring a change of clothes. Tasshja will bring you food and drink later. You best stay here, in the den, until it's time to catch that ship.'

Jaysin accepted the candle and descended the steep steps gingerly, his ankles stinging. The trapdoor closed above him, and he heard the bed scraping into place.

The candlelight revealed an area similar in size to the bedroom. A pile of bedding filled one corner, a waste bucket sat in another, and five three-legged stools were arranged in a circle at the centre. The walls were earthen and damp, and cobwebs covered the ceiling and tops of the wall corners. He put the candleholder on a stool and sat on another. *Why are these people willing to help?* he pondered. Recent events taught him to be mistrustful of the Kermakk, but Iris and Jandis seemed committed to defying the authorities. *Is hatred for the war so deep?* he wondered. *Why would the Kermakk leader – the Karudar Marfek – pursue a highly unpopular war?*

Dull candlelight tempted him to create a light sphere, but he learned from his encounter with Mezzin that conjuring magic led to trouble. Iris might be trustworthy, but he already told her more than he should. His

146

nose was sore, his face swollen, cuts and bruises ached on his arms and legs and his back was sore, and raw skin stung on his ankles. He felt miserable.

The bed slid above the floorboards and Jaysin waited for the trapdoor to open. Iris descended, carrying a bag, followed by Tasshja balancing a bowl of warm water. 'Let's get you cleaned up,' Iris said. 'Strip down.' When Jaysin hesitated, she said, 'I've seen more men naked than you have, young man. Strip. I need to make sure you have no cuts that are going septic.'

Jaysin stripped, self-conscious that he was filthy and stank, but Iris did not seem to care. She told him to sit before she took a cloth from Tasshja, dipped it in the water bowl, and washed his shoulders and back. 'Nothing bad back here,' she said. 'Some shallow cuts to daub.' She asked Tasshja to pass her a small canister and she smeared cold cream across sections of Jaysin's shoulders and back. 'Bring down those clothes for the young man,' she told Tasshja, before she ordered Jaysin to stand and turn around. She washed his chest, stomach and legs, as she continued to inspect his wounds, and she daubed cream where she saw a need. She made him sit again and she worked gently around his ankles. As gentle as she was, her touch made Jaysin grimace, but the cream quickly soothed his discomfort.

Tasshja returned with an armful of clothes and a pair of moccasins and placed them on the floor. 'Try these on,' Iris instructed. 'It's a rag-tag mixture, but that's what sailors wear. Pick stuff that's too big for you rather than too tight.'

Jaysin expected Iris and Tasshja to leave him to dress, but they waited and watched him fossick, choose and put on a pair of loose dark grey trousers, a light blue woollen tunic, and a black jacket with multiple patches.

'I chose the moccasins,' Iris explained, pointing to the red footwear as Jaysin adjusted his outfit. 'They won't rub your ankles. It will be chilly on the ocean, but you don't want the pain, I assure you. They should fit, but if they're too large we can pack loose material in them. And you'll need this.' She handed him a small pull-string purse.

Jaysin took the purse and felt coins within. 'I can't take money,' he said.

'You'll need coin,' Iris said. 'Without it, you'll be doing what you were doing here, and you might not get lucky. It's not much, but it will buy you a drink and food.'

'I brought down this hat,' Tasshja said, holding up a black knitted skull cap.

'You'll need to keep that red hair of yours out of sight,' Iris said. 'I can cut it for you, if you like.'

'I'll manage that,' Jaysin replied. He took the cap and tried it on. 'How do I look?'

'Like sea refuse,' Iris said. When she saw Jaysin's querying expression, she laughed, and said, 'That means you look like the sailors who come by. Perfect.'

Fourteen

Jaysin uttered his illusion incantation and the air crackled. He glanced around the warehouse to be certain his transformation was unseen before he calmly joined the line of sailors lugging goods aboard *The Divine Wind*. He shouldered a sack of grain, so unprepared for the weight that he stumbled, but he steadied and followed the line of men onto the dock, up the gangplank and aboard.

'Hurry up!' a gravelly voice bellowed. 'Sun's nearly set. Offering coming, and then we have to be in port before dawn! You know the drill, scum! Get it done!'

Jaysin followed the lead of the man ahead and heaved his sack into the open hold before he looked around to see who was doing what. Iris advised him, before he left her place, to join the sailors in the hold and pretend he was asked to stack and count goods. 'You can read,' she said. 'Most can't. That will cover your purpose if they query what you're doing.' She handed him a rolled parchment and a quill. 'Pretend you're recording information on this. The Bosun's name is Lam Naykel. You'll recognise him. He bosses everyone around. The ship's captain is Natan Jevid — Captain Jevid to you. You won't see much of him, if at all. If anyone challenges you, tell anyone who asks that Lam gave you the job.'

'How do you know everyone's names?' Jaysin asked.

Iris winked and replied, 'I have many different visitors.'

Jaysin smiled at the memory. Iris was a person of secrets who he hoped to meet again. He looked left and right before he descended the rickety ladder into the hold.

A wiry individual, his brown hair tied in a short ponytail, looked up from a pile of sacks and asked, 'What are you doing, mate?'

Trying to disguise his accent and voice, Jaysin rasped, 'Lam says I have to count to make sure the right number of everything is down here.' He remembered Iris' advice if he was challenged and prepared for the next question, if it came. And it did.

'Never seen you before.'

'One of the lads is still with that woman who gives out favours,' Jaysin replied. 'His good luck is my good luck.'

'Who was that?' the sailor queried.

'How would I know?' Jaysin asked. 'I never worked on here before. I don't even know you. Do you do the inventory?'

'The what?'

'Do you check we have everything we're meant to have?'

'Nobody checks that stuff, mate,' the sailor said, and he spat.

'Well, Lam says I do now,' said Jaysin. 'You want to question Lam?'

'Don't be a wise arse,' the sailor answered sullenly. 'What's your name?'

'Markoo,' Jaysin said. 'And you?'

'Call me Notch.'

'All right, Notch, I better get on with my job,' Jaysin said. 'What are you doing?'

'Eh, don't go pretending you got any rank, mate,' Notch warned.

'Sorry,' Jaysin said. 'Just asking.'

'I'm on the bilge pumps,' Notch said. 'Feel free to come below and help out when you finish your invention job. Always needing more hands to pump the bilge on this sieve.'

A gong sounded and rang multiple times. Notch sank to his knees and put his fingertips to his forehead, covering his face with his hands. Sailors climbed into the hold and adopted the same position as Notch, so Jaysin copied them. He heard the men whispering, but he couldn't hear the words. They repeated the same phrases over and over, remaining on their knees and keeping their hands across their faces for several moments before they rose, one or two at a time, and climbed out of the hold. Notch stood and Jaysin did the same.

'Now we're in the hands of He-Who-Cannot-Be-Named,' Notch said. He picked up a lantern and lit it, throwing the yellow light across the cargo. 'Let's see if He is watching over us.'

Another sailor nimbly dropped into the hold and tapped Notch on the shoulder. 'Water rats below!' he said, and the sailor started for a ladder descending deeper in the hull.

A third sailor climbed down from the deck to join Notch. 'Ship's weighing anchor and about to turn to windward, old son. Down we go.'

'Always welcome to join us,' Notch reiterated to Jaysin, before he followed his colleagues into the bowels of the ship, taking the lantern with him.

Jaysin heard Lam bellowing orders overhead and chains rattled fore and aft. The boards beneath his feet shifted, losing solidity, and the ship creaked and groaned and wallowed in the waves. Jaysin glanced up at the darkening evening sky between the flapping sails. *Time to hide*, he decided. He searched the hold for a suitable spot among the crates and sacks where he could secrete himself and keep an eye on anyone coming into the hold, and he crept into a gap between two stacks of heavy crates.

The ship shuddered and heaved and pitched as it battled the waves, and he listened to the wood groan and creak, the sail cloth snap, and yelling from men busy keeping the ship trim. Wrapped in the odours of salty water, tar and mould, he arranged a sack for comfort and settled in to wait out the journey behind a pile of heavy crates. He let his disguise slip to conserve energy for the morning arrival in Vussar Karemachet. His plan was simple. If anyone threatened to discover him, he would resume his guise and have his parchment and quill ready to pretend he was completing the list.

He woke when a rat scampered across his shoulder, heightening his senses for a period as he anticipated another encounter, and sleep took its time returning. He woke again to close voices and cowered as lantern light swung across the hold, eventually comprehending that Notch and his companions were being relieved of their bilge duties by another group.

Jaysin sat among the crates for a time, thereafter, hoping he would not be asleep when the ship berthed. He imagined what Tam and Harmi might be doing, hoping that Tam was recovered from her injuries. He also hoped Chasse was alive. As much as he envied his older brother's physical prowess and his popularity in Harbin and Machutzka, he loved him, and that was why he was in the hold of a ship, cold, damp, afraid, hoping he could find Chasse and take him home.

And an unexpected memory crept into his mind. He stood in the main room of his Harbin home, watching his mother rolling dough, her thick arms white with flour, her white-streaked red hair tied back, and flour smudged on her cheeks. Morning light filtered through the window and the waves smacking against the ship's hull became waves breaking against the rocks below Watersdrop. He stared at his mother, and she smiled at him, and sadness washed through his being. And he was suddenly standing in a crowd at Watersdrop, and the Dragon Heart was singing his father across the dark oceans to Varst, and his sadness became a deep sorrow he could not deny. 'I tried to save him,' he whimpered. 'I wanted to save him.'

Boots clomped across the deck above him, and Lam was bellowing orders. Grey light angled into the hold. Jaysin wiped his cheeks and rose warily, checking that he was alone. Chains rattled. Sailors emerged from the bilge and climbed to the deck. Cries echoed and mingled with ropes sliding, sails flapping as they were hauled in, and the deck thumped and creaked as the ship wallowed in the swell. The hull thudded against a solid object and shadows broke the shaft of light illuminating the hold.

'Get to it!' Lam ordered. 'I'm hungry and I intend to eat an early breakfast! Shift that cargo!'

Sailors climbed into the hold. Jaysin conjured his illusion, stooped to manhandle a sack onto his shoulders, and emerged from between the crates. He dropped his burden on the winch board and returned to collect another. Second sack delivered, he climbed out of the hold and joined the men who were carting sacks from the winch board down the gangplank and onto the dock. The wharf was busy with sailors and workmen, wagons and drays lurching between cargo piles to cart away goods to warehouses and buyers. He avoided eye contact and made sure Bosun Lam didn't notice him.

Sack stacked, he looked for the most convenient way to leave. He waited for a passing wagon to mask his escape, but as he went to step behind a wagon a voice called, 'You!' Jaysin pretended not to hear and walked behind the moving wagon, but a figure came around the rear to confront him. 'Where do you think you're going?' a brawny, black bearded sailor challenged.

'I need to piss,' Jaysin replied.

'Piss on the wharf,' the sailor replied. 'Stop shirking.'

'Who are you?' Jaysin contested, attempting to bluff the man.

'I might ask the same,' the sailor replied. 'Never seen you in our crew before.'

'Just joined,' Jaysin said. He fished inside his tunic and extracted the parchment. 'Know what this is?' he asked.

'No, and I don't care,' the sailor said.

'It's an inventory,' Jaysin told him. 'It lists everything we carried. Lam wants it given to the Harbour Master.'

'Never heard of that before,' the sailor said.

'New rules,' Jaysin said. 'Don't believe me, go ask Lam. He'll sort you out.'

'I will, mate,' the sailor said. 'And you can come with me. I'll have a piece of you, if you're lying.'

'I'm taking this to the Harbour Master,' Jaysin said. 'I'm not disobeying Lam.'

Jaysin tensed because the sailor looked like he was going to tackle him, but the man spat and headed for Lam. Disguise about to be exposed, Jaysin ran for the nearest street leading from the docks, where he paused to look back. The sailor was talking to Lam and pointing to the spot near the sack pile. The ruse was over. He spotted an alley between the buildings and headed for it.

Save for an empty wagon with a bone-thin horse flagging in its harness, the alley was empty, so Jaysin dispelled his sailor's guide, threw off the black jacket, and assumed Jandis' image. He stroked his goatee as he stepped into the street and headed for a building with a sign proclaiming it as The Mermaid's Promise.

The inn was a single room with a long bar to the right and a dozen round tables with stools spread across the rest of the room under low ceiling beams. Patrons sat at the tables or stood at the bar, a smoky hearth crackled in the left wall, and smoke haze drifted across the beams and ceiling. Spying an empty table by a window close to the door, Jaysin sat and waited for an attendant, until he realised the patrons were buying drinks at the bar. No one paid him attention, so he relaxed and considered his options.

He had to find out who the Lekna were and where he could find them. Then, he had to find the one holding his brother — if that was Chasse's fate. *Someone in here might know*, he contemplated, and he scanned the patrons for a face that looked friendly enough to approach.

The inn door swung open and five sailors marched in. Jaysin recognised Lam and the man who confronted him at the docks and he stiffened with anxiety. And Notch was with them. They surveyed the patrons, Latch looking directly at Jaysin. *The spell is working*, Jaysin reminded himself uneasily.

'Anybody seen a wayward sailor?' Lam bellowed, stifling the inn conversation.

'Only that one,' a man said, pointing at Jaysin.

Lam glared at Jaysin, and swore, replying, 'Not the bastard we're looking for.' He gestured to his companions, who began filing back out through the door. 'Hey, Gorvin!' Lam yelled to the innkeeper. 'We'll all be back later for the usual!'

'I'll be waiting!' Gorvin yelled in reply.

Jaysin stayed seated after the sailors departed, calming his nerves, grateful for his illusion. Eventually, he stood and approached the bar.

'What's yours?' Gorvin asked through his thick brown beard.

'Beer?' Jaysin asked.

'Black beer or Empire brew?' Gorvin asked.

'Black beer,' Jaysin answered, although he had no idea what he was ordering.

'Two bits,' Gorvin said. Jaysin retrieved two rectangular coins from his purse and put them on the bar. Gorvin snatched up the coins and dropped them in his dirty grey apron, took a pewter mug from under the bar, filled it with frothy liquid from a barrel, and set it before Jaysin. 'Just come in?' he asked.

'Yes,' Jaysin replied.

'Which ship?'

'Uh,' Jaysin hesitated, and replied, '*The Sea Dragon.*'

Gorvin raised a querying bushy eyebrow. 'Never heard of that one. Where from?'

Aware a couple of men were also listening, Jaysin improvised. 'West coast.'

'Who's the captain?' a man to Jaysin's right asked.

'Captain, ah, Kevan,' Jaysin replied, resorting to his father's name.

'First time in this port.'

The man winked and asked, 'Is he needing more hands?'

'Full crew,' Jaysin replied.

'How long you in port?' Gorvin asked, but before Jaysin could answer another patron drew the innkeeper's attention and he moved further along the bar.

Jaysin retreated with his mug to the table before anyone else could ask questions. He wasn't expecting to think on his feet so frequently. Everyone wanted to know what everyone else was doing, who they were, where they came from and where they were going. Everyone was intrusively curious. He sipped the beer, surprised it was far more bitter than the one Iris fed him. It was a thicker, darker brew and he wasn't sure that he liked it.

As he surveyed the room again for a potential person to broach the matter of the Lekna, two men came from the bar and sat uninvited at his table. One was the man who asked if there was a need for more sailors. His hair was long, although he was bald across his pate, and his beard was straggly. His left eye was odd, discoloured and glassy. His companion was swarthy in skin tone with a thick black beard and no moustache across his upper lip, and his black hair was tied tightly in a bun. Tattoos of writhing sea creatures ran from his temple hairline down his cheeks and onto his neck. Both men placed their mugs on the tabletop.

'I'm Arch Kardinya,' the balding man announced. 'This is my good friend, Scrag. That's all I know him as.'

'Only my mother knew my full name,' Scrag said, 'and she was taken by the plague fifteen years back.'

'What's your name?' Arch asked.

'Jandis Neyma,' Jaysin replied, confident the man from Cheznah would not be known in the capital.

'And you say you're from the west coast,' Arch said.

'We sailed there,' Jaysin replied, realising he was in the guise of a man who would not have been born on the west coast.

'What brings you here?' Scrag inquired.

Jaysin recognised an opportunity. 'Captain Kevan is interested in the Lekna and the Karushta.' He noticed how Arch's left eye didn't move and lacked energy.

'You been to the Karushta?' Arch asked.

'No,' Jaysin replied.

'You should ask your captain to come with us,' Scrag said. 'Next event is when?' he asked, looking at Arch.

'Two days' time,' Arch confirmed. 'How long is your captain staying in port?'

'A few days,' Jaysin replied. 'He hasn't set a sail point.'

'And where's your captain staying?' Arch asked.

Remembering Alban's false generosity, Jaysin replied, 'Captain stays aboard overnight, as we all do.'

Scrag laughed and slapped his leg. 'Sounds like your captain is afraid he might lose crew to the Empire.'

'He has a point,' Arch said. 'Imperial Army is taking everyone they can march away.'

'Where are you staying?' Jaysin asked.

Arch glanced at Scrag and laughed. 'I stay at Drinkers Paradise,' he said. 'Nice place on Bridge Road. If your captain ever allows you to stay ashore, I'd tell you get a room at Drinkers Paradise. Good food, good beer, good women.'

'He says that because he owns it,' Scrag interjected. 'Don't let him take your money.'

'If your captain is interested in seeing the Karushta, Jandis, tell him to meet us in two days' time at midday at the bridge on Bridge Road. Events start when the midday bell tolls. Don't have to go in straight away. Normally, the first part is praying to He-Who-We-Can't-Be-Bothered-Naming.' Arch lifted his mug, downed the contents and stood. Scrag copied him. 'Midday, two days' time,' Arch repeated. He put his arm over Scrag's shoulder and the pair headed for the exit.

Jaysin sipped his beer. The bitter, dark liquid did not improve with more drinking, but he used it as his pretext to wait for some time before leaving. If Arch and Scrag were planning to rob him, or sell him into slavery, or draft him into the Imperial Army, they would have to wait quite a while for him to emerge.

When he prepared to leave the inn, he peeked out the window at the murky sky and estimated that, by the sun's position, it was well into the morning. The street was busy with merchants and sailors and travellers, and again he was surprised by the absence of women and children. If Arch and Scrag's invitation for Captain Kevan to join them at the Karushta was genuine, he had to stay in Vussar Karemachet for two days and generate a different illusion to meet them. He needed lodgings.

Iris told him, before he left, to seek a dwelling with a green pitch roof in Lower End Road. 'Go straight up Rising Road from the docks to The Main Way. Turn left and walk for a distance until you find an inn called The Barking Dog. Go right there along Carriage Street and on your left one of the roads is Lower End Road. At the house, tell whoever opens the door that Iris sent you. Give the woman named Halian this.' She handed Jaysin a rolled parchment, tied with a thin length of green ribbon.

Jaysin left his half-empty mug on the table and went outside, warily checking for anyone watching him. Two Hakamati sauntering along the far side of the street paid him no attention. He wondered if Lam and the crew had given up searching for him and headed for an inn. His frantic escape from the dock meant that he had no idea if the street that he was on was the right one, so he stopped a merchant wheeling a barrow and asked if he was on Rising Road.

'Two streets over that way,' the merchant told him, gesturing with his head.

Jaysin thanked him, headed for the closest crossroad and veered left.

The Imperial Palace, called the Udarvesna to the Kermakk populace, dominated the view as he veered from Rising Road into The Main Way. Golden spires and cupolas threatened to pierce the low hanging grey clouds and the Udarvesna's pink walls rose higher than the nearest buildings. Jaysin tried to orient himself, recalling his journey with Gabnar and Mezzin after he was bought in the slave market. They must have taken him directly south of the docks to the small hills in the southern district because he had not seen the Udarvesna's majesty then, only glimpsed the towers. Now, he could see the city's true size. Beyond the port, Vussar Karemachet was a hive of activity. Smoke from foundries and factories stained the sky, merchants and travellers traversed the streets, and he was conscious of the military traffic along The Main Way: soldiers, cavalry, supply wagons, and a small convoy of siege weapons.

Jaysin located The Barking Dog inn and walked quickly along Carriage Street, turned into Lower End Road and when he arrived at the house with the green pitched roof he knocked and waited. The door opened and a child in a ragged blue smock stared at him with wide dark eyes. Jaysin said, 'Iris sent me.' He couldn't tell if the child was a boy or a girl beneath the tousled and long black hair, and when the child kept staring blankly Jaysin wondered if he was at the right house. 'Is there someone else I could talk to?' he asked.

A woman's face appeared around the door with her head wrapped in a dark blue shawl. 'I apologise,' she said, shuffling the child behind her. 'What do you want?'

'Iris sent me,' Jaysin repeated.

The woman appraised him with her dark green eyes, before she opened the door wider and invited him to enter.

Jaysin stepped into a main room that opened into a long, shadowy corridor. 'I'm looking for Halian,' he said.

The woman closed the door, ushered the child ahead and said, 'I am Halian.'

Jaysin fumbled inside his tunic and coat to withdraw the rolled parchment and handed it to Halian. 'From Iris,' he explained.

Halian took the parchment without opening it. 'How many nights do you need?' she asked.

'I don't know,' Jaysin replied.

Halian paused, weighing up her options, before saying, 'Follow me.' She collected a burning lamp from a cupboard and led Jaysin into the corridor. They passed several doors and stopped at the last on the left, where Halian produced a ring of keys from within her garment and unlocked the door. 'You can use this room. One bit a night. Hand back this key before you leave,' she instructed as she unhitched one key from the bunch. 'If you need anything, I am in the front room. If I'm not there, you have to wait until I get back.' She leaned in and Jaysin could smell her sweet perfume. 'The other guests do not like being disturbed. No one asks questions. Am I clear?'

'Yes,' Jaysin replied.

'If anyone comes looking for you, I won't be telling them you are here, not even if they claim to know you. This is a sanctuary. When you walk in the front door, you don't exist until you walk out again. If the Hakamati or the army come, you'll hear that bell above your door tinkle. Leave by the window. Get clear of the area. Any questions?'

'Where can I eat?' Jaysin asked.

'Safest place is the end of this street. It's a tiny establishment. Serves wholesome food and beer. Called Jakine's. He looks out for people like you,' Halian said. 'Any other questions?'

'Any Lekna nearby?' Jaysin asked.

Halian stiffened. 'Why would you want to know that?'

'I'm looking for a warrior who's been taken prisoner,' Jaysin explained. 'There's a chance he was bought by a Lekna.'

'A very good chance,' Halian confirmed. 'The good Lekna don't live around these parts. They live in the eastern district, in the fancy mansions.

Poor trainers, those starting out or bad at the business, have property closer to here. They are a callous and nasty lot. I wouldn't be nosing around them, if I was you. Anything else?'

Jaysin heard the woman's irritated tone, so he replied, 'No. Thank you.'

'I'll leave you to whatever you intend to do,' Halian said, and she left.

Jaysin went to the window and discovered that it opened onto a narrow alley running the length of the building. If trouble came, that was his escape route.

The room was sparsely furnished: a single bed with a black hide blanket, a stool with a wash bowl on it, and a wooden clothes rack. He noted the little metal bell above the door and the wire running into the ceiling. He wondered if anyone else was in the adjoining room and, if there were others, who they might be. He let his illusion spell dissipate so that he could relax and re-energise, and he lay on the bed to rest.

Fifteen

Jaysin sauntered towards the stone pillars of the bridge, noting the Hakamati on duty at the approach. He recognised Arch and Scrag in a larger group of men and wondered whether he was walking into a trap, but it was a necessary risk to find information about Chasse.

The previous day, he journeyed to the bridge to memorise the area along Bridge Road in case he needed to translocate to escape. It was a bold escape plan, one that would expose his magical ability and mean he would need a new disguise, but he was not going to be caught like he was by Alban and Mezzin. He sat in his room throughout the morning as himself to conserve energy and he decided to adopt the features of the Machutzkan market vendor he impersonated in the past to be Captain Kevan. He had no idea how long the Karushta events would take, but, if he avoided taking on his disguise until he was ready to leave, he could sustain it until evening.

After taking a room at Halian's refuge, Jaysin spent the intervening two days looking for Lekna in the district around Carriage Street. He was careful with whom he spoke and he avoided attracting the interest of Hakamati by presenting himself as a Sarchah merchant interested in selling slaves. He was introduced to two men who operated premises where they prepared slaves and prisoners for the Karushta, but both were small-time trainers whose charges were offered up as sacrifices to the larger operatives, and they knew nothing about the Machutzkan warriors other than there were foreign prisoners being used in the Karushta. As Halian told him, the successful Lekna lived in districts further east in the city foothills. He had little choice but to accept Arch's invitation and attend the Karushta where he could learn who were the successful Lekna.

Jaysin studied the group with Arch. The men were dressed in Kermakk-style baggy trousers, tunics and large cloaks, no different to the Kermakk merchants. He crossed the road, sidestepping a wagon laden with barrels, and recalled his conversation with Halian the previous night. The woman kept to herself, as she promised, but Jaysin needed to understand more of the Kermakk world, so he sat in the front room where she was reading and asked, 'Can I ask you some questions?'

Halian looked up from her book. 'You know the rules of this house.'

'I don't want to know who comes and goes, or why,' he said, 'but I am curious as to why there are no women or children in the streets, only men.'

Halian lowered her book. 'You're from the west coast, yes?'

'Yes.'

'Iris wrote about you in her message,' Halian said. 'You were taken as a slave. You're not Kermakk and you've never travelled here before.'

'True,' Jaysin confirmed.

'The first thing you must do to survive, even as a man, is pretend to believe in He-Who-Cannot-Be-Named,' Halian advised. 'If someone asks if you are a Believer, you respond with "There is One True God. All others are false." In doing so, you reveal yourself as a Man of Faith.'

'Why is that so important?' Jaysin asked.

'It's how men identify each other as friend or foe. Believers see non-believers as nothing of value,' Halian said. 'They can kill non-believers without compunction as an act of cleansing in the name of their god. The Hakamati and soldiers are blind to such acts of cleansing.'

'But what has that to do with women and children?'

'According to the Word of Faith, He-Who-Cannot-Be-Named has given control of this world to Men of Faith. Only to men.' Halian paused to meet Jaysin's gaze, before she continued. 'Women exist for procreation and service to men. We belong to them in the same way as a horse or a house is owned. Women cannot be trusted because we tempt men into sin with our looks and our ways, so we must stay indoors and keep ourselves covered for the safety of men. The only day we may venture onto the streets to shop is on Shebaal. On Shebaal, all the men are in the Vesnahdi, praying to He-Who-Cannot-Be-Named.'

'That makes no sense,' Jaysin replied.

Halian smiled wryly. 'It does to men who want to control everything. Where you come from, women would still be required to serve their men, yes?'

'Yes,' he conceded, 'but they're not prisoners in their homes. My mother and my sister are powerful women.'

Halian shook her head. 'I would hazard they are only powerful because men allow them to be that way to suit their own purposes.'

Jaysin wanted to argue that his sister was more powerful than any man as a wizard with a dragon, but that was information he could not share, even with someone who appeared to be trustworthy. Instead, he asked, 'And children?'

'Children come of age at ten years,' Halian said. 'Girls are married soon after and kept at home. Boys start working for their fathers and uncles or go into service in the clergy or the military. Until then, they either serve their mothers in the home or are schooled.'

'Schooled?' Jaysin asked.

'They gather at a house daily and they are taught how to be good Kermakk,' Halian explained. 'Boys learn to be men and girls learn to be women.'

As Jaysin reached the group at the bridge, he cleared his thoughts and introduced himself. 'I am Captain Kevan,' he said. 'I am mean to meet a man named Arch Kardinya here.'

'And you have found him. Good that you could join us,' Arch said, smiling. 'This is our visiting maritime friend,' he said to the other men. He indicated each man individually. 'This is Scrag.' Scrag nodded. 'And this is

Lenardi, Wajin, Orvak, and the chubby one here is Bezza.'

'They are jealous of my beautiful belly,' Bezza returned, patting his rotund gut. 'This represents many years of cultivation.'

The men laughed and Scrag put an arm over Bezza's shoulder. 'So, our merry band can now enjoy today's events,' Arch said, and he led the group onto the bridge.

As he crossed the bridge, Jaysin looked down at the barges plying the river, searching for any that were carrying slaves or prisoners as had been his fate. 'It's always busy,' remarked Wajin, the tallest of the Kermakk. 'The barges with the blue and red pennants belong to Lenardi.'

'Lenardi is a river rat,' Scrag teased.

Lenardi, his long black hair plaited in a single strand down his back, turned to Scrag and replied in a surprisingly deep voice, 'There are more rats in this city than sea dogs, my friend. Don't annoy the rats.' The men laughed, although the cause for their amusement escaped Jaysin.

'Scrag owns three merchant ships,' Wajin explained. 'I'm assuming that's why he invited you to join us. He will almost certainly have a business proposition for you. Be careful,' he warned as he patted Jaysin's shoulder.

Jaysin viewed the Karushta from the far side of the bridge the previous day, but as the group reached the entrance its scale seemed to magnify. The red stone walls were four storeys high and the open black entrance gate was at least ten spans wide. Men flowed through in groups and pairs, pausing to pay at two booths stationed on either side of the gateway. 'How many bits to enter?' Jaysin asked, conscious he had limited funds.

'No cost to us,' Scrag replied. 'Arch is paying. He had a good week with his miners.'

'The man owns gold and silver mines, and a rock quarry,' Bezza informed him.

'And several establishments,' Scrag added. 'Probably has more money than all of us put together.'

'That's why he's our friend,' Wajin said.

Jaysin followed the men through the gate to a covered flight of steps that led onto an open terrace of seats, but he was suspicious, now that he knew his hosts were wealthy, as to why rich Kermakk merchants would bother inviting a foreign sea captain to attend the Karushta.

Back in the open air, Jaysin saw that the terrace was one of many stretching around the ovoid Karushta and the seats were filling rapidly with more people than Jaysin previously saw assembled in one place. The centre of the structure was an open oval where soldiers paraded to the beat of drums, bearing green Kermakk pennants. The drums echoed around the Karushta, and sections of the assembling crowd cheered.

'Ah, the Imperial forces,' Arch said as he gestured for Jaysin to take a seat to his right between himself and Lenardi. 'We missed the full display.'

'But we will get the invocation,' Scrag noted from Arch's left.

'I hear you've never been to the Karushta,' Lenardi said to Jaysin.

'No,' Jaysin confirmed.

'Then you're in for a treat, Captain,' Lenardi affirmed. 'Mijeff Nevorn is displaying his prize fighters today, for the first time.'

'Oh, yes,' Arch joined in. 'This will interest you. Rumour is that he has a west coast champion in his team.' He turned to Jaysin. 'You sail there, I believe.'

'Yes,' Jaysin replied calmly. 'I do.'

'And there goes the army,' Bezza said, as the soldiers streamed off the arena in three disciplined lines through a gate.

'And here comes the Voice of God,' Scrag announced with a clear tone of dismay.

'I thought we'd miss this,' Bezza said.

'Are you a Man of Faith?' Lenardi asked.

Jaysin remembered Halian's advice, but he modified it with, 'I am learning that there is only One True God. All others are false.'

Lenardi smiled, as he replied, 'The journey to faith is strewn with

166

pebbles and boulders, but the man who takes the journey will overcome them all.'

Jaysin guessed Lenardi's observation was associated with the faith. Seeing the other men focusing on the arena, he returned his attention to the centre where men were assembling on a portable dais. One man in a bright green robe and a square yellow hat, his arms and chest adorned with gold chains, stood with his arms stretched wide, facing a pavilion at the western side of the Karushta. An assistant held a golden funnel before the man in the green robe which amplified the man's voice.

'Do you think the Karudar Marfek will ever actually come to the Karushta?' Bezza asked.

'The Mistress of He-Who-Cannot-Be-Named doesn't approve of the spectacle,' Lenardi replied.

'She approves of the spectacle of men being slaughtered across the war fronts,' Scrag said.

'I have it on good authority that she sees the wars as necessary and the Karushta as unnecessary,' Arch shared.

'That explains why she pardons so many fighters,' said Scrag. 'She invites them to serve in her army.'

'And slaughters them regardless,' Bezza quipped. 'Shame. I'd rather they died entertaining us.'

Jaysin studied the distant pavilion where colourfully adorned people sat in cushioned chairs, observing that the central and most opulent high-backed chair was vacant. 'The Karudar Marfek can pardon fighters?' he asked.

'The Karudar Marfek can do whatever she likes,' Lenardi said.

The anomaly and irony struck Jaysin. Kermakk men ruled over women as their owners, but a woman ruled over them all because their god decreed it to be that way. *Why does she allow women to be oppressed*? he wondered.

As the Voice of God finished his ceremonial opening of the day's event in the name of He-Who-Cannot-Be-Named, and processed from the arena, accompanied by his assistants, the men around Jaysin placed their fingertips on their foreheads and closed their eyes, and the Karushta was filled with a common declaration from thousands of Kermakk voices: 'Adeh na akehu tusou, o udar shemata usz ha lonia, martut madeh Kermakii, karzekk usz ha shematakar!' Jaysin imitated the hand gesture to avoid arousing attention, remembering the action from the ship.

'Now the fun begins!' Bezza announced, as he lowered his hands.

Gates opened in the arena and a man in red and gold livery rode to the centre on a white horse. Like the Voice of God's assistant, he held a funnel-shaped instrument to his mouth to amplify his voice and Jaysin reflected on how much simpler it would be if they could use the amplification spell.

'First event is going to be a horse contest,' Arch said. 'Three teams of riders have to simultaneously defend a flag and steal the other two. Each rider has a wooden baton. If a rider falls, he's eliminated from the game.'

'And there are no rules other than that,' Bezza added. 'The fewer the rules, the better the contest!'

Jaysin watched the event unfold. Three teams of five riders wheeled and clashed and fought. Tactics emerged as the green and red teams coordinated to bring down the blue riders. Even while two red riders attacked the surviving blue rider, cheers and cries rose in the crowd when it was obvious that the green team was betraying the reds as they stole the red flag from under the watch of a red rider who they unhorsed. Incensed, the three remaining red team riders regrouped and charged the green team, but they were outnumbered, and the green team scooped up the blue flag and rode toward the Karudar Marfek's pavilion with all three flags flapping in the breeze. The crowd cheered as the triumphant riders trotted to the gates. A crew of slaves emerged to retrieve the horses and their injured riders and clean the arena, and the rider on the white horse returned to announce the next event.

'This should be good,' Lenardi said, leaning forward. 'Nevorn's new team are being matched against Dierdran's champion team.'

A group of fifteen soldiers marched into the arena, each carrying a crossbow with a javelin strapped to his back and a sword at his side. 'They are well prepared,' Arch said. 'Dierdran has his team in full Imperial armour. That must have cost him a small fortune.'

'If it's the same team he presented the last three times, they are unbeaten and unmatched,' Bezza said. 'These are the best fighters in the Kermakk Empire.'

'They were assembled from several places,' Scrag contributed. 'The big one, the one in the Captain's kit, is named Shengat. He's a Yargu warrior. Takes three men to bring one Yargu down on the battlefield, so I heard.'

'I heard it took ten men to subdue him,' Orvak chimed in. 'Phenomenal strength and stamina.'

'And here's Nevorn's offering,' said Arch. 'A new batch of hopefuls to the slaughter.'

A second team of fifteen entered. The men wore loose leather armour, and each bore a weapon; some axes, some swords. The broad figure at the front of the team, red hair braided tightly, was Chasse and Jaysin's heart pounded as he fought his compulsion to call to his brother.

'That's the west coast champion,' Arch said, turning to Jaysin. 'They call them dragonwarriors on the west coast, Kevan, correct?'

'Yes,' Jaysin said, trying to hide his emotion.

'The red hair is the clue,' Scrag explained. 'There are six more in that team. The rest look like the usual mongrel mix from all over the place.'

'Hate to say it, but this will be a lop-sided encounter,' Wajin argued.

'Fully armoured and hardened fighters against inexperienced prisoners and slaves is not a fair fight.'

'Don't underestimate the slaves,' Arch warned. 'They were warriors.'

'Before they were captured,' said Orvak. 'They obviously weren't good enough warriors to win their last battles.'

'I concede your point,' Scrag agreed.

'Watch and see,' Arch said. 'I will bet on Nevorn's team. One hundred bits if anyone is game.'

'I'll take that wager,' said Wajin. 'Easy money.'

'Count me in,' Orvak added.

'And me,' Bezza said.

'I'll side with Arch,' said Scrag.

'Lenardi?' Wajin asked.

'I'll watch this one,' Lenardi replied.

'What about you, Kevan?' Wajin asked.

Jaysin shook his head.

'Leave the man alone,' Arch intervened. 'He's a seadog,' and he winked at Jaysin.

'It's on,' Orvak announced.

Shengat's soldiers formed three ranks of five and marched towards Chasse's team. Chasse gestured to his companions who fanned out, running to form a circle around Shengat's team, but the soldiers responded by forming a triangular defence, five men on each side. They unhitched their loaded crossbows and took aim.

'Dierdran has drilled his team better than the Imperial army,' Wajin noted.

Chasse bellowed an order in Menin and the fanning warriors changed direction and closed in on the soldiers. Crossbows fired. Eight warriors fell and the crowd cheered and applauded. The remaining seven warriors ducked or dodged the bolts and charged into the soldiers.

'That severely dented your hopes,' Wajin said to Arch, grinning.

'And that might make your wager shaky,' Scrag retorted, as one side of the defending triangle collapsed.

Jaysin stayed focused on Chasse who crashed into one line of soldiers and knocked three of the five backward with the force of his impact. He knocked two down with one sweep of his sword and slammed into the side of a third who crumpled. Two warriors with him were Menuii who cut down the remaining soldiers and opened up the defence triangle. A second side was under pressure from the surviving four warriors and began to lose shape, so the unaffected line wheeled to face the onslaught and what was ordered military manoeuvring dissolved into a free-for-all melee. Chasse stabbed and hacked, working with brutal efficiency, dodging and fending aside sword sweeps and thrusts, bringing down two more opponents.

'Five on seven,' Wajin called.

'And now four on seven,' Lenardi corrected. 'The flame-haired warrior is a force.'

'As is Shengat,' Wajid retorted, as the big Yargu warrior, arms and legs bulging with muscles, swept aside a Menuii who crumpled, clutching his thigh.

'Three on one!' Orvak yelled as men fell. 'Have that money ready, Arch, my friend!'

Jaysin was horrified. In a matter of moments, the battle came down to Chasse facing three enemy, one of them the Yargu warrior.

'This will be interesting,' Wajid said. 'I'm tipping Shengat will leave the finishing blows to his two companions. That would be Dierdran's instruction. No need to unnecessarily risk your best man at this point.'

'Seems that you're right,' Lenardi confirmed.

The big warrior stepped back to let his two companions stalk Chasse.

For the first time, Jaysin saw blood smeared across his brother's cheeks and down his arms and legs and his fear rose. He could create a diversion, distract everyone so Chasse could escape. He could use energy bolts to kill Chasse's opponents and help his brother escape. But none of those ideas would work. Even if they escaped the Karushta, they couldn't escape the city. He had to watch and hope that Chasse could find a way to win.

Chasse circled back a few steps, but Jaysin recognised that his brother was poised, balanced, waiting for his opponents to commit. When the first fighter attacked, Chasse easily knocked the thrusting blade aside. And he did so again on the next attack. The second fighter edged to Chasse's left, looking for an opportunity while the first distracted him, and when the first man lunged the second stepped right. Chasse struck so quickly that Jaysin was astonished by his brother's speed. Two flashes of Chasse's sword and both men crumpled. The crowd roared with delight and applauded by stamping their feet.

'Nevorn has a magnificent champion!' Scrag cried, clapping excitedly. 'Did you see that move?'

'But now he has Shengat to deal with,' Lenardi said calmly. 'We will see what this west coast warrior is really made of.'

'Dierdran will rue accepting this challenge,' said Arch. 'He's lost considerable investment and reputation today.'

'It's not over,' cautioned Wajin. 'It's far from over.'

Standing before Chasse, Shengat, a full head and shoulders taller and his chest broader, reminded Jaysin of Natias. Shengat flexed his arm muscles to delight the crowd and, as they cheered, he slipped his sword into its sheath and unhitched his javelin, taking it in one hand by the end.

'Smart,' Orvak said. 'Greater reach. The warrior won't get within range to strike him.'

Chasse moved to the right, stepped in and dodged out as Shengat swung the javelin, the point whistling past Chasse's cheek. Chasse took several steps further around and lunged in and ducked as Shengat thrust the javelin.

I know what you're doing, Jaysin thought, as he watched the contest unfold.

Chasse started to circle again, but Shengat charged, stabbing with the javelin as he closed the distance, forcing Chasse to backpedal. Chasse tripped, and rolled right, and narrowly avoided being pinned as Shengat stabbed again. On his feet, Chasse jumped back a handspan, balanced and faced Shengat. The big fighter hurled the javelin, but Chasse adroitly caught it and stuck it in the earth and the crowd cheered. Shengat drew his sword.

'Here we go,' Orvak said, delighted with the impending clash.

Reach and strength on his side, Shengat waded in, thrashing his sword left and right, thrusting, sweeping, forcing Chasse back as Chasse blocked and deflected the big man's blade. Jaysin rose, along with the cheering crowd, begging his brother to win, to find a way. And it happened. In an instant, Chasse was inside Shengat's reach, under his broad arm and spinning out behind the man, ducking a desperate flailing late swing from Shengat. The Yargu warrior toppled as he turned and thudded against the arena earth and did not move, and the Karushta echoed to cheers and foot stamping. A portion of the crowd in the northern seats began chanting, 'Ne-vorn! Ne-vorn!'

'I believe, my good friends,' said Arch, with a broad smirk and his hand held out symbolically, 'I am now three hundred bits richer.'

Sixteen

'How often do you sail to the west coast?' Scrag inquired, as he poured beer into Jaysin's mug.

'Leave the Captain alone,' Wajin complained. 'We're celebrating losing our wager. Your money-making ventures can wait for tomorrow when our heads are clear.'

'Best time to make new agreements,' Orvak said, lifting his mug. 'Beer makes men more agreeable.'

'Free beer even more so,' Lenardi chimed in. He raised his mug and nodded to Arch who smiled in return.

'Paid for out of our losses,' Wajin protested.

'Makes it taste even better,' Scrag said, and he tilted the jug to top up his mug.

Jaysin sipped his beer, careful not to drink as eagerly as his new companions because the day was getting late and his energy for sustaining his illusion was rapidly waning. More so, he wanted to rescue his brother, having found him.

Earlier, as he watched Chasse herded from the arena after his victory, he asked Arch, 'What happens to the warrior?'

'That one?' Arch rhetorically replied. 'I imagine Nevorn will have him cleaned up, bathed in oil and dressed for display this evening at Nevorn's mansion, and then he'll be given a choice of women as his reward.'

'And, tomorrow, he'll be back at training as if none of today happened,' Lenardi added.

'He might be put up for sale,' Orvak suggested.

'I doubt it,' Lenardi disagreed. 'After this demonstration, that one will be a prized performer for Nevorn's stable. He showed himself to be better than any recent warrior in the Karushta and the crowd already adores him.'

'What is a display?' Jaysin asked.

'A display?' Arch repeated. 'Lekna who have outstanding fighters put them on display so that others can fawn over them. They charge an admission to their house or stable to raise more money, and men go to ogle.'

'Can anyone attend?' Jaysin asked.

'If you have the coin, and know where to go, anyone can attend a display,' Arch replied. 'Are you keen, Captain?'

'I am,' Jaysin replied.

'Then I'll see what can be done,' Arch promised. 'First, however, there are more events to enjoy, and then we celebrate at my venue.'

Arch's venue, the Drinkers Paradise, was busy with patrons when they arrived. The ground floor was a large bar area with at least fifteen tables, but Arch took the company upstairs to a smaller, private room, where a woman served from a smaller bar and three girls, not boys, waited on the four tables in the room.

'I thought women were not allowed to work or be out of their homes,' Jaysin said to Wajin after the retinue sat.

'Of course, they're not,' Wajin said. 'These are Arch Kardinya's daughters. That's his wife at the bar. This is their home, at least in this room.'

'They would not dare go down those stairs,' Orvak said. 'Arch would kill them.'

'Really?' Jaysin asked.

'If a woman brings shame on her husband or father, He-Who-Cannot-Be-Named sanctions killing the woman,' Wajin explained. 'It is an ancient Sacred Decree.'

Jaysin did not pursue the topic. Everything about this culture was abhorrent to him in its treatment of women. He eyed the three girls, noting they were of a similar age, two almost identical in appearance with their long hair tucked under a head scarf and dark eyes.

'Jerpa and Neywin are twins,' Wajin explained, as if he knew what Jaysin was considering. 'Aleya is a year older.'

Conscious that he was being watched, even as he was watching, Jaysin relaxed and waited to see how the episode would unfold.

Scrag sat beside him and said, 'Let's talk about possibilities between your ship and my trading businesses.'

Jaysin waited for a break in the conversation and drinking between Arch's friends, but when it became clear that the group was settling in for a long night Jaysin rose and excused himself.

'So soon?' Wajin asked, rising with Jaysin.

'I have a crew to oversee,' Jaysin replied. 'I have to set the standard.'

'A leader who leads!' Lenardi declared and he stamped his foot to show approval. 'I am impressed! You are part of a dying breed, my friend.'

Arch also rose and leaned toward Jaysin to say, 'I will organise a ticket for you at Nevorn's. Go to the front gate and say your name. The rest will be arranged.'

'Where is Nevorn's house?' Jaysin asked.

'You can't miss it,' Arch said. 'It is at the end of Ocean View, a road that rises into the eastern hills off The Main Way. You'll see it. All the lanterns will be burning and people will be coming and going.' He clapped Jaysin on the shoulder. 'I look forward to meeting you again, Captain.'

Jaysin headed downstairs, weaving through the crowded inn and onto The Main Way. The sun was almost set. Birds circled above the river and harbour, returning to their roosts. Fewer merchants travelled the road. As he walked toward The Barking Dog inn, gongs sounded across the city and the men diverted and headed into nearby buildings, leaving Jaysin eerily alone with abandoned horses, carts and dogs. Feeling conspicuous, knowing his presence outside signalled him as not being a Man of Faith, he retreated into an alcove and waited. Exhaustion seeped through his body from maintaining the illusion. After a short time, men re-emerged to go about their business, and Jaysin continued his walk to Halian's refuge. Outside the house, he gratefully dispelled his illusion as Captain Kevan, entered and went to his room, conjured a light sphere and lay on his bed to rest.

His emotion remained heightened at seeing Chasse alive, and he wished he had his bracelet to communicate the news with everyone. Although it was hard to tell at distance, he was certain Chasse no longer had his bracelet. If he did, Harmi and Tam would surely have come for him. *If Tam recovered consciousness*, he remembered. *I wish I knew.*

To appear at Nevorn's display as Captain Kevan, Jaysin needed to recuperate his energy. *I'll sleep a short while*, he decided. *It should be enough. If I walk to Nevorn's house as myself, but cloaked, I can assume the illusion outside the entrance. It should be enough.* He dispelled the sphere and closed his eyes.

The thoroughfares through Vussar Karemachet were dark patches broken by random slits of lantern and lamplight spilling from windows and doorways. Every now and then, the moon briefly bathed the streets in a silvery glow before disappearing behind clouds. Jaysin walked quietly, his cowl covering his hair and face, avoiding the patches of light wherever possible and crossing them briskly where they could not be avoided.

Exactly as Arch promised, Nevorn's house was unmissable, even before Jaysin ventured from The Main Way onto the street leading up the hill, because the building was ablaze with lanterns and bonfires and the street was busy with men ascending and descending the hill.

Realising that he was losing the opportunity to transform into his disguise if he continued, Jaysin searched for an alley or alcove and settled on the porch of a small house hidden by a hedge. The dark front windows suggested the house was either uninhabited or the people within were asleep. He made certain no one could observe him before he uttered the necessary phrase to adopt the illusion of Captain Kevan.

Alteration made, hood down, Jaysin stepped onto the road and approached the gateway to Nevorn's property where two burly men were asking visitors for invitations and taking payment for entry. One man held out an arm to block Jaysin's way, but Jaysin introduced himself with, 'I am Captain Kevan.'

The man turned to his companion to ask, 'We know anything about a Captain Kevan?'

His companion replied, 'Arch Kardinya's guest.'

'You can enter,' the first man said, lowering his arm, and he turned his attention to the man behind Jaysin.

Jaysin traversed a paved pathway through a lavish garden and up stone steps to the house entrance. He skirted five men talking at the double door entry and entered a domed ceiling foyer where several men were studying the oiled, loincloth clad, red-haired fighter displayed on a pedestal like a living statue.

So close to his brother, Jaysin trembled with exhilaration and wrestled with his instincts to reveal himself and embrace Chasse, but disclosure would be fatal, pointless. He had to maintain his disguise. It hurt to see Chasse so close and yet out of reach as he listened to the observers praising his brother's physique, commenting on his handsome features, his red hair, tattoos and scars, and assessing whether they believed he was a long or short term prospect in the arena.

'Nevorn will invest in this one,' a man commented beside Jaysin. 'I'd buy one of his spawn. The athleticism, the looks and the physique would add value to my stock.'

Jaysin realised the man was talking to him. He looked down at the round-faced grey bearded man and asked, 'Are you a Lekna?'

The man's face creased in a smile as he replied, 'More of a speculator. I buy good merchandise and on-sell it to Lekna who understand value. Would you be interested?'

'Perhaps,' Jaysin replied. 'Price is important. I'd buy this one, if he was for sale.'

The man laughed again and grabbed Jaysin's arm. 'Nevorn won't sell this one. Not unless he suffers a serious injury in the Karushta, and I don't think Nevorn will risk that with so much interest being given to this fighter.' He steered Jaysin away from Chasse toward the next room, saying, 'Have you met Mijeff Nevorn?'

'I am new to the city,' Jaysin replied, looking over his shoulder at his brother.

'Then come, and I will introduce you,' said the man. 'By the way, what is your name?'

'Kevan,' Jaysin answered.

'Family name or birth name?' the man asked.

'My only name,' Jaysin replied.

'Ah,' the man said, nodding knowingly. 'I am Bendrak Kelahn. You can call me Bendrak.' He ushered Jaysin past two groups in the next room and into a third room lit by a multitude of small lanterns arranged in a cluster in the middle of the ceiling where three men were conversing, each holding a glass of red liquid. Bendrak interrupted and directed his words to a lithe man with a dark beard and cropped hair and a significant scar running from his forehead across the bridge of his nose and along his left cheek. 'Mijeff, allow me to introduce Kevan. He's very impressed with your new stable addition.'

Nevorn faced Jaysin, and Jaysin felt as if his shining dark eyes threatened to pierce his illusion. 'Sea-going man, by your attire,' Nevorn noted. 'Which ship?'

Jaysin hesitated, caught by the question, and replied, '*The Sea Dragon.*'

Nevorn turned to a broad-shouldered, grey-haired companion and asked, 'Heard of it?'

The individual shook his head and he asked Jaysin, 'When did you drop anchor?'

'Three days ago,' Jaysin replied.

'I don't recall your ship or your name in the Port Register,' the man said. He squinted, studying Jaysin, and asked, 'You did register?'

Jaysin had no idea what the Port Register was, but it was obvious if he was a ship's captain that he should have registered, so he improvised. 'Registered as soon as we unloaded our cargo,' he said.

'And what cargo was that?' the third man queried, a thin individual with a goatee.

'Grain. Wood,' Jaysin replied.

'Who was the procurer?' the third man asked.

Again, guessing the purpose of a procurer by the tone, Jaysin improvised. 'Arch Kardinya,' he said, hoping his choice was logical.

The second man was about to speak, but Nevorn cut him off with, 'Gentlemen, I think we might be subjecting our visitor to an unnecessary interrogation.' He turned to Jaysin. 'You have an interest in the fighting trade?'

'I trade along the west coast,' Jaysin replied. 'I could find more men like the one you have on display.'

'Then we should talk,' Nevorn said. 'Come by tomorrow evening, after Shebaal, and we can see if what you can obtain will pique my interest further.' He turned to Bendrak. 'Take your new friend away. And thank you for introducing him.'

Bendrak bowed his head and took Jaysin's arm, but as they left the room Jaysin noticed the two men with Nevorn were observing him and he knew his story was unconvincing. Captain Kevan's time in Vussar Karemachet was over. 'How long does the display last?' Jaysin asked, as Bendrak stopped at the foyer entry.

'I would say Nevorn will close his house soon,' Bendrak replied. 'I apologise for the questions from the Port Manager and Karzekk of the Hakamati. They are always untrusting.'

'I didn't mind,' Jaysin replied. 'I might go back to my ship.'

'Are you a Man of Faith?' Bendrak asked.

'There is One True God and –'

'The answer is yes,' Bendrak interrupted, smiling gleefully. 'You should join us for Shebaal tomorrow in the Vesnahdi.'

'Where is that?' Jaysin asked.

'At the foot of the eastern wall of the Udarvesna,' Bendrak replied. 'If you follow The Main Way to the Udarvesna, you will see the great pavilion with the bright green dome. That is where the best men worship on Shebaal.'

'I will come,' Jaysin promised, but he knew he would not keep that promise. 'Does Nevorn attend?'

'As I said,' Bendrak confirmed. 'The best men worship there.'

'But there are so many men in the city,' Jaysin said. 'Where do the others worship?'

Bendrak laughed and apologised, saying, 'Sorry. I should not laugh. I forgot you have never been here before. There are smaller versions of the Vesnahdi all across the city, even for the poorest of men to worship on Shebaal. Everywhere that you see a building with a domed green roof, you see a Vesnahdi. Your crew can attend the closest ones to the dock, if they are Men of Faith.'

'I will tell them, Jaysin replied. 'But, now, I must go to them, or they will think I am a bad captain. Thank you for hosting me this evening.'

'A pleasure, my friend,' Bendrak said, stopping before Chasse to stare at the warrior. 'A truly magnificent specimen.'

I will be back for you, brother, Jaysin silently promised.

Jaysin woke to rain slanting across the square window. He threw aside his bed clothes, dressed quickly and assessed the weather, guessing it was early morning, possibly immediately after sunrise, judging by the grey light filtering through the rainclouds. Being Shebaal, the Kermakk men would be making their ways through the downpour to their preferred Vesnahdi to spend the day in worship, talking, drinking and more worship, until the sunset gong released them to return to their homes. Women and children would be preparing for their day in the markets and shops, released from their household prisons to mix and talk and share food. Shebaal, so Halian told him, came every tenth day.

'We are cooped up for nine days and allowed to pretend we are free for one day,' Halian said, unable to hide her bitterness. 'One day in ten, we can be people. One day in ten.'

Jaysin crept from his room along the corridor, lantern light in the main room warning him that Halian was already up, but he didn't expect to find two more women in the room. All three looked at him. None wore headscarfs. 'I'm going to Shebaal,' Jaysin mumbled apologetically. When no one answered, he pulled up his hood and stepped into the rain.

He strode along the streets and roads towards the eastern district, hood up against the rain and to hide his appearance. Occasionally, he passed women venturing into the rain to enjoy the freedom of being out and about despite the weather and he spotted a pair of men ambling towards a smaller Vesnahdi, late to worship. He also passed men who were obviously not Men of Faith, sailors and merchants from places outside the Empire. He was surprised to see a trio of Hakamati on The Main Way. He crossed the road to avoid the Hakamati.

At the base of the hill leading to Nevorn's residence, he conjured a portal and recalled the room where he was introduced to Nevorn. The plan was simple: enter Nevorn's house, learn where the fighters were kept, and rescue his brother. He stepped through the blue haze.

Startled by screams, he retreated a step and took in where he appeared. The room was the one in which he met Nevorn, but two young women cowered against the wall. 'I'm not here to hurt anyone,' Jaysin reassured them, holding out his hands.

'Where did you come from?' the shorter woman asked timorously, as she pulled up her headscarf to hide her dark hair.

'Who are you?' demanded the second woman, also covering her head.

'Where are the fighters quartered?' Jaysin replied.

'Not in here,' the taller woman told him.

'Then where?' Jaysin asked.

'In the stables,' the first woman said. 'But it's Shebaal. They are worshipping.'

'You should know that,' the second woman said accusingly.

'Who are you?' the second woman repeated, straightening and becoming bolder.

'A merchant,' Jaysin lied. He strode out of the room towards the foyer. The larger chamber he passed through was empty, so he looked over his shoulder and, confident the women could not see him, he conjured a portal and translocated to the road. 'I am an idiot,' he chided himself. Thunder rumbled across the distant ocean and rolled over the city, and the rain intensified. Dejected, he headed for Halian's house.

'Broth?' Halian asked when Jaysin entered. He discovered the same two women seated by the hearth as when he left, and a man in a long dark green robe was leaning against the mantlepiece. 'You are among friends,' Halian said, seeing Jaysin's hesitancy.

'You can sit here,' the grey-haired woman offered, tapping a stool beside her.

'After you remove that wet cloak,' Halian ordered.

'I thought everyone kept to their private spaces,' Jaysin said warily.

'It is Shebaal,' said the man, his voice modulated and melodic. 'Only women, misfits and miscreants remain beyond the Vesnahdi.'

'I saw Hakamati,' Jaysin replied.

'That's because the Men of Faith fear the faithless will rob their homes while they pray,' said the woman who offered the stool.

Jaysin lowered his hood and removed his cloak, which Halian took and hung beside the hearth. 'Sit,' she said. 'I'll pour the broth.'

Jaysin sat and held his hands toward the crackling flames. 'You have slender fingers,' the man remarked. 'Fine hands.'

Jaysin looked up. The man was a good height, a little shorter than himself, his hair was dark with the beginnings of grey wisps and hung loosely to his shoulders, the ends curling gently under, and his features were finer than the Kermakk who Jaysin met, more like Jaysin's own, or like Chasse's; a long nose and thin, high cheekbones. The most striking aspect was his bright green eyes.

'I take it you don't work for a living,' the man added.

'I thought Halian's guests didn't ask questions,' Jaysin retorted.

Halian handed Jaysin a steaming bowl and a wooden spoon, and said, 'The four of you have a common interest. You should talk.'

'I am Laseen,' said the grey-haired woman on Jaysin's right.

'Karelan,' the brunette woman added.

'Paten Nedrek,' the man said. 'We are citizens of the Assandan Kingdom.'

Jaysin sensed they were waiting for him to identify himself, so he said, 'Jaysin.' He looked at Halian. 'Is this a meeting of some kind?'

'Of some kind,' Paten answered. 'You have an interest in the arena fighters. So do we.'

'How?' Jaysin asked.

'I have a very good friend who should not be among them,' Paten said.

'I have a husband among them,' said Karelan.

Jaysin asked Laseen, 'And you?'

'Karelan's husband is my son,' Laseen replied.

'My brother,' Jaysin shared.

'And what are you hoping to do?' Paten asked.

Jaysin glanced at Halian, deciding if he was making a mistake, before he said, 'I intend to save him.'

Paten smiled, and Jaysin liked the man's smile because it was warm, genuine. 'There is only one way to save your brother,' he said.

'How would I do that?' Jaysin asked.

'A pardon from the Karudar Marfek,' Paten replied. 'That is the only way arena fighters are set free.'

'And you are all seeking a pardon for your people?' Jaysin asked.

Paten looked at Karelan and Laseen, and said, 'Yes. We are.'

Seventeen

'We are foreigners and women,' Laseen reminded Jaysin. 'How would we even be allowed to approach the Udarvesna?'

'But, as a sheykermett, an ambassador from the Assandan Kingdom,' Paten said, coming forward to place a gold clasp in the shape of a rearing horse on Jaysin's cloak, 'you will be received.'

'We will go over the necessary protocols again,' said Halian, when Paten stepped back to admire his handiwork. 'Let's begin with your title and name.'

'I am Sheykermett Davin Arkan,' Jaysin said, as he adjusted the maroon cloak Halian provided.

'Who do you ask for?' Paten asked.

'The Karmatimett,' Jaysin replied.

'And his name?' Paten asked.

'Fassen Lemodin,' Jaysin answered. 'But I never use his name, unless he invites me to.'

'Correct,' Paten confirmed.

'And why do you need to see him?' Halian queried.

'It's a delicate matter of regional importance,' Jaysin replied. 'I have a message from King Nati fit only for delivering in the presence of the Karudar Marfek.'

'And if you are refused?' Halian continued.

'I tell whoever I am speaking to that the Kermakk Empire may be fighting wars on four fronts instead of three,' Jaysin said.

'And if you are asked why you make such a threat?' Paten asked.

'I repeat that the information is only for the ears of the Karudar

Marfek, because only she has the power to appease my king.'

'Very good,' Halian declared.

'And when you do have an audience with the Karudar Marfek?' Paten asked, 'what do you ask for, and what do you offer?'

'I tell her that King Nati is very upset that three of his prized shanti – did I pronounce that correctly?' Jaysin asked.

'Shjaan-tchee,' Paten pronounced. 'Yes, very good.'

Jaysin continued. 'I tell her the King is upset and wants his three prized shanti returned, and as a show of good faith in exchange he will supply a full contingent of Assandan medja –'

'Mee-dya,' Paten corrected.

'Meedya,' Jaysin repeated, and continued, 'to support the Kermakk forces in the southern troubles. He will also send monetary compensation to be shared with the Kermakk Lekna whose investments are affected by this request.'

'Perfect,' Paten commended.

'You are a good man to do this for us,' Karelan told Jaysin. 'We have no other way to free my husband or Paten's partner.'

'I can do this on my own,' Jaysin said to Paten. 'It's too risky for you.'

Paten chuckled and replied, 'A sheykermett arriving at the Udarvesna without an escort would be deemed suspicious. Besides, you can't speak our language. I can intervene if needed.' He stepped back, opened his maroon cloak to expose his mauve tunic and purple trousers, and asked, 'How do I look?'

'Official,' Halian replied. 'Stand beside him,' she told Jaysin.

Jaysin complied and stood beside Paten. Halian and Laseen nodded approval. 'You look the part,' Halian said. 'We are lucky the sewing women could quickly prepare the outfits we need.'

Jaysin knew that, while he was making a failed attempt to free Chasse the previous day, the people in his refuge were conspiring to engage him in a more effective, if daring, rescue of their people. Dying his red hair dark brown eliminated the need for an illusory disguise to play his part, and that allowed him to keep his arcane skills hidden from Halian and her companions. If matters turned bad, he had a way out. Paten's choice to accompany him complicated his escape options, but Paten was making a choice that wasn't entirely Jaysin's concern.

At midday, Jaysin and Paten walked The Main Way to the Udarvesna, the massive pink walls expanding under the grey sky as the pair neared them. Men, horses, carts, and small herds being shepherded to and away from markets moved haphazardly along the road, separated by columns of Imperial troops in green livery marching east or toward the docks.

'The whole country is embroiled in the wars,' Paten remarked. 'I cannot imagine how many men are involved. The Empire must be vaster than my people estimate.'

The concepts of a nation's size in land and population were new to Jaysin. Before leaving Harbin, his world was contained at the foot of Dragon Mountain and bordered by an ocean that only the dragonwarriors ventured upon. Reading Eric's books and the journey to Machutzka broadened his view that the world was far larger than he imagined and that view was reinforced by his arrival in Sarchah, Cheznah and Vussar Karemachet, but the vastness of a world in which hundreds of thousands of soldiers marched and sailed to destinations beyond anywhere he knew existed made Jaysin dizzy with possibilities.

Arriving at the gates, Paten reminded Jaysin that, as his servant, he would introduce him wherever necessary. Paten approached the soldiers on duty at the Udarvesna gates and, while Paten spoke with a soldier, Jaysin took in the size of the gates. They were twice as large as the gates guarding Machutzka and they were constructed of dark brown wood reinforced with thick bands of dark grey metal. He guessed they would resist considerable force if anyone tried to break them down.

Four soldiers emerged from the gatehouse and ushered Jaysin and Paten into an expansive courtyard and a garden filled with trees and bushes. Despite the wintry conditions, the garden displayed cultivated patches of bright flowers and coloured birds hopped between the vegetation clumps. A curved and light grey paved road cut through the courtyard towards a central triple-storey building constructed from the same pink stone as the outer walls. Tall windows dominated the facade, designed to make the building appear light and airy, as if it floated in the grounds. Six thin round towers topped with gold pinnacles jutted from the sides and reached well above the walls.

The central building was flanked by equally imposing structures. To the right, built from yellow stone and ornately adorned with masterfully crafted statues and sculptures and capped by a series of eight square towers with gold pinnacles, a two-storey barracks pressed against the walls and extended from the centre around the walls almost to the gatehouse. The building to the left, however, was at odds with the beauty and intricacy of the other two, although it was impressive in its brooding atmosphere and design. Its circular structure of dark grey stone rose the equivalent of three storeys, capped by a massive gold dome, with four hexagonal towers equidistant around its circumference, each tower visible beyond the walls.

The soldiers escorted Jaysin and Paten along the garden road, veering towards the grey building at a junction and they halted before another squad of eight soldiers who were guarding the building at the base of a flight of stone steps the width of the facade. An exchange occurred between the soldiers before the escorting quartet headed for the gatehouse.

'We wait here,' Paten informed Jaysin as a soldier ascended the steps and entered the building. 'This is the Karfeshnar,' he explained. 'Kermakk Feshnari meet here to discuss matters of state and make laws. The Karmatimett resides within.'

Jaysin studied the courtyard, spotting several fountains spouting water from fish and animal statues scattered around the grounds. He also observed there were wagons parked near the steps with servants tending the horses and chatting. A raindrop kissed his cheek, and another, so he shielded his eyes to look up at the clouds and, as the rain steadily increased, he asked Paten, 'Should we get under cover?'

'Where?' Paten asked.

'Inside,' Jaysin replied.

Paten smiled as he said, 'We won't be going inside unless we are invited.' He pulled up his hood. 'So, we hope we are invited inside soon.'

Jaysin raised his hood. Annoyed to be made to wait in the rain, he rehearsed what Paten and Halian taught him. The two Assandan men he was meant to retrieve were Zerana Timaki and Welan Godrun. Both were important men in the Assandan kingdom and favourites of King Nati, but they were taken from an inn on the Assandan coast by a raiding party who sold them to Kermakk traders who sold them to Kermakk Lekna. The same raiding party captured his brother who was a prized bodyguard of the Assandan men.

A soldier accompanying a young envoy in green robes descended the steps, and the envoy approached, bowing his head. He spoke in Assandan, but Paten interrupted by informing him, 'The Sheykermett is well-versed in Kermakk.'

The envoy spoke in Kermakk to Jaysin. 'The Karmatimett has asked you to wait in the library until he calls.'

Jaysin glanced at Paten, who replied, 'Take us there.'

The envoy led Jaysin and Paten up the steps and out of the rain, and in the expansive foyer another young man approached. 'Tosyn will take your cloaks and see that they are returned to you, dry,' the envoy explained. Jaysin and Paten allowed Tosyn to take their cloaks, and the envoy led them to a large open door. 'Please wait in here,' Tosyn said. 'I will come for you when the Karmatimett is ready.'

Jaysin was overwhelmed by the chamber's size and its contents. He counted fifteen rows of double-sided wooden shelves, each rising at least four spans high and extending more than twenty paces into the chamber. The quantity of books astonished him.

'The Kermakk waste their time with amassing words,' Paten remarked dismissively.

'I will be among the shelves,' Jaysin replied. He drifted into the first row and searched the spine titles, only to be disappointed when he discovered that many were untitled, but when he saw each shelf was labelled, identifying the topics of the stored books, he shifted his attention to the labels, hoping to find a collection of texts devoted to learning magic. No such collection appeared. The labels concerned politics, religion, social organisation and sundry dry topics.

'Why so much interest in parchment and paper?' Paten asked, joining Jaysin in the aisle.

'Texts are voices,' Jaysin replied, remembering a statement that Shika the Librarian used. 'They are windows of the world and doorways into people's minds and hearts.'

Paten shrugged. 'Eyes are the windows into people's souls,' he retorted. 'Their spoken words and actions reveal their minds and hearts.' He pulled a book from the shelf and opened it. 'What is this one about?'

Jaysin leaned in to read the first page. 'It's a collection of stories by someone named Gordo Tomi.'

'Stories about what?' Paten asked.

'I can't tell without reading it,' Jaysin replied. 'May I see?' He took the book from Paten and flicked through the pages, briefly reading sections. 'This person travelled through different kingdoms and lands, and he recorded what he saw and heard.'

'What good is that?' Paten asked.

'We may never travel through these places,' Jaysin replied, 'but if we read what Tomi wrote we can travel there in his words.'

Paten laughed and said, 'I'd rather travel there myself. To smell a place, listen to the people, eat the food - that's travelling.'

Jaysin wanted to argue, but a voice interrupted, echoing through the library. 'Where is the Assandan Sheykermett?'

Paten nudged Jaysin's arm. 'I am here,' Jaysin replied.

The envoy appeared at the end of the aisle. 'The Karmatimett will you see you now.'

Jaysin and Paten followed the envoy from the library into the foyer and crossed to a large door where the envoy stopped to say, 'Only the Sheykermett goes beyond this door.'

Jaysin glanced at Paten, before replying, 'My assistant goes everywhere with me. That is the King's orders.'

The envoy's expression became stern as he said, 'No one but Sheykermetti enter this door. That is the Karudar Marfek's law. Your King's rule does not apply here.'

'I will wait for you here,' Paten told Jaysin. Jaysin followed the envoy through the door.

A smaller foyer beyond opened into a circular space dominated by a raised bench at the farther end, lit by suspended lanterns, behind which sat three men. The central figure, white-haired and white bearded, wore an Imperial green robe and a tall green headpiece, adorned with gold braiding and a large white plume on the left side. The men either side, beards greying, wore green robes similar but less impressive to the central figure, and their cowls hid their features. Behind the bench rose another platform with steps leading to a large and ornate throne. As he entered, Jaysin also became aware the space was an auditorium with men seated in tiered seats around the closest half of the circle. Soldiers in green uniforms stood at loose attention, one every five paces around the space.

'The Karfeshnar welcomes the Assandan Sheykermett!' announced the man to the left of the central figure. He motioned for Jaysin to come forward.

Jaysin expected to meet the Karmatimett in a less public, less formal room, not be a central player in an Imperial performance. He approached the raised bench, entering the brighter light thrown by the lanterns.

'Welcome, Sheykermett Arkan,' the Karmatimett greeted. 'How is King Nati?'

'In most respects, the king is very well, thank you,' Jaysin replied in Kermakk. 'But I would not be here if it wasn't for the fact that my king is not happy.'

'And why is your king unhappy?' the Karmatimett inquired.

'With respect,' Jaysin replied, remembering the phrasing Halian and Paten taught, 'King Nati has a very personal request to make of the Karudar Marfek.'

'You have an audience,' the Karmatimett said. 'State your king's request.'

Jaysin met the Karmatimett's gaze, and said, 'Again, respectfully, but King Nati's personal request is not for public ears.' He purposely shifted his gaze to encompass the Feshnari seated in the auditorium.

The Karmatimett spoke quietly, in turn, with the men seated either side of him, before he faced Jaysin to say, 'Shalan unas nassay eshanya.'

Startled by the unexpected expression, Jaysin replied, 'I apologise, but I do not understand.'

'The Karmatimett asked you to roll up your sleeve,' said the man on the right side, who lowered his cowl. Jaysin recognised Bahti. 'Surely an Assandan Sheykermett would understand his own language?'

'I was simply not paying attention,' Jaysin hastily replied.

'You were asked to roll up your sleeve,' the Karmatimett said. He motioned to the soldiers on the perimeter and they moved closer, lances lowered. 'I recommend that you roll up your sleeve.'

I should have used an illusion, Jaysin thought angrily. He slowly rolled up his sleeve to reveal Mezzin's slave scar.

'This man is an imposter!' Bahti yelled.

'Seize him!' the Karmatimett ordered. 'Take him to the matishem!'

Jaysin considered resisting, but he knew it would end only with his death. He anticipated the soldiers would bind his hands, upon Bahti's advice, so he was surprised when they didn't. Instead, they prodded him to leave the chamber under close escort and Jaysin realised that Bahti did not recognise him with brown hair and Assandan robes. He was joined by Paten in the foyer, and they were marched to a door that opened to a set of steps leading deeper inside the Karfeshnar. At the foot of the stairs, they entered a dingy torchlit space where two men rose from their chairs and asked the soldiers what they were doing.

'The Karmatimett ordered these two to be imprisoned,' a soldier explained.

'This way,' the leaner man directed, and he led the party along a narrow corridor to a T-junction. Jaysin winced at the rancid human body and faecal odours assailing his senses. 'Third door should do it,' said the jailer. He unhitched a set of heavy rusty keys from his belt and unlocked a wooden door. 'In you go,' he indicated.

Jaysin and Paten entered the narrow cell, the door thudded shut behind them and they were cloaked in darkness. 'What happened?' Paten asked.

'I was exposed,' Jaysin replied. 'Sorry.'

'How?' Paten asked.

'I'm not sure,' Jaysin said. 'One of the men with the Karmatimett bought me as a slave.'

'You were a slave?' Paten asked. 'Why didn't you tell us this?'

'You didn't ask,' Jaysin replied. 'I didn't think it was important. Halian knew.'

'And this man recognised you?'

'I'm not sure he knows who I really am,' Jaysin said, reflecting on how the arrest transpired. 'He knows something about me that should have made him wary, but he didn't react as if he remembered.'

'I don't understand,' Paten said. 'How did he recognise you?'

'Now that I think about it,' Jaysin said, 'I don't think he recognised me at all. He set a simple trap and I fell into it.'

'A trap?'

'He asked a question in your language.'

Paten was silent in the darkness, before saying, 'He suspected you. Something you did gave him a clue.'

'I'm sorry you are here with me,' Jaysin said. 'I should have insisted that I came alone.'

'You would not have made it through the front gate,' Paten said. 'I wonder what they plan to do with us?'

'Watch your eyes,' Jaysin warned. He conjured a light sphere.

'In the name of the Seven Gods!' Paten gasped.

'It won't hurt,' Jaysin assured him. 'It would, if I intensified it.'

'What are you?'

Jaysin grinned and said, 'More than these people anticipate.' He surveyed the narrow cell. No bed, no stool, no waste bucket. 'I'm not impressed with this accommodation. I think we should speak to the Karudar Marfek.'

'How do you intend to do that?' Paten asked.

Jaysin whispered a phrase and a blue oval light appeared against the cell wall. 'Follow me,' he said, and he vanished through the light.

Jaysin caught Paten before the man stumbled when he appeared in the Imperial garden. Rain pattered on the leaves and ground. 'I assume the Karudar Marfek is in the main building. We can visit her there,' Jaysin said, and he whispered another arcane phrase.

'This can't be happening,' Paten muttered, looking around. 'How did we get here?' He looked to Jaysin and met the Karmatimett's level gaze. Shock filled his face.

'It's me,' Jaysin announced calmly. 'This is how we enter the main building.' Seeing Paten's reaction, he urged, 'Don't stare at me. Come on.'

Jaysin strode to the steps of the palace, with Paten fearfully trailing, and he confronted one of eight soldiers on guard in the rain. 'I have an urgent matter that must be conveyed directly to the Karudar Marfek,' he announced. The addressed soldier stiffened and glanced at Paten. 'Do not invoke the wrath of the Karudar Marfek!' Jaysin snarled. The soldier bowed his head and strode up the stairs into the palace.

'We should hurry,' Paten whispered, gesturing at the grey Karfeshnar. 'The assembly is ended. The Feshnari are leaving.'

Jaysin saw carts and wagons drawing up at the base of the Karfeshnar steps, and men waiting in the shelter of the porch. He returned his attention to the palace doors. The soldier reappeared, accompanied by a man in black attire. The man in black gestured for Jaysin to ascend the steps and, as Jaysin and Paten reached him, the man said, 'Apologies for making you wait in the rain, Karmatimett. The Karudar Marfek was indisposed.' He scrutinised Paten with a disparaging expression.

'This is Sheykermett Nedren. He has an essential message for the Karudar Marfek,' Jaysin explained. 'I brought him personally for this meeting.'

'This way,' the man in black directed, and he led the pair into the palace foyer.

The foyer's opulence – mirrors, glass and marble glittering in the flickering light from countless lanterns suspended in clusters from the vaulting, ornate ceiling – astonished Jaysin, even more than the Karfeshnar library. Obsidian beams created squares and angles through the surfaces, and large murals of idyllic settings and battles decorated the walls. Pairs of guards in green and gold livery, with polished bronze breastplates and tall halberds, stood at attention before five double black doors, three on the opposing wall, and one at each side of the foyer.

The man in black led Jaysin and Paten to the left door in the rear wall, and a guard opened the double doors as they approached. Inside, the man in black said, 'The Karudar Marfek will speak to you here, as usual,' and he withdrew, closing the doors in his wake.

Although a smaller space, long and narrow, the chamber was opulently furnished like the foyer. Paintings of individuals and scenes adorned the right wall between embroidered hangings. One painting, running from floor to high ceiling, depicted a sailing ship with full canvas on three masts, three-quarter facing, crashing through high waves, and a figure in an emerald jacket and baggy pants, long black hair splayed in the breeze, stood defiantly on the ship's prow, pointing out of the painting at his unseen destination. It reminded Jaysin of a similar piece in Alban's inn. Tall windows filled the left side, looking onto a small courtyard garden and fountain and another wall of a separate wing of the palace. The far wall was dominated by a fireplace and white marble mantlepiece covered with a variety of golden and silver and glass objects, and a black door squatted in the right corner. At the chamber's centre, an arrangement of five high-backed and plush armchairs, the material a pattern of plants and flowers in muted colours, was placed around a low dark wooden table, the table displaying an assemblage of glasses and decanters.

Paten paced nervously along the windows, while Jaysin studied the paintings. 'What if the real Karmatimett arrives?' Paten asked, halting at the chairs.

'Let's hope he doesn't,' Jaysin replied.

'If the Karudar Marfek does give us an audience,' Paten said, approaching, 'you must let her speak first. Don't dare question her. Don't stare at her. Despite anything you might think, here she is the Kermakk god incarnate.'

'Is that how you treat your king?' Jaysin asked.

'Yes,' Paten replied. 'Every leader believes they are all-powerful.' He smiled. 'And they are all-powerful.'

The small black door opened and a servant in black entered to hold the door. A second figure entered, a tall woman wearing a long green robe embroidered with gold lace and encrusted with an assortment of red, gold, yellow, white and blue jewels in patterns sweeping over the shoulder and across her breasts to her waist. A thin silver metal belt, like strands of twisted rope, circled her narrow waist. Her hair was hidden beneath a large green turban adorned by a white plume like the one Jaysin imitated in his illusion of the Karmatimett, only the Karudar Marfek's turban also had a prominent orange jewel clasped to its front. A white dog, wolfish in appearance and fluffy, walked beside her.

A figure trailed the Karudar Marfek, a thickset and tall individual clad entirely in black cloth from head to feet, face masked behind a black mesh. The servant closed the door and stood stock still, almost imperceptible against the background, while the Karudar Marfek settled in a chair facing Jaysin and Paten and the dog sat dutifully beside her. The figure in black stood behind the chair.

'Come forward, Fassen,' the Karudar Marfek invited.

Assuming Fassen was the Karmatimett's name, Jaysin approached the ring of chairs. Paten remained behind.

'You have an important matter that could not wait for our usual session?' the Karudar Marfek inquired.

'Yes,' Jaysin replied, trying to imitate the Karmatimett's voice.

'Well?' the Karudar Marfek asked.

'I would like the Assandan Sheykermett to speak for himself,' Jaysin stated politely.

'Are you unwell?' the Karudar Marfek asked.

Jaysin glanced at Paten before asking, 'Why?'

'You are not who you pretend to be.'

The accusing voice came from the figure in black, a woman's voice. She stepped from behind the Karudar Marfek's chair, a soft warm glow enveloped the Karudar Marfek, and Jaysin sensed magical energy rising in the chamber, making the hair on his arms and neck rise. The air around him crackled faintly and his illusion dissipated.

'So, who exactly are you?' the woman asked.

Exposed, Jaysin replied, 'I'm here to save my brother from the Karushta.'

'And the Assandans!' Paten blurted.

'Silence!' the woman ordered, turning her head toward Paten. He retreated, his head bowed.

'Who are you?' Jaysin asked.

'I asked first,' the woman reminded him. 'Or perhaps I should have asked "What are you?"'

'I came to ask the Karudar Marfek to pardon three fighters,' Jaysin replied.

The woman in black approached and walked around Jaysin, in the same manner as Mezzin appraised him, and her manner angered him. 'I am not a slave,' he said firmly.

'No,' the woman agreed when she stood before him. 'And neither are you a mas, a wizard in your language. Bahti informed us that he had caught a mas, and the mas promised to use his oozim to help in the wars.' She paused before explaining, 'A wizard and his dragon, as you might call them. But now that I see you, I see that you are not a wizard, but something else entirely.' She returned to stand beside the Karudar Marfek.

'Who are you?' Jaysin asked, unable to mask his frustration.

'You are speaking with the Karudarteta,' the Karudar Marfek said from her chair. 'She is my advisor.' She looked up at the woman and asked, 'What do you advise, my love?'

'Listen to what this one has to say and offer,' the Karudarteta said.

'Well?' the Karudar Marfek asked.

Jaysin swallowed and said, 'King Nati would like three men taken into servitude by Kermakk Lekna to be returned to him. In exchange, he offers to supply a contingent of Assandan troops to support the Kermakk Great Army and he offers to compensate the Lekna an agreeable amount for the fighters they will lose.'

The Karudar Marfek turned to the Karudarteta, and they conversed in voices too low for Jaysin to hear, until the Karudar Marfek spoke to Jaysin.

'I believe one of the fighters is your brother, correct?'

'Yes,' Jaysin replied.

The Karudar Marfek beckoned for Paten to approach, and to him she said, 'Return to your king. Tell him we will accept his offer and we will release the Assandan men when the promised Assandan troops arrive in our port, along with the compensatory coin for our Lekna who will be upset to be robbed of their wares. This is my decision.' She waved her hand and added, 'You are dismissed.'

Paten glanced at Jaysin, before he withdrew obediently.

When the door closed, the Karudar Marfek said to Jaysin, 'You have taken a courageous but unwise path to rescue your brother. Did you really believe that you, alone, could steal him from me?'

'I wasn't stealing him,' Jaysin replied. 'I came to seek a pardon for him.'

'In the guise of someone else,' the Karudar Marfek said. 'Hiding behind the façade of a sheykermett and making false offers. In fact, you came here pretending to be my Karmatimett. That is treason of the highest order. I should have you executed.'

Jaysin prepared to translocate, bracing himself for a quick conjuration and escape as he did when Bahti cornered him.

'At this moment,' the Karudarteta remarked, 'you are thinking "How can I escape?" probably even readying a spell to do so. I advise that you don't.'

'What is your brother's name?' the Karudar Marfek asked.

'Chasse,' Jaysin replied.

'No family name?' she asked.

'Savages along the west coast don't use family names,' said the Karudarteta. Seeing Jaysin's expression, she added, 'Yes. You dyed your hair, but everything about you identifies where you come from.'

'And where is your brother?' the Karudar Marfek asked.

'He – he is a fighter for Nevorn,' Jaysin replied.

'Ah, the new Karushta champion,' the Karudar Marfek,' said, nodding.

'Yes. I've heard Nevorn has a new fighter.' She raised an eyebrow. 'And he is your brother?'

'Yes,' Jaysin confirmed.

The Karudar Marfek shook her head. 'Nevorn will not let his prized champion leave,' she said. 'You are asking me to make an important man very unhappy. I would need a significant incentive to consider granting a pardon to your brother, given the pain it will cause.' Jaysin saw the Karudarteta lean forward and whisper in the Karudar Marfek's ear. The Karudar Marfek studied Jaysin as she stood before she asked, 'What are you willing to offer to save your brother?'

'Whatever it takes,' Jaysin replied.

'Would you give your life for his?'

Jaysin almost blurted, 'No,' but he hesitated, weighing up what might be the consequences of offering his life in the circumstances. 'I risked my life to stand here,' he replied.

'Would you give your life for his?' the Karudar Marfek repeated.

'Yes,' Jaysin confirmed, his heart racing. 'I would.'

Eighteen

Jaysin trailed in the wake of the black garbed Karudarteta along a wide corridor that penetrated deeper into the Imperial Palace. The Karudarteta walked softly, her black slippers whispering across the grey marble tiles, making Jaysin feel clumsy because his boots clumped oafishly on the floor in comparison.

As with the chambers, the corridor walls were adorned with paintings of people and places and inlaid with streaks of gold layered into the masonry. Black-robed attendants waited at every door along the corridor and when the Karudarteta reached the last door the attendant opened it and stepped aside. Wordlessly, the Karudarteta entered and began ascending a spiral staircase and Jaysin followed, fascinated by the stone structure he understood was one of the Palace's six towers.

The stairs reached a landing and a door, but the Karudarteta continued climbing past a second landing and door and beyond to a third landing where small slit windows appeared in one side of the wall, allowing shafts of natural light to fall across the stairs. The staircase wound higher until it ended at a metal door that opened into a circular room, illuminated by four windows.

Jaysin's gaze was drawn to a round table topped with a pile of books and rolled parchments and a half-melted candle and blue lamp. A curved sleeping space lay along a section of the wall between windows. Two more sections of the curved wall were filled with bookshelves.

'You can read?' the Karudarteta asked.

'Yes,' Jaysin replied. 'Why have you brought me here?'

'Sit,' the Karudarteta instructed, indicating a stool by the table. Jaysin sat, listening to the rain thrumming on the wooden roof. 'You have chosen to give your life for your brother's freedom,' the Karudarteta said as she turned to watch the rain. 'Some would call that noble.' She faced Jaysin, and it annoyed him that he could not see her face behind the gauze. 'You, however, believe you can escape, once your brother is safe.'

'I have made an offer,' Jaysin said. 'I will honour it.'

'Words are meaningless from the mouths of those who have other thoughts,' the Karudarteta said.

'If you don't trust me, why have you brought me here?' Jaysin challenged.

'Because I believe that, when you see what your prison can offer, you will stay.'

'This is my prison?'

'For now,' the Karudarteta replied.

'And my brother?' Jaysin asked. 'How can I be sure your Karudar Marfek will honour the bargain? I need to see my brother being released. I should accompany him to freedom.'

'And escape with him,' the Karudarteta said. 'A simple plan. But the Karudar Marfek is not so gullible.' She sat opposite Jaysin. 'It will take several days to organise for your brother's release from Lekna Nevorn. Protocol. Meetings. Promises. Monetary exchange. Political and economic matters. All very boring, but very necessary. Nevorn cannot lose public opinion after exhibiting a prized fighter in the Karushta. That his fighter should be pardoned by the Karudar Marfek so soon after a winning performance would smack of opportunism on the part of our leader. The matter will need careful resolution. In that time, you will remain here. Food and drink will be brought from the buttery. There is a garderobe on the level below. A servant will guide you to it. But first, we talk.' She leaned forward. 'Who taught you magic?'

Jaysin weighed up the possible consequences, before responding, 'I taught myself. Mainly.'

'Not possible,' the Karudarteta said bluntly. 'You had a mentor, a source. Who?'

'I taught myself,' Jaysin repeated.

'Then you are the spawn of a mas,' she said. 'Who was your father?'

'Kevan of Harbin,' Jaysin answered. 'He was the Dragon Head.'

'What is a Dragon Head?'

'Like your Karudar Marfek,' Jaysin explained. 'He was the most important person of our village.'

The Karudarteta sat back, and Jaysin wondered what her reaction meant, especially as she already labelled his people savages. Without a face to read, he couldn't tell. 'I've seen your illusion, your ability to appear as another. It is strong magic,' the Karudarteta said. 'What other magic can you do?'

'What can you do?' Jaysin countered. 'How did you break my illusion?'

'Like this,' the Karudarteta replied. As she waved her hand, the books on the table and shelves vanished and the rain outside the windows ceased.

The transformation startled Jaysin. 'This is an illusion?' he gasped, and he rose from the stool.

'Sit down,' the Karudarteta ordered, snapping her fingers. The books and shelves reappeared and the gloomy rain resumed.

'How?' Jaysin queried.

'You know how,' the Karudarteta said. 'Show me an illusion.'

Jaysin considered his options, still struggling with the ease by which the Karudarteta conjured and dispelled her illusions. He transformed into a replica of Chasse.

The Karudarteta raised an eyebrow, and said, 'Impressive. I presume this is your brother's appearance?'

'Yes,' Jaysin admitted.

The Karudarteta waved her hand and Jaysin's spell evaporated. 'It's called dispelling,' she said. 'You already do it when you end or cancel your spell. In this form, it is designed to break another's spell. Very useful when dealing with other arcane users.' She chuckled, shaking her head. 'Not many opportunities for that.'

'How did you learn magic?' Jaysin asked. 'I know you don't own a dragon.'

'No one owns dragons,' she responded. 'Mas and oozim are one. One does not exist without the other, once they are bonded.' She stood and moved to a bookshelf to extract a volume. 'This is a book you should read, while you await the outcome of your request for your brother's pardon.' She placed the book on the table before Jaysin. 'I would like to stay longer and play this game of questions and avoided answers, but the Karudar Marfek is busy, and my task as advisor is to ensure that she has a mind sharing the burdens of the Empire. Read. You will find answers to your questions. Then we can talk again.' The Karudarteta closed the door.

Jaysin walked around the donjon's confined circumference, glancing out each of the four windows to ascertain his position in relation to the Udarvesna and the city. The rain was persistent and heavy and water cascaded in tiny waterfalls from the corbels and finials along the stonework of the buildings and walls. He paused by the bookshelves to touch the leather binding and read the inscribed titles: *Controlling the Crowded Mind*, *Fascinating Creatures of the West*, *Diplomacy Reimagined*, *Four Directions: Six Possibilities*, *Curing Maladies and Ills*, titles confirming that he was in a repository of magic with new texts and spells to learn.

He returned to the book the Karudarteta placed on the table and ran his fingers across the purple textured leather cover. It was untitled and embossed with a symbol like a stylised flame and dragon's claw. He opened the book to the first page and the title and author, but the script and language were foreign. He flipped a few pages and realised that he was given a book he couldn't read. *What is your game*? he pondered. *Why this unreadable text*? She said he could come and go in the tower. He would explore it, then, and plan his escape when it was time to leave.

He closed the book and went to the door, pulled on the handle, and discovered it was locked. He hadn't heard the Karudarteta lock it. He pulled harder, but the door did not budge. She did tell him this was his prison. No matter. He would translocate. He remembered the Udarvesna layout. He paid attention to location details for this very reason. Escape. He looked back at the library of books. *What else does she have stored here*? he wondered. He knew he could escape. Perhaps he had enough time to select a text or two to take with him.

The light faded, thunder rumbled across the Udarvesna, and the rain morphed into a torrential downpour, drumming loudly on the wooden tiles. Leaks appeared in the ceiling and drops pattered on the stone floor. Jaysin conjured a light sphere and commanded it to follow him while he scanned the bookshelves for interesting tomes.

Some titles were in Kermakk, but most were untitled, or in languages he did not recognise. He pulled books from the shelf and opened them one by one, using illustrations to guess at their content, but he paused when he lowered a Kermakk book titled *Meddamettum A Har Mettum*, which he interpreted to mean *Translating the Lost Tongues*. He opened the rust orange leather cover to see the title repeated and an author named Mmda A Sheyker. 'I am a stranger,' he whispered, translating the Kermakk name into his Harbin words. He took the book to the table, sat, and read.

Jaysin peered through the window at the night. The rain had ceased, but clouds hid the moon and stars. Flickering torches and lanterns formed a veneer of light across Vussar Karemachet that spread up to the surrounding hillsides and out across the river mouth and harbour, revealing the city's size in a surprisingly striking manner. He had lost track of time. He expected the Karudarteta to return, but she did not. She told him food and drink would be brought to him, but none was. He was hungry and thirsty. He would fetch refreshments for himself.

He returned to the table and stared at the book. If he understood and memorised the contents correctly, he had learned a new key to knowledge, a new spell. He pushed the book aside and drew the purple leather-bound item forward that the Karudarteta challenged him to read, caressing the soft cover and embossed icon with his fingertips before he opened to the first page and stared at the alien script. 'Let's see what happens,' he whispered.

He recited the Kermakk phrase, 'Feyla akehu loka, harmetta usz sheykum.' As when he generated an illusion, energy rippled in the pages, the book shimmered, and his eyes watered, and the script morphed into a Kermakk title: *Orphans of the Wizards*. He hesitated, fascinated by the transmutation, before he read the opening words: "Among us dwell rare individuals who share mighty powers thought only to belong to the dragons and their wizards. They are the key to the final eradication of the dragon menace that plagues our world. Find them. Grow them. They are the future."

Jaysin sat back, reflecting on the opening lines, his curiosity piqued. *This is why you intend to keep me*, he ruminated. He bent to read.

The glimmer of sunrise coloured the eastern horizon when Jaysin finished reading the *Orphans of the Wizards*. Driven by hunger and thirst, he uttered a familiar conjuration and passed through the metal door, smiling at his expertise, and the black clad servants looked surprised when he strolled into the buttery. 'I was promised food and drink,' he said. 'I'd appreciate some now. And I need to piss.' Wordlessly, the two servants set to organising a platter and a jug, while Jaysin used the garderobe. When he emerged, the servants picked up the tray of nourishment to follow him to the chamber, but he asked, 'Do you have the key to the donjon door?'

The servants looked at each other before one replied, 'No, Zekk.'

He anticipated the servants would have a key to his prison, so when they denied it he was perplexed as to why the Karudarteta would tell him he would be fed and not give the servants access to the donjon. 'Awkward,' he noted. 'Then I will eat here.'

The servants put the tray on the preparation bench and stepped back.

'Thank you,' Jaysin said. He sat on a long bench and ate the collection of vegetables, nuts, fruit, and part of a slab of cultured cheese, but he pushed aside the cuts of meat. The jug contained a familiar yeasty brew. 'Do you have water?' he asked, turning to the servants. One fetched a water jug and placed it on the table. Jaysin drank from the jug.

Meal finished, Jaysin ascended the tower and passed through the locked door. He originally thought the lock may have been magical, given the Karudarteta's handling of matters, but it was only a common lock and key which disappointed him because, for a moment, when he passed through, he imagined he had solved the riddle of the metal door on Shika's library. Not so.

How long he had to wait before the Karudarteta returned was a guessing game and it annoyed him. He wanted a guarantee for Chasse's release, tangible evidence that the Karudar Marfek would uphold her end of the bargain. Using the passing spell was an act of bravado, but all they knew of his ability was that he could cast an illusion and perhaps now realise that he could walk out of their prison if he so chose. Exhaustion was pressing down. Reading all night was a mistake, he decided, as he sat on the bed. Morning sunlight struggled to pierce the clouds, but enough light filtered into the donjon to be annoying. Nevertheless, he laid down and closed his eyes. His stomach was appeased and his thirst slaked. His body needed rest.

When Jaysin opened his eyes, the donjon walls were lit by afternoon sun.

'I wondered how long it would take,' said the Karudarteta. 'What did you learn?'

Jaysin rubbed his eyes and sat up to stare at the woman in black standing between the bookshelves. He assumed she was looking at him from behind her black mesh veil. 'You are the orphan of a wizard,' he said.

'As are you,' the Karudarteta replied.

Jaysin rose from the bed. 'Not at all. I know my parents. I am not an orphan.'

'You think you know your parents,' the Karudarteta said. 'Children believe what they are told. You know one important truth, however. Magic can be learned, but only by spirits closely connected to the arcane web, spirits touched by dragons. Wizards and dragons are one, so wizards are completely in tune with the web. Orphans, like us, separated from the wizard who gave us life, must make the connection through intelligence and experimentation. But we can change and alter what the wizards and dragons cannot because we are not wedded to the arcane web like they are. We can grow our power.'

Jaysin shrugged. 'Yes, I read that. But you still haven't answered my question.'

'Which was?'

'How did you learn magic?'

The Karudarteta said, 'Look around. This is a trove of magic. I gathered it. I inherited some from the wizard who abandoned me. Some books were brought to me by servants and slaves. Some I wrote.'

'Any books of magic in the Karfeshnar library?' Jaysin asked.

'That has everything except books of magic,' the Karudarteta replied scornfully. 'Histories, political treatises and philosophies, personal stories, fiction – it's all there, but not what matters, not these books and scrolls.' She approached Jaysin, looking up at him, as she said, 'You can create illusions, pass through objects, create light, and Bahti reports you can translocate and generate energy bolts. I'm sure there's more we haven't seen. You are a unique individual. Bahti wanted to bring you before the Karudar Marfek to enhance his standing and his status across the Empire, but you frustrated him.' She snorted behind her veil, before continuing. 'I admire you for that. Bahti deserves to be put in his place, only my – the Karudar Marfek won't let me do that.' She sat on a stool and gestured for Jaysin to do the same. When he was seated, she said, 'I have been searching for you for more than half my life.'

Her statement astonished Jaysin. 'Why?' he asked.

The Karudarteta reached up and removed her black coif and mesh veil, revealing grey hair that fell beyond her shoulders and a face sagging with age. Dark green eyes stared from dark sockets. 'My name is Inaya Oozimneba,' she said.

'Dragon child,' Jaysin mouthed, translating her second name.

'Yes,' Inaya said, nodding. 'That is the name I was given. Not by my father, as is the custom, nor by my mother, who gave me away, but by the woman who became my mother.'

'But you said you inherited books from your father, the wizard.'

'Yes,' Inaya confirmed. 'I was raised by a woman who was a servant in the Udarvesna to the Karudar Marfek's father, the Karudar Karzekk, but it was common knowledge that I was the orphaned child of Mas Tomas, a wizard who visited Vussar Karemachet with his dragon, extorting payment in exchange for protecting the eastern border and not letting his dragon run amok. When the Kar Oozim Ushta, the Great Dragon War, reached its peak and my absent father and his dragon were slain, the Karudar Karzekk had his library and possessions brought to the Udarvesna, as was done with the libraries of all wizards who were killed or executed. I was still a child, perhaps eight cycles old, when I learned the books were stored in the Karfeshnar library. I stole them, one at a time, and hid them and read them.'

'If you were raised by a servant, who taught you to read?' Jaysin asked.

'My best friend,' Inaya replied, smiling. 'The Karudar Karzekk's daughter. My surrogate mother brought me to help her clean in the Udarvesna, but the princess was lonely, so we played together almost every day. She taught me to read.'

'She played with you because she had no brothers or sisters?' Jaysin asked.

'The Karudar Marfek had three brothers and a sister,' Inaya explained. 'Her sister, Martik, was eldest, almost ten years older, and she was to become the Karudar Marfek, but she died from a horse fall when she was fourteen.' Inaya paused, and Jaysin saw the tragic memory was still raw. Inaya breathed in and continued. 'Her brother, Akin, was killed in the Astikan Rebellion. That was forty years ago. Lamos, the brother closest to her age, was taken prisoner by the Jug Anya during a war in the southern lands and he disappeared. The middle brother, Sardin, is the current Karwema, the General of the Great Army fighting the eastern kingdoms.'

'I don't understand this land,' Jaysin said. 'Men are in control of everything, own everything, and they treat women badly, but the leader is a woman. Why is that?'

Inaya smiled. 'Religion, young man. Men control religion. He-Who-Cannot-Be-Named, the Eternal Being, is male, and someone, a man, decreed long ago that, while the only rightful ruler of the Kar Shematta's Udaryuna is He-Who-Cannot-Be-Named, his earthly representative would be his mortal wife, the Karudar Marfek. If the Karudar Marfek dies before her successor is named or of age, a man, perhaps her father, as was the case for the Karudar Marfek, can hold the office until a new wife for He-

Who-Cannot-Be-Named is chosen.'

'The Karudar Marfek has an earthly husband?' Jaysin asked.

'No,' Inaya replied. 'She has me.'

'But succession?' Jaysin queried. 'She needs a daughter, yes?'

'She can choose any female successor she wants to choose,' Inaya replied. She stood, and said, 'Enough political history.' She sniffed disdainfully. 'You stink, and that dreadful dye you put in your hair is not flattering. We can talk magic later. You need to go down to the bathing room and clean up. I'll have servants provide fresh clothes and I will come back at midday.' She rearranged her head covering and withdrew, leaving Jaysin to ponder what he learned and why she was so concerned by his odour.

Nineteen

Jaysin whispered the phrase that Tam taught him. Slowly, easily, the chair rose from the floor until it hovered before Inaya's face.

'Impressive,' she said. 'Now put the chair against the wall, without touching it.'

Jaysin held his concentration, but admitted, 'I can't do that.'

'Release the chair to me,' Inaya instructed.

Jaysin relinquished his spell and watched the chair remain suspended as Inaya directed it through the air and placed it against the wall under the window.

'Transfer and direction,' Inaya said.

'You don't look like you concentrate,' Jaysin said.

'Concentration is an inner capacity, one operating below the conscious mind,' she replied. She gestured at a bookshelf and a book floated to Jaysin. 'Read this. Learn. Kartum wrote it several generations ago.'

Jaysin placed the book on the table beside five other tomes he was reading. 'Teach me how to dissolve magic,' he said.

Inaya's expression hardened and she said, 'No. You are not ready.'

'When did you learn it?' Jaysin asked.

'I had to learn it by myself.'

'Why?'

'A story for another time,' Inaya replied. 'When you are ready to learn the unmaking spell, I will tell you the story.'

'It's here in one of these books, isn't it?' Jaysin proposed.

'No,' Inaya replied. 'I don't keep that knowledge where someone might stumble upon it.'

'You are afraid I'll use it against you,' Jaysin said.

Inaya shook her head. 'I am not afraid of you, young man.' She sighed. 'Enough for today. Time for you to study and for me to play politics.' She crossed to the door.

'You could translocate to wherever it is you are going,' Jaysin noted.

Inaya said, 'Yes. I could. But I walk the stairs because it is good for my health. Magic unlocks longevity, but healthy living sustains it. You will do well to learn that lesson.' She passed through the closed door.

Jaysin glanced at the new book to read before he walked to the window and gazed over the city toward the port. Ships sat at anchor in the bay, five were moored at the docks loading and unloading, and two sets of sails were visible further out to sea. The river wharves were busy with workers packing and unpacking barges and boats. At the edge of his view, smoke rose from foundries and tanneries and other industries, and buildings spread into the foothills and along the coastline.

Despite the distraction of learning new spells, extending his range of skills and gaining knowledge, and his fascination with the woman who was keen for him to become her protégé, he was restless. His bargain with the Karudar Marfek for his brother's freedom was unfulfilled. He pestered Inaya for news every time she visited the donjon, but she told him to be patient because the negotiations and the reparation required were complex and sensitive. He didn't understand. He offered an exchange of his freedom for his brother's freedom. Simple. He understood there was a monetary matter to resolve with Lekna Nevorn. Again, simple. Three days was a long time. *What if Nevorn decides to put Chasse in the Karushta before the deal is struck? What if Chasse is injured – or worse?* he pondered. *What then?*

And there was Inaya.

She was intent on keeping him in the tower. There were no locks to hold him in, only her request for him to remain out of sight while the negotiations for Chasse's freedom took place. He acceded, partly for

Chasse's sake, and partly because Inaya was laying a cornucopia of magic before him to convince him to stay. He knew that she knew he planned to double-cross the Karudar Marfek, if he could. His original intention was to ask to be allowed to accompany Chasse into safe hands as proof of his release and then abscond using magic. Simple plan. Easy enough to see through. *Why would I expect otherwise?* he asked.

But everything was becoming complicated. The longer he spent in Inaya's company, the more the idea of remaining to learn magic appealed to him. Her sources were different to what he found in the Herbal Man's cave or Shika's library, and Inaya's ability to dispel magic was alluring because it could lead him to unlocking the metal door in Shika's library. What lay beyond that door teased him constantly, especially as Harmi and Tam warned him to leave the door locked. It had to be potent magic.

He watched a raven glide over the rooftops. One Kermakk enslaved him to bring him to the Karudar Marfek to enhance his status. Another was coaxing him to stay and serve the Karudar Marfek because she claimed she was waiting for him. *Not me, specifically*, he reasoned, *but an apprentice*. He would draw from Inaya what exactly it was she had been waiting for when she came again.

Jaysin turned from the window, sat at the table, and opened the book by the long-dead wizard Kartum. It was written in an ancient script like many of Inaya's books, but he muttered his recently acquired incantation and the words rippled into Kermakk meaning. He read the opening comment: "We are slaves to what we think. We must make what we think a slave to us."

'Nevorn is willing to release your brother.'

Inaya's announcement thrilled Jaysin.

'You are called before the Karudar Marfek,' Inaya continued. 'The servants are waiting for you downstairs. You will be bathed and appropriately dressed for the occasion.'

'Will you be there?' Jaysin asked.

'I am always with the Karudar Marfek,' Inaya replied. She paused, before warning, 'Outside this chamber, we are not known to each other. You understand what I am saying?'

Jaysin hesitated, considering the message, before replying, 'I think so. I am still a prisoner, after all.'

Inaya smiled. 'If it was that simple, it would be plain enough. For now, let's leave it as that. You are a prisoner. I will see you again when you come to the Karnishem.'

'Where is that?' Jaysin asked, translating the Kermakk word into the "Great Room."

'You will be escorted,' Inaya replied. Again, she paused, before quietly warning, 'Be on your guard. You will be tested.' She vanished, leaving Jaysin perplexed by her comment and unexpected translocation.

Jaysin turned over the book he was reading before Inaya's arrival and checked his memory of its contents. Titled *Imur Ad Barneduus*, it revealed a broad range of fire-based spells that complemented and extended what he already knew. In five days, Inaya unlocked a world he previously barely understood. He rolled his hand over, whispered 'Cha!' and a small, green flame ignited a finger space above his palm. He remembered learning the basic spell from Tam to light fires when they travelled from Harbin through the mountains and he especially enjoyed Chasse's surprise when he showed his brother that he could conjure flames from damp wood. *Everything has latent energy*, he reminded himself. *Magic is harnessing the energy and transforming it*. He extinguished the flame and patted the black book cover. His new knowledge allowed him to harness the latent energy of the air to create a potent version of the original spell. He merely needed time to perfect and grow it.

Jaysin descended from the donjon to the second floor where he was met by four servants who guided him toward a large steaming ceramic bath. Bathing done, the servants produced a white robe with gold trimmings and sandals, and a green cloak. He dressed, appreciating the quality of material Inaya chose, and admired his appearance in a long mirror held by two servants while allowing another to adjust his garb, before the servants indicated he should follow them.

The servants led Jaysin downstairs and along the wide corridor he traversed when he was first imprisoned and they stopped before a large recessed double black door guarded by two Imperial soldiers. The guards stepped aside, one opening the door in the process. Jaysin turned to the servants, but the four men retreated along the corridor toward the stairs. The guards retained an implacable stare into space. He was alone.

As he walked through the doorway, he realised that he was entering a side entry into a large space, the ceiling vaulting high overhead into a gold framed dome covered with intersecting panes of glass that let light into the Karnishem. The main chamber entry, to his right, was a pair of massive dark doors at least ten arm spans high and five spans wide. A wide aisle led from the doors between five tiered bench rows into a central circular section of floor. The floor was covered with variegated green tiles surrounding a mosaic, the image of which he couldn't discern. The bench tiers swept in semi-circles to halfway on either side of the walls, and twelve dark green pillars supported the outer lower ceiling covering the benches. To his left rose three tiers of high-backed chairs capable of hosting an audience of sixty, but only a few men occupied seats. The central space was dominated by a raised gold and silver dais, split at three levels similar to what he saw in the Kar Feshnar, but far more opulent.

At the foot of the dais stood a grey bearded man in dark green robes. Equally spaced on either side were three Kermakk soldiers. On the first level, five steps up, men in dark green and gold armour stood vigil, each bearing a halberd, their helmets displaying the Imperial white plume. Five steps above them stood three men in black robes and black turbans displaying smaller white plumes. Five more steps up on the top layer, the Karudar Marfek sat on a broad golden throne, the base sculpted into the form of a sleeping dragon, the backrest a half circle of gold padded with dark green fabric.

The Karudar Marfek sat regally on the throne, wearing the same green turban with the orange jewel clasp and white plume, and green robe that Jaysin recalled her wearing when he first met her, and her white wolfish dog lay at her feet. On a simple red cushioned stool beside the Karudar Marfek sat Inaya, the Karudarteta, clad in black from head to foot like a shadow resting beside the ruler of the Kermakk Empire.

Assuming the assembly was waiting for him, Jaysin adjusted his white robe and green cloak and walked towards the dais, escorted by two guards. The man in dark green robes gestured for Jaysin to stand directly before him and, when Jaysin stood in position, the man announced to the Karudar Marfek, 'Most High Leader, the Machutzkan Sheykermett stands before you.'

The unexpected title caught Jaysin unawares. He looked up at Inaya for a hint of explanation, but her face was hidden behind her black mesh. What he did feel was faint tingling along his cheeks and the air rippled perceptibly with magic.

'The last time we spoke,' the Karudar Marfek began, her amplified voice clear and strong, 'you made a significant request for a particular arena fighter to be pardoned.' She paused to catch her breath and continued. 'As a gesture of goodwill towards the people of Machutzka, I have agreed to grant this request on several conditions. First, you will serve the Empire as the Machutzkan Sheykermett. Second, you will serve the Empire as I see fit. Third, you will ensure that the Machutzkan people acknowledge my sovereignty and peacefully concede to becoming servants of the Empire.' She gestured to the man at the foot of the dais who handed Jaysin a parchment and a gold ring. 'The Udarvesnahaka has given you my decree to be shared with the people of Machutzka,' the Karudar Marfek said. 'You will take this to their Mena and Meysa and you will return with their answer. The ring is your seal of rank in the Imperial offices. Wear it. Use it to display your authority where necessary.'

'You are dismissed,' the Udarvesnahaka bluntly stated.

Jaysin returned to the side entrance, where the guards admitted him into the corridor. He rolled the ring in his fingers, noting it was inscribed with the image of a crouching catlike creature. He examined the rolled parchment, sealed with a large green wax stamp, pondering his sudden change in status and what it meant. *Can I come and go as I please?* he wondered. *Am I free?*

'I would be wondering the same.'

Jaysin looked up to find Inaya in the corridor. 'You can read my mind?' he asked.

'It's a magic I tried to master,' she replied, 'but no, not here. There's no art to understanding what you are thinking right now.'

'You arranged all this, didn't you?' Jaysin asked as he approached the Karudarteta. He looked for a door she had to have used to be in the corridor, but none was evident. 'You translocated?' he queried.

'One question at a time,' Inaya replied. 'First, I did not translocate. That would be too showy in the Karnishem. I left the dais and discretely passed through the wall behind a curtain.'

'You amplified the Karudar Marfek's voice,' Jaysin stated. 'I can do that.'

'It's a very simple spell,' Inaya said disdainfully.

'And all this?' Jaysin asked, holding up the parchment.

'I warned you that you would be tested. Put on the ring.'

'I have to broker submission of the Machutzkans to your Imperial rule?' Jaysin asked, as he slipped the ring onto the forefinger of his left hand.

'You simply have to deliver the message,' Inaya replied. 'The Machutzkans can decide their fate.'

'Isn't The Man a friend of the Karudar Marfek?' Jaysin asked. 'He ought to be delivering this, not me.'

'He betrayed his people,' Inaya explained. 'He informed us of the Machutzkan plans to resist and revealed your plan to create an illusion that the city was abandoned. You know he did.'

'Where is he?' Jaysin asked.

Inaya said, 'Dead. Inevitably so, after a betrayal of that magnitude.'

'Who killed him?'

'Your brother,' Inaya replied. 'Revenge appropriately served, I think.'

Jaysin assessed the information, before saying, 'By this, you are trusting me to take my brother to our home, act as an ambassador, and return.'

'A test,' Inaya confirmed. 'Any other questions?'

'When do I see my brother?'

'Tomorrow morning, when you leave,' Inaya replied. 'I have to return to civic duties. I will see you in the tower at sunset.' She stepped through the stone wall.

Jaysin contemplated what he heard. *I'm being tested*, he thought. *I'm going back to Machutzka.*

Jaysin watched the sun set over the mountains. As a boy, he watched it dissolve into the ocean between White Eagle Ledge and Nakiades' Watch in a blaze of fiery colour and wondered how it could disappear every evening and magically reappear over Dragon Mountain every morning. Even now he wanted to know what made the sun come and go, how it moved effortlessly through the sky, and where it went when it disappeared.

'If I told you the sun is a star like other stars you see at night, only this one is very close to us, what would you say to that?' Inaya asked.

Jaysin faced the Karudarteta. 'I'd say how do you know? Can you prove it?'

'The Aytahrem watch the skies and chart the stars,' Inaya explained as she flicked through the pages of a book on the table. 'They have done this for generations and can predict which stars will be where and when. One man, Sajinkareen, from the Amenad Kingdom, far away to the east, studied the oo – the sun – and showed us that it is a star like all other stars, and we travel around it.' She looked at Jaysin. 'Before Sajinkareen's study, our ancestors believed the sun died every day in the west and a new sun was rekindled every day in the east by Vashki, the Goddess of rebirth.' She laughed for the first time in Jaysin's presence and continued. 'Of course, the men who believe in He-Who-Cannot-Be-Named assign the sun's creation to their god and said He-Who-Cannot-Be-Named set it in motion for the good of all Men of Faith.'

'But what about Sajinkareen's study?' Jaysin asked.

'Disregarded, after he died,' Inaya replied. 'His disciples were murdered.'

'How do you know all this?'

'The library, of course,' Inaya explained. 'Sajinkareen's original texts are stored there. Read, and you will learn much more than hearsay and oral superstition.' She closed the book on the table. 'The servants will bring a meal,' she said. 'You will be escorted to the barge at first light. A wema cohort of Imperial soldiers and two servants will accompany you to Sarchah and on to Machutzka. The region is dangerous. The Machutzkans are resorting to guerrilla warfare, unfortunately.'

'They will recognise my brother,' Jaysin said.

'And that might only spur them on to rescue him,' Inaya warned.

'They also know me,' Jaysin argued.

'But not the soldiers or servants travelling with you,' Inaya rebutted. 'You are a sheykermett of the Kermakk Empire and their lives and safety are your responsibility. After we eat, I will teach you a spell that you haven't studied. It will enable you to protect yourself and the company who travel with you.'

'What spell?' Jaysin asked, curiosity piqued.

'It's a defence spell. I learned it from an ancient scroll. You energise the air within twenty paces to create a barrier that allows nothing in or out, so long as you sustain the spell,' Inaya explained.

'Teach me the Dissolution spell,' Jaysin urged.

'I told you that I would do that when you are ready,' Inaya replied.

'I am ready,' Jaysin asserted. 'If you want me to return to Machutzka, I need to know that spell.'

'Why?'

Jaysin wondered how much he needed to share to get Inaya to agree. 'I found a small chest,' he improvised, 'a silver one, but someone locked it with a spell.'

'Wizards and dragons locked objects like that if there is a reason for not opening them,' Inaya said. 'Perhaps you should bring it to me.'

'Please teach me the spell,' Jaysin begged.

A knock at the door interrupted as Jaysin was about to improvise more detail. 'First, we eat,' Inaya said, lifting her mesh veil into place before opening the door. 'Then, you learn.'

Jaysin rolled over and sat up. He was tired, but sleep persisted in evading him while his thoughts pursued conversations and possibilities and fears. The Karudar Marfek not only accepted his plea for Chasse's release but also elevated him in Kermakk society and gave him status to move freely through the Empire. The cost was high. Freedom in the Empire ended his freedom in Machutzka. He was a servant of the Karudar Marfek. He could not return to stay with his sister or brother. He was to negotiate Machutzkan compliance and capitulation. He was the enemy.

But there were great advantages. In Vussar Karemachet, he was not the little brother, the less important child, the odd one. He was a stranger, yes, but also a man accepted by one of the Empire's highest officials, the Karudar Marfek's Karudarteta, her advisor and partner. She was offering to mentor him, to allow him to become what he knew was in his being, his purpose. Tam and Harmi eked out magic to him as and when they saw fit, so he learned much of what he knew by himself, and he learned faster than Tam could teach him. He needed someone like Inaya to let him reach his potential.

The spells that Inaya taught him after the meal were spells he was certain neither Tam nor Harmi would share freely with him, especially the dissolution spell. But he had to know what was behind the metal door in Shika's library. He had to know. *Am I betraying my family?* he wondered. *Is it wrong to be who I want to be?*

Moonlight flowed through the window, bathing the floor and table in soft blue light as it crept to the edge of his bed. He rose and held his hands over a book on the table, willing the air to form the protective barrier that Inaya taught him while he practised conjuring from within without speaking. The air crackled with energy and a tiny almost imperceptible energy dome glowed over the book. Keeping focus on the dome, he reached for the copper cup and dropped it onto the dome. The cup bounced and danced in an eruption of sparkling energy and dissolved, leaving a lingering taint of melted metal. Jaysin allowed the dome to dissipate and smiled at his experiment. The journey to Machutzka began in the morning. He had time to decide. 'I need a sleep-inducing spell,' he murmured.

Twenty

Two black garbed servants, one bearing a green flag, and eight Kermakk soldiers marched across the dock to the barge in the dawn light and crisp air. At their centre walked Chasse, his red hair and solid physique wrapped in a dark green cloak, his wrists bound. Jaysin waited until the group was close, before lowering the cowl of his white robe.

Recognising his brother, Chasse cried, 'Jaysin!' and he pushed aside a protesting soldier who attempted to stop him going to Jaysin. 'I would hug you if it was possible,' he said, holding up his arms.

'Then let me hug, you,' Jaysin replied, and he encircled Chasse, acutely conscious of his older brother's muscular solidity.

Chasse stepped back, appraising Jaysin. 'What is all this?' he asked. 'How did you find me?'

'I am the Machutzkan Sheykermett,' Jaysin announced, enjoying his brother's astonishment, and he held out his hand to display his gold ring of office.

'How?' Chasse asked.

'A long story for our journey,' Jaysin said.

'You are taking me home?'

'Let's get aboard and you can tell me your tale and I can tell you mine.' Jaysin gestured for a soldier to unchain Chasse's hands. When he saw the soldier's reluctance, he said, 'This is my brother, and I carry the seal of the Karudar Marfek. You will do as I ask.'

The soldier removed Chasse's bonds before Jaysin led his brother onto the gangplank with the servants and soldiers dutifully following. Jaysin waved to the barge captain who issued orders for the bargemen to release the mooring ropes and push away from the dock. Jaysin ushered Chasse to the bow where he sat on a crate and waited for his brother to sit, before saying, 'Tam will be surprised to see you.'

'And you,' Chasse said. 'You've grown taller.' He squinted. 'I think there are hairs on your chin.' He rubbed his own red beard, grinning.

'I expected to find you outside Sarchah,' Jaysin said. 'I came looking for you.'

'We were betrayed,' Chasse said. 'The Kermakk were waiting to ambush us.'

'The Man,' Jaysin said. 'I heard.'

'Who from?'

'The Karudarteta.'

'Who?' Chasse asked.

'The Karudar Marfek's advisor,' Jaysin explained. 'So, tell me what happened.'

He listened to Chasse tell the tale of his adventure while the bargemen poled the barge, weaving between river traffic as the sun gilded the roofs and trees along the bank, and glittered on the water. Black and white birds skimmed the river surface, hopeful fishermen dangled lines and netting from their boats, and a black dog cavorted in the shallows with three children.

'We were set upon by the Kermakk, and they separated us and wore us down. Some escaped. Many died,' Chasse said, and he swallowed to suppress his sorrow. 'Kini was struck by a stone. She was close to me, and I turned, and she was lying on the ground, and she –' He stifled a deep sob and tears welled. Jaysin wanted to comfort his brother, but before he could speak, Chasse continued. 'I fought as hard as I could. I tried to reach her, but there were too many Kermakk. We were being overwhelmed, and I accepted I would also die. We waited for Harmi to come, but she did not.'

'Harmi was injured,' Jaysin told him. 'I found her unconscious in the forest. She couldn't come to your aid.'

'What happened to her? Who attacked her?' Chasse asked.

'It's what happened to Tam,' Jaysin explained. 'She was crushed when the roof of her bedroom collapsed. Because she is connected to Harmi, when she lost consciousness Harmi was also knocked out.'

'Is Tam all right?'

'I don't know,' Jaysin admitted. 'I left her with a healer and came searching for Harmi and you. After I found Harmi, she went back to Tam. I haven't heard since.'

'Your bracelet?' Chasse asked.

'Taken when I was imprisoned,' Jaysin said. 'I had no way to communicate.'

'As was mine,' Chasse said.

'How did they catch you?'

'The Kermakk surrounded those of us who remained, and The Man was sent forward to convince us to lay down our weapons. He promised that, if we surrendered, the Kermakk would let us return to Machutzka. Some of my warriors wanted to fight to the death, but I told them it was better to surrender and live so we can defend our homes. We laid down our weapons.' Chasse shook his head despondently, and said, 'They didn't let us leave. Instead, as we were walking away, they used a giant net to trap us. We were tied up, stripped of all we had and sold at the market to whoever bid for us. I was bought by a slaver who shipped me down the river and sold me to Lekna Nevorn. He made me fight for the pleasure of the Kermakk and paraded me in the same way a man in Machutzka might display a prized horse.' He turned to Jaysin. 'How did you find me?'

'I saw you in the Karushta.'

'When?'

'When you beat Shengat,' Jaysin said.

'I don't understand,' said Chasse. 'How did the Kermakk let you into the city?'

Jaysin rolled up his sleeve to reveal the slave brand. 'Like you, I was taken prisoner and sold at the market,' he said. 'Only I escaped. I used illusions to disguise myself.'

'Illusion?' Chasse asked.

Jaysin theatrically waved his hand across his face as he adopted Bahti's features and Chasse's shock at his changed appearance made Jaysin quietly smile. 'I pretended to be one of them and that way I could walk the streets without fear of arrest by the Hakamati or wema – their lawkeepers and soldiers.' He waved his hand to end the illusion. 'I was invited to the Karushta the same day you fought the champion.'

Chasse twisted his arm to reveal his inner forearm brand. 'They treat everyone like animals,' he said. 'It is a bad place. But how did you get me released?'

Jaysin glanced at a bargeman pushing his pole into the water, before he said, 'I didn't have an axe to exchange for you.' He grinned and continued, 'I managed to get an audience with the Karudar Marfek.' He wanted to add details about how the illusion he used to obtain the audience was exposed and how Inaya showed him a world of greater possibilities, but he also felt that wasn't necessary for Chasse to know – not yet.

'And ambassador?' Chasse asked.

'Sheykermett,' Jaysin translated, and continued. 'I'm not exactly sure why they chose to give me that role, except to take a proposal to the Meysa. The Karudar Marfek told me that you killed The Man, so I assume she wanted someone else to be the go-between and I was conveniently there.'

Chasse looked down at his feet momentarily, raised his head and said, 'I thought they would execute me for killing The Man.'

'How did you do it?' Jaysin asked.

'One arrow,' Chasse said. 'I was angry. We were all angry that he betrayed his people.'

'But how? I thought they caught you in the net?'

'I cut myself free of the net when it fell on us. I could have escaped. I wanted to. But I saw him watching the Kermakk herd the Menuii, so I tackled a soldier who had a crossbow, disarmed him, and took one shot. He saw me taking aim and tried to flee. It didn't matter,' Chasse said.

'Why didn't you escape then?'

'Too late,' Chasse said. 'If I lift my robe, you will find a long scar across my back. A soldier struck as I fired. Like I said, I expected to be executed, but it was as if they didn't care that I killed The Man. They even bound my wound – although I suspect that was only to make sure I was saleable in the market.'

Jaysin stood. 'I will have the servants fetch food and water. Going upstream to Sarchah will take three days, according to the barge captain. We stop once at a town. We sleep on the barge the other night.'

The morning brightened as the barge moved up the river, passing vessels travelling downstream, and Jaysin and Chasse shared more of their experiences at the hands of the Kermakk, but by midday the daylight faded to grey, the wind picked up, rippling the river surface, and the weather soured under a leaden sky.

The barge captain informed Jaysin that he ordered the servants to set up shelter at the stern and, later, grey rain swept across the landscape, forcing Jaysin and Chasse and the two servants to shelter under the canvas. Jaysin peered through the rain at the soldiers huddled against the piled cargo, their cloaks wrapped tight and hoods up, while the bargemen continued to pole the barge forward as if they were oblivious to the elements. He remembered his journey downstream, bound and stowed beneath canvas while the rain poured, and shivered at the memory.

'You should learn a spell for controlling the weather,' Chasse chided as he paused from chewing a dried lamb strip.

'I'm confident there are spells of that magnitude,' Jaysin replied. 'Only I haven't found them yet.'

'Ask Harmi or Tam,' Chasse suggested.

The barge captain appeared at the edge of the canvas shelter, rain dripping from his broad brim leather hat and coat and the end of his nose and beard. 'There's a storm sweeping in behind this rain,' he said. 'We're pulling in to shelter at a fishing village called Dadnadichet, if you agree.' Jaysin agreed and the captain withdrew.

'Guess we might take more than three days,' Jaysin said to Chasse. 'Pass me the metal bucket.'

After Chasse handed Jaysin the bucket, Jaysin put his hands on it and it began to glow, radiating warmth. Chasse held his open palms toward the heat, and said, 'I envy what you can do.'

The comment made Jaysin feel a glow within, knowing that Chasse appreciated his talent. He leaned against a sack and closed his eyes.

Five forlorn and shadowy fishermen's huts and a ramshackle inn with a barn huddling on the riverbank between straggly willows defined Dadnadichet. By the time the barge moored, the rain shrouded sky rippled with thunder and flickering lightning briefly exposed the countryside and choppy river. Jaysin and Chasse disembarked and headed for the inn, trailed by the soldiers and the flag-bearing servants, leaving the bargemen to secure the barge and its cargo.

The inn was a tiny room with a roaring hearth and half a dozen local fishermen sheltering from the storm. It was not a room designed to accommodate an additional crowd of twelve men, with the five bargemen yet to arrive. The conversations stopped and a portly chap with a flourishing dark beard and a red apron approached. 'I'm Yanos the festata,' he said in a surly voice. 'Can I help you?'

'We're seeking shelter,' Jaysin said. 'It's too wild on the river.'

Yanos appraised Jaysin and Chasse. 'You're not Kermakk,' he said.

'No,' Jaysin replied. 'I am the Machutzka Sheykermett. These are my servants and my soldiers.'

'Don't get important people here,' Yanos said. 'You can see I have no rooms. It's a simple place for simple people.'

Jaysin glanced at Chasse, before saying, 'What about the barn at the back?'

Yanos snorted. 'If you can fit, and you don't mind the stink of pigs, you're welcome.' He held out his hand, and added, 'For a fee.'

Jaysin had not considered costs. He ought to have organised a purse before leaving Vussar Karemachet. 'I have no coin,' he said.

'Zekk Sheykermett?' said the servant with a thin face and straggly goatee. Jaysin turned to him. 'The Karudarteta assigned me to see to such matters.' He produced a large coin pouch. 'How much is needed?'

Yanos' eyes sparkled. 'One bit per man,' he said quickly.

The servant tipped coins into his companion's hands and counted. 'That would be seventeen bits,' the servant said, handing the coins to Yanos. 'The count is right.'

Yanos shook the coins in his hands. 'The barn is yours for the night,' he said, and he headed for a door at the rear of the room.

'Thank you,' Jaysin said to the servant. 'I don't even know your names.'

'Zekk Sheykermett,' the servant said, bowing his head, 'it is not important to know our names.'

'But tell me anyway,' Jaysin urged.

The servant hesitated, glanced at his companion, and replied, 'I am Guss. He is Janno.'

Jaysin glanced at the second servant, also a thin man with a fuller beard and squinty eyes. 'I will tell the Karudarteta you acquitted yourself well,' he said. 'Why do you carry the banner everywhere?'

'Zekk Sheykermett, it tells everyone you are an important Imperial official,' Guss explained. 'It is protocol.'

Jaysin turned to Chasse and said, 'No point staying huddled in here.

The barn it is.'

Jaysin led the group through the driving rain into the barn where the stench of pig was stronger than he anticipated. He conjured a floating light sphere, to the amazement of the servants and soldiers, which revealed a derelict space with a pile of hay and a rudimentary pen containing six sows in mucky squalor. A swayback blue roan horse stood abjectly in one corner staring at the intruders. Rain dripped through the thatch roof and the wind whistled through gaps in the wooden walls. 'Better than being drowned on the barge,' Jaysin remarked.

'Not so sure,' Chasse replied.

'Look for a large stone, or similar,' Jaysin said. 'I'll create a heat source.'

'I saw a pile of rocks outside,' Chasse said. 'I'll fetch one.'

Jaysin told the soldiers and servants to find space to sleep and he cleared a circle at the centre of the barn. When Chasse returned bearing a large wet rock, Jaysin had him place it in the cleared circle before he held his hands above it. The rock glowed with heat, steam rising as the moisture evaporated, and the soldiers and servants watched in wonder. 'This is for all of us,' Jaysin said, gesturing for the others to gather around.

'I still think that's the best spell you learned,' Chasse said, drying his hands over the rock.

The Kermakk soldiers took places around the rock, but the servants held back. 'Why the reluctance?' Jaysin asked. 'The magic won't hurt you.'

'It's not our place to sit with you, Zekk Sheykermett,' Guss explained.

Jaysin grinned and rolled up his sleeve to reveal his slave scar. 'I was the same as you,' he said. 'And I say you can sit among us.'

Guss and Janno stared at the scar, before Guss said, 'Thank you, Zekk. We did not know.'

'And now you do,' Jaysin replied. 'Get warm and dry.' He watched the servants squat near the glowing rock beside Chasse, Janno glancing warily at the soldiers. *Having authority and power feels good*, Jaysin mused. *I am the leader here. No more little brother*, he gloated. *I like this.*

Chasse asked, 'Where are the bargemen?'

'I'll fetch them,' Jaysin said.

'I'll come with you,' Chasse offered.

'No,' Jaysin said. 'Stay. You're already drying off.' He pulled up his hood and headed for the door.

Inside the inn, Jaysin discovered the bargemen seated at a small table, drinking a warm brew. He was also aware that the conversations at the other two tables stopped when he entered and that the men were not the fishermen who were previously in the room. He approached the barge captain and said, 'The innkeeper is letting us stay in the barn tonight.'

The captain lowered his mug and replied, 'It's all right. We're regulars here. Yanos is looking after us. We'll see you lot in the morning.' He grinned at his companions, raised his mug, and they cheered before quaffing their drinks.

The captain's dismissive response annoyed Jaysin, especially as the bargemen were receiving preferential treatment. Yanos was staring at him sternly, so he approached the innkeeper and asked, 'I thought you had no room?'

'I don't,' Yanos said bluntly.

'Where are the bargemen sleeping?'

'Out back,' Yanos replied.

'Why didn't you offer that to us?'

'Doesn't fit seventeen,' Yanos replied. 'Fits five.'

'I'm a sheykermett,' Jaysin reminded him.

'And you're not a river man.'

'What is that meant to mean?' Jaysin asked. Sensing movement, he turned and saw three men rising from the closest table.

'Is this one causing you trouble, Yanos?' asked the leading man, a florid, thickly bearded individual with a bird tattoo above his left eye.

'I was asking about accommodation,' Jaysin replied.

'I think you were trying to act important,' the man said, leaning forward so that Jaysin could smell ale on his breath, 'and I don't take kindly to those who think they're more important than any of us.'

Hearing the menacing threat, Jaysin turned to leave, saying, 'The matter is closed.'

The man grabbed his arm, squeezing hard and he spun Jaysin to face him. 'I don't like fancy people being rude to me, or my friends.'

'Let go,' Jaysin said, fighting his panic to sound calm.

The man shoved Jaysin's arm against his chest, sending him stumbling against the wall beside Yanos.

'No need for trouble,' Yanos said.

'Too late,' the man said, pushing his hand hard against Jaysin's chest. 'There's a storm. This poor sod drowned in the river, eh lads?' His two companions closed in.

'Let go!' Jaysin screamed. He prepared to conjure an energy bolt.

'Let him go!' a voice boomed.

The man kept pressure on Jaysin's chest, while he turned his head to see who spoke. Chasse stood in the doorway. 'Another red nut!' the man said. 'We can accommodate both of you.'

'Start with me,' Chasse said, taking off his cloak. 'Beat me and you can do what you like with him.'

The man pushed Jaysin aside, and faced Chasse, his companions squaring up with him. The barge captain yelled, 'Back down! He's an arena fighter!'

'He could be the Karudar Marfek for all we care,' the man snarled. 'He's about to be fish food.' He stormed forward, and Jaysin saw three more men rise from their table, two drawing long knives.

Chasse erupted into a controlled dance of punches, blocks and high kicks that sent the first man and his two companions sprawling against the tables, before he spun sideways and stopped a knife wielder with an elbow to the throat. He wrenched the knife from the man's hand, ducked under a sweeping swing from the second knifeman and stabbed him in the quad, before punching him in the face. The sixth man backpedalled, hands up to avoid fighting. The first man clambered to his feet, wiped blood from his mouth and beard, and charged, but Chasse neatly sidestepped and pushed his assailant through the inn door to sprawl in the mud outside.

Another man staggered to his feet, holding up his hands, saying, 'Enough. No more. We're done.'

'Out!' Chasse ordered.

The men grabbed their cloaks, one assisting the man with the knife jutting from his leg, and the group exited, helping their leader outside to his feet. The bargemen sat wide-eyed at their table. Yanos began resetting the furniture.

'Are you hurt?' Chasse asked, turning to Jaysin.

'Only my pride,' Jaysin replied.

'That was a mistake,' Yanos said.

'Why?' Chasse asked.

'They're Magros' men,' Yanos replied. 'They don't like anyone causing trouble.'

'They started it,' Jaysin said.

'No,' Yanos said, facing Jaysin. 'You started it with your uppity attitude. They don't take kindly to Imperial bullies. They're free men. You made a stupid mistake.'

'I only queried why you didn't offer us room inside,' Jaysin retorted.

'Because it's river custom to offer room to those who work and live on the river. Your city customs don't apply out here,' Yanos explained. 'We look after our own, like you do.'

Chasse lifted a toppled chair. 'We'll give you hand to clean up,' he said. 'Then we'll go back to the barn.'

'I don't need your help,' Yanos said.

'No, but we're giving it anyway,' Chasse replied. He gestured to Jaysin. 'Come on. It wasn't his fault this happened.'

Jaysin hesitated, annoyed that his brother seemed to take the innkeeper's side, but he acquiesced and tipped a chair into position.

A rough hand woke him. Jaysin sat up, rubbing his face. 'What?' he asked. It was dark, although he glimpsed faint grey light lining the barn door and flooding through cracks in the wall.

'Shh,' Chasse warned, and said quietly, 'I'll wake the others. There's trouble.'

Jaysin stood. The soldiers moved like shadows through the barn. 'What is it?' Jaysin whispered.

'We have company outside,' Chasse replied.

Jaysin crept to the door and peeked between the gaps. Against the backdrop of grey fog wreathing through the trees and buildings and sitting heavily on the river, a line of silhouetted men faced the barn. At a quick estimate, he reckoned on thirty or forty individuals. 'What do they want?' he whispered as Chasse joined him.

As if responding to Jaysin's query, an individual stepped forward from the line to shout, 'We know you're in there! We don't want any trouble with the soldiers! We only want the Machutzkans! Send them out, and the rest of you are free to leave!'

'He can't be serious,' Jaysin said. 'The Karudar Marfek will purge this place if they touch an Imperial official.'

Chasse glanced at the soldiers behind them and said to Jaysin, 'You better check their loyalty before we answer anything.'

Jaysin faced the soldiers. He knew none of them. He realised that he hadn't even determined who was their leader. 'Who is in charge?' he asked.

A soldier replied, 'I am, Sheykermett.'

Jaysin met the man's steady gaze. He was solidly built, like all Kermakk soldiers, with bushy eyebrows and a full beard, but he had a handsome line to his features. 'What is your name?' he asked.

'Lokan Ambinya,' the soldier said.

'You heard what they want?'

'Yes, Sheykermett,' Lokan replied.

'And?'

'We are sworn to protect you, Sheykermett,' Lokan confirmed.

'To the Karudar Marfek?' Jaysin asked.

'No, Sheykermett,' Lokan answered. 'To the Karudarteta.'

The answer pleased Jaysin. Inaya would have chosen loyal men. He said to Chasse, 'They won't hand us over.'

'Then we need a plan,' Chasse said. 'Forty against twelve.' He paused to assess the slaves. 'Against ten, isn't good odds.'

'We could sneak out the back,' Jaysin suggested.

'There are more out the back,' Lokan told them, bowed his head, and added, 'Sheykermett.'

Jaysin hurried across the barn to where a soldier was keeping watch and peered through a gap in the wall to see more shadowy figures in the fog. 'At least another thirty,' he called to Chasse, his fear rising.

'Not good,' Chasse said. He turned to Lokan. 'I need a weapon.'

Lokan looked to Jaysin. 'Find him a weapon,' Jaysin said. Lokan drew his sword to hand to Chasse.

'No,' Chasse said. 'You need it. I'll find something in here.' He searched the barn, spotted a pitchfork by the hay, tested its integrity, and announced, 'This will do fine.'

'No more waiting!' a voice yelled from outside. 'You've made your choice!'

'Ready yourselves!' Chasse yelled. The soldiers drew their swords.

'They're going to burn us out!' yelled the soldier at the rear of the barn.

'Won't work!' Chasse shouted. 'Everything is too wet!'

236

'It will create a lot of smoke, though,' Lokan warned.

'That might work in our favour,' Chasse suggested.

Jaysin listened and judged the unfolding situation and considered his options. He recalled spells from the *Et Kar Shaz* book. He learned several on the night before Tam was crushed under the ceiling collapse. Two that he learned would serve now. 'Open the door,' he said.

'What?' Chasse asked.

'Open the door,' Jaysin repeated. 'Trust me.'

'They will rush us!' Chasse argued.

Jaysin turned to Lokan and ordered, 'Open the door.'

Lokan wrenched the rickety barn door open to reveal a wall of men bearing swords and pikes and clubs closing in. Jaysin stepped into the opening, yelling to his companions, 'Get back!' and he spread his arms and cried, 'Oosha!' The air sparked with intense energy and burst into a wall of flame along the length of the advancing enemy, igniting individuals and sending the men screaming and dancing in retreat. Jaysin turned to his left, where astonished men were staring at what they were witnessing, spread his arms again and repeated his cry of 'Oosha!' Fire exploded and burning men fled past the inn into the forest. Jaysin looked for further threats, before he pointed his finger and drew a line of flames from one side of the barn to the river edge and another from the river around the inn to the other side of the barn, forming a protective ring of fire. He dropped his arms to stare at the river and the moored barge, his energy drained from the conjuration. Chasse's hand on his shoulder startled him.

'It's me,' Chasse said. 'How did you do that?'

'A spell I learned,' Jaysin replied. He was aware of soldiers warily walking into the open ground before the inn, several, including Lokan, staring at him. The bargemen and Yanos emerged from the inn, their faces filled with wonderment. 'We better get onto the river before they come back.'

'I don't think they will be returning,' Chasse said.

Jaysin snorted and said, 'They will when they work out the fire is an illusion. We best leave quickly.'

Chasse bellowed orders for everyone to get aboard the barge and Lokan and the barge captain urged the others into action.

Jaysin approached Yanos and said, 'You knew they would come back, didn't you?'

Visibly shaken by the ring of fire, Yanos replied, 'You are a mas.'

'No,' Jaysin replied. 'Answer my question.'

'Yes,' Yanos said.

'Why didn't you warn us?'

Yanos looked at his feet, before replying, 'Magros and his men were victims of that one's warriors.' He gestured at Chasse. 'They hate the Machutzkans.' He shuffled his feet. 'I did not warn you because I have to live here among these people. The wrong word and I lose everything.' He shook his head and looked up at Jaysin. 'Besides, it seemed obvious that, even with the fighter, you would be dead this morning.'

'Bad gamble,' Jaysin said.

'I didn't know,' Yanos said.

'But now you do,' Jaysin said. 'Remember it. Make sure Magros and all the people here remember what they saw tonight. I will not be so lenient if anything like this ever happens again.' He watched Yanos lower his eyes, and he heard Yanos apologise and he relished the sense of power the moment presented.

'Jaysin!' Chasse yelled. 'We're leaving!'

Jaysin headed for the barge, crossed the gangplank, and stood beside Chasse as the bargemen pushed away from the bank. With a small hand gesture, he dissolved the ring of fire.

Twenty-one

Taunted by rain and wind and turbulence, the bargemen expertly poled the vessel along the waterway while Chasse and Jaysin sheltered and talked and fished and watched the river life, waving to people aboard boats and barges heading downriver. The barge captain opted for mooring on the river when night fell and the soldiers and Chasse set watch against threat.

Sarchah came into view mid-afternoon of the third day. Jaysin thanked the barge captain as he disembarked and Guss paid the man. In the company of Lokan's soldiers and the servants, Jaysin led Chasse across the market square to the street where he remembered horses were hitched and bought and sold. He instructed Guss and Janno to organise horses for their band and he waited for the servants to return.

'I have bought fourteen horses,' Guss informed Jaysin. 'Two are for supplies. The vendor will buy them back on our return.'

'Good work,' Jaysin replied. 'Have everyone get ready. I have an acquaintance to visit before we leave.' He pulled up the cowl of his leather cloak.

'I'll come with you,' Chasse offered.

Jaysin shook his head. 'This is a private matter. I need you to stay to make sure the group are ready to leave.' Chasse acquiesced, and Jaysin headed across the busy and crowded market square toward an inn.

Under the swinging sign of The Market Pot, Jaysin studied the market and the streets, noting the patrolling Hakamati and their routes. He stepped aside to allow two patrons to exit, before he entered the smoky interior, observing little was changed since his first visit. He spotted Alban pouring ale at the bar as the serving youth made a beeline for Jaysin.

'Can I get you something?' the youth asked.

'I've come to speak with your master,' Jaysin replied, and he walked to the bar.

Alban looked up and asked, 'Can I help you?'

Jaysin noticed Alban staring at his shadowed visage, so he announced imperiously, 'I am the Machutzkan Sheykermett. I'd like a word in private, if I may.' He showed his ring finger as proof.

Alban called the youth and threw a small wet towel at him, saying, 'Mind the bar.' He gestured for Jaysin to follow him through a door.

The kitchen beyond was as Jaysin remembered it, with Alban's wife and mother busily preparing food and washing bowls. 'Give me a moment,' Alban said to Jaysin. 'Seria!' he yelled. 'Take Mother and yourself into a bedroom. I need to talk.' Jaysin watched Seria tug on the older woman's sleeve and lead her from the kitchen. 'Now,' Alban said, facing Jaysin. 'What is this about?'

Jaysin lowered his cowl and watched Alban's expression change. 'You know who I am,' Jaysin said. 'Good.'

'I didn't know who you were,' Alban said quickly. 'If I knew –' He fidgeted with his sleeve.

'How much was I worth?' Jaysin asked. 'How much did Mezzin pay you?'

'What do you want?' Alban asked. 'Why are you here?'

Jaysin smiled as he replied, 'You know why.'

'I don't have the money,' Alban said shuffling against the kitchen bench. He picked up a knife. 'You would be stupid to threaten me,' he warned. 'I didn't get to run this inn without throwing out a few idiotic customers.'

Jaysin gestured with his left hand and another knife rose from the kitchen bench and hovered before Alban.

'How?' Alban blurted, shuffling back from the floating blade.

'When I return to Sarchah, I will sell you into slavery,' Jaysin said. 'I have the authority to do so. I owe you that.'

'I have my wife, my old mother,' Alban begged. 'My son is out there serving. You saw him.'

'Then you have someone who can petition for your freedom,' Jaysin said. 'Perhaps they can organise enough money to buy you back at the market.'

'You're mad!' Alban spat.

Jaysin's smile widened. He flicked his hand and the airborne knife embedded point first into the bench, startling Alban. 'Enjoy the little time you have left,' Jaysin said. He pulled up his cowl, exited the kitchen, crossed the inn to the main door and stepped outside, satisfied that Alban understood he was marked for revenge. He walked through the market to his company and indicated that he was ready to leave.

'Who did you see?' Chasse asked as Jaysin mounted and reined in beside him.

'A man who owes me a debt,' Jaysin replied.

'Did he pay?' Chasse asked.

'When I come back through,' Jaysin told him. 'Let's go.'

'We might only get a short distance this late in the day,' Lokan said, reining in beside Jaysin. 'Perhaps we should rest overnight.'

'No,' Jaysin replied. 'The further we get from Sarchah, the better. We'll find a place on the road.'

'Do you know somewhere?' Chasse asked.

'A hamlet,' Jaysin replied. 'I remember passing it, but I don't know what it is called,' and he prodded his horse into motion.

Lokan organised the Kermakk soldiers to ride in pairs at the front and rear, with Chasse and Jaysin and the servants in the middle and Jaysin appreciated the stares the company received from men as they rode through Sarchah's outskirts.

The ride into the hills was leisurely, although Jaysin was conscious of the encroaching rain clouds hugging the mountains and the fading daylight. From his first morning ride into Sarchah, he remembered passing a cluster of buildings no larger than the Dadnadichet fishing village that would suffice for the night, although he couldn't remember there being an inn. The ride also reminded him of the encounter with the Kermakk soldiers and the wolf pup, Shar, and Garva and the devastation they discovered at Nekdonchet, and that set him to wondering if Chasse knew what happened to Machutzka after his Menuii force was routed.

Chasse and Jaysin chatted as they rode, reminiscing on times spent on Dragon Mountain, sharing memories of their parents and their journey through the mountains to Machutzka. 'I wish we knew Mother's fate,' Chasse said. 'We should have gone back.'

'To what?' Jaysin asked. 'Harmi and Alan told us the village was abandoned.'

'Mikane and his men took everyone south. Mother and Banni and Jara would be somewhere, probably in Jebaran. We could find them,' Chasse proposed.

'I dream about it,' Jaysin said wistfully.

Chasse met Jaysin's gaze and said, 'I dream about it, too. Often.' He sighed changed topic. 'If your negotiations with the Meysa are successful, then what?'

'I return to Vussar Karemachet,' Jaysin replied.

'You wouldn't stay with us?'

'I'd like to,' Jaysin confirmed. 'I really would. But I offered my life in exchange for yours. I'm obligated to return.'

Chasse reined in, forcing the company to stop. 'You did what?' he asked, but he didn't wait for an answer. 'You shouldn't have done that.'

'Why not? You would have done the same for me.'

Chasse snorted. 'You don't know that.'

Jaysin cocked an eyebrow and said, 'I think I do. You are braver than me, Chasse, and I know what you would sacrifice. I'm not as brave. And I haven't given up my life freely.' He lifted his ring finger.

'You want to serve the Empire?' Chasse asked.

'For now,' Jaysin replied.

'Why?'

'To learn,' Jaysin said.

'Magic?' Chasse queried. 'Tam and Harmi will teach you.'

'Tam and Harmi do not know what the Karudarteta knows,' Jaysin said, and he urged his horse into a walk to end the conversation.

The company rode on, following the river, and, as the evening settled across the mountains, hills, and forest, Jaysin took time to search for the presence of wolves, casting his mind wide to find wolf consciousness in the hope that Shar might have stayed close to the road, especially when they passed the point where they were separated by the Kermakk soldiers. He startled a variety of creatures as he touched a variety of minds, but none were the consciousness of wolves and the absence saddened him.

Lokan called the party to a halt when they spotted a solitary light flickering at the base of a tall hill and he sent a soldier to investigate. The soldier returned and reported to Lokan, who turned to Jaysin and Chasse to say, 'It's a small village.'

'We will stay overnight here,' Jaysin said.

The hamlet had eight houses, a small foundry, an animal common where a cow and two goats grazed, and a tiny nameless inn. Jaysin, Chasse and Lokan entered the inn to be greeted by a man who introduced himself as Roughie.

'Welcome to Nyichet,' he said. He looked at the three men and Jaysin noticed the man's bearded visage adopted a quizzical expression. 'It's a curious world when Kermakk and Menuii ride together.'

'Why do you say that?' Jaysin asked.

Roughie scratched his thinning scalp before replying, 'Only recently watched them killing each other.' He eyed Jaysin and asked, 'And what are you meant to be?'

'A sheykermett,' Jaysin replied. 'An ambassador.'

'And what's that do?' Roughie asked.

Jaysin grinned and said, 'Deliver messages.'

Roughie looked over the men's shoulders at the party and horses outside and said, 'I got one room.'

Jaysin surveyed the small inn, its two tables and six stools, two barrels against the wall, and its cold hearth, and said, 'You don't seem to have much business tonight. I think we could sleep in here. How much?'

'I haven't cut firewood for the hearth. Wasn't expecting travellers,' said Roughie.

'Leave that to us,' Jaysin replied. 'How much?'

Roughie ruminated, twisting his fingers, and said, 'Twelve of you. One room. Make it six, no, eight bits.'

'What about food?' Jaysin asked, puzzled by how the innkeeper arrived at his cost.

'I can do a solid gruel,' Roughie offered. 'That would be an extra two bits.'

Jaysin looked at Chasse and Lokan, and said, 'As long as it can feed twelve.'

By the time Roughie had the steaming gruel dolloped in wooden bowls, Jaysin had the hearth glowing with warmth and the soldiers and servants were sitting on the stools and floor, chatting. Roughie shared out the bowls before asking Jaysin, 'Would you like a drop of Roughie's Best?'

'Ale or mead?' Jaysin asked.

'Neither,' Roughie replied gleefully. 'Better. I make it myself. Cleans your teeth and warms your gut.'

'How much?' Jaysin asked.

Roughie shook his head and said, 'To see Kermakk and Menuii sharing one room, it's free.' He headed past the two barrels to a large ceramic jar mounted on a side table in the corner, assembled thirteen mugs, filled each with a clear liquid, and distributed them, handing Jaysin and Chasse theirs at the end. 'Here's to peace,' he toasted, and he drank the contents of his mug, exhaling heavily as he finished, and he exclaimed, 'Now that clears the head!'

Jaysin wished that his horse would walk more steadily and that the world would stay still. He expected to lose his balance and fall at any moment, and part of him did not care if he did. He clung to his reins and kept his eyes closed against the daylight glare and while the misty rain was soothing on his face the throbbing pain would not ease.

The party of twelve rode along the twisting pathway in single file, every man silent, wrapped in his own hangover. They pressed deeper into the foothills where the mountains loomed over them, and above the mountains hung mournful grey clouds. They passed silently through the ruins of Nekdonchet, Jaysin glancing briefly at the charred wood and the ash as he remembered what he found there with Garva.

Later in the morning, they were met by a column of Kermakk horsemen heading for Sarchah. The lead riders talked briefly to Lokan before riding on. Jaysin wanted to know what was said in the exchange, but his head hurt far too much. *I will ask later*, he decided, and he sank back into his misery.

Roughie's Best was the cause. The innkeeper was far too generous with his brew. Jaysin remembered the soldiers started singing loudly, Chasse won a series of arm wrestles with Lokan and other soldiers, Guss danced on a table, and Jaysin made coloured lights burst from his hand to the astonishment and amusement of his companions. He couldn't even remember where that particular spell originated. At some point in the evening, he must have fallen asleep. He woke, leaning against Guss who was leaning against a barrel. The room stank. Lokan roused the others and Guss and Janno organised the horses, but everyone seemed to be moving in mud, slowly, carefully, quietly. Except for Roughie. He showed no ill effects from the night's carousing. He was jovial and busily tidying his inn and offering water and porridge to anyone able to stomach them.

When the rain intensified, Lokan led the party into a stand of trees where the canopy provided protection. He dismounted and said to Jaysin, 'We should eat and drink. How much further is it to Machutzka?'

Jaysin processed the question slowly, fighting the residual alcohol fog as he composed his guess. 'Two days, as we are travelling,' he replied, and then he remembered that on the outward journey he spent time waiting for Harmi to awaken. 'Less, even. We should arrive in the afternoon, tomorrow.'

'Any more villages or inns?' Lokan asked.

Too many questions, Jaysin silently complained. 'No,' he said, and he closed his eyes.

'A night under the stars it is,' Lokan concluded. He walked away to inform his men.

'I can help you down.'

Jaysin opened his eyes and focussed on his brother. He wanted to say, 'I am fine,' but instead he reached out with his arm and slid from the back of his horse into Chasse's embrace.

'We stopped in time,' Chasse remarked, lowering Jaysin to sit. 'I know how you feel. That was a very potent drink.'

'I haven't learned,' Jaysin muttered. 'I was drugged by a Kermakk innkeeper and sold because of drinking. I should not have done what we did last night.'

Chasse sat beside his brother and put an arm over Jaysin's shoulder, and said, 'From time to time, a drink with friends does little harm and a lot of good. Last night's sojourn bonded this party. Look around. They trust you, now, because you are one with them.'

Jaysin squinted. The soldiers were busy creating a temporary shelter out of boughs and bushes, and chatting with the servants who were helping them set the campsite. A soldier glanced in Jaysin's direction, and nodded, before continuing his task of laying rocks around a makeshift hearth.

'I will help the soldiers,' Chasse said. 'Choose a dry place to sleep near the hearth.'

Annoyed with his groggy headache, Jaysin assisted two soldiers to place bushes across a structure of boughs. When the shelter was finished, he retreated deeper into the trees and stood beneath one, letting the cool rain soothe his face. *I will never drink like that again*, he decided. *Never again*.

The party rode through dull light under the leaden clouds until the sun burst through mid-morning and threw colour across the landscape, easing everyone's mood. The soldiers talked and pointed out features on the mountains and in the forest. They spotted animals darting for cover and a herd of deer on a hilltop watched imperiously as the company passed.

Though the air remained cool, the sun's touch on Jaysin's face made him smile. He slept solidly overnight, only waking when Chasse roused him. He was glad to discover his malady gone, although the cold and his heavy sleep left him with aching muscles and reinforced his promise to never drink again when he readied to leave the camp. He also resolved to find a spell that could assuage headaches. As they rode, he pondered other spells, considering how he could embellish or modify them. He loved decoding the spells and exploring ways to improve them, change them, link them with other spells and he silently practised Inaya's ability to cast without speaking.

Chasse travelled part of the morning beside Lokan and, when he returned to ride beside Jaysin, Jaysin asked, 'How do you reconcile being civil with a man you might have killed before you were captured?'

'Lokan?' Chasse asked rhetorically. 'In another circumstance, he would be a comrade. He serves his army as a Menuii serves Machutzka and the dragon. He is honourable. I respect that, as does he.' He paused, before adding, 'Difference is a matter of perspective.'

Jaysin considered Chasse's answer, recognising in it why he was willing to learn from Inaya and do the Karudar Marfek's bidding. Perspective was an interesting concept – no, a reality. "To see truth," he remembered reading in a text in Inaya's library, "the seeker must see what is before her from every angle." *I first saw the Kermakk world from the eyes of an enslaved outsider*, he mused. *And now I see it from the eyes of an ambassador. It looks different. It feels different.*

'Look,' Chasse directed.

Jaysin raised his gaze, aware that the lead soldiers were stationary on the crest of a rise. He reined in beside Lokan and stared at the familiar vista opening ahead.

The road spilled down a gentle slope onto another low hill where a large Kermakk army was encamped. Green tents and flags, wagons, and siege engines, corralled horses and men strolling and squatting, working, dominated the length of the hilltop. The road cut through the camp and rolled up to the open iron gates in the mottled Machutzkan walls. Jaysin recalled his first view of the town when he arrived over three years earlier with Tam, Chasse, Harmi and Natias, and his awe at its presence and magnitude, the walls the height of ten men enclosing seven thousand inhabitants. It seemed a large town back then, but Vussar Karemachet dwarfed it. *Perspective*, he mused.

The presence of the Kermakk army comfortably camped outside the city with the city gates open puzzled and troubled him and he glanced at Chasse who was staring at the scene. When he rode away with Garva and Akanda, the Machutzkans were repairing the damage inflicted by the Kermakk army and it seemed as if the work was completed, but the cluster of ramshackle buildings and structures at the base of the walls where the Pushka resided was in ruins and abandoned.

Lokan turned to Jaysin to say, 'With your permission, Sheykermett, I will find who is in charge and ensure we can enter the city.'

'It's our city,' Chasse said. 'We don't need permission to enter.'

Lokan faced Chasse. 'Respectfully, friend, but what I see before me is a town occupied by our Imperial troops.'

Chasse frowned as he stared at Machutzka.

'Lokan may be right,' Jaysin calmly asserted. 'We should use caution.' He expected Chasse to agree. He didn't expect his brother to lean forward, wrench Lokan's sword from his scabbard, and urge his horse into a wild gallop. 'Chasse!' Jaysin yelled, but his brother charged headlong through the Kermakk camp.

Bellowing orders, Lokan led his men in pursuit with Jaysin in their wake, the banner-bearing servants cantering in the rear. Soldiers strode into Chasse's path to bar his way before leaping aside when they realised the red-haired warrior flailing a sword was not stopping, and Lokan followed, yelling in Kermakk for the soldiers to let Chasse through.

Jaysin spied a cluster of larger tents to his right where a group of men were watching the incident unfold. One pointed towards the gates and Jaysin saw that soldiers were forming a line to block Chasse's entry. They produced lances and braced to meet the rider's charge, but when Chasse reached the flat ground he showed no sign of slowing his pace. Realising that his brother was rushing headlong into a pointless clash, Jaysin reined in and conjured a translocation portal. He urged his horse forward, but the horse baulked, so Jaysin slid from the horse and strode into the blue haze.

Jaysin's unexpected appearance a few paces ahead of the soldiers' line made Chasse rein in sharply. Horse puffing in Jaysin's face, Chasse demanded, 'What are you doing?'

Jaysin pushed aside the horse's muzzle and replied, 'Saving your life again.'

'Let me through!' Chasse demanded.

'They won't stand aside, Chasse, and then you will fight them, and for what?' Jaysin asked.

Lokan and his men closed in. A larger troop of Kermakk horsemen were descending from the camp.

'Are you stupid?' Chasse roared. 'Tam? Harmi? Where are they if the Kermakk hold the city?'

Understanding flooded Jaysin. He involuntarily looked up, as if he expected to see Harmi hovering overhead. Chasse was right. *Why didn't I think of that*? he silently brooded.

Lokan reined in beside Chasse and held out his hand. 'Return my sword and I'll order these men to stand aside,' he offered. Chasse met his gaze and saw the rapidly approaching troop over Lokan's shoulder. 'I will explain to the others why we are here,' Lokan said. 'Take the Sheykermett and his servants into the city or die here. Choose.'

Chasse glanced at Jaysin before returning Lokan's weapon. Lokan lifted his hand, ordered, 'Fetch the Sheykermett's horse and stand aside!' A rider trotted up with Jaysin's horse in tow and when he mounted the soldiers parted to allow entry.

Chasse urged his horse into a canter, with Janno holding the banner riding in his wake, and Jaysin followed with Guss and four of Lokan's men. Jaysin saw that the soldiers lining the street at intervals adopted aggressive stances when they spotted Chasse, but they relaxed when they recognised the Sheykermett's banner and Jaysin's white robes. Chasse led the party into the central square, past the shattered Dracovamin, and down another street to the Dracoshaza jakusharm. The building's top floor was a pastiche of broken stones and wood. He dismounted and entered the open front door. Jaysin followed.

The ground floor was a chaotic mess of shattered and displaced furnishing, evidence of ransacking. The first floor was in similar disarray and part of the ceiling was collapsed. The stairs to the second and third floors remained intact, but when Jaysin reached the corridor landing where Tam and he lived he was shocked to find more of the building destroyed than when he left and the rooms were looted and empty of furniture. He stood in the doorway beside Chasse, who declared, 'They've taken her!'

Chasse spun to descend, but Jaysin caught him at the head of the stairs and said, 'Wait. It's worse than when I was here, but this damage isn't from a second attack. This all happened because there was a stone, maybe two, from the war machines on the roof from the first attack. The weight of the stones made the roof cave in.'

'Then, where is Tam?' Chasse demanded.

'We have to ask,' Jaysin suggested. 'Perhaps she is safe somewhere else.'

'The Kermakk hate dragons,' Chasse reminded Jaysin. 'They would hunt Tam and Harmi.'

'If they caught them,' Jaysin argued. 'Surely, we'd see evidence of that. I would have heard about it in Vussar Karemachet. They even thought I was the wizard. They definitely haven't found Tam or Harmi.'

Chasse shook his arm free of Jaysin's hand. 'Perhaps you're right,' Chasse agreed. 'We need to ask what happened.'

'Find The Woman,' Jaysin said. 'And ask the Meysa to meet. I have to speak to them. They will know where Tam and Harmi are.'

'Shouldn't you come with me?' Chasse said. 'You are the ambassador.'

'I will ask people I know if they know where Tam is,' Jaysin replied. 'I'll join you at the Mena's house. Gather the Meysa there.'

The brothers emerged from the jakusharm to find a small crowd congregated in the street and individuals called out.

'Have you come to free us?

'Where is the dragon?'

'Why are you with the Kermakk?'

'Where are our Menuii?'

Jaysin ignored the calls and shouts as he urged Chasse, 'Go to the Mena.' He beckoned for Guss to dismount and told the servant, 'Go with my brother. Take everyone. I will join you in a short while.'

'As you wish,' Guss replied, bowing his head.

'Protect my brother,' Jaysin said to a mounted soldier who relayed the instruction to his companions.

'You should come with me,' Chasse said. 'This is no longer the town we knew.'

'I am safe,' Jaysin said. 'I am the Imperial Sheykermett, remember?'

Chasse mounted, nodded to Jaysin, and led the small party along the street.

After the riders departed, Jaysin asked the small crowd, 'Do you know what happened to the Dracoshaza?'

'The dragon carried her away,' a woman replied, and the others agreed.

'We prayed that the dragon would return and drive back the Kermakk, but the dragon did not come,' said a man.

'The Kermakk took our city and ransacked what they could,' another man shared.

'And they took people as slaves,' added another woman. 'They took my daughter.'

'Why are you wearing Kermakk clothes?' a man challenged. 'Are you not the brother of the Dracoshaza?' His question raised angry murmurs.

'I come to bring peace,' Jaysin replied hastily, feeling the crowd's mood change. 'My brother, the Dracomenu, is gathering the Meysa. There will be peace. Trust me.'

A man spat at Jaysin's feet. 'We trusted you and took you in, and this is how we are repaid,' he accused. 'Betrayal!'

Hearing the rising threat, Jaysin silently conjured a portal and, when the blue haze crackled into view and startled the crowd, he stepped through.

Twenty-two

Jaysin appeared in the street outside Shika's library, scaring three dogs sniffing among the building debris, and the dogs retreated, growling, circling. A man with a load of material on his shoulders was heading for the market, but other than the dogs and the man the street was empty. Jaysin was disheartened to see the library door caved in.

When he entered, he found empty shelves. Several were overturned, and a handful of torn pages lay scattered across the floor. He remembered Inaya telling him that the Karfeshnar library contained all known books across the Empire. The Kermakk must have confiscated Shika's books.

At the foot of the stairs leading to the next level, he called, 'Shika?' His voice echoed in the room, but no one answered. He climbed, emerging in a room as large as the library. It was rudimentarily furnished – a table, four chairs, a sleeping space, two open cupboards, their contents scattered like the pages downstairs, and an orange lounge chair. A tabby cat sprang out of the chair and onto the windowsill, glaring at Jaysin. 'Shika?' he called again. The cat leapt out the window.

Jaysin retreated downstairs, concerned that his friend no longer resided in her house. *What would the Kermakk want with a librarian?* he pondered as he headed to the rear wall. Significant chunks were hacked from the stone around the metal door, and the metal bore new scars, long gashes and indentations, but the door was intact. *What if they broke through the side or rear walls?* he wondered. Logic told him he should go outside to check, although he wanted to see if Inaya's spell could unlock the ward left by the Herbal Man. He vacillated between his choices, before deciding to examine the external walls.

As Jaysin stepped into the daylight, a voice asked, 'What are you looking for?' The man's wrinkled face suggested a great age sat on his shoulders. His hide coat, tunic and worn and patched baggy trousers were the style work by a Machutzkan merchant or carter.

'Do you know where Shika the Librarian is?' Jaysin asked.

The old man studied Jaysin and asked in reply, 'Are you the Dracoshaza's brother that came here all the time?'

'I'm Jaysin,' Jaysin replied, pleased to be recognised. 'Yes. Who are you?'

'Dantin Kor,' the old man replied. 'Shika's brother.'

'I didn't know she had a brother,' Jaysin admitted.

Dantin shook his head. 'Well, she does. She had two, in fact, but I'm the one that's left.'

'Where is she?'

'The Kermakk took her. And her books.'

'Do you know where they took her?' Jaysin asked.

The old man shook his head. 'She was a fighter, my little sister,' he said.

'Fighter?' Jaysin asked.

'They had to drag her from the library,' Dantin said. 'She gave out a few bruises before they got her out.' He chuckled, as if remembering what transpired. 'I should have helped, but I'm too old.'

'But where did they take her?' Jaysin persisted.

'I don't know,' Dantin replied, shrugging. 'They took a lot of people away.' He pointed at the library building. 'What do you hope to find in there?'

'I don't know,' Jaysin replied.

'Well, I wager there's nothing left to find,' Dantin said, and he walked on, ending the encounter.

Jaysin considered the buildings that were jammed against the library walls on either side. One, a bakery, was rubble and broken frames. If the Kermakk tried to burrow into the rear chamber that seemed the likely place and might explain why it was destroyed.

He climbed over the rubble and examined the stone wall adjoined the library. It showed signs of fervent digging and large chunks were hacked from the stone, but the library wall wasn't penetrated. His confidence rose. The ward protecting the chamber behind the metal door obviously extended around the chamber, not only the door. He returned to the street and re-entered the library, heading for the rear wall.

'The Dissolution spell demands great patience and energy,' he remembered Inaya warning before she taught him the arcane recipe. 'Even if I teach you this, it might not be enough to breach a mas locking seal. And it may contain traps designed to kill anyone who meddles with the lock.'

'I will take that risk,' Jaysin told Inaya.

The door was a collection of shadow and dull light in the gloom, but he knew the seal embraced the entire chamber. He focused and quietly recited the ancient words Inaya taught him. As he finished, a faint purple luminescence emanated from the door and the wall, and within the glow were shimmering runes and segments of script.

'How will I know when I have broken the seal?' he had asked Inaya.

'There will be no more light,' she told him.

Jaysin recited the words again. The purple light shifted hue to a faint green. Again, ancient words and runes floated within the glow. He repeated the phrase a third time and the light shifted colour to dull crimson.

'How will I know if it's not working?' he asked when Inaya showed him a simple example on a locket she wore.

'You won't,' she said. 'It depends how many layers the caster applied and how patient and accurate you are in dissolving the seal.'

He repeated the words over and over, and each time the glow along the wall and around the door changed through variations of blues, greens, yellows and reds, until it returned to the first purple glow, leaving Jaysin frustrated and weary.

Apart from the seal's glow, no natural light filtered into the library. He conjured a light sphere and understood that he was thirsty and hungry. *Is it evening already?* he wondered, looking at the front door. The outside world was dark. He stared at the glowing metal door. *How many layers did the Herbal Man create?* he wondered. 'It doesn't matter,' he murmured. 'I will break them.' He recommenced reciting his litany, aloud now because his energy was rapidly fading, and the seal shifted again through its rainbow colours as he finished each recitation.

Jaysin lost count of recitations and the cycle of colours as he unravelled the seal. He lost fear of traps embedded in the magical lock. He lost sense of place and time. He lost consciousness.

When he woke, he was on the floor in darkness. The air was chilly and he was exhausted, but the door and the wall no longer glowed. He felt a glimmer of hope. As futile as he knew it would be, he stood and pushed on the door. It did not give. *Locked*, he remembered. *The key eaten by the Herbal Man's dragon.* 'So be it,' he rasped. He summoned the last fibre of his energy, recited the phrase, *'Ate ekam hooda shetra'* as he imagined himself ceasing to exist, stepped forward, passed through the door, and collapsed again.

He was in a murky forest, surrounded by heavy-boughed trees with broad trunks, gnarled roots and an impenetrable canopy. Multi-winged insects darted from leaf to bough to leaf, pausing to hover mid-flight before veering away. A wolf appeared, emerging from the undergrowth, dark grey pelt flecked with lighter grey and white, and the wolf stared with languid amber eyes, filling him with compulsion to follow the animal. As if sensing his intention, the wolf slouched into the shadows and Jaysin trailed

in its wake, pushing through the branches and bushes effortlessly, until he stood at the edge of a large glade.

The wolf vanished as it began to trot across the space and a small black and grey dragonesque creature materialised at the centre, sitting on its haunches, holding a green fruit in its tiny forepaws as it chewed. The creature's scales seemed softer than Harmi's scales and it lacked wings, but in every other aspect it looked like Harmi looked not long after she hatched. He stared at the creature, rapt by its charm and innocence, as he always was by the presence of a fawn or wolf pup.

Shapes moved at the edge of the glade, but the little dragon was oblivious to their presence, content with its meal. Man-like creatures emerged, tall, lithe, with long silver hair and green robes, and they formed a circle around the dragon and they were chanting, although the language and its meaning were lost to Jaysin, like voices in an adjoining room. The little dragon began to glow, its eyes widening as it realised it was the centre of attention, and as the light intensified the little creature screamed.

Jaysin opened his eyes to pitch black. His cheeks were chilled. His neck, shoulders, back and legs ached. He was tired, as if waking from a restless sleep. Fragments of the dream faded. He rolled into a sitting position and created a light sphere, the glow cascading across a stone floor to reveal a table and stool, a bookshelf, a wooden casket and a grey marble pedestal topped with an obsidian bowl. A black staff leaned against the wall. He eased to his feet and brightened the sphere's radiance. Scrolls were piled in the corner.

The staff attracted Jaysin's interest first because Tam owned one like it. The top had a tiny but exquisitely carved creature with dragonesque shape absent of wings and memory of the dream flitted through his mind. The base of the figurine was carved into stylised flames. As he picked up the staff, it exuded warmth in his palm and faint, amber runes glowed along the shaft. He rotated it to examine the runes, but they were indecipherable, written in a language he had not encountered.

He lay the staff across the table, approached the pedestal and looked into the obsidian bowl. It was shining in the light of his sphere, but empty. Tam showed him an object like it in the Herbal Man's cave and he wondered if, filled with water, it was a similar vessel for seeing and communicating.

Jaysin examined the bookshelf, disappointed that there were only three books, two covered in black leather, the third in an unusually textured green material. He selected the green one because it was a slim volume. The cover was etched with leaves and a single rune like those on the staff, and the texture reminded him of forest leaves and wood. The pages were of a similar material, but thinner, and filled with elegant, spiderweb thin runic script. Curiosity ignited, he perused the volume and it felt as if it was expanding, revealing more pages than it appeared to contain, as if it was drawing him into its depths, taking him over. He shut the book. He was breathing quickly, his pulse racing. The experience fascinated him, shocked him. He returned the book to the shelf and chose another.

The first black book was weighty, so he lugged it to the table. Like the green book, it had no title, but the cover was plain. He opened to the first page and discovered a familiar ancient language that he learned in Inaya's donjon. The book was a compendium titled, "Karsim Na Fekartima" – *Methods of Unmaking* – compiled, it seemed, by five contributors: Mekan Avet, Berannion Goss, Chessan Shekar, Lania Da Jakine and Jasna.

The title drew him in. Inaya's spell to unlock the chamber almost certainly came from a collection like this, he assumed. He flicked through the pages, reading titles that highlighted sections on new spells: "Breaking

Chains", "Unravelling Cloth", "Reversing Curses", "Dissolution." He stopped at the last one, expecting to find more details on the spell that Inaya taught him, but the entry was not as he anticipated. Not only did the script describe how to use the spell to unlock wards and magical locks, but it also described how to break down a soul, how to dissolve a person's will and beliefs; how to unmake a person.

Jaysin read for a long time, recognising the book was a volume containing destructive recipes, magic to generate chaos by annihilating order, spells to disrupt powerful magic. It detailed how to burrow to the very core of matter, living or non-living, and consume energy or destroy it utterly. He closed the book. There was much to learn and he was ready to learn it.

He retrieved the second black book. Intrigued by the image of a skull embossed on the front and rear covers, he opened it, expecting to find the same language as in the first black book, but it was a different script, scrawling, blunt characters, accompanying varied illustrations of strange creatures and anatomical diagrams. Like the green book, he could not translate the text, even using the translation spell.

Lastly, determined to ignore his hunger and thirst until he explored everything, he collected the scrolls from the floor and placed them on the table. Each scroll was enclosed within a wooden cylinder inscribed with runic symbols like those in the green book and sealed at both ends with green wax. He broke the seal on one and extracted it from the cylinder.

Like the green book, the scroll was made of a compound more primal, more earthy than the usual vellum or paper with which he was familiar. He unfurled the scroll to discover it was written in tiny runes, another language he could not translate. He opened a second cylinder to discover a scroll like the first; densely scribed and illegible to him. He replaced it in its case.

Jaysin surveyed the chamber for more loot, noticing only a grey sack in the bottom of the bookshelf. *So, this is what everyone wanted to hide*, he mused. *Three books, some scrolls and a staff.* The brevity of goods disappointed him. He expected more impressive items. He yawned and accepted that he was still desperately thirsty and hungry. He picked up the grey bag and packed it with the books and scrolls, disappointed by its unwieldy weight when he hoisted it from the floor. He collected the staff, extinguished the light sphere, and passed effortlessly through the metal door.

Surprised to see grey light in the library entrance and heavy rain falling, he paused to assess the situation. It was definitely daytime, despite the gloomy light obscured by the downpour and leaden clouds, but it felt as if it was early morning. He arrived in the library after midday to explore the chamber. He recalled waking to darkness after he collapsed from exhaustion, but perhaps he was confused. He studied the daylight. *Did I sleep an entire day?* he wondered.

Panic rose in his chest. He was meant to meet the Meysa with Chasse in the afternoon. *If I slept*, he thought, *I missed the meeting.* He held his hand out in the rain, caught a smidgeon in his palm and lifted to his lips, savouring the moisture. *I am so thirsty*, he realised. He held out both hands to catch more rain and drank the water eagerly to slake his parched mouth and throat. He wiped his hands on his coat before conjuring a portal and translocating to the jakusharm.

Jaysin searched the building, hoping to find Chasse and his servants, but it was empty. The horses were gone. If Chasse wasn't staying in their Machutzka home, the only other place he would be was in the Menuii barracks, Jaysin decided. He stowed the sack in a corner and covered it with a rug, determining to portal back to retrieve it after he found Chasse. As much as he wanted to avoid trudging through the muddy streets, he pulled his cloak tight, lifted the cowl, and headed through the city to the barracks.

Very few people were on the streets, apart from Kermakk soldiers who huddled under shelters or stood forlornly in the rain with their hoods up.

He didn't bother with wondering who might look at him as he navigated the city, but when he reached the Menuii compound he discovered soldiers guarding the gates. He approached the soldiers and said, 'I want to go in.'

'On whose orders?' a soldier challenged.

'I am the Sheykermett,' Jaysin replied. 'I am the Karudar Marfek's representative.'

'Respectfully, Sheykermett,' the soldier said, 'but the buildings inside the compound are empty. There's no one here.'

'What about the Machutzkan Dracomenu?' Jaysin asked. 'Did he come by?'

'No,' the soldier replied.

Jaysin headed for the city market. The rain was easing, although the streets were muddy and the market stalls were quiet, half not even open. He targeted a greengrocer stall and stepped under a sagging water-laden brown awning to speak to the owner, a thin woman who wore her hair wrapped beneath a green turban in the manner that Jaysin associated with the Kermakk.

Smiling on seeing a customer, she asked, 'What would you be wanting on a sodden day like this?'

'Do you recognise me?' Jaysin asked, lowering his cowl.

The woman's eyes widened, and she answered, 'The Dracoshaza's brother!'

'It is,' Jaysin confirmed.

'We thought you were long gone, like your brother and your sister,' she said. 'Can't say we can blame you under the circumstances.'

'When did my sister leave?' Jaysin asked.

'No one knows for sure. She was gone the same day the Kermakk army returned,' the woman told him, confirming what he heard before he left for the library.

'Have there been any instructions from the Meysa?' Jaysin asked. 'My brother met with them, yesterday afternoon.'

The woman shook her head and said, 'It wasn't yesterday afternoon. They met three days ago. Your brother left the city yesterday.'

Her response bewildered Jaysin. 'Are you sure?' he asked.

'Everyone was talking about your return and the meeting, and how you didn't show up,' she said. 'Your brother searched for you. So did the soldiers. When they couldn't find you, your brother left.'

'Did he say where he was going?'

'I heard he rode out without saying anything to anyone,' the woman told him. 'Were you hiding from your brother?'

'No,' Jaysin replied angrily. 'I had business to attend.' He lifted his cowl and retreated into the market, weaving through the stalls, heading for the city gates, but he was forced to seek shelter under a veranda when the rain became heavier, and he used the moment to catch his breath and sort his troubled thoughts. *How long was I asleep*? he wondered. *I should have bought food from the woman.* He snorted. *I have no coin. Where has Chasse gone? Perhaps I should still meet the Meysa. How long did I sleep?*

A party of Kermakk soldiers rode past, cloaks tight, cowls dripping water, horses plodding through the mud. Perhaps he could speak to the Mena, the Woman. Chasse would have spoken with her, so she might know where Chasse was going. She might know where Tam and Harmi were.

Jaysin stepped into the sodden street and headed for the Mena house, avoiding eye contact with everyone he passed, although most people on the streets, even the soldiers, were too wrapped in their wet weather misery to be interested in him.

The Mena house was a two-storey building and similar in style to the jakusharm, but he was disappointed to discover Kermakk soldiers at the gates into the Mena garden. *I am the Sheykermett*, he reminded himself. He approached the guards and held up his hand to reveal the gold ring. 'I wish to speak with the Mena,' he said.

'There is no one here,' a guard replied.

'Where is the Mena?'

The guard looked at his companion, before saying, 'If you mean the Machutzkan woman who lived here, she was executed for treason some time ago.'

Jaysin took a moment to digest the soldier's response, before he mumbled, 'Thank you,' and he walked away, rationalising what he learned and knew. The Man and the Woman were dead, the Menuii defeated and dispersed, the Meysa disempowered. Machutzka was under the control of the Kermakk army, absorbed into the Empire by force in the same manner as Mikane took control of Harbin. His task as Machutzkan Sheykermett was redundant begore he left the capital. Tam, Chasse and Harmi had fled. He was alone. He strode in the steady rain through the city to the main gates, ignoring the soldiers' gaze as he passed, and climbed the slope towards the Kermakk camp.

Twenty-three

Jaysin acknowledged Lokan across the crackling campfire before he resumed reading under the warm glow of his light sphere. The scroll was the only one written in a language close in form to ancient Kermakk or whatever title the old kingdoms held before recent times, and it succumbed to the translation spell. He tried interpreting the other two scrolls, but their runic inscriptions were impenetrable, like the content of the green book. The translatable scroll was the code to a simple spell called Shan – decay.

Satisfied that he understood the command, Jaysin rose, walked to a tree, pulled a leaf from a bough, cupped it in his palm and whispered 'Shan ek anul.' The leaf curled, lost colour and became dust. He blew it away. He glanced at the soldiers and servants clustered by the fire, noting that Guss turned away, pretending he wasn't watching. Jaysin returned to where he was sitting, rolled up the scroll, replaced it in its wooden cylinder and stashed it in his saddlebag. He leaned against a tree trunk and watched the lustrous fire sparks circle skyward.

Leaving Machutzka wasn't easy. When Jaysin went to the Kermakk Matihaka, the army commander, his intention was to find out what the commander knew of Chasse leaving and if he had news of Tam or Harmi. If he learned promising information, he would pursue his siblings.

When he reached the commander's pavilion, Guss and Janno were waiting dutifully for him, and Lokan came to explain. 'The Karudarteta ordered me to return to the capital with you. I had to wait.'

'What if I ran away?' Jaysin asked.

Lokan smiled and replied, 'The Karudarteta was confident you would return.'

Jaysin met with the Kermakk Matihaka, a broad-shouldered, grey bearded veteran named Yakiz Arden, who gruffly answered Jaysin's questions. 'The dragon flew away before the full army arrived, so I was told by those who witnessed it. The consensus is your sister left with the dragon.' He grimaced, an odd expression Jaysin thought, and added, 'According to the watch, your brother rode out in the middle of the night, into the mountains. I sent a party in pursuit. They found nothing.'

'And what of Machutzka?' Jaysin asked. 'How long will you stay here?'

'This is Kermakk land now,' Arden replied. 'We stay until we are certain the people are complying with Kermakk law.' He studied Jaysin, as if assessing his trustworthiness. 'You're not Machutzkan.'

'No,' Jaysin replied.

'Then why do you care what happens here?'

'I don't,' Jaysin replied. 'I had family here. But they're gone.'

The conversation ended. Jaysin arranged for Guss and Janno to portal with him into the city to retrieve the books and scrolls, which Guss stored in saddlebags. Lokan and his men waited for them to return, and the party rode out from the army camp, heading for Sarchah.

Jaysin wondered if he was making the wrong choice by leaving. He loved his sister and brother and the pull to join them, wherever they were hiding in the mountains, was intense. They were all that remained of his family and his original home. Tam opened the door to magic by teaching him to read and letting him consume the contents of the Herbal Man's books. Without her, he would not be becoming his true self. And Chasse – Chasse was so much like their father, Kevan, only kinder and more understanding. He was stupid to leave.

But Inaya was offering far more than Tam or Chasse could ever offer. She was not only letting him learn magic; she was offering an unbridled right to learn whatever he wanted to learn. She gave him the skill to unlock even the magic that Tam and her mentor, the Herbal Man, denied to him. Tam was acting like his mother, keeping him in a place where she could control him; like people always tried to do to him in Harbin, even in Machutzka. And Chasse didn't fully appreciate what Jaysin did to rescue him. He didn't acknowledge how powerful Jaysin was becoming, more powerful than Chasse and his warrior fixation and limitations. In Harbin, everyone considered him to be a strange little boy. In Machutzka, he was the third stranger, the brother of the Dracoshaza and Dracomenu, important only by association. But in Vussar Karemachet he was a sheykermett, an individual wearing the Imperial seal, an important official under the direct protection of the Karudarteta. He had power and status, and much more was promised to come.

Jaysin relaxed against the trunk and closed his eyes. *Why would I spend my life hiding in the mountains, homeless, a fugitive, when I can live in a great city and become what I know I can become?* he mused. *Besides, I will bring Tam and Chasse to me. I will ask the Karudar Marfek to pardon them. It will turn out good for everyone.*

The party arrived in Sarchah at midday on the third day and Jaysin excused himself with the reason that he had important business to complete before they poled downriver to Vussar Karemachet. He charged Guss with organising a place for them all to stay overnight and he told Lokan that he was free to allow his men time to relax.

'They will appreciate that,' Lokan said. 'I will accompany you.'

'This is the same errand as when we came through,' Jaysin said. 'I don't need protection.' He pointed to The Market Pot inn. 'I'm in there.'

'I am thirsty,' Lokan said.

'Feel free to drink at the inn,' Jaysin said. 'I will be talking to the owner.'

Jaysin headed across the market square with Lokan beside him and two soldiers in train, aware that people were watching as he passed along the aisles between the stalls and onto the street. A child at the front of the inn turned and bolted through the entrance.

'Seen that before,' Lokan noted. 'Someone's being warned.'

Jaysin did not comment. Five men emerged, stepping aside when they saw Jaysin in his Sheykermett robes accompanied by soldiers, and when Jaysin entered the smoky interior conversations stopped and patrons stared. Alban, the innkeeper, was conspicuously absent. Jaysin also noted that the child who ran inside was not in the room.

Alban's son came forward, and said, 'My father said you should meet him round the back.' Jaysin started toward the door behind the bench, but the youth tugged his sleeve, saying, 'Not that way.'

'How do I get there?' Jaysin asked.

'Outside and down the left. It's an alley to the back,' the youth explained.

Lokan asked, 'Want company?'

'No,' Jaysin replied. 'Enjoy a drink.' He addressed the youth and said, 'Soldiers drink for free, yes?'

Flustered, the youth hesitated before he answered, 'Yes,' and he headed for the serving bench.

'Enjoy,' Jaysin told Lokan, and he grinned as he warned, 'Don't drink the mead.'

The market babble assailed Jaysin's ears as he stepped outside, but his eyes were relieved to escape the smoky inn. He entered a narrow alley squeezed between the inn and a neighbouring establishment, barely wide enough for him to fit through, and a fat rat scrabbled up the wall and disappeared into the eaves. The alley opened into an unkempt yard littered with a chaotic stockpile of empty and full bottles and crates and jars and barrels and a brindle cat perched on a barrel hissed before slithering through a gap in the pile and vanishing. The yard was bounded by rough wooden fences, the rear one with a large double wooden gate, presumably opening onto a street or larger alley where the inn's goods were delivered. The rear of the inn was a ramshackle collection of crude building additions created from a variegated mixture of materials – old wood, stone, boxes, hessian.

As Jaysin scoured the yard for Alban, the innkeeper's head and shoulders emerged from a cellar by the rear door. Jaysin opened his mouth to greet the man, but Alban disappeared into the cellar.

Jaysin smiled wanly, thinking, *I understand you're not keen to see me again*. He approached the cellar, stopping at the head of the steps to listen and measure the situation. Lamplight spilled from the cellar to the steps. The cellar was quiet, but Jaysin smelled smoke, the kind he associated with the pipes that the men favoured in the inn. *And you're not alone*, Jaysin surmised. He descended, ready to cast a spell if Alban attacked, wondering how many companions the innkeeper assembled in waiting.

At the bottom of the steps, he faced a cellar larger than the inn's common room. Burning lamps hung from the exposed beams, throwing yellow light over a dozen tables, and at least a dozen or more men sat at the tables looking at him. Alban was at the back.

Jaysin stepped into the room and said, looking at Alban, 'You know why I'm here.'

'You don't scare me,' Alban replied. 'It's not only you and me this time.' As if Alban's statement was a cue, several men got to their feet, producing knives and swords.

'I am a Sheykermett of the Kermakk Empire!' Jaysin announced. 'This is business between that man and me. It doesn't concern the rest of you.'

'The Empire doesn't concern any of us down here,' a thick bearded, pot-bellied individual replied.

'Out of respect for your rank, Sheykermett,' another man said, 'we'll let you walk back up those steps and leave.'

The rising threat jangled Jaysin's nerves. He spotted the child who warned Alban lurking in a corner. He half-expected Alban would resist when he imagined how this moment of his return might play out and he was resolved that he might have to subdue Alban to cart him away, but he didn't anticipate Alban would lure him into a trap where the innkeeper was defended by a company of men. He was about to order Alban to come with him when he heard footsteps behind him and eight Kermakk soldiers pushed into the cellar to stand at his side.

Lokan smiled and asked, 'Anything we can do to help, Sheykermett?'

Jaysin saw the aggressive demeanour of the men defending Alban diminish and was grateful that Lokan masterfully tipped the scales. 'As I said,' Jaysin began, 'my business is with Alban.' He glanced at Lokan before continuing. 'I will forget the insult you cast at the Karudar Marfek if you leave now.' He watched his offer take effect.

Alban's supporters looked at each other, muttered, and one by one the men headed for the steps. Lokan gestured for his companions to stand aside to allow the men to leave.

'Hey!' Alban pleaded. 'Jakset! Mondi! Wait!' He grabbed the arm of the thick bearded man who first spoke and said, 'Pol. You promised me.' Pol shook his arm free and walked between the soldiers, glaring at Jaysin. Alban tried to follow Pol, but Lokan stepped in his way. The innkeeper backpedalled and faced Jaysin, visibly shaking and white-faced.

'This man is to be sold as a slave at the market in Vussar Karemachet,' Jaysin informed Lokan.

'I'll arrange for him to appropriately prepared,' Lokan replied.

'You can't do this!' Alban cried, and he dropped to his knees. 'My wife! My family! They need me!'

'How many people did you sell before me?' Jaysin asked. 'Did you ask them about their families? Did you even care?'

'But I'm a citizen!' Alban cried. 'I am Kermakk! Slavery is humiliation!'

Jaysin headed up the steps, ignoring Alban's desperate pleas. In the yard, he was met by Alban's wife and son, and he stopped before Seria, seeing tears in her eyes. 'You know why I am doing this,' he said. Seria nodded. He looked at the youth, observing his seething anger. 'I don't know your name,' Jaysin said. The youth glared defiantly.

'His name is his father's name,' Seria said.

'You have a business to run,' Jaysin told the youth. 'In time, if you are careful with money, you can buy back your father's freedom.'

'We won't know how, or where to find him,' Seria sobbed.

'You will,' Jaysin said, looking at the youth. 'When the time comes, ask for Sheykermett Jaysin in Vussar Karemachet and I will tell you where to find your father.'

'And I will find you and kill you!' the youth snarled.

Jaysin shook his head, and said, 'Save your father and yourself.' He led the soldiers single file down the alley and into the market.

'I hope this is suitable?' Guss asked when Jaysin arrived at the dock in the early morning.

Jaysin cast an eye over the flat deck, the small cabin at the front and single mast. Four river men waited expectantly on the deck. 'No cargo?' he asked.

'No.' Guss replied. 'This boat is used to carry people along the river. I thought it was more appropriate for you, Sheykermett.'

Soldiers, servants, prisoner and Jaysin aboard, the bargemen untied the vessel and poled into the river until the downstream current set to work. Fog sat on the grey river. The pale sun peeked over the tree line on the eastern horizon. The voices of men at work, on the docks and aboard vessels setting out to carry cargo south to the capital and north to towns and cities unknown to Jaysin, echoed across the river and into the fog.

'Revenge has a sweet taste,' said Lokan, as he stood beside Jaysin at the entry to the cabin.

Jaysin glanced at Alban trussed against a pole, remembering how he felt when he was enslaved and ferried down the river. 'He'll learn what he did to others,' he said.

'Sarchah will not be safe for you, hereafter,' Lokan warned.

'I have no intention of returning to it,' Jaysin replied. He turned to Lokan and said, 'Thank you for disobeying me at the inn.'

Lokan grinned as he replied, 'I guessed that you would encounter a trap.'

'Good guess,' Jaysin said.

'It was a familiar situation,' Lokan answered.

'You've accompanied other sheykermetts?' Jaysin asked.

'I've served the Karudarteta for a long time,' Lokan explained. 'She has trusted me to protect the people she values.'

Jaysin glanced at Alban again, before inviting Lokan into the cabin where Guss and Janno were organising food and drink on a rudimentary table. 'Make sure the soldiers and the bargemen are fed,' Jaysin ordered.

Guss issued instructions for Janno to see to the others, before asking Jaysin, 'Is there anything else I can do, Zekk?'

'No,' Jaysin replied. 'Thank you.'

'I will help Janno feed the others,' Guss said, and he withdrew.

'Can we talk?' Jaysin asked, indicating that Lokan should take one of the three stools.

Lokan sat, and as Jaysin perched on a stool he noted, 'Your servants like you.'

'I didn't know them before this journey,' Jaysin replied. 'Inaya – the Karudarteta provided them.'

'She is grooming you,' Lokan said. 'She chose you, and I see why.'

'What can you tell me about her?' Jaysin asked. Seeing Lokan's hesitancy, he added, 'What is said here is between us only. I trust you.'

Lokan drew a calming breath before he began. 'The Karudarteta is a powerful person, second only in authority to the Karudar Marfek and a very close confidante. Some whisper she is the real ruler of the Empire.'

'What do you believe?' Jaysin asked.

Lokan glanced past Jaysin at the door. 'She stays silent at public events, stays in the shadows whenever she can, but I think she has much more to say in the private chambers.'

'How long has she been Karudarteta?' Jaysin asked.

Lokan scratched his beard and Jaysin noticed the grey flecks in it for the first time, wondering why he didn't notice them before. 'Longer than I know,' Lokan said.

'And how long is that?'

Lokan chuckled. 'This will be my forty-first cycle when the season of Alam begins. I enlisted with the Imperial Armies when I was your age, perhaps younger. How old are you?' he held up his hand and said, 'No. Let me guess. Not yet eighteen cycles. Yes?'

Surprised to be asked, Jaysin shook his head, smiling and replied, 'I will be sixteen summers when Gok commences. Where I was born, it would be my entry to manhood.'

'We are made into men at fourteen,' Lokan said. 'That was when I became a soldier and the Karudarteta was already advising the young Karudar Marfek.'

'She doesn't look so old,' Jaysin replied, and he recalled Inaya's conversations about how she came to know the Karudar Marfek as a child.

'Everyone believes she is the forsaken spawn of a mas,' Lokan replied. 'No one ever sees her face.' Lokan grinned. 'Some even think she is immortal, the same Karudarteta for every Karudar Marfek.'

I've seen her face, Jaysin reflected, but he kept that to himself, and asked, 'What of her powers, her magic? What have you seen?'

'Not much is seen in the capital,' Lokan replied. 'I suspect the powers accredited by observers to the Karudar Marfek belong to the Karudarteta.' He hesitated, as if considering what to say, before continuing. 'I have only seen what she is truly capable of twice. The first time, I was serving as a soldier in the Janur Matichettar, during the Kemze Ushtar, the second war, and the Kemze rebels were amassing a great army to overrun the Imperial Army. On the third day of battle, the Karudarteta arrived, and she climbed a tower to see what was happening. When the Kemze army began its assault, a strange blue mist flowed across the fields and the town, enveloping the Kemze, and lightning flashed in the mist. We heard the Kemze screaming, but we couldn't see anything except the lightning. The mist evaporated and we were ordered to charge. As we rushed in, we saw bodies of men and horses strewn across the field and along the streets, and the ones still alive scattered when they saw us, so we chased them down and killed and captured them. The survivors were terrified. It was the easiest battle I ever took part in.'

'Did you see the Karudarteta create the mist?' Jaysin asked, excited by Lokan's description.

'No,' Lokan answered. 'No one saw anything like that. When we returned from the battlefield, the Karudarteta and her entourage were gone.'

'And the other time?' Jaysin asked.

'Have you seen a Kelan giant?' Lokan asked. When Jaysin shook his head, Lokan said, 'A Kelan giant stands twice the height of the tallest man.'

He assessed Jaysin and said, 'You are taller than most. Imagine a man twice as tall as you, and with your brother's physique. Kelan giants sell their physical prowess as mercenaries to the highest bidders and are formidable foes in battle. It often takes twenty men to bring one down.'

'Are there any in the Imperial Army?' Jaysin asked.

'No,' Lokan replied. 'The Kelan swore an oath on the corpses of their forefathers to never kneel before or serve a Karudar Marfek.'

'Why?' Jaysin asked.

'Generations past, the Karudar Marfek of the time led her armies against the Kelan to force them to submit to Imperial rule. The Kelan were few in number and knew they could not win against the Imperial Army, so they destroyed their villages and salted their lands and wells and retreated beyond the eastern mountains rather than submit. Only a few remained behind to fight a rear-guard action to protect the rest as they escaped. Those few were slaughtered, eventually, although at great cost to the Imperial Army, but the Kelan survivors swore their oath and their descendants continue to fight the Empire,' Lokan explained.

'But how does this relate to the Karudarteta's powers?' Jaysin asked.

'Let me tell you,' Lokan said. 'Three cycles ago, I was leading a contingent in the Andamar Metta. We were tasked with subduing the tiny Vessanine kingdom, but, when we reached a fort where the king was making his stand, we were confronted with a Kelan giant on the only bridge into the fort. I sent a body of fifty men to take him down. They weren't able to. I sent word to the siege machine operators, and they tried to bombard him with missiles without damaging the bridge, but he knocked the rocks and bolts aside with his shield and defied us. I sent word to the Karzekk that we could not cross the bridge. Instead of more men, the Karudarteta arrived on a white horse. She said nothing to me or my men. She walked through our ranks and down the road to face the giant, pointed her arm at him and a bright bolt of energy, like a burning arrow, flashed across the space between, tore through his shield, his armour, his body and exploded against the fort's gates. As the dying giant crumpled to his knees, she walked back up the road, through our ranks again, mounted her horse and rode away.'

Jaysin contemplated Lokan's experiences. Inaya could control the weather. He knew the ability was possible, but he never imagined exactly how. She could teach him. The dispatching of the giant was less impressive, he decided. *I can do that*. 'And when did you start to serve her?' he asked.

'From that day,' Lokan replied. He met Jaysin's gaze and added, 'And now I will serve you.'

Twenty-four

'Our next offering is an individual with a background in serving others,' the auctioneer announced, as Alban was hustled onto the platform. Jeers rose from the buyers. 'I know. Not your usual specimen suitable for labour. This one is most likely best for menial tasks.'

'I was festata of The Market Pot in Sarchah!' Alban yelled. 'I shouldn't be here!'

The auctioneer gestured to his minions who gagged and restrained Alban. 'This one might benefit from an owner who doesn't mind disciplining their slaves,' he said. 'I think this one will demand a little roughing up.'

The small crowd chuckled. 'Maybe your lads ought to rough him up a bit before anyone buys him!' one man yelled.

'Won't devalue that piece of trash!' quipped another, and the men laughed.

'Let's open the bids at a hundred bits,' the auctioneer announced. 'Who wants to start?' When no one spoke, he said, 'Let's be generous. I know some of you could take this one to the bog pits or maybe he could be used to clean your animal enclosures. Who's bidding?'

The crowd were silent, until a merchant toward the back yelled, 'Twenty bits!'

'Twenty bits?' the auctioneer replied. 'Are you mocking me?'

'He must be!' another man yelled. 'I wouldn't part with five bits for that one!' Laughter rose.

'We think you're mocking us!' another man yelled. 'Give the man at the back this free sample and let's move on to better stock!'

'Surely someone would offer fifty bits?' the auctioneer asked.

'Twenty!' the merchant at the back yelled.

'Sell the mongrel to the bidder!' a man yelled. 'Get it done!'

The auctioneer looked across the heads to the merchant wearing a grey turban and grey robes, and said, 'You got yourself a bargain, my friend. Twenty bits it is. Payment to my money keeper at the side of the stage.'

The auctioneer's minders bundled Alban from the stage and down to the side where he was made to wait until his merchant buyer appeared, a wizened older man with a grey straggly beard. 'Twenty bits,' the chubby money keeper said, holding out his hand. The merchant placed a gold coin in the money keeper's hand and said to Alban, 'Follow me.'

'What about these chains?' Alban asked, holding up his bound wrists.

'Follow,' the merchant repeated, and he walked away with Alban clumsily trailing in his wake, his hobbles hindering his stride.

The merchant led Alban across the docks and into a small street squeezed between two large warehouses. The street rose steeply, and Alban found walking difficult because of the slope. 'At least take the hobbles off,' he pleaded.

The merchant ignored him, walking on fifty paces before halting at a point where a narrow alley opened between two dwellings. As Alban staggered to the place where the merchant waited, he was surprised that two soldiers stood inside the alley entrance. 'What is this?' he asked fearfully.

'You are my possession,' the merchant said. 'That means I can do anything to you that I want.'

'I'm a citizen!' Alban cried. 'I'm a free man!'

The merchant chuckled and shook his head. 'The moment I made you into a slave, you ceased being a citizen. You are nothing, less than my dog or my horse.'

'I have a wife, a son, an ailing mother!' Alban pleaded. 'They need me!'

'You should have thought of those things before you chose to sell others into slavery,' the merchant said.

'It was money!' Alban said. 'I needed it!'

'So, you took the risk and here you are,' the merchant replied. 'How does it feel?'

Alban dropped to his knees. 'Please!' he begged. 'I will buy my freedom!'

'With what?' the merchant asked. 'You are a slave. You have nothing.'

'Please!' Alban begged. 'Please!'

The merchant ignored him and nodded to the soldiers before he walked further up the street. Several paces on, he stopped beneath a jutting veranda to observe the soldiers with Alban, waved his hand across his face to break the illusion and became Jaysin. He didn't need to hear the conversation between Alban and the soldiers. He watched the soldiers hand Alban his clothes, a small money purse and point to the docks. Alban stared in his direction, at which point Jaysin continued up the hill toward Guss and Janno who were waiting with Lokan and the rest of the soldiers.

Jaysin adjusted his crisp white robe and green cloak while he waited in the antechamber outside the meeting room. After so many days wearing the same clothes with little opportunity to bathe, he revelled in the cleanliness of his skin and fresh garments. He carried his recently acquired black staff to enhance his appearance. The Karudar Marfek summoned him as soon as he arrived at the Udarvesna, but Inaya, disgusted with his dishevelled and unwashed appearance, ordered Guss to take Jaysin to the bathing room and find replacement robes befitting a sheykermett who was preparing for an audience with the Karudar Marfek.

Two Imperial guards were on duty in the doorway. Being whisked away to be washed and dressed allowed Jaysin no opportunity to talk with Inaya or to relay his adventure, and he was unsure exactly what the Karudar Marfek would ask. He expected to be received in the same lush room as when he first arrived with Paten to plead for Chasse's release, but the antechamber he waited in was an entirely new space and he wondered exactly how many rooms there were in the Udarvesna. He heard rumours that it contained a thousand rooms, and while he doubted the veracity of those rumours the palace clearly had a great many rooms.

The main door opened and a servant in Imperial green bowed his head and gestured for Jaysin to enter. The room was very different to what Jaysin anticipated. Instead of comfortable chairs, a hearth and walls decorated with paintings, the room was dominated by a large square table, there were no chairs, and the dark green walls were adorned with a plethora of maps and weapons.

The Karudar Marfek and Karudarteta waited on two sides of the table. The Karudar Marfek wore familiar green robes, a green turban and jewellery, and the Karudarteta was hidden beneath her formal black garments and headwear. The Karudar Marfek's white dog was notably absent. 'Welcome to the War Room, Sheykermett Jaysin,' the Karudar Marfek said in greeting. 'Come to the table.'

The tabletop was a detailed and colourful map in three dimensions, with mountains rising three finger widths, patches of ocean and water glistening blue, and cities and towns in abstract relief. The physical representation of the Kermakk Empire and its surrounding regions was a revelation and Jaysin studied it, trying to determine exactly what was represented and where.

'The current Empire,' the Karudar Marfek said. 'Have you seen this before?'

Jaysin shook his head.

'Here,' The Karudar Marfek explained, pointing to a city, near the central section of the table, 'is where we are – Vussar Karemachet. This end of the table is the north. You stand at the south. The lands directly in front of you, across the Shekkarsussar, are the Shekkarem and Assandan kingdoms. To the east are the Okkari kingdoms and tribal lands.'

Jaysin noticed that patches close to the end of the map in the east and south were blank.

'Yes,' the Karudar Marfek said, as if she understood his mind. 'There are places beyond what we know, although there is a great deal of trade that comes from beyond the borders of this map.' She pointed to the wall on Jaysin's left. 'The maps represent what we know of those places beyond our reach. But to the matters at hand,' she said, drawing Jaysin's attention. 'What do we know of the Machutzkan dragon?'

The blunt question caused Jaysin to hesitate and consider what he could say in response that would be meaningful. 'The dragon is in hiding,' he said.

'And your brother?' the Karudar Marfek asked.

'He has gone in search of our sister,' Jaysin replied.

'As for the dragon, you understand why we cannot allow it to roam free in the Empire?'

Jaysin knew Tam and Harmi were a threat to Kermakk authority, but he shook his head.

The Karudar Marfek pointed to the south-eastern portion of the map. 'Beyond that corner lie lands that were once the realm of the Oozim, the dragons, a very long time ago. The dragons were feared because they were magical creatures with powers beyond the understanding of people. They were voracious, brutal, irrational monsters that ate livestock and burned villages to ash. They decimated entire armies and their scaly hides made them virtually unkillable except through poisons and the like. To make matters worse, individuals entered bizarre pacts with the dragons to acquire their magic and became mas, wizards in your tongue, and they used their power to usurp rulers and coerce nations. Inevitable war broke out between the wizards with their dragons and humankind. In time, the wizards and dragons were defeated, the last of them hunted down and killed, and it was believed they no longer existed,' The Karudar Marfek locked eyes with Jaysin and her determined gaze disturbed him. 'Until now.' She hesitated, before asking, 'Where did this dragon come from?'

'An egg,' Jaysin replied. 'It was left in my sister's safe keeping.'

'By whom?' the Karudar Marfek asked.

'The Herbal Man,' Jaysin replied.

'A wizard,' the Karudar Marfek flatly stated. 'You saw his dragon?'

Jaysin nodded.

'And where are they?' the Karudar Marfek queried.

'They left,' Jaysin replied. 'They flew west, across the ocean.' He glanced at the tabletop map. 'Across the Karrekarsussar.'

'And left you with an egg,' the Karudar Marfek said.

Jaysin nodded.

'And this is the truth?'

'I am telling the truth,' Jaysin replied sharply. *I am betraying my sister*, he reflected shamefully.

'He is telling the truth,' the Karudarteta affirmed. She leaned forward and whispered to the Karudar Marfek.

'For now, the fates of your sister and brother are in their own hands,' the Karudar Marfek said. 'But know that you will be tested in the future as to where your loyalty truly lies.' Her eyes narrowed. 'I am persuaded by my advisor that we can trust you, and that you have returned because you want to learn how to serve the Empire. Is this true?'

Jaysin glanced at the Karudarteta, before answering, 'I would like to serve. I want to learn.'

'You want greater power,' the Karudar Marfek noted. 'The Karudarteta wants you to be her protégé, her batan. Do you accept this offer?'

Again, Jaysin glanced at the Karudarteta. 'Yes,' he said. 'I do.'

'Then I give permission for this to happen,' the Karudar Marfek determined. 'You are hers to train as she sees fit. You will be given full citizenship and a title befitting your role. And you will obey all Kermakk law and renounce all affiliation with the Machutzkan people, and with any others to whom you feel you might have belonged before this moment. Am I understood?'

Jaysin briefly considered the profundity of the offer and its implications for his identity, and when he realised the Karudar Marfek was impatiently awaiting his answer he said, 'I understand.'

'Good,' said the Karudar Marfek. 'And one last thing. Why are you holding a staff?'

Jaysin blushed. 'I found it,' he replied.

'Is it magical, or for show?'

'I don't know, yet,' Jaysin replied.

'Find out,' the Karudar Marfek ordered. 'If you're carrying it merely for effect, don't. It looks ludicrous.'

Inaya closed the wooden door and removed her face covering. She approached the table to study the three books that Jaysin brought from Machutzka, her hand caressing the covers and exploring the textures. Looking up, she said, 'I see why you wanted to retrieve these, especially the Aelendyell Lore Book.'

'The what?' Jaysin asked.

'This one,' Inaya said, lifting the green book.

'What is the Aelendyell?' Jaysin asked.

'Who,' Inaya corrected. 'The Aelendyell were an ancient race, descendants of the fabled Elvenaar. They lived in the oldest forests in lands far from here and were the first to create and harness the arcane energies. They stored their wisdom and knowledge and spells in texts they called *Gealdorbec*, Lore Books. This is one.'

'You've seen one before?' Jaysin asked.

'No,' Inaya said, turning the book in her hand reverently. 'This is the first.'

'How do you know what it is, then?'

Inaya returned the book to the table. 'The same way I know most things,' she replied. 'Through study and research. These books are mentioned in other writings. Wizards sought to find them because they believed the Aelendyell Lore Books could unlock access to power greater than anything even the wizards knew. I have a dozen books, each from writers living at different times, referring to the mythical Aelendyell *Gealdorbec*. The oldest of those writers claims to have seen such a book and he records scraps of Aelendyell language that suggests he actually did find one. But this is the first I've ever seen. The wizard who locked this away was either exceptionally wise or monumentally stupid.'

'Can you read Aelendyell?' Jaysin asked.

Inaya picked up one of the black tomes as she answered. 'No. If what I deduced from what I read is true, you don't read an Aelendyell Lore Book. You become immersed in it. You flow through it like a fish swimming in a stream.'

Jaysin was about to describe what he experienced when he opened the pages, but he held back from telling Inaya.

'You know I know what you are thinking,' Inaya said. 'Don't hide what you want to say. You felt it, didn't you – the book drawing you into its depths.'

'Yes,' Jaysin replied awkwardly.

'How long did you immerse yourself?' Inaya asked.

'Not long,' Jaysin replied. 'I wasn't sure what to do. I closed it before it drew me in.'

'Then I will test the book first before you try again,' Inaya said. 'It may be dangerous.' She flipped through the pages of the book in her hand, saying, 'This one is interesting. It is like a healing guide, only it describes how to create the opposite effect – how to make others ill, how to create curse and plague spells.'

'I couldn't read it,' Jaysin admitted.

'The language is Wushu, very old,' Inaya replied. 'We would call it witch-speak.'

'What is that?' Jaysin asked.

'A language developed by women for spellcasting,' Inaya explained.

'How did you learn it?' Jaysin asked.

'By chance,' Inaya replied. 'I stumbled upon a book in the library that was a history and translatory. Wushu was banned a thousand or more cycles past. Men saw the threat and crushed the power of women. The ancient arts were lost. Luckily, someone was wise enough to record them.' She stopped to cursorily read a page before she put the book down and reached for the second black tome. She opened it. 'Unmaking spells. Eshamata. I've seen some of these.' She flicked through the pages. 'This is quite a collection. You've read these?'

'I learned some,' Jaysin proudly announced.

Inaya raised an eyebrow in response to Jaysin's boast. She placed the book on the table. 'And scrolls?'

'Each one is a specific spell, I think,' Jaysin clarified. 'They are in the same language as the green book.'

'Aelendyell,' Inaya reminded him. 'And the staff?'

Jaysin glanced at his staff leaning against the wall. 'It was in the chamber with these books and scrolls.'

Inaya picked up the staff and studied it.

'There are Aelendyell runes along the shaft,' Jaysin told her.

Inaya examined the shaft. 'Where?' she asked.

Jaysin approached and was surprised to see no runes. 'They glowed when I picked it up,' he said.

Inaya handed the staff to Jaysin and as he grasped it the runes glowed. 'Fascinating,' Inaya murmured.

'Why does it glow for me, but not you?' Jaysin asked.

'I don't know,' Inaya replied. 'We will have to learn why.' She stared at the staff and refused it when Jaysin went to return it to her, saying, 'No. The staff is yours. I can feel strong power emanating from it. You must learn how to use it. First, however, you will have to learn Aelendyell.'

'How?' Jaysin asked. 'You said there are no books translating it.' He saw Inaya's eyes glance at the green book and understanding dawned.

'I will read the Aelendyell Lore Book,' Inaya said. 'It will have the answer.' She looked around the chamber, and asked, 'Was there anything else?'

'No,' Jaysin said, and then corrected himself. 'There was a bowl on a pedestal. It looked like one I saw in the Herbal Man's cave. Tam called it a Seeing Waters bowl. This one was empty of water, and it was too heavy to bring back.'

'A scrying pool,' Inaya said. 'It's of little consequence. The wizards used them to communicate with each other. There is an old one in a cave outside the city, but it has lost its energy and there's no one left to communicate.' She picked up the Aelendyell Lore Book. 'The black books and the scrolls can stay with you, for now. Eventually, they must be stored in the tower library.' She crossed to the window and gazed at the vista, the palace gardens and trees, the wall, the blue sky pocked with white clouds, before turning to Jaysin. 'We have a lot of work to do,' she began. 'You have much to learn. The fate of the Empire sits with us, and you will be an integral tool for all that is needed to ensure the future of the Empire is magnificent.' She walked toward Jaysin as she continued. 'You chose to return because you want power and authority, and, because you chose to return, I will give you all that you want. But those things require absolute commitment by you to the greater glory of the Kermakk Empire, and utter, unquestioned devotion and loyalty to the Karudar Marfek.' She stood before Jaysin. 'You are being entrusted with secrets no one has known before. You will become famous and powerful, a force beyond the comprehension of those people outside this chamber, an unstoppable, all-conquering energy, greater than any wizard of the past. All will bow before you. And you, in turn, will bow only to the Karudar Marfek.' She made certain he was looking directly into her dark green eyes before she continued. Jaysin saw a flame flare in each pupil. 'Only I will be more powerful than you. Always remember that. Remember who gave you your power. Remember to whom you owe your loyalty.'

Jaysin saw the flames flicker, and vanish, and Inaya's eyes darkened, sinking into their shadowy sockets. He watched her lift her veil and hood into place and his icy fear eased, even as his mind raced to understand what he heard.

'This is your chamber,' Inaya said. 'Anything you need or want will be provided. You have Guss and Janno to serve you and they have a room next to this one. Lokan is assigned as your personal guard and he has thirty men under his command to ensure you are safe. Food, wine, women — yours as you need. My advice — be wise in your choices. Every day, at my discretion, I will command you to attend training. Read. Learn. Learn everything you can. Learn everything I teach you. Understood?'

'I have one question,' Jaysin said.

'Yes?'

'What did you do with the librarian?'

Inaya paused before asking in return, 'I presume you mean the woman from Machutzka?'

'Yes.'

'When she recovers from her discipline and retraining, she will be set to work in the Karfeshnar library.'

'And her books?'

Inaya chuckled. 'Most were copies of what we already have. Some were worth keeping. They will be added to the Karfeshnar library. Anything else?'

'No.'

Inaya knocked on the door, a servant opened it, and she left.

Jaysin headed for an armchair to sit and reflect. He surveyed the chamber with its four plush green fabric armchairs, the round wooden table, the empty bookshelves waiting to be filled, the big multi-paned window framed by thick dark green curtains, the doors into a private garderobe and a spacious bedroom. He had servants and soldiers waiting beyond his door to serve him. His return to Vussar Karemachet was exhilarating, even as it was daunting. All he anticipated and hoped for was unfolding. Inaya and the Karudar Marfek were pleased with him, and they were giving him status in the Kermakk Empire. He was allowed to learn everything he could to do with magic. He was unlocking magical secrets that Tam and Harmi tried to keep from him.

The scars of the Kar Oozim Ushta, the Great Dragon War, were deep in Kermakk culture. The Karudar Marfek made it clear that she could not tolerate Tam and Harmi's existence. But Jaysin knew that when he proved his trustworthiness and wisdom, he would redeem Tam and Harmi in the eyes of the Kermakk. He would prove his worth to his family.

Jaysin rose and retrieved the tome of unmaking spells and settled in the chair to read, memorise and expand his magic repertoire. Before Inaya started formally training him, he intended to surprise her with his skills. He was disappointed that she took the Aelendyell Lore Book. If Inaya's knowledge of its contents was accurate, it was a source he could master before anyone else. Perhaps she recognised that he could and intended to retain her status as his mentor by learning the Aelendyell magic before him. *A small price*, he decided, as he opened the *Methods of Unmaking*.

Twenty-five

The chair floated an arm span above the table.

'Place it by the door,' Inaya instructed.

Jaysin levitated the chair across the chamber and lowered it to the floor.

'Now the table,' Inaya said.

Jaysin shifted his focus to the round table and made it rise an arm span.

'Higher,' Inaya ordered.

Jaysin lifted the table another arm span.

'To the window,' Inaya told him.

Jaysin directed the table to the window and lowered it in place.

'Rest,' Inaya said.

Jaysin relaxed. The afternoon practice was wearing, not as draining as he anticipated, but Inaya's daily training was frustrating him. Every spell session was repetitive, almost boring. Levitate this. Again. Again. Pass through the door. Come back. Through again. Warm this stone. Dispel it. Warm it again. He was reminded of the brutal training that Chasse endured in the mountains under Natias Hunda. He wanted to be involved in unpacking the spells, analysing and modifying them, making them more agile and powerful. She seemed determined to drill him.

'Ready?' Inaya asked. Jaysin nodded. 'Return everything to their places,' she said.

Jaysin closed the book and rose from his chair. His chamber was illuminated by three floating spheres, and he admired them, satisfied that he was mastering the ability to conjure self-sustaining spells. At least with the light sphere spell, he could leave the spheres glowing and floating while he went elsewhere, the energy of the air from which they were formed no longer reliant on his focus or his presence.

He selected a vase from a small pedestal by the window. Lilac in hue, with painted images of plants, it was inconsequential to him. He lifted the vase and dropped it, smashing it on the wooden floor. He studied the shards, large and small, noting the tiniest fragments were scattered wide, before he spread his hands and conjured the mending spell. Almost instantaneously, the shards and tiniest fragments flashed, and the vase reassembled at the point of the floor where it shattered. He picked it up, looking to see if there was indication of damage. Pleased that it was whole, he placed the vase on the pedestal. Then he silently recited a phrase, touched the rim, and the vase crumbled to dust, some dust spilling onto the floor. He spread the dust with his foot, aware that particles clung to his sole, before he recited the mending spell. The dust flew from the floor, his sole tingled, and the vase reassembled. He smiled.

'Concentrate,' Inaya ordered.

Jaysin was tired of her voice. *I know what I am doing*, he thought, as spear-bearing soldiers surrounded him in the garden. The air sparkled and changed texture when he conjured a protective barrier. 'When you're ready,' he said. He watched Inaya on the balcony overlooking the garden gesture to a soldier, who leaned back and hurled his spear. The missile sped across the gap and dissolved in a sparkling shower as it hit Jaysin's barrier.

'Attack!' Inaya yelled, and a dozen spears whistled toward Jaysin, exploding in sparks as they struck the barrier. 'Jaysin! Help!' Inaya screamed.

Startled by her unexpected cry, Jaysin looked up at the balcony. Inaya was laughing and a spear buried into the grass beside his left foot. He stumbled back and glared at a soldier who clearly had not thrown his spear with the others.

'Never lose focus!' Inaya yelled.

Jaysin was furious. He touched the spear and it crumbled to dust.

Jaysin was reading when Inaya appeared in his chamber in the morning. 'You should knock,' he complained.

Inaya approached his table, placed the Aelendyell Lore Book on it, and lowered her hood and veil.

'You've read it?' he asked. 'What did you learn?' Inaya wore an expression that made him uncomfortable. 'What?' he asked.

'I can't read it,' she said bitterly.

'What do you mean?' Jaysin asked. 'The language is too old?'

'Read it,' she prompted, edging the book towards him.

'I couldn't,' he replied. 'I told you it –'

'Drew you in,' she finished. 'Exactly. That's what it is meant to do, according to the older writers. An Aelendyell Lore Book is not a reading experience. It is an immersion.' She looked at him. 'Read it.'

'Now?' he asked.

'Now,' she said.

Jaysin looked at the green cover, the embossed pattern. 'Are you sure?' he asked, remembering his experience in Machutzka.

'Read it,' Inaya commanded.

Jaysin picked up the book and opened to the first page. As before, the page shimmered and shifted and he was drawn into the text, the strange runes enveloping him, expanding and opening their meaning. He was awash in a different time, an alien culture with unfamiliar rites and customs and aphorisms and magic. Everything was infused with magic. Runes flashed, sharpened in intensity like beacons before fading, replaced by other runes, other script, elegant, spiderweb thin, ancient, a tapestry created from language and energies. He shaped water to fire, fire to mist, mist to light and back to water. Crystals formed and vibrated, generating energy that caught fire and cooled to ice. He was running through dense forests, swimming in crystal waters, standing in misty rain, warmed by crackling hearth fires and cooled in milky moonlight as snowflakes circled him. White horses galloped across a clearing and slender winged creatures flashed through the forest canopy, plants blossomed and wrapped tendrils around and through him, creeks rushed over waterfalls, strange almond-eyed children laughed, warriors clashed across vast battlefields, fires raged through the trees and fog swallowed the open plains. Thunder boomed. Dark caverns opened yawning mouths in the cliffs. Stars raced across the sky. Light flared and was extinguished by darkness.

And then it was silent. Empty. Breathless. Only his beating heart thudded against oblivion.

When he opened his eyes, he was on his back on the floor. His pulse was racing. He was sweating and confused. The chamber was shadows and moonlight. Something beside his head glowed green. He sat up and looked at the Lore Book, but as he focused the green glow dissipated and moonlight replaced it. Forest images flitted through his mind and faded.

Inaya.

He stood and looked around the chamber. He was alone. He started reading the Lore Book in the morning when Inaya brought it to him and demanded he read it. *What time is it now?* he wondered. He walked to the window. A full moon sat high in the southern sky and moonlight glistened on the wall parapets. The gardens were awash with soft silver light. A solitary guard stood in the shadows exposed by moonlight glinting on his halberd.

Jaysin returned to the book and picked it up, his hands tingling as he held it, and images of glittering runes flashed through his head. He put the book on the table, stepped back and breathed deeply. On a whim, he lit a sphere and headed for the black staff leaning against the wall near the door. When he grasped it, the runes along the shaft glowed amber. He flipped the staff lengthways and read the runes: *arodscipe metod. Energy maker*, he translated silently. *How do you work?* As if somewhere within the answer to his question was heard, he understood. 'This staff sustains creative energy,' he murmured. 'I use it to maintain my energy when I spell cast.' *How did I know that?* he wondered. He glanced at the table. He was exhausted. *Time to sleep.*

Jaysin was dressing when he heard Inaya in the adjoining room. 'I know you're there,' he called. He buttoned the clasp of his green cloak and walked through the door for effect, materialising in the main chamber. Despite sleeping soundly beyond sunrise, he was tired from the night's events 'I was going to bathe and wash my hair,' he explained when he saw Inaya staring quizzically.

'What have you done to your hair?' she asked.

'What do you mean?'

'Have you seen your hair?'

'No,' Jaysin answered.

'Go look,' Inaya urged.

Jaysin retreated into the bedroom and stood before the dressing mirror and was shocked. He turned side on. His hair was white – no, silver. He remembered how Tam's hair turned white when she was bonding with Harmi. *Is this what the Lore Book did?* he wondered. Inaya appeared in the reflection. 'I don't understand,' he said.

'When did you wake up from reading the Lore Book?' Inaya asked.

'The middle of the night.'

'Are you hungry?' she asked.

Jaysin realised he was very hungry, and thirsty. 'Yes.'

'You should be,' Inaya told him. 'You were unconscious, or dreaming, or whatever was happening to you for two days.'

Her revelation astonished him, but then he remembered what happened when he was unlocking the chamber in Shika's library. 'I didn't realise,' he said.

'I watched over you,' Inaya told him. 'I had Guss and Lokan check in to see if you were waking when I was elsewhere.' She touched his silver hair. 'The Lore Book changed you.' She stared into his eyes. 'Outside and in.'

'I don't feel any different,' Jaysin told her.

'But you are very different. Look at your eyes.'

Jaysin moved closer to the mirror and peered into it. His eyes were naturally green. Now they were ice blue. He turned to Inaya. 'My sister changed when she joined with Harmi. Her hair went white, as if all the colour drained from her hair into the dragon's scales.'

'Ancient magic,' Inaya said. 'Something triggers it in you. Something makes you different to me.' She went to the main room and waited for Jaysin. 'This afternoon, after lunch, we will travel out of Vussar Karemachet. Be ready to leave,' she said. She passed through the door.

Jaysin returned to the mirror and studied his appearance. He looked older, but more impressive, he decided. *The Lore Book did this*?

He walked into the main chamber to the table and examined the Lore Book. The embossed rune on the green cover was an Aelendyell symbol for knowledge, accented to emphasise the importance of the knowledge within the text. *But I can't read Aelendyell*, he mused. He stared at the rune. He could read it. He expected his hand to tingle at touching the book, but it didn't, and when he opened the book the pages were blank. He flipped through the pages, but they were all uninscribed. *Inaya has taken the original*, he decided. *But why leave this behind*? But he knew why the book was blank. He had consumed the knowledge, absorbed it into the fibre of his being. The Aelendyell knowledge was his. That was how Lore Books worked. He opened his right hand and whispered *'Bael,'* and a tiny green flame ignited in his palm. He whispered *'Acwence,'* and the flame vanished. He grinned. Creating a magical flame was nothing new. How he created this flame was entirely new. He could speak Aelendyell.

He expected to travel on horseback out of the city, so he was curious when Guss led him downstairs into the palace undercroft where Inaya was waiting with Lokan and ten soldiers armed with crossbows. A portal shimmered in the centre of the cellar. When Lokan and the soldiers entered the portal, Guss returned upstairs.

'This is a test,' Inaya told him.

'What kind of test?' Jaysin asked. 'Loyalty again?'

Inaya replied, 'No. Survival,' and she gestured for him to enter the portal.

Jaysin appeared in a glade on a hillside. Lokan and his soldiers were at the edge of the glade, peering through the trees.

Inaya materialised beside Lokan. 'And?' she asked.

'They're assembling in the quarry,' Lokan replied.

'As we were informed,' Inaya said. 'How many?'

'At least fifty,' Lokan told her. 'Maybe more.'

Jaysin peered through the trees at a stone excavation site forming an amphitheatre. People were arriving and milling in the quarry, men and women, all of them common folk. 'What's going on?' he asked.

'Dissidents,' Inaya replied. 'Enemies of the Karudar Marfek. They're plotting to kill her.'

'How do you know that?' Jaysin asked.

'We have a web of spies operating in every city, town and village,' Inaya explained. 'Through them, we hear every word spoken against the Empire. We know every malcontent, every plan of insurgency, every ill word. Sometimes they're nothing more than angry or drunken fools who make noise and do nothing. Soldiers pay those fools a visit and they crawl into their fear and behave. Sometimes, they gather like this group, give themselves a name and a cause, and plot rebellion and assassination. We eliminate these people before they give others reason to believe they can change things.'

'Why am I here?' Jaysin asked.

'To learn,' Inaya said.

'To learn what?'

'How to survive by eliminating rebels,' Inaya replied.

'How am I meant to do that?'

'Watch,' she said.

Inaya strode through the trees separating the glade from the quarry and stood on the quarry rim. Lokan and his men followed Inaya and Jaysin trailed them. Inaya spread her arms wide and spoke, her voice magically amplified, while Lokan's soldiers loaded their crossbows and aimed at the assembly.

'Enemy of the Empire,' Inaya began. 'In the name of the Karudar

Marfek, I sentence you to death. Make your peace with He-Who-Cannot-Be-Named.'

Angry voices retaliated, yelling hateful words.

'Your fates are sealed,' Inaya said firmly. 'You made your choice by assembling here. I simply apply the law.'

Over the rim, Jaysin watched the crowd. Individuals pushed to the front, facing Inaya, brandishing swords and spears, while others, terrified by the Karudarteta's presence, retreated to the quarry rock face or were running toward the road leading into the heart of the excavation.

A big man stepped forward and hurled a spear toward Inaya, but she waved her left hand and the spear ignited and burned to ash before it reached her. She made another gesture with her left hand and the quarry wall along the road collapsed, blocking the path of those trying to escape. Lokan's soldiers fired. The big man and several around him pitched back, struck by the crossbow bolts, and their companions panicked and retreated into the cowering crowd.

'I apply the law!' Inaya announced.

With a flourish of her arms, a wall of flame erupted at the quarry margins and flowed towards the crowd. People screamed. Several people charged the flame wall, catching fire as they burst through, their run rapidly deteriorating into staggers as the flames enveloped them and they fell, writhing. Jaysin watched in horror as the flaming wall engulfed the crowd, eating through the terrified, burning victims, until the circle met at the centre and sprayed a spiralling shaft of flames into the sky.

'There!' Lokan yelled.

Jaysin followed Lokan's direction and spotted a small group who must have separated from the crowd and were scrambling up the quarry cliff, slipping and desperately clinging to jutting stone. The soldiers jogged closer, loaded their crossbows and methodically picked the men and women off the wall.

Struck with abject fascination by the slaughter, Jaysin flinched when an arrow whistled past his shoulder and he spun to discover a gaggle of men loping across the rim of the quarry towards Inaya, Lokan and himself. Lokan and Inaya were unaware of the threat. Jaysin conjured a shield dome, the energy crackling as the spell took effect, and the charging men who hit the static wall created a shower of sparks as they screamed and fell back.

Lokan drew his sword and Inaya turned and the attackers halted and stared. Their companions who hit the wall clambered to their feet clutching burned arms and faces. The archer loosed another arrow that hit the invisible wall and exploded in sparks.

'Drop the wall,' Inaya ordered.

Jaysin wondered if her order was wise, but he dissolved the spell and prepared to fight. The attackers separated, three men running into the trees, the remaining fifteen, including six injured by Jaysin's spell, deciding what to do next. Inaya raised her arms and the area where the fifteen were gathered exploded in a ball of flame, the heat reaching Jaysin's face.

'Kill the others!' Inaya ordered.

When Jaysin realised she was speaking to him, he went in pursuit of the three who ran into the trees, wondering how he would kill them. *Energy shaft*, he decided.

The escapees had a start, but he spotted the first emerging in the glade. He focused and shot a sharp burst of energy and the man catapulted and fell. The thrill of power energised him. He searched for the other two. A shadow detached from a tree to his left and ran. Jaysin knew he was too far ahead and too fast to catch, but he measured the distance, cast his spell, and an energy dart flashed through the stand, searing leaves before it punched through its target. *Two*, Jaysin counted proudly. *One more*. He listened as he searched for signs of the third man. His quarry wasn't running. He glanced back at the point where the men enter the trees and estimated a line between it and where the two he shot lay. The third man was hiding in that arc.

A soldier walked toward him. Inaya was still near the quarry. Jaysin began quietly searching, ready to cast his spell. As he passed a dense bush, he heard the faintest rustle and sensed a shadow in the midst of the foliage. 'I know you're in there,' he said. The shadow was silent and still. 'I won't hurt you,' Jaysin said. 'Come out. Don't run. There's nowhere to run.'

'I don't want to die,' a trembling voice replied.

'You don't need to,' Jaysin said. 'It's over.'

'I don't want to die,' the voice repeated, a reed-thin, childlike voice.

'I won't kill you,' Jaysin promised. He noticed the soldier circling to the other side and he shook his head. 'Come out,' Jaysin said.

The bush rustled and a skinny youth emerged, ragged grey tunic and pants, straggly black hair, gaunt face smeared with dirt and tears. Jaysin estimated he was barely in his teens. He was terrified and gaping with wide eyes at Jaysin.

'I'm Jaysin. What's your name?'

The youth faltered, eyes fixed on Jaysin's hands, before he stuttered 'Willid.'

'Why were you –?' Jaysin began, intending to say 'here', but he gasped as the soldier stabbed the youth in the back. Willid's eyes bulged, his mouth fell open, and he crumpled at Jaysin's feet. 'Why did you do that?' Jaysin asked, staring at the soldier.

'Because there can be no prisoners,' Inaya's voice replied from behind. 'None.'

Lying on his back in his bed, a solitary moon ray angling through the curtains across his bedspread, Jaysin wrestled with the day's events and Inaya's lesson. Images of people running, burning wretches, terrified faces, Willid's pop-eyed shock as the soldier killed him cycled through his thoughts, disrupting his logic with emotion and confusing him.

'Power does not come from being weak,' Inaya told him as he knelt beside Willid's corpse. 'Power comes from being strong, determined, willing to go further and do more than those around you.'

'He was a child,' Jaysin argued.

'Were you a child at his age?' Inaya asked.

No, Jaysin thought, remembering his trek from Harbin and the responsibilities he undertook while escaping with his sister and brother.

'He came here because he already believed in the destruction of the Empire,' Inaya continued. 'He believed it was possible, like all the others. He believed he could be powerful, more powerful than the Karudar Marfek and the Imperial Armies, more powerful than me and you. That belief made him dangerous. To become powerful, you have to believe you can become powerful. One follows in the footsteps of the other. Think of yourself. No one thought you could be more powerful than your sister or your brother. And yet, you believed it was possible, and now you are.'

Those people died unnecessarily, Jaysin mused. *Why didn't the Karudarteta talk them out of what they were planning?* Memories of his father's clashes with Trask and Mikane emerged. Talking with enemies wasn't constructive if they weren't prepared to listen.

That was Inaya's message, later in the afternoon in the Udarvesna, when she told him, 'Killing our enemies is far more efficient than trying to convert them to being submissive. You might see it as cruel, wrong even, but you haven't ruled an Empire. The Karudar Marfek's father put his enemies in jails and left them to rot there. Cruel to his enemies and wasteful of Imperial resources. If he killed them, he wouldn't need the jails or guards to guard them and his enemies wouldn't have suffered for the rest of their miserable lives. His father forgave one of his enemies as an example of clemency and his enemy's gratitude was to assassinate him. Hard way to learn a lesson. When someone hates you, they have reasons to do so, right or wrong, and they clutch those reasons close to their hearts where they fester until they believe the only way to deal with you is to kill you. Let them fester and plot long enough and they will kill you. Dead enemies don't plot. Dead enemies don't fester their hatred. Dead enemies can't kill you.'

Inaya carries an enormous load of bitterness, Jaysin decided. *How does she live with so much bitterness*? He rolled onto his left side. Inaya's last statement to him was a challenge.

'We are at war with many people,' she told Jaysin as she stood in the doorway to his chamber. 'To the north, we are in a great war with the Five Kingdoms. To the east, the Okkari kingdoms are unwilling to accept our authority and they harbour raiders who disrupt our trade routes and exact exorbitant taxes on our merchants. To the south, across the ocean, the Assandan kingdom, which was our southern province for two hundred cycles, has rebels rising against our authority, sanctioned by their king. And, within our own people, there are those, like the gathering this afternoon, who believe it would be better if they could throw off the Imperial yoke and descend into their little villages and fend for themselves in a form of localised freedom. Their brand of freedom sets the lawless thugs loose and the ruthless and desperate and selfish can prey on the weak without the constraint of laws or fear of retribution. We have greater ideals for the people. Without us, there would be chaos and the innocent would suffer under the tyranny of the selfish, cruel and greedy. We want a better world.'

A better world, Jaysin reflected. *A better world*.

Twenty-six

He was drawn to a glimmering ring of fire in the dark. At its edge, he stared at dancing forms in the centre, awkward flaming figures gyrating as part of the inferno. As fascinating and curious as the scene was, he knew it was not beautiful but tragic. And the scene morphed into a deep lush forest with mist weaving between thick gnarled tree trunks and spilling over grasping roots illuminated by golden light. A woman appeared in the mist, and he moved toward her, but, as he reached her, she became a dragon looming above him and he felt threat and fear even as he realised the dragon was Harmi. And everything erupted in flame.

Breathing rapidly, his heart pumping hard, Jaysin sat up, chasing the dream's vestiges as they dissolved and left him afraid and lonely. There was a disconnect in the arcane web. He felt it, but he didn't understand it. The dreams were warnings.

Jaysin padded to the window. The city was waking. A solitary lantern shone on the closest Udarvesna tower. The eastern horizon glowed with an impending sunrise, the sky bleeding from gold to amber to azure, dotted with indigo gilt-edged clouds. Ships sat in the harbour, their masts dark against the sky and ocean. Not so many weeks past, he was walking the devastated streets of Machutzka, deciding whether he would escape with Chasse to find Tam and Harmi, or return to Vussar Karemachet. He chose to return. During his waking times, he was satisfied with his choice, even filled with exhilaration as he mastered new knowledge and skills, but in his dreams Tam and Chasse and Harmi whispered to him, luring him back, and those moments filled him with immense sadness.

It was mid Alamu, the season of growth, and he was studying, practising and experimenting every day, learning new spells, refining known ones, and coming to understand the impact of the Aelendyell Lore Book on his capacities to generate magic. He could conjure food and drink, read signs in the forest and the weather, recognise and utilise plants and trees and understand and communicate with animals. He could read the Aelendyell scrolls and learned from them how to heal and infect, how to make himself invisible to others, how to enter another's mind. In a very short time, he knew how to cast and dispel, make and unmake, create and destroy, give life and death. His hair was silver, his eyes bright blue, and he was content with that as well.

After his return from Machutzka, he believed he was still a prisoner because Inaya was reluctant to let him outside the Udarvesna without her company, despite her promises that he held great status. And then she arrived one morning, a few days after the execution of the rebels in the quarry, to announce, 'You are being presented to the Karfeshnar. Today, you will be installed in the Imperial Order as the Kar Saleem – the Great Sorcerer. Once installed, you answer only to me and the Karudar Marfek. Guss will dress you.' She gave him no further explanation.

Guss dressed Jaysin in a light green robe and emerald cloak and hung a gold chain around his neck. 'Where did this come from?' Jaysin asked, fingering the diamond star pendant on the chain.

'The Karudarteta, Zekk,' Guss replied. 'She insisted you wear it as your badge of office.' Guss adjusted the cloak and stood back to admire Jaysin. 'The green beautifully matches your silver hair, Zekk,' he said.

Jaysin carried his ebony staff into the Karfeshnar, trailing the Karudar Marfek and the Karudarteta. He remembered the dull auditorium with its members on tiered seats and soldiers spaced around the perimeter, and, as he anticipated, three men sat at a raised bench, the Karmatimett at the centre in his green robe, green turban and white plume, and Bahti on his right. He didn't yet know the third individual. All three rose from their seats, as did all the Feshnari. *Will Bahti recognise me?* Jaysin wondered. Bahti inspected him as the Karudar Marfek processed past the bench and ascended the steps to the chair above and behind. *Will it matter if he does?* Jaysin mused. The Karudarteta and Jaysin followed the Karudar Marfek up the steps and stood either side of the chair.

From his elevated position, Jaysin surveyed the chamber, counting the Feshnari in the tiered seats, noting their varied garbs and headwear identifying the Imperial regions and kingdoms they represented. He wondered who his replacement ambassador to Machutzka was.

The Karudar Marfek motioned for the Feshnari and Karmatimett to take their seats and Jaysin felt the air texture change, recognising the amplification spell being cast by Inaya. 'May the members of this chamber be blessed by He-Who-Cannot-Be-Named and walk always within his protection,' the Karudar Marfek intoned.

'Fa na se,' the assembly responded, a Kermakk expression that Jaysin translated as 'Let it be so.'

'I bring before you,' the Karudar Marfek continued, 'a new member of the Imperial Court who you will observe and obey as if you are obeying myself. I present to you the Kar Saleem!' She gestured for Jaysin to step forward and, as he straightened, the men in the Karfeshnar stamped their feet three times in affirmation.

Jaysin moved from his bedroom window. Since his installation, he discovered he was free to go wherever he chose, so long as he remembered to attend training sessions with Inaya. He walked through the Udarvesna, along the wide corridors and the marble colonnades, up and down the wide wooden staircases and through the halls and rooms. The only section of the Udarvesna prohibited to him was the Karudar Marfek's private chambers. Otherwise, soldiers bowed and stepped aside, servants waited on him if he asked for food or water, and Lokan and Guss and Janno shadowed him everywhere he ventured.

Six days ago, he approached the Udarvesna gates and asked the guards to open the small side entry. They complied and stood aside as he walked through and onto the street, with Lokan and Guss and Janno in his wake. He ordered Guss and Janno to return inside. Guss bowed and led Janno back through the gates. He turned to Lokan, who was speaking to a guard, and said, 'I want to walk a little way on my own.'

Lokan replied, 'You may walk wherever you choose, Kar Saleem, but not without me or my men.'

Jaysin noted the guard withdrawing into the Udarvesna. 'What if I order you to stay here?' he asked.

Lokan replied, 'I would still go with you.'

'But I have the authority to order you to stay,' Jaysin insisted.

'Respectfully, Kar Saleem,' Lokan tactfully answered, 'but you do not, in this case. I answer to the Karudarteta for your protection and she ordered me to accompany and protect you at all times. So, I will.'

Jaysin saw the gate guard returning with a squad of soldiers. 'And six men,' he said sardonically.

Lokan grinned. 'Yes, Kar Saleem.'

Accepting the situation, and quietly appreciating Lokan's protective presence, Jaysin headed along the road, enjoying the fresh air, the city sights and sounds and smells after too many days cooped in the Udarvesna and his chamber. His wandering took him downhill toward the docks, and only when he recognised familiar streets and alleys did he consider visiting Halian's house to learn the fates of the people he met there and the outcome of Paten's plea to rescue the two Assandan men. Except he couldn't. With Lokan and his guards, he would jeopardise the safety house and its occupants, even if he was careful not to disclose the truth. He let the urge dissipate and returned to the Udarvesna.

At his table, in the shadowy dawn, Jaysin generated a small light sphere and perused the Empire map. Today, at the Karudar Marfek's command, he was to travel from Vussar Karemachet to a town on the eastern front called Mentan where Kermakk troops were encountering strong resistance from Okkari rebels who called themselves the Ooshemata, the Fire of God. Rumour abounded that the rebels were supported by three shessmari, women with magical powers. His task was to put the rumours to rest, eliminate the shessmari if they did exist, and thereby lead the army to victory.

'Why send me?' he asked Inaya when she informed him that he was going to Mentan.

'Your fourth test,' she replied. 'You've proven your loyalty and trustworthiness. Now you must prove your ability.'

'But you could do this,' Jaysin argued.

'I could,' Inaya agreed, 'but I am needed here to protect the Karudar Marfek. That's why you must go. One of us can ensure stability remains in the capital. One of us can ensure success on the borders. If you can do this, your place in Kermakk society and history is assured.'

Jaysin rang the gong at his door and Guss and Janno entered. 'Is everything ready?' he asked.

'Yes, Kar Saleem,' Guss replied. 'As you ordered.'

'Then let's begin.'

Jaysin was enjoying the parade in the mid-morning sunlight through the city along The Main Way. As Kar Saleem, he rode at the head of the procession on a grey horse, proudly wearing his green robes and gold badge of office, his silver hair in a single thick braid, a style that surfaced in his memory – no, not his memory; an Aelendyell memory. Sometimes, he found himself remembering things that had no part in his life, as if his memories were expanded beyond himself. The effect was confusing and vague, an effect he wanted to understand but could not because a veil lay between those new ancient memories and his control of them.

Lokan rode beside him. Behind them rode two Kermakk matihaki, followed by long triple columns of soldiers in green uniforms. The supply wagons and servants, including Guss and Janno, trailed in the wake of the columns.

Men gathered on the roadside stamped their feet and shouted encouragement and blessings from He-Who-Cannot-Be-Named and Jaysin soaked in the adulation and deference to his authority. This was his sixteenth summer. He was a man – not the kind of man he might have been forced to become in Harbin, but a man of power and influence in the Kermakk Empire, an achievement far beyond his father or mother's wildest imaginations – one even he never imagined existed. But he was here, now, and he was happy.

Jaysin didn't see the protesters run into his path. His horse baulked and reared and he fell, tumbling across the horse's haunches and hitting the gravel road heavily, knocking the wind from his lungs. As he gasped for air, arms grabbed him and hauled him to his feet and bodies pushed and milled around him. He heard shouting, and a scream.

A man yelled, 'Death to the Karudar Marfek!'

Jaysin regained his senses and saw that he was surrounded by soldiers with their backs to him. Cheers rang out and Lokan faced him, asking, 'Are you hurt?'

'No,' Jaysin replied, but his left leg and shoulder throbbed from the fall. 'I am fine.'

'I'll help you remount,' Lokan offered. Jaysin's horse was brought forward by a soldier.

'I'm fine,' Jaysin repeated. He took the reins, put his foot in the stirrup and swung onto the saddle. As he straightened, he heard another burst of cheering and foot stamping from the onlookers. Five soldiers with drawn swords stood over three men who were on their knees, heads lowered. Two bodies lay at the edge of the road.

Lokan remounted and pulled alongside to say, 'We're ready, Kar Saleem.'

Jaysin urged his horse forward and the procession recommenced. A few paces on, Jaysin asked Lokan, 'Who were they?'

'Disgruntled citizens,' Lokan replied.

'Why did they attack me?'

'You represent the Karudar Marfek,' Lokan replied. 'A blow against you is a blow against the Empire.'

'But they're citizens,' Jaysin said. 'Why are they angry?'

'They are sick of the wars,' Lokan explained. 'They're sick of having sons taken from them to die on foreign land. They're angry that they have to pay taxes to keep armies armed and fed. They see the riches in the Udarvesna and know how poor they are.'

'How many people are like that?' Jaysin asked.

'Too many,' Lokan replied.

'But the Karudar Marfek must know this?'

'The Karudar Marfek knows everything,' said Lokan.

'Then why doesn't she do something about it?'

'It is not for me to question what the Karudar Marfek does,' Lokan replied. 'The Karudar Marfek is the bride of He-Who-Cannot-Be-Named and does what she must. And we are her servants, and we do what we are told.'

'Even if it's wrong?' Jaysin asked.

'What is wrong?' Lokan queried. Before Jaysin could pursue the matter of ethics, Lokan wheeled his horse and rode along the ranks, leaving Jaysin to wrestle with the question, *Who decides what is wrong and what is right?*

Beyond the city, the troop followed a winding road that rose into forested hillsides, passing through hamlets and crossing creeks and a larger river. Jaysin observed the varied wildlife in the countryside – numerous coloured bird species, small furry animals, a larger herd of shaggy creatures with thick curved horns, a cat-like animal that sat high on a ledge to watch them pass, a black bear raising its honey-smeared head from a beehive. He was thrilled when he spotted wolves loping across a glade and it left him wondering on the fate that Shar might have endured after she escaped the Kermakk attack. He should have searched for her more thoroughly on his journey to Machutzka, but he was confident she would have found a pack to join. The Aelendyell knowledge of animals gleaned from the Lore Book bubbled beneath his consciousness, urging him to make psychic contact with the animals, but he resisted, knowing that spellcasting would halt the army's progress and Lokan was keen to rest the army overnight at a town called Danyisar bordering the vassal Vessanine Kingdom.

Danyisar sat on the fork of two streams in a wide, fertile valley and the army arrived as the last vestiges of sunlight angled across the upper eastern verdant slopes. A gong echoed across the valley as the army descended the western road and through the trees he glimpsed farmers herding animals into enclosures and people hurrying into the town. The army stopped and the soldiers and servants began the evening prayer ritual to He-Who-Cannot-Be-Named while the Kermakk matihaki rode ahead with a dozen cavalry.

'You do not observe prayer,' Lokan observed when Jaysin remained mounted.

'Neither do you,' Jaysin noted.

'I was going to follow your lead, Kar Saleem,' Lokan said.

Jaysin looked over his shoulder at the soldiers kneeling with their hands over their faces. 'I think He-Who-Cannot-Be-Named has enough prayer being offered,' he dryly remarked. 'But feel free to join your men.'

'I will wait with you,' Lokan replied.

When the short prayer session ended, the soldiers and servants returned to their positions while Jaysin and Lokan waited for the contingent sent into the town to return. The matihaki rode back and reported that the townsfolk were waiting to receive Jaysin. The army set up camp along the stream, and Lokan, Jaysin, Guss and Janno rode into Danyisar.

Lokan reined in outside a substantial two-storey inn bearing the name The Passing Fancy on a sign accompanied by a picture of a jug and plate of food. Two old men outside the inn offered to take the horses into an adjoining stable.

'You know this place?' Jaysin asked as he approached the door with Lokan.

'The owner is a woman named Channine Ayam,' Lokan said. 'She is very accommodating.'

'A woman?' Jaysin asked, stopping Lokan. 'But women are not allowed to own public businesses.'

'Before the Vessanines joined the Empire, they had very different social structures,' Lokan explained. 'Women had the same freedoms as men, perhaps a little like where you came from. When the Vessanine king capitulated, among his requests was one that women be not made subservient in the manner they are in the Kermakk Empire. The Karudar Marfek approved that request.' Lokan grinned. 'She, too, is a woman.'

'So, why doesn't she free all Kermakk women?' Jaysin asked.

'Religion,' Lokan replied dismissively. 'The laws of He-Who-Cannot-Be-Named.' He gestured to Guss, who opened the door to allow Lokan and Jaysin to enter. 'Let's go inside.'

Within was a cosy and tidy room, with tables and chairs and a curved bar filling the left side. A small fire burned in a large hearth, giving warmth in the cooling evening. Jaysin was surprised at the absence of patrons, although three women sat at the table closest the bar and a fourth woman stood at the bar facing them.

'Channine!' Lokan called in greeting as he strode towards the woman at the bar. Jaysin watched them embrace before Lokan said, 'May I introduce the Kar Saleem.'

As Channine bowed her head, Jaysin studied her. Average in height, she was amply proportioned and her dark hair was tied in a thick ponytail that hung down her back. She wore a dark blue smock and a cream apron, and when she lifted her head Jaysin saw her brown eyes were large and alluring. Her face was worn with time, but she was still remarkably attractive.

'Rooms are prepared,' Channine said. 'Food and drink will arrive soon.'

Jaysin thanked Channine and sat at a table and Lokan joined him, while Guss and Janno spoke with Channine before withdrawing through a side door into the sleeping quarters. 'How many times have you been here?' Jaysin asked, curious about Lokan's relationship with Channine.

'I can't say exactly,' Lokan replied. 'Perhaps eight or nine times.'

'On tasks for the Karudarteta?'

'The last three times, yes,' Lokan replied. 'Before that, as a soldier, on different campaigns.'

'Campaigns?'

'Wars.'

'Are there always wars?' Jaysin asked. The concept astounded him that people would be constantly fighting.

'Always,' Lokan replied.

'Why?'

'Many reasons,' Lokan answered. He paused as plates of food and a frothy jug were placed on the table. 'Mostly, it's over who is ruling what. Warlords rise to power and lead rebellions to shake off the evil Empire. Vassal kings or queens think they should be supreme rulers and set out to suppress the warlords. Some groups pursue whatever concept of freedom they believe and take up arms against the warlords and the kings and queens. The rich push down on the poor and sometimes the poor push back. And wars keep the incumbent ruler safe from internal revolutions – mostly. Wars unite kingdoms against a common enemy and deflect attention from the incumbent ruler – unless the war goes badly.'

Jaysin listened to Lokan's explanation of the causes for war while he ate. Power, security, freedom and greed seemed the common reasons, although at the centre of the wars sat the Kermakk Empire, the Karudar Marfek and He-Who-Cannot-Be-Named.

When Channine came to sit with them, at Lokan's invitation and with Jaysin's permission, Jaysin asked why the local patrons were not in the inn.

'You are here, Kar Saleem,' Channine replied with a broad smile. 'The inn is yours tonight. They will come again tomorrow night.'

Meal and drinking done, Jaysin's head fuzzy from the long day of traveling on horseback and the alcohol, he allowed Guss to escort him through the side door and into the first room where Janno stood beside a large tub of steaming water. 'We thought you would appreciate a warm bath, Kar Saleem,' Guss said, bowing.

'Thank you,' Jaysin acknowledged. He glanced at the large and inviting bed with its sizable and plentiful cream pillows and purple counterpane, the gilt-edged dress mirror on the wall and the formidable carved wooden robe. 'This is an impressive room,' he noted.

'This room was used in times past by the Vessanine king on annual sojourns around his kingdom,' Guss explained. 'Do you like it, Kar Saleem?'

'I do,' Jaysin said. As he undressed, Guss retrieved his clothes and folded them neatly. Jaysin climbed into the tub and the warm water was immediately soothing. He leaned back and closed his eyes.

'Shall I bathe you?' Janno asked.

'I'll soak awhile,' Jaysin replied. He took a deep breath and relaxed, and murmured, 'Stay, though.'

The town was wreathed in fog and the air was chill as Jaysin mounted his horse. Lokan's breath came in clouds, mingling with the horses' steamy exhalations. He was glad to be riding out of Danyisar.

The previous night was unpleasant, despite the comfortable bed and the room's warmth, because it included an unwanted intrusion. As he settled under the covers, a dark-haired woman, one of the three in the inn, climbed into his bed and cuddled against him, startling him so abruptly that he leapt out of the bed, calling for Guss.

'What is it, Kar Saleem?' Guss asked when he entered, holding a sword.

'Get her out!' Jaysin ordered, pointing at the disappointed woman sitting up in his bed.

Guss hesitated, as if the order didn't make sense, but he gestured for the woman to accompany him from the room. As she left, she apologised, looking upset, which gave Jaysin a sharp pang of guilt.

Guss returned and asked, 'Are you all right, Kar Saleem?'

'Yes, thank you, Guss,' Jaysin replied, but as Guss began to close the door Jaysin asked, 'Where did you get that sword?'

'I always carry it outside the Udarvesna, Kar Saleem,' Guss replied. 'Is there anything you need?'

'No,' Jaysin replied, dismissing his servant.

After the door closed, Jaysin assessed the events. He never asked for the woman. Someone must have sent her to him. But who? Guss? Lokan? Channine? *I've never asked for women before*, he mused. In fact, the idea of sleeping with a woman hadn't registered with him. *I am sixteen summers. In Harbin, I would have been expected to choose a wife before winter. What would I have done?* He climbed into the bed and snuggled his head against the pillows. *I never thought of choosing a wife*, he thought. *The girls in Harbin didn't interest me and none of them liked me anyway. What would I have done?* He rolled over. *Who sent her in?* he wondered. *Why?*

And then he wondered why he never noticed Guss carrying a sword. *Does Janno have one as well?* He was so wrapped in his pursuit of magic that he was missing details around him. *That could be dangerous. I need to be more observant*, he decided.

Questions and thoughts raced through his head, defying sleep for a long time, and when sleep finally came it was troubled with dreams he could not remember this morning, only a lingering feeling that the dreams contained anger and frustration and sadness.

'Another day's ride across the Lendarian Hills, and then we stay overnight in Mardressa, a large town that served for a time as the Vessanine capital,' Lokan explained as they rode. 'That was four hundred cycles ago. Much of the old city is in decay, now, from wars and neglect. After that, we travel half a day, cross the Hunjakker River, and we will arrive at Mentan.'

Jaysin let his reins loose momentarily to adjust his leather cloak's collar to keep out the cold, and then he took hold of the reins and eased into the day's riding, his mind buzzing with questions.

Twenty-seven

Smoke rising from Mentan clouded the horizon throughout most of the morning's ride before they climbed the last hill outside the town and entered the army camp. Siege weapons dotted the slope and men wandered between the tents or stood on duty behind the fortifications. Rows of green canvas and hide Kermakk tents covered the hilltop and flowed down the hillside to an abatis fortification. Beyond the abatis line to the riverbank lay an open field strewn with corpses and blackened remnants of huts and siege machines. The eastern bank rose into a stone wall, damaged sections revealing the buildings beyond. A stone bridge arched over the river, littered with more corpses, and led to a scorched and battered wooden gate with a charred siege vehicle lying on its side before it. Black birds circled above the field and sat on corpses. The stench of putrefying death permeated the air.

Lokan led Jaysin to a pavilion on the hillside where guards took their reins while they dismounted. Four men emerged from the pavilion to greet them.

'I am Karzekk Corten,' a tall, grey-bearded, dark-eyed man said. 'Welcome, Kar Saleem. We are expecting you.' Indicating his companions in turn, he said, 'I introduce Matahaki Naebinya, Jakubi and Lozantika.' The matahaki bowed their heads. 'Please,' Corten said, gesturing for Jaysin to enter the tent.

The pavilion was richly furnished with armchairs and beds hidden behind sheer curtains. Oil lamps provided light. A large table with a map and movable pieces dominated the centre. Three servants stood attentively to the side.

'Can I offer mead or wine?' Corten asked. 'Perhaps you are hungry from your journey?'

'Neither,' Jaysin replied politely. 'Tell me what I need to know.'

Corten stood at the table to explain and the matahaki joined him. 'We are here,' Corten said, pointing to a collection of objects. 'We control most of the surrounding countryside and have the town blockaded.'

'So, you could starve the people into submission,' Jaysin said, wondering why the Karudar Marfek sent him to a battle where being patient would see the army ultimately win.

'We tried,' Corten replied. 'But they are not starving. The shessmari use magic to sustain the people.'

'And attacking the town?' Jaysin asked.

'The shessmari burn everything we send across the open ground,' Corten explained.

'With magical fire?' Jaysin asked.

'Yes,' Corten confirmed.

'Have your archers tried to kill the shessmari?'

'I have archers waiting to do that,' said Jakubi. 'But the women never venture beyond the walls.'

Jaysin studied the map. 'How accurate is the street charting?'

'Prisoners and merchants helped with details,' Naebinya explained.

'I have been in the town,' Lokan said.

Jaysin looked at him. 'On one of your many journeys?'

'Yes, Kar Saleem,' Lokan replied with a sly grin.

'Where are the shessmari most likely to be in the town?' Jaysin asked.

Naebinya answered him. 'The prisoners say the shessmari are sisters. They live in the gardens of the Basmura, the Okkari man who is like our Karudar Marfek in this town. He leads the Ooshemata.'

'And where does he reside?' Jaysin asked.

'Here,' Naebinya replied, putting his finger on a large compound at the centre of the town. 'This is his Udarvesna, his palace.'

Jaysin rested on a log, watching the sunset fade across the clouds above Mentan. A gong sounded through the Kermakk camp, signalling the Kermakk call to prayer. Torches flickered to life along the town walls in the twilight and moved with the sentries. The air was rapidly cooling, stinging his cheeks with its icy caress.

He spent the afternoon, after Corten's briefing, and a meal with the Kermakk general and captains, planning how he would deal with the shessmari. He wondered if making his presence known might lure them out in challenge, but he dismissed that idea. The shessmari were secure in their town and the information shared with him showed they intended to remain so. The only way to reach them was to go to them.

He could boldly approach the town, using his magic as protection, and demand entry, but he didn't know the extent of their powers. They might be able to dispel his magic and expose him to attack. He decided on stealth.

Then there was the issue of what to do when he did confront them. Subdue them? Kill them? When he left Vussar Karemachet, he was under the impression the shessmari were not necessarily able to use magic – that their power was a rumour – but Corten assured him they could create fireballs that destroyed siege machines and conjure food to sustain a population under siege. They must have significant magic, he deduced, and that prospect made him curious.

As far as he knew from his readings and experiences, magic belonged only to people associated with dragons, either directly, as with his sister Tam, or indirectly, as with Inaya and her wayward wizard father. *Except for me*, he remembered. *I am an exception*. But that didn't explain the existence of the shessmari. *Is it possible there are other exceptions?* he mused.

Hearing an approaching footfall, he turned to Lokan's shadowy outline and rose. 'I am ready,' Lokan said. 'Matahaka Naebinya provided the Okkari clothing.' He handed Jaysin a bundle.

'For this to work, you have to remain close to me until we breach the wall,' Jaysin explained, as he changed out of his robes into the grey and cream Okkari tunic, trousers and jacket. 'And we have to move quietly. The spell hides us, but it doesn't suppress sound. Once we are in the town and free to move around, it will matter less because you will look like one of them but stay close.' He adjusted the jacket and stood before Lokan. 'How do I look?'

'You need a hat or a hood to hide your hair,' Lokan recommended.

'I'll fix that when we are inside the walls,' Jaysin replied.

Jaysin and Lokan descended the hill in the twilight to the fortifications where soldiers showed them a narrow, concealed path through the field. Crossing the field in the dark was treacherous because they had to negotiate bodies and wreckage and dips and rough ground and the decaying stench in patches made Jaysin gag. He wished they could follow the road because it was level, but it was also strewn with corpses, giving no respite from the odour, and they would be easily spotted against the road's lighter hue when the moon rose.

Naebinya did tell them where they could cross the river. A sortie against the town in the early stages of the siege left a section of crumbled wall clogging the river where a log bridge was jammed across the water for the soldiers. While the defenders drove back the Kermakk attackers, no one subsequently managed to dislodge the bridging log.

A short distance from the riverbank, the rising moon illuminated the world, filling it with grey light and shadows. Jaysin conjured his spell and whispered to Lokan, 'Stay close. The spell is active.'

'How will I know where you are?' Lokan asked. 'I can't see you.'

The realisation of the impact of invisibility dawned on Jaysin. 'Here,' he said, cancelling the spell, and he held his hand toward Lokan.

Lokan took the hand. 'If I let go, I'm balancing,' he said.

'I'll wait if you do,' Jaysin replied. He recast the spell.

Hand-in-hand, Jaysin and Lokan reached the river where Jaysin saw the extent of the log bridge. He expected a single log to be in place, but the remaining bridge was made of multiple logs, wide enough for five people to cross side-by-side. He tugged Lokan onto the bridge and carefully made his way over, feeling Lokan adjust as he adjusted when either of them shifted their balance.

The stone pile presented a new challenge. Climbing across and up required both hands. Jaysin whispered, 'This part we have to do alone.'

'If you climb one step at a time, I can touch your foot after each step to stay in touch,' Lokan suggested.

The climb into the town was painfully slow, Jaysin waiting after each move of his right foot for Lokan to find it and tap the invisible boot, but they stayed close and slipped past the soldiers defending the gap, only stopping one time when Jaysin dislodged a stone that clattered down to rest near the soldiers. Unable to clearly understand the Okkari language, only the intent, Jaysin listened to the soldiers argue as to what caused the stone to dislodge, anticipating they would ascend the rubble to investigate, but they did not come closer. When he was satisfied they were not a threat, Jaysin led Lokan to ground level and across the street to the shadows of a building where he cancelled the invisibility spell.

'That was weird,' Lokan said. 'I couldn't see my feet.'

'Like moving with our eyes shut.'

'Yes,' Lokan replied.

'Now we find the shessmari,' Jaysin said. 'First, I need to look like you.' He focused and adopted the illusion.

Lokan gasped. 'That is uncanny,' he said, examining his reflection in Jaysin's appearance. 'We are twins.'

'This will get us into the street,' Jaysin said. 'When I find a more suitable appearance, I will change. Looking too much alike might draw unwanted attention.'

Jaysin and Lokan stepped out of the shadows and walked along the street toward the main thoroughfare into the heart of Mentan. Jaysin glanced at the Okkari rebels lounging against walls or working to repair the town's fortifications and decided Lokan and he looked like an ordinary pair of Okkari on patrol. He tapped Lokan on the shoulder and gestured for him to wait when they reached an inn, while he entered and scrutinised the half dozen men within. He returned and indicated to Lokan to walk on.

At the entrance to an alley, Jaysin incanted a change to his appearance modelled on a patron of the inn. 'Now we don't look exactly alike,' he said to Lokan.

They entered the main street and headed for the town centre, silhouettes and shadows shifting in the light of smouldering fires and lamps and torches and moonlight. For a town under siege, the mood among the residents was buoyant. Inns were open for business, and people sat on doorsteps and on rubble eating, drinking and chatting. Some watched Jaysin and Lokan walk by, but no one challenged them.

The main street entered a large market adjoining a high wall with wrought iron gates at the centre. Six Okkari men wearing bronze chest plates and armed with halberds guarded the gates. Beyond the gates, Jaysin glimpsed the moonlit outlines of trees and bushes – a garden – surrounding a two-storey building, its upper storey windows lit with lanterns.

'This is the place,' Lokan confirmed. 'The shessmari live in there.'

'Good,' Jaysin said. 'Let's go to the other side.'

The pair passed through the market. Most stalls were dark and quiet, but several food stalls were lit and open with customers eating at them. On the right side of the compound, Jaysin halted and said to Lokan, 'Stay here. Keep watch and listen until I return.'

'How will you get through the gates?' Lokan asked.

'I'll go through the wall,' Jaysin replied.

Jaysin couldn't see Lokan's face in the dark, but he guessed his companion was puzzled by his answer. He imagined himself momentarily not existing and he passed through the stone wall and emerged in a garden.

His boots were under water. He grinned because he stood in a pond and he remembered the importance of knowing what was beyond a wall before passing through.

He stepped out of the pond and waited, observing and listening. The compound was quiet, the only sounds coming from beyond the walls. He crept through the garden, until he reached a gravel path encircling the central building and followed it to a door. Its position and size reminded him of the side entrances in large Kermakk houses, so he assumed it led into servant quarters. He passed through.

He was in a darkened corridor, but flickering light peeping from sills on either side revealed that the corridor ended at a flight of rising steps and a second set descending. He listened at the first door and heard voices and sounds of food preparation. Beyond the second door, voices conversed. He cast the invisibility spell again and climbed the stairs into a lit hallway opening onto a balcony. Doors were spaced equidistantly along the balcony wall.

Jaysin walked onto the balcony, noting that it swept around half the building, before ending at a door on what was the third side of the space. A window filling the fourth wall afforded whoever was in that room a view into the space below. A staircase dropped directly into the space from the balcony. He looked down to discover a square banquet hall with a long table diagonally stationed across the centre being set for a meal. Servants scurried through the room, placing plates and cutlery on the table and decorative flowers on pedestals around the outer walls.

When he looked up again at the window opposite, he was startled to see three women. The shessmari. He calmed his nerves while he studied them. They were mirror images – dark, shoulder length hair, short but slender framed, all three wearing dark blue robes. They were talking as they gazed on the activities below. A shessmar lifted her eyes and looked directly at him and he tensed, ready to react in case she had the power to see through his invisibility spell, but she turned to her sisters and continued the animated conversation. They moved from the window.

Now what? Jaysin wondered.

As he considered whether to confront the shessmari in their chamber, a door opened to his right and a man emerged in ceremonial silver armour, an older man, perhaps Lokan's age, his cropped hair greying along the sides. Three servants followed him along the balcony and the group entered the shessmari room. His arrival complicated the situation. Jaysin guessed that the man was the Basmura, the town leader. Inaya wanted the shessmari eliminated. She said nothing about the Basmura.

Retaining his invisibility, Jaysin crept along the balcony to the door into the shessmari chamber. To enter, he either had to open the door while he was invisible or pass through and appear because one spell negated the other. He opened the door and entered, noting that no one initially paid attention, until a shessmar said, 'Who opened that?' All eyes turned to where he stood, but no one could see him. He stepped aside.

'Close it!' the Basmura snapped, and a servant hurried to the door.

The room was spacious. A suite of dark blue armchairs and a lounge occupied the area before the window that overlooked the banquet hall. Behind the chairs was a table with eight chairs, and bottles and food were scattered across the tabletop. Further back against the wall were three wardrobes and three beds draped in luxurious dark blue quilts. Paintings and tapestries adorned the walls and separated four tall thin windows. Lamps hung from the high ceiling. The shessmari and the Basmura were seated at the table.

Jaysin estimated his best chance at completing the assassination. Four quick energy bursts would be efficient. A fireball would fill the room and kill his targets in one burst, but it would arouse too much attention. It occurred to him he would like to know how the shessmari used magic. *I could take one with me*, he contemplated.

Sudden pain in his calf broke his concentration and his invisibility spell. He yelped and looked down to find a small black dog sinking its teeth into his leg. He shunted the dog away and conjured an energy bolt at the closest shessmar. As he cast, he heard screams and the Basmura drew his sword and charged. Jaysin loosed another bolt, and the man collapsed and slid along the polished floor. The remaining shessmari were conjuring so he loosed a third energy bolt at one. And a solid object smacked the back of his head.

The woman's crystal green eyes brimmed with burning hatred and her lips curled as she mouthed silent words. Fire crept along his skin. He screamed.

When the pain subsided, he saw her face again and she snarled, 'Feel it. Feel every prickle, every biting agony. This is the agony inside of me that I return to you for murdering my sisters!'

Searing pain flared across his skin, and he screamed, as he had screamed time and time again since she started torturing him. This time, though, he retreated within, drawn by an ancient spell he couldn't remember learning, yet he knew it, an ancient Aelendyell enchantment. It wrapped around his senses to protect him from the anguish coursing through his skin, so that the torture was elsewhere, not where he was, happening to a body in which he no longer dwelled. The invocation soothed him, created a space where he could assemble his thoughts devoid of pain, cloaked him in green coolness, like standing in a forest glade. The woman could not touch him here. He could collect his emotions, his thoughts, his self, and plan. She was using an incantation to burn him; not real fire, magical fire that seared his nerves but did not damage his skin. She also held him in chains – real ones with magic binding them tight. He needed to unlock her magic before he could break the chains.

The glimpses he managed between bursts of searing pain revealed he was still in the shessmari chamber, bound atop a bench or table he could not remember seeing. Perhaps it was secreted in an adjoining room. First, he needed to break the binding spell, but that meant venturing outside of the psychic haven he was hiding within. It meant enduring the pain. She would be witnessing his resistance and wondering what he was doing. *Is she alone?* he wondered. Two shessmari and the Basmura were dead. He was certain of that. *No. Someone – a servant – hit me from behind.* There were three servants. *Did she summon others while I was unconscious?* He could risk emerging from the green space within to see who else was in the room, but that wouldn't work because the pain she inflicted blinded him. *I need to find the binding spell.*

He summoned his courage and crept out of his refuge, searching along his arm and leg sinews for the magic that held him fast. She was waiting. Pain flared, racing along his skin in pursuit, savaging his senses as he fled into his safe place. He could not hear himself, but he felt himself scream, his muscles tensing, his jaw taut, his lungs forcing out air. The magic was not binding his ankles or wrists. Those were metal manacles. She held him rigid elsewhere. He had to find where.

He eased out of the green haven, searching his body and found his target – a necklet clasped around his neck. He withdrew as she sent his body into another paroxysm and waited for respite before he probed the necklet, analysing its properties, searching for the key. He mistimed his retreat and shuddered when ferocious pain scorched him and left him fighting to keep his conscious mind from drowning in a wave of nausea and agony. *How long does she intend to torment me?* he wondered. The binding magic was simple, not complex like the lock on the library door in Machutzka, and he was confident he could quickly unravel it. The challenge was how quickly. Her pain pulses would break his concentration if she caught him unguarded, and he would have to start again. *I have to make her stop torturing me*, he decided, and, to do that, she would have to believe he was unconscious.

He focused on the green forest light and allowed it to draw him deep within its glow, infusing his spirit, filling him with peace, calming his heart and pulse, soothing his mind. A face formed in the green light, an elongated, handsome face with high cheekbones and almond eyes framed by intricately braided strands of hair, and the eyes were kind, consoling, uplifting. He felt that he should let go of his desire to resist and stay where he was, beyond the world of mortals, outside the realm of pain and sorrow. To remain would be easy. The face promised he belonged there.

No, he whispered. *Now.*

He drew on his will to push out of the haven, through his chest to his neck, cast his spell to shatter the binding spell, flexing as he yelled the ancient word to dissolve the shackles. He rolled from the tabletop to his feet, spread his arms dramatically and sent a crackling wall of flame rushing from his body, igniting everything in the room as it spread and climbed the walls, the window glass shattering from the heat, the servants screaming. As the shessmar writhed in a flame wreath and staggered back, Jaysin conjured an energy bolt and sent it ripping through her left leg, crippling her. She collapsed to the scorched floor, kicking and screaming.

He cancelled the fire spell, focused and pushed his mind into hers. *Now the pain is yours!* he snarled. He waited for her response, but she kept screaming, her mind a fractured vessel, so he withdrew, conscious of the stench of charred wood and flesh and smoke, and cast a soothing spell over the prostrate woman and he waited for her to cease twitching and quieten.

Noise drew his attention. Though the broken viewing window, he spotted soldiers rushing onto the balcony and the door swung open. 'Gelucan!' he yelled. The door slammed shut, knocking the intruders back onto the balcony. 'Oeggian!' he added, to lock it. The door glowed with a faint red aura.

Knowing the door was secured, he attended to the woman on the floor. The fire blast had burned away most of her robes, her hair was scorched and her skin blistering red. She stared at him, unblinking, when he squatted beside her. 'Where did you learn your magic?' he asked.

She stared silently.

'You don't have to die like this,' he said. 'I can heal you.'

'Why would I want to live anymore?' she replied, anger rippling in her rasping voice.

He remembered his conversations with Inaya. 'To learn,' he said.

'Learn?' the woman asked. 'Learn what?' She drew a grating breath. 'How to serve men? How to crawl in the shadow of your god? How to obey your leader?'

'Learn magic,' Jaysin replied.

'I know the craft,' the woman replied. 'That's what makes men afraid of us.'

'How did you learn it?' Jaysin asked.

'You will never know,' the woman replied. 'Kill me like you came to do. Others will take my place.'

'What's your name?' Jaysin asked. The woman's lips moved, but he couldn't hear. 'Again,' he asked.

'Closer,' she whispered.

Jaysin glanced back at the door to check his spell was holding before he leaned down to listen to the woman.

'Death,' she whispered. He didn't remember seeing an object in her hand. He felt a blade bite deep under his ribs and she let out a bloodcurdling scream, 'Die!' She kicked at him, and he nearly fell sideways, but he grabbed her arm and uttered the unmaking phrase. The woman made a muffled whimper and dissolved to dust.

Jaysin sank to all fours, the dagger sticking from his side and he curiously explored the throbbing pain before he sank onto his haunches, gripped the dagger hilt and repeated the unmaking spell. The dagger dissolved. Blood flowed freely from his side. He put his hand over the wound and mumbled a healing spell, again fascinated by the sensations coursing through his body at the site of the injury, the rising warmth, the coursing blood and throbbing pulse.

A grappling hook clunked on the floor by the viewing window and was pulled back to take hold against the frame. A second grappling hook appeared. The Okkari were climbing up to the room.

Jaysin took one more look at the charred bodies and detritus scattered around the chamber and he noticed a tiny amber crystal in the dust pile that had been the shessmar. He retrieved the crystal, feeling it faintly tingling his fingertips before he tucked it into his pocket, conjured a portal as a head appeared in the window frame, and stepped into the blue haze.

Twenty-eight

'You're injured,' Lokan noted, examining Jaysin's bloodied tunic and trousers.

'I'm fine,' Jaysin replied. He altered his appearance to look like an Okkari and examined the dark street outside the compound. Shouting rose beyond the wall.

'The shessmari?' Lokan asked.

'Dead,' Jaysin told him.

'Then we should leave,' Lokan recommended and he turned to head for the main thoroughfare.

'No. They will be searching everyone. This way.' Jaysin conjured a portal and urged, 'Step through.'

Jaysin materialised beside Lokan by the log at the edge of the Kermakk campsite. 'Why didn't we go into Mentan like that?' Lokan asked.

'No connection,' Jaysin explained. Seeing Lokan's confused expression, he explained, 'To make a portal, you have to know exactly where it must connect. I'd never been in Mentan.'

'I said I was there before. I could have described it,' Lokan said. 'That would have been easier than crossing the river.'

'Your description wouldn't help,' Jaysin replied. 'I need to exactly visualise the destination point to cast the spell.' He gazed at the town in the moonlight. The town appeared unchanged, but he knew there was chaos ensuing as word spread that the Basmura and the shessmari were dead. 'We should let Karzekk Corten know the threat is eliminated,' he said.

Corten looked up as Jaysin and Lokan were admitted into the pavilion.

The Kermakk Karzekk was alone, holding a mug of mead. 'Couldn't get in?' he challenged. His eyes strayed to the blood on Jaysin's garments, and he lifted his left eyebrow.

'The shessmari are dead,' Jaysin informed him.

Corten's expression changed to astonishment, but he coughed to clear his throat and assemble his emotion, before saying, 'All three shessmari?'

'All three,' Jaysin replied. 'And the Basmura.'

Corten glanced at Lokan who nodded confirmation. 'Impressive,' Corten said, shaking his head. 'And your injury?'

'Nothing,' Jaysin said. 'The town is yours. Attack whenever you're ready.'

'The Empire will be forever grateful for what you have done tonight,' Corten said. 'Less men will die.'

'Too many have already died,' Jaysin said. 'If there is no other need for us, we will return to the capital.'

'I will order a feast before you go,' Corten said. 'This deserves celebration.'

'No celebration,' Jaysin said. 'We will go immediately.'

'Tonight?' Corten asked. 'It is not safe to travel in this region after dark. The rebels are active beyond the town.'

'We will be safe,' Jaysin said. 'When will you attack the town?'

'In the morning,' Corten said. 'The men will be rested and the Mettuzhashemata will give a blessing from He-Who-Cannot-Be-Named to protect us in battle.'

'Then may the blessing be lucky,' Jaysin replied. 'We are leaving.' He exited with Lokan in his wake.

'Are we seriously leaving tonight?' Lokan asked, as they walked to the campsite where Guss and Janno had set tents. 'It's getting late and the Karzekk is correct about the risks on the road.'

'We won't be riding,' Jaysin told him. 'Collect your things and meet me at the log as soon as you can. We will leave from there.'

After instructing Guss and Janno to organise the necessary gear and to leave what wasn't necessary, Jaysin walked to the lookout and stood in the moonlight beside the log. Mentan's torches and lamps glowed in the town's silhouette. The silver river snaked across the landscape past the town and the road curved down from the hills into the town, before a thin sliver of it appeared in the distance, framed by dark trees. The ground between the river and the edge of the Kermakk camp that ran up the hill, littered with the detritus of war, was a tapestry of variegated shadows and light. In the morning, men would ride and run and haul siege machines across it, as they had for many days, this time believing they held the advantage with the shessmari gone.

The shessmari, he reflected. He fossicked in his pocket to withdraw the amber jewel and held it up to glitter in the moonlight. It tingled his fingers, and he knew it was magical. 'How did this help you?' he whispered to the night. He rotated the crystal, studying how its facets caught and reflected the light, reminding him of the amber crystal in the Dragon Mountain cave and Tam's amber dragon ring. And the amber bracelet Tam gave him to stay connected. An ancient memory sparked. An Aelendyell memory. The Genesis Stone. He pocketed the crystal.

In the thrill of the mission, the anticipation of the fight, the unexpected attack by the dog, the struggle with the third woman, he had little time to reflect on the consequences of what he did. He reacted. He survived. He did what he was asked to do. 'I would have liked to talk with you,' he whispered. 'I could have learned from you.' *But I killed you.* The thought saddened him. He remembered the quarry and Inaya's slaughter of the rebels. 'Is this what I am becoming?' he whispered. 'A killing machine?' 'Learn to survive,' he imagined Inaya replying.

'We are here,' Lokan announced, interrupting Jaysin's reverie.

Guss and Janno stood behind Lokan, loaded with backpacks and bags. 'Is all that necessary?' Jaysin queried rhetorically.

'Why are we meeting here?' Lokan asked.

'We are leaving from here,' Jaysin replied. He conjured a portal, the blue light crackling with static momentarily before settling into a comfortable haze. 'After you,' he invited.

Settling into the bath's warm embrace, Jaysin closed his eyes and let the soothing water relax his body. The return from Mentan to Vussar Karemachet via the portal was a successful experiment, confirming for him that his power had substantially expanded since absorbing the Aelendyell Lore Book. Rather than report directly to the Karudar Marfek, or even Inaya, Jaysin went directly to his chambers to sleep until the morning. He asked Guss to inform the Karudarteta of their return, dismissed Janno to unpack the bags and offered Lokan the opportunity to sleep in the Udarvesna in his chambers.

Lokan declined, saying, 'Thank you, Kar Saleem, but I will sleep in the soldier's quarters as usual. If you require me again, I will be ready.'

Jaysin watched Lokan walk along the Udarvesna hallway, appraising the older man's stature and presence, before he entered his chambers and stripped off his bloodstained clothes to slip into the comfort of his bed.

He slept almost immediately, exhausted, but dreams rushed in and made his night restless. When he woke in the morning, only vestiges of the dreams remained and he considered them as he waited for Guss to prepare a bath for him. In one dream, he was watching a dragon circle below the clouds in the distance, while he stood atop a hill, surrounded by army tents. He felt alone. That was all he could recall. Fragments of another dream were clearer. A woman with green eyes laughed at him, saying, 'You will never know,' before she crumbled to dust and was swept away by a raging river. A second woman took her place and said, 'Men should be afraid of us,' and, as she faded into the background, a third woman appeared and said, 'All is not what you like to think it is.' She also crumbled to dust, but in her place was Inaya and she was smiling. A third dream was about Lokan, but he couldn't recall details.

Before he bathed, he studied his reflection in a mirror. A whole lot was changed, not merely his silver hair. His face was beardless and smooth, and there were subtle but evident altered structures in his cheeks and jawline. He was the Kermakk Kar Saleem. Within a few days, news of his role in breaking the siege of Mentan would spread throughout the Empire and strike fear in the hearts of Kermakk enemies while lifting him to legendary status among the people. All that Inaya promised was evolving for him as she said it would. But there was a terrible cost. Lives. That cost gnawed at his conscience.

Refreshed, dressed in clean green robes, his hair braided in a single cord and the golden seal of his office dangling from his neck, Jaysin allowed the six karhaka, the Udarvesna guards, to escort him to the Karudar Marfek's personal chamber, one of several Jaysin understood were scattered through the Udarvesna. A banquet of meats, breads, fruits and cheeses and delicacies was presented on a square table in the chamber and the Karudar Marfek and Inaya were waiting.

Inaya rose from her scarlet armchair to greet him. 'A welcome return, Kar Saleem,' she said, smiling. 'The Karudar Marfek thought you might appreciate refreshments after your difficult journey.'

Jaysin bowed his head toward the Karudar Marfek and replied, attempting formality, 'The food is appreciated.'

'You should sit at the table,' Inaya directed, indicating a chair.

Jaysin did as asked, noting neither Inaya nor the Karudar Marfek intended to join him in partaking of the food.

'I am told that you successfully and effectively completed the task I set for you,' the Karudar Marfek said from her dark green armchair.

'Yes,' Jaysin replied, eyeing the fruit and nuts hungrily.

'You may eat as you answer our questions,' the Karudar Marfek graciously offered.

Jaysin smiled appreciatively and selected fruit.

'So,' began the Karudar Marfek. 'What did you learn of the Okkari shessmari?'

'Not much,' Jaysin said between mouthfuls. 'They have some ability with magic, but it is limited to fire spells.'

'Which would suit the needs of the Okkari Ooshemata,' the Karudar Marfek concluded. 'Of little consequence, it seems.' Jaysin noticed that she was staring intensely at him, as she said, 'Inaya told me that you have read very ancient books that caused you to mutate somewhat. I see what she means. No more beautiful red hair.' Jaysin blushed. 'Do you feel different?' the Karudar Marfek inquired.

'A little,' Jaysin replied.

'You are certainly more powerful,' the Karudar Marfek stated. 'One shessmar can be a potent enemy and yet you despatched three in a single encounter. How did you do that?'

'Surprise,' Jaysin replied. 'I was able to attack them before they could defend themselves.' He paused and then asked, 'What do you know of the shessmari?'

The Karudar Marfek's left eyebrow rose as she glanced at Inaya, before she replied, 'I thought the Karudarteta told you what you needed to know.'

Jaysin also looked at Inaya and said, 'I was told the three women used magic and I learned they were sisters.'

'Then you know what you needed to know,' said the Karudar Marfek. 'Did you learn anything else about them?'

'No,' Jaysin replied. He raised his mental defences to prevent Inaya peering into his thoughts. 'They were weaker than I expected.'

The Karudar Marfek was fleetingly astonished by his response, but she resumed her composed demeanour and said, 'Your success means we can commence a new military operation in which you will play a pivotal part.'

'What is that?' Jaysin asked.

'I will inform you when it is time,' the Karudar Marfek told him. 'For now, you have earned time to rest and relax. Enjoy the meal.' She rose from her chair and left the room without further comment, and Inaya followed silently, leaving Jaysin to eat and drink in the company of two attendant servants.

Although he expected to be called to attend or be visited by the Karudarteta, Jaysin heard and saw nothing of Inaya for six days and when he attempted to visit her chamber her guards told him that she was unavailable. Feshnari came and went from the Karfeshnar daily and sheykermetti gathered in the Udarvesna, but he was not invited to assemblies or meetings and no one could tell him what was driving the increased political activity.

Shunned and isolated, Jaysin buried himself in reading and researching magic and Guss and Janno attended his usual requests while he worked. He unpacked the ancient power within his black staff and learned that it not only conserved the energy of the bearer but also contained protection and warding spells and light spells. He was fascinated by how many new spells he could call upon that must have become part of him when he subsumed the Lore Book and he discovered in an Aelendyell scroll that the shessmar amber crystal could further amplify his spells. The last breakthrough sent him exploring how to best apply the crystal, finally deciding to meld it with the diamond on his neck chain using an Aelendyell making spell that ended with the diamond adopting a soft amber hue.

Experiments and research kept him deeply occupied every day and late into the evenings, but despite his pre-occupation with magic a desire to visit Halian nagged him and he decided he should visit her, if only to thank her for keeping him safe when he arrived in the capital. Conscious of Lokan's stifling protectiveness, he waited until Guss and Janno cleared his breakfast one morning before he cast his spell to adopt his servant's appearance and he headed out of the Udarvesna, amused at the irony that a servant like Guss could freely come and go while he, the Kar Saleem, was constantly observed and far less free to do whatever he wanted outside of the Kermakk place.

The morning was warm and clear as he strolled along the Main Way. Merchants and vendors spruiked their wares, organised their shops and served customers, and he passed a troop of soldiers and wagons heading east to the frontlines. The war, it seemed, was never-ending, like Lokan described, and he was beginning to understand why the protestors were angry and frustrated with the Karudar Marfek and the Feshnari for waging constant war. He wondered how many soldiers died the morning after he left Mentan.

When he found Carriage Street, he made sure no one was following before he headed downhill to Lower End Road. He looked for the green pitched roof identifying Halian's safe house and stopped in shock. Where the house had been was a ruin of charcoaled wood and charred stone. The buildings either side were scarred from the fire that burned the house between them. His heart sank. Was the fire a tragic accident, or the outcome of a more sinister act? Did Halian perish in the inferno? He contemplated the ruin and the possibilities, and then he began retracing his steps to Carriage Street until an urchin ran into his path. 'You want something?' Jaysin asked.

'Are you looking for someone in particular?' the child asked in reply.

The child's unkempt long hair and dirty face reminded Jaysin of when he first came looking for the safe house. 'Do you know where Halian is?' he asked.

'Who's asking?' the child chirped.

Jaysin hesitated. His disguise as Guss made him unknown to anyone who might have seen him when he was staying with Halian. He replied, 'A friend of Iris.'

The child ran away, deviated into Carriage Street, and disappeared, leaving Jaysin to wait to see what his message would bring in reply. He leaned against a stone wall, but as time dragged he sank to sit on the ground. A merchant wheeled a barrow of vegetables by and a curious red mongrel trotted to him to sniff his boots before heading into Lower End Road and disappearing between buildings. A pair of Hakamati patrolled Carriage Street, one casting a cursory glance at Jaysin as they passed.

Deciding that the child wasn't returning, he walked to the intersection to head to the Udarvesna, only to be stopped on Carriage Street by the urchin calling, 'This way, zekk.'

Jaysin turned to find the child waving for him to follow. *Halian must still be alive*, he decided, as he trailed the child down the sloping street.

The child led Jaysin into a narrow alley off of Carriage Street and at the end of the alley the child pointed to a large unpainted and rotting wooden warehouse door, and said, 'In there.'

'Halian?' Jaysin asked.

'In there,' the child repeated and scampered away.

Jaysin studied the door. It was in poor condition, but he noticed that the hinges were oiled and clean, so it was regularly used. *It might be a trap*, he considered, Halian was always vigilant, so he prepared to cast a protection spell if needed. He looked up to see if anyone was observing from the second story of the building, or the roof, but no one was obviously visible. *Inside it is*, he decided, and he turned the handle and pushed on the door.

The space was a large warehouse filled with erratically piled crates and boxes and full of darkness and shadows, save for the shaft of light from the open door. Jaysin anticipated someone coming from his left or right to confront him, but the warehouse was silent. That only made him more wary. 'Hello?' he called.

'Close the door,' a male voice instructed.

Jaysin closed the door, alert for attacks, estimating the direction to the speaker.

'Who sent you?' the voice asked.

'Iris,' Jaysin replied. The extended silence warned him that there was a problem with his answer.

'Lie on the floor,' the voice ordered.

The voice came from behind crates piled to his right and ahead. He lay on the floor, focussed on keeping his illusion spell secure. Boots approached. An object was pressed against the back of his neck and hands grabbed his arms. His wrists were bound firmly. A bag was placed over his head. He was hauled to his feet.

'Walk,' ordered a new voice by his left ear.

If he needed, he would translocate outside. The bonds were no challenge. He complied and walked. Several steps on, he was stopped. He heard shuffling and whispers.

'Hold still. Don't struggle,' the escorting voice ordered.

Jaysin was lifted and lowered. His hands and his side scraped against hard surfaces. *Underground*, he noted.

More shuffling, before the voice said. 'Good. Walk.'

Hands steered him. The walk continued at least a hundred paces, with his guides steering him through four bends or corners until the procession stopped. Hands untied his wrists. A door closed behind him.

'You can remove your blindfold,' said a woman.

Jaysin lifted the cloth. He was in a room illuminated by lanterns, and he was facing Halian. Her dark hair was uncovered, cropped short, and she was studying him with her piercing eyes. Three women had hand-held crossbows targeted on him.

'Let's keep this short and simple,' Halian began. 'Iris is dead. So, why are you here? And why shouldn't we make you disappear?'

'I didn't know Iris was dead,' Jaysin replied.

'Obviously,' Halian retorted.

'How?' Jaysin asked.

'Butchered by your Karudar Marfek's Hakamati,' Halian said. 'Your turn.'

'Can I talk to you alone?'

'And why would I let an uninvited guest do that?' Halian challenged, 'Especially one who serves the new Kar Saleem?'

Surprised to be recognised as Guss, Jaysin asked, 'How do you know who I am?'

'We know every single individual who creeps through that place,' Halian replied. 'Now, answer my question. Why are you here?'

'My master knows you,' Jaysin said. 'He wants to talk to you.'

'About what?'

'Paten. And the Assandans.'

'Why would the dead concern your master?' Halian asked.

'Dead?' Jaysin asked.

Halian shook her head. 'The Karudar Marfek had them executed the same day that she befriended your master. We are at war with the Assandan Kingdom. Your master would know that.'

'I thought the Karudar Marfek pardoned them.'

Halian laughed ironically, shaking her head. 'Is that what they tell Udarvesna servants? Do they tell you the Karudar Marfek is benevolent and wise and forgiving? They feed you lies to keep you compliant and happy.'

'My master didn't know,' Jaysin explained. 'If he had known, he would have intervened.'

'Why would the Kar Saleem care about an enemy of the Empire?' Halian asked.

'What happened to the house in Lower End Road?' Jaysin asked.

Halian squinted and her brow furrowed. 'The Hakamati burned it down on the Karudar Marfek's orders. They came in the middle of the night. If we hadn't been alerted, we all would have perished in the fire. But it didn't go that way.'

'How did they find you?' Jaysin asked.

'They tortured Paten Nedrek until he confessed everything,' Halian said. 'Simple. Cruel. Effective.' She stared at Jaysin, and he heard the chill in her voice. 'We assumed that your master also gave them information. Whatever the reason he might have, your master sent you to find me. You have. That is unfortunate for you, because he cannot know where I am.'

Jaysin heard the threat. He incanted and vanished.

In the alley, outside the warehouse door, illusion dissolved, sharp pain in his left shoulder, he conjured a portal and stepped through, into his chamber, stumbled to his armchair, dissolved the crossbow bolt protruding from his shoulder, cast a healing spell on the wound, and sagged into the chair, exhausted.

Twenty-nine

The alien face in his dream was familiar. He should remember her, but he was certain that he never met her. He watched her watch him stumble into the forest, aware of the oddity of observing the observer. A wolf loped towards him and lay at his feet and he knew it was Shar when she looked up with liquid amber eyes. 'I have been waiting for you,' she said, and he was not surprised the wolf could talk. 'You should come back.' He wanted to say he would if he knew how but tingling on his wrist distracted him. He rubbed his wrist, expecting to find the amber bracelet that Tam gave him, but it was gone. Who took it? Alban. He forgot to ask Alban where the bracelet was. 'I will go back,' he promised. But even without the bracelet, the tingling in his wrist – no, through his body – was strong, and there was a soft glow in his chest and, when he looked down, the diamond pendant was amber. No chain. The pendant was on his chest – no, it was in his chest. How could that be? he wondered. 'How could it not be?' the observer asked.

'We have a new task for you, Kar Saleem,' the Karudar Marfek announced when Jaysin arrived in the Karfeshnar.

Jaysin acknowledged the seated Feshnari, noting the five Karzekk including Corten were standing before the Karmatimett's raised bench. He had never seen the Karzekk assembled on one place and he believed that at least three were leading armies in remote regions. Somehow, the

Karudar Marfek brought them from their posts to the capital and their presence made the mood ominous. He hesitated, thinking that he should climb to take his place beside the Karudar Marfek, but when he understood that he was the focus of the assembly he remained where he stood in the centre of the chamber.

'You have all heard how the Kar Saleem resolved the impasse at Mentan,' the Karudar Marfek said, her voice echoing. 'A new power is born in the Empire and our enemies now understand how futile their rebellions and petty resistances are against the might of He-Who-Cannot-Be-Named. Already, the Okkari are sending envoys to sue for peace, and I was informed this morning that a similar plea will come from each of the Five Kingdoms in the north. That leaves only the southern kingdoms to comply.' She paused, before adding, 'And the mas and her oozim rebels in the western mountains.'

Tam and Harmi, Jaysin wondered. *Why them? What were they doing?*

'Tomorrow,' the Karudar Marfek continued, 'we will send the largest army ever assembled in the Empire across the ocean to the southern kingdoms and we will crush them to complete the unification of the Empire.' She looked directly at Jaysin. 'And the Kar Saleem will sail with that army and he will bring us quick and glorious victory.'

The chamber echoed with foot stomping from the Feshnari and Jaysin felt the new weight of responsibility rest heavily on his shoulders. *More killing*, he contemplated.

'At the end of the campaign, the army will return, march into the western mountains, and rout the last pocket of resistance. The Kar Saleem will destroy the wizard and the dragon. The Kermakk Empire will be complete!'

The chamber echoed again with fervent stomping.

'All glory to the Kar Saleem!' the Karmatimett yelled.

'Fa na se!' the men chorused.

'All glory to the Karudar Marfek!' the Karmatimett bellowed.

'Fa na se!' the men repeated.

'All glory to He-Who-Cannot-Be-Named!' cried the Mettuzhashemata, rising from his seat on the bench.

'Fa na se!' the assembled men shouted enthusiastically.

'Adeh na akehu tusou, o udar schemata usz ha lonia,' the Mettuzhashemata began and Jaysin translated his Kermakk prayer as it unfolded as 'We are your servants, oh Mighty Maker of all things, Keeper of the Kermakk people, Lord of all Creation.'

At the end, the assembly chorused, 'Fa na se.'

The religious fervour in the Karfeshnar chamber astonished Jaysin. Aware as he was of the Kermakk monotheistic belief, in his time in the capital he witnessed very little public expression of it, save for the dawn and twilight gongs and calls to prayer, but neither did he visit the temples or shrines and Inaya never mentioned He-Who-Cannot-Be-Named. But more than the fervour, the announcement that he would defeat Tam and Harmi angered him. That he could never do.

He sensed Inaya's attentive gaze and locked eyes with the Karudarteta. 'If you want to be truly great, the path is open to you,' Inaya projected. 'You are at the crossroad. One road leads to glory. One road leads to oblivion. Choose wisely, Kar Saleem.'

Jaysin emptied his mind of emotion and did not reply.

'The world is made up of the strong and the foolish,' Inaya added. 'You are one with the strong.'

The canvas sails snapped tight in the dawn wind and the ocean tang assailed Jaysin's nostrils as the brig drove through the waves into the mouth of the bay. To port, starboard and astern, the bay was crowded with vessels of manifold sizes and forms – sloops, schooners, ketches, brigs like the one he was on – ships loaded with siege machines, horses, supplies and servants – a thousand ships sailing to the shores of the southern kingdoms carrying eighty thousand soldiers, the largest Kermakk army ever assembled. Although he knew he was sailing to a war in which he was to play the main part, he was excited by the impending adventure, the thrill of being at sea and the rush of air, water, nautical sounds and smells inundating his senses.

Jaysin climbed the steps onto the fo'c'sle where he held onto the foremast and revelled in the motion and wind. The first time aboard a ship, transported as a slave to Cheznah, he was ill. The second time, masquerading as a sailor aboard *The Divine Wind* during his escape from Cheznah, the motion made him queasy, but not ill. *This time*, he decided, *I will enjoy the journey.*

Inaya told him the previous night that the voyage to the port of Amanaya would take five full days. She came to his chamber after the evening meal and asked Guss to fetch an ushta board and pieces, and a carafe of wine. 'You've played ushta?' she asked, taking a seat at his table.

'No,' Jaysin replied, curiosity aroused.

'You should,' Inaya said. 'I will teach you.'

'What is the game?' Jaysin inquired.

'It is a contest to see who can dominate the board,' Inaya explained. 'Each player begins with fifteen pieces. One piece is the karzekk, the general. Two are masi, or wizards. Two are oozim – dragons. Ten are soldiers. Only a karzekk can capture a mas. A mas can take any piece on the board, but it takes two masi to capture a karzekk. The oozim can defeat any piece and only an oozim can defeat an oozim, but if an oozim's mas is defeated the oozim is automatically removed from the board. A piece is captured when it is surrounded and cannot move. When a piece is captured, it becomes the winner's piece. There are two hundred and twenty-five areas on the board and the aim is to either capture all the opponent's pieces, trap the opponent in a position where they cannot move any pieces, or own more areas of the board than the opponent.' Guss arrived with the board, pieces and carafe and placed them on the table. 'Excellent!' Inaya said. 'I will show you how to set up.'

Inaya explained the game's intricacies as they played; how to surround an opponent's pieces to capture them, how to own a square, moves to bring the karzekk into conflict with a mas, and how oozim can fly to any space in a move. By the end of the first rapid demonstration game, Inaya owned all of Jaysin's thirty pieces. 'Do you understand?' she asked.

'Yes,' Jaysin answered.

The second game unfolded quickly again, although Jaysin did manage to take one of Inaya's wizards and create minor havoc with his dragons for several moves until Inaya retrieved the initiative. She then trapped Jaysin's surviving six pieces in the corner of the board where he had no choice but to capitulate. 'Better,' she declared. 'Again.'

During the third game, Inaya slowed her moves as she spoke to Jaysin of the impending mission into the southern kingdoms. 'The army is a demonstration of the Empire's strength,' she explained. 'But you will be the demonstration of its power. You arrive in a port under Kermakk control, but two days' journey south of Amanaya is the Assandan city, Shkali, where the Assandan king resides. It is a fortress with a stone wall, twenty spans high, encompassing the entire city, and an army of thirty thousand men and women guard the walls. Wells supply it with fresh water and it has gardens and orchards and stock to maintain food for a very long time. The city has withstood many sieges, including our attacks. The Assandan resistance not only stems from that city; the city is the symbol of Assandan hope and strength. Destroy Shkali and we destroy Assanda.' She looked directly at Jaysin. 'You will destroy the city.'

'Alone?' Jaysin asked.

'Alone,' Inaya confirmed.

'I could assassinate the king,' Jaysin suggested. 'That would be easy enough.'

'It will not have the desired effect,' Inaya told him. 'The Assandan people are resilient. One king is easily replaced with another in their world. Shkali, however, is irreplaceable. It is a city one thousand cycles old. Take that and we break their spirit.'

'The whole city?'

'There must be dust where it stands,' Inaya said.

'And that is my mission?' Jaysin asked.

'No,' Inaya said. 'That is the first part. After Shkali, you will travel south-east with the army to Medha Akkan. It is an underground city built in caves, the holy city of the Shekkarem kingdoms. You will bury the city.'

'And then?' Jaysin asked.

'You return to us and we celebrate your triumph,' Inaya replied. 'The army will subdue those who still do not believe with their own eyes the power of He-Who-Cannot-Be-Named and the southern kingdoms and tribal lands will be absorbed into the Empire.'

Jaysin watched a dolphin pod race beside the ship, the sleek creatures catching the bow wave and leaping and diving through the water, and the vision made him smile. Life held so much beauty. A memory of Harmi learning to fly leapt like a dolphin into his thoughts and he grinned, remembering how the young dragon tumbled down the side of the mountains as she struggled to take flight. And when she did become airborne she was majestic. Beauty was everywhere. Life was everywhere. Life. And death. He had five days aboard the ship to rehearse his raft of spells in preparation to destroy two cities. He was death incarnate, sailing towards the southern lands to deal out death to the living in two cities. The idea numbed him.

Jaysin climbed down from the fo'c'sle, ignored Lokan's inquiring gaze and Guss' offer to be of service, and descended below decks to his cabin. The morning sun was glittering on the waves outside, but he curled up on his bunk and closed his eyes and pondered what he was doing and why.

Jaysin was amazed by the gusty wind and dust. The land leading to the city walls was dry and parched, dotted with ruined remnants of farms, the houses abandoned, the fields cropless and littered with bones. The hot sun was overbearing and relentless.

'Shkali,' Lokan announced.

'Why is everything so brown and yellow and dry?' Jaysin asked.

'Shkali is at the edge of the Great Desert,' Lokan explained.

Jaysin remembered allusions to deserts in texts that he studied, but they were concepts and vague references. A panorama devoid of green or mountains or snow or rivers, a land burned by the sun was alien and uninviting, depressing. 'How do people live in a place like this?' he asked.

'Underground water,' Lokan replied. 'Beneath the surface lie vast lakes accessed by wells.'

'But the farms are dead,' Jaysin argued.

'War,' Lokan said. 'What you see is a landscape where armies have fought for decades. The farmers gave up. When the war is ended and the Empire united, the farmers will return and make the land fertile again.'

Jaysin looked over his shoulder at the vast Kermakk army arrayed across the countryside, stretching as far as he could see. The Kermakk had already met and comprehensively defeated a sizeable Assandan army in one day after disembarking at Amanaya. *Surely the Assandan people can see their resistance is pointless*, he thought, but he remembered Inaya's reply when he said as much to her before leaving Vuss Karemachet.

'When we played ushta last night, how many games did we play?' she asked.

'Six,' he replied.

'And how many times did you lose?'

'Six.'

'And yet, after each loss, you were willing to play another game.'

'I was learning from you,' Jaysin replied.

'Did you think you might eventually win?' Inaya asked.

Jaysin grinned as he replied, 'Yes.'

'But you didn't.'

'No.'

'And yet you kept playing,' Inaya said. 'Now you understand why the Assandan people do not surrender. So long as Shkali resists our armies, they believe they can learn and eventually win.'

'But that's not a game,' Jaysin asked. 'They're fighting for their independence.'

'Everything is ushta,' Inaya replied.

Jaysin returned his attention to the city. *Everything is ushta*, he repeated. The Kermakk word translated to "contest," sometimes to "war." *Everything is war*. 'Wait here,' he said to Lokan.

'What are planning to do?' Lokan asked.

'Play a game,' Jaysin replied, and he urged his horse into a canter along the road toward Shkali.

Jaysin reined in outside the city walls, impressed at the size of the massive iron city gates. Fifteen spans high and twenty spans wide, the battered and scarred gates were embossed with creatures and serpents entwined in brutal struggles against the background of a glaring sun.

'They worship ten separate gods,' Inaya told him before he left. 'They are truly delusional.'

Jaysin wondered if the gate images represented the Assandan gods or simply the struggle of desert life. He conjured voice amplification and announced, 'People of Shkali! Hear and obey! Lay down your weapons! Open your gates and surrender! Choose the path to life!'

He waited. Sweat beaded on his brow. The sun was intolerably hot. His horse pawed the dusty road. When he measured enough time to have passed for sign of a reply, or an envoy to be despatched from the city to meet him, he drew a deep breath and repeated his message, ending with, 'If you do not surrender, the only path is death!'

Again, he waited. He looked back over his shoulder. Lokan was a tiny figure on horseback and three others were beside him, most likely the karzekki. One was Sardin, the Karudar Marfek's brother, the Kermakk Karwema, general of all the generals. The grey-haired man was at least sixty cycles or summers, but with his solid physique, taller than most Kermakk, steel blue eyes, thick grey beard and deep voice, he was a commanding presence. His military career was built on fighting the eastern kingdoms. Now, he would subdue the southern kingdoms with Jaysin's help.

Jaysin faced the city. He was determined to be patient to give the Assandan people a chance to abandon their fortress and live. As he waited, feeling the sun gain intensity as it rose to its zenith, he reviewed the spells he would invoke if the defenders chose badly.

And then a cloud of arrows rose from the walls and arched towards him. He was disappointed. He created an invisible defensive dome and watched the arrows ignite and disintegrate as they hit the barrier. Tiny silhouettes moved behind the parapets and he wondered how the archers and observers reacted when they witnessed their projectiles vanish harmlessly above the target. To his amusement, a second wave of arrows rose and fell, evaporating on contact with his barrier. *They didn't believe it*, he mused, and he anticipated a third arrow storm, but when none followed he began his attack. Whispering, 'Baelegsa scur,' he raised and spread his arms wide.

Above a section of the city, a red, roiling cloud appeared that rapidly expanded, taking the form of rushing, eddying flames. Jaysin swept his arms down and the flaming mass plunged and disappeared behind the walls into the city. An instant later, a ball of fire erupted. Jaysin created a second fire cloud and sent it diving into another quarter. And a third. He shifted his focus and mouthed, 'Waehpoll blaest,' punching both arms in the direction of a section of the stone wall and the wall exploded, showering shattered stone over a wide circle as it opened a broad path directly into the city. Thick smoke rose above the walls into the deep blue sky, and above erratic explosions he heard a muffled cacophony of screaming and yelling voices rising from Shkali.

Jaysin sagged to his knees. He expected to be exhausted from conjuring a batch of powerful spells, especially spells that he learned but never used, and so Lokan was ready to whisk him from danger if he was overcome. Hearing hoofbeats nearing, he turned to find Lokan bearing down on him, but he also saw the Kermakk horsemen charging at the breached wall and the foot soldiers following dutifully in the riders' wake. As Lokan reined in to help him onto his horse, the Kermakk riders thundered past, ten thousand horses churning the earth with iron-shod hooves. Shkali was falling. The Assandan Kingdom was broken.

Medha Akkan fascinated Jaysin. The idea that people would hew a city through underground rock was testament to ingenuity and he wanted to see it, so, when he arrived with the Kermakk army, he advised Guss and Janno and Lokan that he needed to sleep for at least a day to restore his energy for the task of destroying the city and therefore he could not be disturbed. Orders given, he retreated into his pavilion, cast an invisibility spell, and walked to Medha Akkan.

The city gates were carved into a stone cliff, the cliff a remnant in a valley of an ancient and dry watercourse. With the steep valley the only method of approach, Jaysin understood why the city survived numerous attempts to take it. An army had nowhere to deploy. Even the gates, plain, made of a shiny, smooth and unfamiliar metal, allowed only two people abreast through them. Using his Aelendyell knowledge to sustain multiple spells, he passed through the gates like a ghost.

He followed the entry passage until it opened into a labyrinth of underground tunnels, each tunnel like a street in a normal town, with doors and windows opening into facsimiles of above-ground houses. He studied an artisan making pots in a stall and stepped into an empty alcove where he ended his invisibility spell to adopt the potter's appearance, before continuing his journey.

The journey from Shkali to Medha Akkan was punctuated by a series of battles and skirmishes as Shekkarem forces harried the Kermakk army, but the clashes were short-lived and one-sided, and Jaysin's entourage was unaffected. He felt as if he was moving in a bubble through hostile lands, an observer unrequired to participate in events. Even after he created chaos at Shkali and breached the walls, he was neither invited nor wanted to be involved in the city's sacking. Visiting Medha Akkan broke what was a monotonous campaign for him.

Everywhere, lanterns burned to provide light, and Jaysin noted that, although the city builders bored vents through the rock to the surface at regular intervals, breathing was fraught because of the ever-present fumes generated by lanterns.

He wandered through the streets, observing the men and women and children going about their lives, the artisans and merchants, the customers, noting especially the absence of soldiers or Hakamati or anyone with threatening authority. He stopped to listen to a group sharing prayers at a small shrine, although he didn't see visible representation of the god or goddess to whom their prayers were offered.

Two streets on, he discovered children sitting at the feet of an older woman listening to and repeating phrases she shared as though they were her trainees or disciples. The city felt safe, the people content.

As he rounded a corner, Jaysin almost tripped over a child hunched against a wall with his head on his knees, crying. Several more children were playing tag nearby in the street. Jaysin squatted before the child and assembled his limited range of the Shekkarem language to ask, 'Why are you crying?'

The child lifted a tear-smudged face and stared with dark eyes from beneath a cropped but dense shock of hair.

'Lost?' Jaysin asked.

'No,' the boy muttered and sniffed.

'Why unhappy?' Jaysin improvised.

'It doesn't matter,' the boy replied.

Memory stirred in Jaysin, and he looked at the group of children who were laughing and chasing each other. He turned to the boy and said, 'They won't let you play.'

The boy sniffed and rubbed his nose.

'Why won't they let you play?'

'They think I'm different,' the boy said. 'They don't like me.'

'Are you different?' Jaysin asked.

The boy looked at Jaysin and anger flickered in the boy's eyes, as he said, 'I don't want to be like them.'

'Why not?'

'They're silly,' the boy said. 'They only want to play silly little children's games.'

'And what would you rather do?'

Instead of answering, the boy pushed to his feet and ran through the playing group and into another street.

Jaysin watched until the child disappeared, recalling his childhood feelings of loneliness and disconnection, and the memories saddened him. He surveyed the junction, satisfied that he had seen enough of Medha Akkan, created a portal to the astonishment of the children and nearby adults, and disappeared.

Thirty

'You achieved in thirty days what the entire Kermakk army couldn't achieve in two hundred years,' the Karudar Marfek said, her eyes sparkling with admiration. 'Your name will be forever inscribed in the Empire's history: Kar Saleem, Peace Maker.'

Stamping acclamation rang through the Karfeshnar chamber, echoing against the domed roof, and it was sustained for a long time, allowing Jaysin to soak in the adulation bestowed by the Kermakk officials.

Later, alone in his room, Jaysin stood at the window and gazed across the Udarvesna walls at the city, the sound of the Karfeshnar acclamation still ringing in his mind. Single-handedly, he brought the Assandan and Shekkarem kingdoms to their knees. Shkali lay in ashen ruins and Medha Akkan was buried forever. The power he wielded was potent beyond his wildest dreams. He was the Kermakk Kar Saleem, known, feared and held in awe throughout the Empire. Even his mentor, Inaya, could not match him in magical prowess. No one could ever again push him aside, ignore him, treat him disdainfully or call him odd. If his father was alive, Kevan would see that the little boy who did not want to be dragonwarrior, but something far greater, was worthy of his admiration. If he played the game of ushta well in the coming years, he would become even more powerful than the Karudar Marfek.

But recurring memories and feelings nagged him, unsettled him throughout his return journey to Vussar Karemachet. The little boy in Medha Akkan reappeared almost every night in his dreams, except that, when Jaysin looked at him, the face looking back was his own at the same age. Like him, that boy only wanted to become what he was meant to become – except Jaysin buried him when he destroyed the city and that act left Jaysin wondering what might have happened had Mikane caught him in Harbin. *I should not have killed you*, Jaysin lamented. *I am not a killer.*

And he kept seeing Tam and Chasse and Harmi in his dreams, always staring with questioning eyes, although the question lingered unspoken and unanswered. *Is this what I really want to be*? he asked himself.

And there was always that other face in the background of every dream, the exotic, beautiful face, almond eyes observing him, assessing his choices, his moods, his desires. He was compelled to speak to that face, to ask its intentions, its identity, but the will to do so was never fulfilled by his actions. He was mute. Yet the face whispered an instruction to him in the oldest language of magic, words he did not actually hear but understood. Those words circled in his memory and took shape.

As much as he wanted to share his dreams with Inaya, he no longer trusted his mentor. Her loves were the Karudar Marfek and the Empire, and he was a mere tool to ensure her loves were secure. He believed he was being admitted into the inner sanctum of power in the Empire when she encouraged him to stay, but now he knew otherwise. She only told him the truth she wanted him to know – her truth. And he knew that she intended to use him to hunt and kill the last potential threat to the Empire: his family.

Jaysin walked to his table where he had laid his gold chain diamond pendant. The diamond glimmered with amber. Why he had not previously considered the possibility that he was about to explore annoyed him. The obvious was too obvious. He clasped the diamond in his hand and focused his mind on his sister, searching for her. She was out there somewhere. He knew it. He only needed the means to contact her again. 'Tam,' he projected. 'Can you hear me?'

'Jaysin?'

Hearing Tam reply in his mind spurred an unexpected welling of excitement. 'Tam!' he blurted. 'It's me! Jaysin!'

'Oh, Jaysin! Where have you been?' Tam projected.

'I'm here,' Jaysin replied. 'I'm in Vussar Karemachet.'

'Are you all right?'

'I'm fine. Are you all right?'

'We're safe and well,' Tam replied.

'Chasse?'

'He's with us,' Tam confirmed. 'He told me what you did to rescue him from the Kermakk. That was very brave.'

'It's all I could do,' Jaysin replied. 'I had to do something. Is Harmi safe?'

'Again, thanks to you,' Tam told him. 'You found your bracelet?'

'No,' Jaysin replied. 'I created one.' He sensed hesitation at the other end and projected, 'I've learned a great deal since I returned here.'

'I can feel the power in you across the arcane web.'

Harmi's intrusion startled Jaysin. 'Harmi,' he projected.

'Ancient power,' Harmi said. 'Power of our Makers. Where did you find it?'

'Many places,' Jaysin lied.

'Such great and ancient power is very dangerous,' Harmi cautioned. 'Be careful how you use it.'

'Are you coming to us?' Tam asked.

'I wanted to warn you,' Jaysin said.

'Warn us of what?' Tam asked.

'The Karudar Marfek and Karudarteta are sending a great army to hunt for you,' Jaysin explained.

'An army doesn't bother us,' Tam replied. 'One has already tried and got lost in the mountains. We are safe.'

Jaysin swallowed, before saying, 'They want me to kill you.' Again, he felt a hiatus.

'You might find that more difficult to do than you realise,' Tam calmly responded.

Jaysin projected, 'I don't intend to try. There's no reason to hunt you. The Empire already has all it needs.'

'Not everything.'

Startled by the intruding voice, Jaysin discovered Inaya in her flowing black garments standing in his chamber. The door behind her opened and Lokan entered with ten armed guards. Jaysin closed his connection with Tam.

'Your loyalty to family is touching,' Inaya said, approaching Jaysin. 'Show me.' She held out her hand indicating that she wanted the amber-infused diamond.

'No,' Jaysin said, but he flinched as the pendant vanished from his grasp and appeared in Inaya's hand.

She twisted it, inspecting the jewel. 'You have exceeded yourself,' she said. 'A fine piece of crafting. Thank you.'

'For what?' Jaysin asked, contemplating how he would react to an attack from the Karudarteta.

'For revealing where the mas and oozim are hiding,' Inaya said.

Jaysin felt the magical surge and began a response, but he faltered as he wrestled with Inaya's spell enfolding his mind. Immersed in psychic darkness, invisible tendrils wrapping around his limbs, his thoughts were shattered and disrupted. He vainly tried to conjure defences against her mental intrusion, but the harder he fought the stronger she seemed to be. He desperately bundled his energy to burst free, discovered himself infused with light, and the light vanished.

Jaysin woke to find he was strapped to his chair in his room. Wispy smoke swirled in a soft breeze coming from the shattered window and he was within a faint glowing sphere. Inaya stood beyond the glow, her expression grim, determined, visibly sweating. He tried to move, but he was fixed fast to his chair.

'The spell will secure you,' Inaya said. 'It's one I doubt that you know. I learned it to lock masi away if ever I encountered them. It diffuses magic.' She twisted the pendant in her hand. 'I see, now, why this is so important. The amber jewel amplifies power. Curious. It explains why the shessmari, who really have very little magical talent, can do what they do. I take it you took this from one of them?'

'Why are you doing this?' Jaysin asked.

'Why are you doing what you're doing?' Inaya retorted. She twisted the pendant again, and said, 'This allows me to find your sister and her dragon.'

'How?'

Inaya smirked. 'You have so much more to learn. Your little communication leaves a path on the arcane web from source to source. I simply find it and follow it.'

'You know they are more powerful than you,' Jaysin challenged.

Inaya laughed. 'Like you? How did that turn out for you? Power without intelligence is wasted.'

Jaysin wanted to retort, but Inaya's astonished expression stopped him. Unable to move, he could only watch his tormentor's eyes narrow as she began conjuring, but she was enveloped in a pool of light and shock filled her face before she could react. At the edge of his vision, Lokan and his men drew their swords, and shouts and clashing metal rang as a fight ensued. The air around him crackled with energy and the embracing glow evaporated. Freed from Inaya's spell, he sprang to his feet and looked around.

Tam was engaged in an arcane battle of wills with Inaya. Chasse was keeping Lokan and his men away from Tam. And Tam also stood beside him. 'I know,' a voice whispered inside his head. 'Confusing.'

'Harmi?' Jaysin asked.

'Yes,' Harmi replied. 'You're free to help Chasse. I'll help Tam.'

Jaysin fired three energy blasts, killing three soldiers attacking Chasse. Two assailants panicked and bolted for the door. Another three Kermakk soldiers lay wounded on the floor, but Lokan and the remaining two soldiers continued to press Chasse.

Inaya crumpled to her knees before the twin images of Tam. Seizing the opportunity, Jaysin reached for the neck chain while one image of Tam maintained control of Inaya and the other generated a portal in the centre of the room, but Inaya's fierce grip on the pendant did not relinquish.

'Go,' Tam projected to Jaysin.

'The pendant,' Jaysin argued.

'Go!' Harmi urged.

'Not before Chasse,' Jaysin replied, turning to defend his brother. Two more wounded soldiers lay on the floor, leaving Lokan facing Chasse. One on one against Chasse, Jaysin knew Lokan would fall and an unexpected welling of loyalty for the man surged through him. Lokan was his protector, his confidante, his friend. He did not deserve to die. He conjured a sharp gust and slammed Lokan against the wall, winding him, and ending the fight. 'Chasse!' Jaysin urged.

'Go!' Tam ordered. Chasse glanced at Lokan, grabbed Jaysin's arm and pulled him through the blue portal haze.

The western ocean glittered in the sunlight, defying anyone to stare at it for an extended time, but Jaysin was content and shielded his eyes. The swell rolled towards the shore and broke on the rocks, sending white spray skyward, and gulls and terns circled above Nakiades Bluff as they always had. The soft breeze carried the scents of summer plants, and the sky was sharp blue and cloudless.

'If you squint, you can almost imagine nothing has changed,' Chasse said.

Jaysin looked down from the ledge on Dragon Mountain at the empty village, the abandoned huts and upturned fishing boats, and squinted. 'Everything has changed,' he said. 'Especially us.'

'Especially you,' Tam said.

Jaysin turned to his white-haired sister. 'I learned and saw far more than I wanted.'

'Harmi says you are more like an ancient being,' Tam said. 'Your hair, your face and eyes, even your skill with magic. She used the term "Elvenaar."'

'I broke into the Herbal Man's vault in Machutzka and found the Aelendyell Lore Book,' Jaysin confessed.

'We know,' Tam said. 'Harmi said it was inevitable.'

'Harmi expected me to do it?'

'She said Eric expected you to do it,' Tam corrected. 'Remember? She carries the memories of every dragon before her. Eric and Claryssa left us legacies of all their adventures, the treasures and the secrets. You were always meant to open the vault.'

Jaysin softly shook his head. 'I haven't thanked you for rescuing me,' he said. 'Both of you.'

'All three of us,' Chasse corrected.

Jaysin laughed. 'And Harmi. It's still creepy seeing her looking like you. How did you create a portal to connect so accurately with my chamber?'

'Your pendant is a beacon on the arcane web,' Tam said. 'I only had to target it to locate you and link the portal.'

'That's how Inaya said she could find you,' Jaysin said.

'Unfortunately, she can,' Tam confirmed, 'which is why we didn't bring the pendant and why we can't stay here. She would know we came from here to rescue you.'

'She can't generate a portal that reaches this far,' Jaysin said. 'She doesn't have that much power.'

'She wouldn't come alone,' Tam replied. 'She knows we have Harmi. She will bring the Kermakk army.'

'It will take them a full moon cycle, perhaps even a season to reach here,' Chasse argued. 'Marching an army through the mountains to Harbin will take enormous organisation and effort.'

'They will sail up the coast from Ekkarvuss Emachet,' Jaysin suggested. 'The Kermakk have a massive fleet, all of their ships larger than any dragonship. That would be the way I would come if I was Inaya.'

'Either way, we will go north, deeper into the mountains. The northern mountains are wild and difficult to travel, and almost unpopulated. We can live in peace,' Tam said.

'The Kermakk will keep hunting,' Jaysin persisted. 'They want absolute rule. The Karudar Marfek and Inaya view you and Harmi as the last threat to their Empire.'

'If they hunt us, we will be ready,' said Chasse.

'We can stay here for a few days,' Tam offered. 'Harmi and I located a suitable cavern, further to the north, above a fishing village the local people call Apakin Sha. It means Crystal Waters in our language. We can link portals and transfer goods from the treasure chambers in the dragon cave before we leave.'

'Even the books?' Jaysin asked, remembering Eric's library that they abandoned in the escape from Harbin.

'Everything,' Tam confirmed.

'We start anew,' Chasse said. He looked across Harbin Bay and pointed. Jaysin and Tam followed his direction to see Harmi frolicking in the air above Dragon's Mouth, red scales sparkling in the sunlight as she rolled and twisted, chasing gulls.

'She is still a child,' Tam said, chuckling. She turned to Jaysin. 'We haven't celebrated your coming of age.'

'Sixteen summers,' Chasse said. 'You would have been aboard the dragonship.'

Jaysin shook his head, grinning, and retorted, 'I don't think I would ever have been on the dragonship, brother.'

The leafy canopy threw cool shade across the slope, shielding Jaysin from the afternoon heat. Much of his childhood was spent wandering in the Harbin mountain forest, studying the animals, learning their habits and rituals, making connections. He was glad to be free to roam a final time before they left.

The plan was to ferry the last of the Herbal Man's treasure on Dragon Mountain to their new haven above Apakin Sha and close the portal at sunset. Once they were safe from the Kermakk, there was much to do. They all agreed that they would search for Eesa and Banni and the Harbin people and save them, and that meant planning sorties to the south to learn where Mikane took his captives. And Chasse was keen to rescue Natias and the Menuii enslaved by the Kermakk. That task would prove far more dangerous and difficult because it would inevitably bring them into direct conflict with the Empire.

Tam, Chasse and Harmi's fortuitous arrival in Vussar Karemachet left Jaysin no opportunity to decide a pathway for himself, and yet he understood that their intervention saved him from becoming Inaya's pawn and ultimately a weapon in the Kermakk Empire's arsenal. He appreciated the risk that his family made to rescue him and he told them as much before they began planning their escape from Dragon Mountain. What he didn't admit was that he mourned the loss of the Kermakk libraries, especially the one Inaya accumulated, and he particularly mourned the missed opportunity to be a powerful, respected person, with the grandeur of status and wealth. Truth be known, he also missed

Lokan, Guss and Janno. When it came time to move against the Kermakk to rescue the Menuii, Jaysin knew he would have to be ready to face Inaya. Harmi and Tam, combined, showed they could curb her power, but they would need him to defeat her properly. He would learn everything about his new identity as an ancient Aelendyell spirit in readiness.

Jaysin spotted bear spoor as he walked through the forest, but no bears. Smaller creatures scampered from him and birds flitted between branches or sat on boughs and watched him pass. He slid down a slope and found a familiar path across the Meltsparkle stream before climbing a ridge below Varst's Bluff. Driven by memory, he weaved through the bushes and trees until he emerged in a glade where a natural spring trickled down the slope to join Meltsparkle. He chose a flat stone, sat, and closed his eyes to relish the forest's chatter – the babbling water, trilling birds, rustling leaves in the gentle breeze.

He sensed the mind's presence before an inquisitive black nose appeared between two thick bushes, sniffing, testing the scents. A grey muzzle emerged, followed by a furry grey and black head with ears erect. Golden eyes locked on him. Jaysin projected soft, welcoming images, and he felt the wolf recoil before altering its defensive thoughts to images of curiosity.

The wolf slunk out of the undergrowth and padded slowly to him, head low, eyes attentive, nose twitching, and it stopped three paces short, lifting its head to stare him directly in the face. Jaysin lowered his eyes respectfully. The wolf edged closer and sniffed his boots and his robes, before circling behind to sniff his back, and all the while Jaysin projected soft wolf images of a pack mingling and submissiveness. The wolf came to his left side and stood still, its attention focussed on the bushes from whence it came, and a second animal appeared, smaller and greyer than the first. Behind it came a third and fourth wolf. And a white wolf appeared. The four animals sauntered slowly across the glade and stood before Jaysin, assessing him, while the wolf at his side lowered onto its belly. The smallest grey wolf sniffed his boots before it sat, leaning against Jaysin's feet, and then the other wolves sat on the cool earth. The forest leaves whispered. The white wolf scratched its ear and stretched out on the ground. Jaysin closed his eyes and relaxed. The Shadow Hunters were content that the humans were gone from Harbin.

ABOUT THE AUTHOR

Tony Shillitoe is a multi-genre author of fantasy, young adult, historical romance, science fiction and contemporary novels and short stories. Fantasy novels *The Last Wizard* (1995) and *Blood* (2003) were short-listed for the Best Fantasy Novel category in the Aurealis Awards and the teenage fiction *Caught in the Headlights* (2003) was listed as Notable Book for Older Readers in the Children's Book Council of Australia Awards.

A former high school educator, part-time TAFE and university lecturer and tutor, writing workshop convenor and writing mentor, International Baccalaureate teacher trainer, sports coach and player, amateur actor and radio show guest and very poor guitar player and singer, Tony is committed to fulltime writing to complete an array of projects while enjoying coffee and good times with family and friends.

BOOKS BY THE SAME AUTHOR

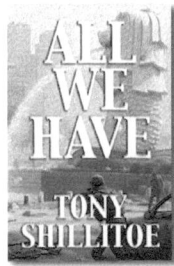    

  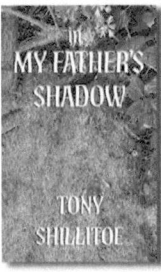  

www.ingramcontent.com/pod-product-compliance
Lightning Source LLC
Chambersburg PA
CBHW022145010726
47493CB00002B/342